DEVOUR

DEVOUR

KURT ANDERSON

PINNACLE BOOKS
Kensington Publishing Corp.
www.kensingtonbooks.com

PINNACLE BOOKS are published by

Kensington Publishing Corp.
119 West 40th Street
New York, NY 10018

All Kensington titles, imprints, and distributed lines are available at special quantity discounts for bulk purchases for sales promotions, premiums, fund-raising, educational, or institutional use. Special book excerpts or customized printings can also be created to fit specific needs. For details, write or phone the office of the Kensington sales manager: Kensington Publishing Corp., 119 West 40th Street, New York, NY 10018, attn: Sales Department; phone 1-800-221-2647.

This book is a work of fiction. Names, characters, businesses, organizations, places, events, and incidents either are the product of the author's imagination or are used fictitiously. Any resemblance to actual persons, living or dead, events, or locales is entirely coincidental.

ISBN-13: 978-0-7860-3679-0
ISBN-10: 0-7860-3679-6

First printing: June 2016

10 9 8 7 6 5 4 3 2 1

Printed in the United States of America

First electronic edition: June 2016

ISBN-13: 978-0-7860-3680-6
ISBN-10: 0-7860-3680-X

*This book is dedicated to the four points
of my compass:
Tina, Tyler, Carter, and my mother, Nita.*

Prologue

Something was wrong.

Jaarva "Joe" Inuviat stood at the edge of the sun-rotted ice sheet, two miles north of his home village of Naujaat. In front of him a long lead of open water sparkled in the weak April sun, the small black-capped Arctic terns darting over the surface. The days were growing longer, and the ringed seals had begun to surface in the open leads, their small heads rising above water just long enough for a man quick with a gun to make a killing shot. But there were no seals. There hadn't been any seals, or walrus, for weeks.

Something was wrong under the ice.

There was a visiting group of scientists in the village, climate researchers from a place called Stanford. They had theories, these researchers. They said the rapid melting of the landward glaciers had created a dense stream of diluted seawater, a massive river flowing south and east toward Nova Scotia. The Kaala Current, they called it. The krill and the mysids were victims to the Kaala, pulled south mindlessly. The smaller fishes and minnows followed, mindfully. The larger predators hounded the schools, followed in turn by the big marine mammals which for thousands of years had sustained Joe's people. That's what they said.

Joe was a carpenter, and he supported his wife, Akiak, and their two small daughters with a combination of what he earned from Inupiat Construction and what he harvested from the sea. It was the same path his father had followed, a good and honest life, enough to raise a family well. Joe thought of his daughters, a smile spreading across his face, and studied the lead.

He did not know much of science, nor of climate change. He did not know if the researchers were wrong, or right, or somewhere in between. He knew the world changed, sometimes over the course of days, sometimes over many generations. It was foolish to look at today's events and attempt to unravel the world's mysteries.

Besides, he knew the seas were not barren. There was still life here. It was just very, very skittish.

Joe squinted into the brisk northwest wind, staring at the great white expanse of packed snow, and his thoughts turned from his daughters to poor, doomed Daniel Pakak. Danny had been an ultra-traditional hunter, only twenty-three but radical in his adherence to the old ways. Two weeks earlier, Danny had set out on a hunting expedition onto the big ice with three other men looking for walrus. Danny had returned alone two days later, severely hypothermic, his clothes frozen stiff on his body. The other men were dead, he managed to tell them through lips that had gone an unhealthy shade of dull purple. Not from cold or drowning, though.

"Quallupilluit," he croaked, then slipped into his last sleep.

Joe looked out over the ice fields, marked by steaming lines where other leads had opened, and pulled his hood tighter against the frigid wind. The ocean was a mystery, one of the few that were still left in his world. He had always liked mysteries, especially the ones that his grandmother told him at bedtime when he was a boy, the scratchy feel of store-bought wool blankets pulled tight over his face. Sometimes those stories revolved around a monster that lived in cracks of the sea ice.

Quallupilluit, the monster of legend. *Quallupilluit*, who had survived for eons by hibernating in the cold sea mud, buried in the soft floor of the ocean while its brethren flamed out and froze out across the rest of the world. *Quallupilluit*, eater of worlds, emerging every fourth or fifth generation to gorge and reproduce. What a strange last word. Danny must have had some awful visions before he died.

Joe turned to the east, waved at his brother-in-law, Darmuska, and put a hand to his mouth. Darm nodded. They would eat now, a leisurely lunch of caribou jerky dipped in fermented seal oil. As they ate, the sun would warm the surface layer of the water, and the krill would become active. The baitfish would rise up to eat the krill, and the cod would follow. Soon the seals would begin to hunt, and then the Arctic air would crackle with gunfire.

Joe started toward the rest of the hunters. The

hunger he'd felt for the last hour was gnawing at him, and he didn't want to be distracted when the seas came alive. It was time to eat.

Over a hundred feet below the ice, a pod of ringed seals swam for their lives.

There were three adult females in the group, their thick backs undulating in the icy water. Behind them, tucked in tightly just behind the females' pelvic flippers, were two nearly grown pups. The third pup, a small male born with a malformed flipper, had disappeared. He had been a weak swimmer, too slow to keep up with the rest of the pod. Now he was gone, swallowed up by the ocean.

The seals flashed through the water, their stream-lined bodies faster than the cod they lived on much of the year, faster even than the skittering char that ran up the Crowkill River. In unison the pod banked hard to the right, their disturbance sending a small mass of krill scattering in the water column like tiny white shotgun pellets. The seals swam with their eyes nearly shut, long whiskers pressed tight against their snouts. They were nearly out of air.

The water behind the seals was dark and feature-less, marked only by striations of light where the leads had opened above. Then, out of the darkness, a shape appeared, closing in rapidly on the seals. It swam with a pronounced up and down bobbing, almost as though it were nodding to itself. Huge black pectoral flippers propelled the killer whale forward, closing the distance between it and the fleeing seals. It was a bull, just over twenty-four feet long, six tons of death mov-

ing through the water at over thirty miles per hour. It blasted through a bar of slanting light, its massive curled fluke sending billows of krill spiraling out to the side.

Fifty yards ahead of the bull, one of the remaining seal pups slowed. Its muscles saturated with lactic acid. It drifted to a stop, watching the pod grow smaller in front of it, and then turned up toward the light of the lead. Air, just seventy feet above.

The killer whale reached the pup within seconds. The young ringed seal saw the bull at the last moment and tried to turn away, a small stream of bubbles exploding out of its nostrils. But the killer whale kept swimming, a giant black-and-white monster streaking toward deeper water.

The pup, out of air and nearly unconscious, never saw the killer whale's pursuer. A huge form materialized out of the deep, a pair of slitted eyes a dozen feet apart. Then there was only teeth, and darkness, and death.

Darm was telling a story around a mouthful of food, gesturing with the jerky strip he held in his hand, spraying the snow with flecks of venison. Joe, who was an only son, loved his sister's diminutive husband like a brother. But it was difficult to be around the man when those ancient twin urges—eating and talking—overcame him at the same time.

There were four of them standing with their backs to the wind. Joe and Darm had hunted together for twelve years. Nuqtak and Paarvu were cousins of Darm, younger men who worked on Joe's construction crew. They had been hunting for only a few years, and they were worried about the ice, worried they would end up like Danny Pakak. Dying from the cold, of all things. It was a disgraceful way for an Inuit hunter to liberate his *anirniq* from his body.

"Think about how Danny hunted," Darm said, showing a mouth full of masticated caribou jerky. "Always on the edge, always pushing things." He tapped the side of his hood. "He didn't listen. There was a big current the day he went out. You could hear the ice pop from a mile inland."

"Hard for you to hear the ice pop when you are nestled between Marjuk's *narnugs*," one of the other men said. Darm joined their laughter, more flecks of dried venison spraying on the ice. Marjuk was Darm's wife, Joe's sister. She was a plump woman, well-insulated from the cold.

It's a different way to hunt, Joe thought, listening to the men joking, arguing, giving each other shit. A different way to *be*, actually. He could not remember his father hunting with a partner. Trapping, yes, it was too hard and dangerous to be a solitary trapper in these frozen expanses, where a lame dog or fouled spark plug for the snowmobile could mean death. But the day-trip hunting expeditions had been solemn, just father and son and few words. No lewd jokes, no bantering, no camaraderie. He liked the new way better in many regards, he liked the men and liked the little lunch breaks. And yet he missed those days on the ice when it was just he and the sky and the wind, the small opening in the ice front of him where a seal might emerge to breathe. Everything drawn into a tight focus. Feel the ice under you contracting like thick, cold skin.

Think about the sea, so barren on top, teeming with rich and unknown life below.

Now Nuqtuk and Darm were wrestling, playfully, the steel Yaktrax on the bottoms of their boots scraping across the ice. Joe watched, smiling, but inwardly disappointed. The seals would hear the noise, and they knew the sharp scratches on the ice meant hunters, or polar bears. They would not surface in this lead now, instead seeking out other, safer—

He caught a blur of movement out of the corner of his eye and instinctively reached for his rifle. He brought the rifle to his shoulder and dropped the barrel down so that the sight nestled just above the eye of the smallest of the four seals, just fifty yards away. Younger seals were the best eating, with the least amount of toxins in their meat.

He clicked the safety off and squeezed the trigger, and three of the seals dipped back below the water. The fourth flopped several times and then went still, bobbing in the open lead, its blubber keeping it afloat. Joe turned to the men, who were staring at him, and grinned. He was about to say something about their youth, something about his skills, when he heard the water splash behind him. Their jaws dropped, and he realized their mouths weren't open because of his shooting prowess. Joe spun back to look at the lead.

He saw nothing. The water was empty, the seal gone.

The predator was still hungry.

It had been asleep too long, its muscles atrophied and stiff. Its reflexes were sluggish, its eyesight blurry. The only sensation that it possessed with any clarity was hunger, a sharp need that drove it onward. The several smallish seals in its belly were not nearly enough to dull the hunger pains. It wanted more, needed more, but the sea life was not as abundant as it had been the last time it had emerged. And the scattered prey that remained were too fast for predator's current condition. So far it had been only been able to catch the weak, the injured.

The predator circled fifty feet below the open lead, its immense body cutting through the water. It needed more food, enough sustenance to bring it back to a fuller state of consciousness. The seas might be thin with prey, but there were sounds transmitting through the ice above, small vibrations that the predator picked up both in its rudimentary ears and the lateral-line nerves that ran along its sides. It repositioned its great bulk with surprising agility, oriented itself at a forty-five-degree angle, eyes dilating as it looked toward the bright surface.

The predator had many attributes, but above all was its ability to adapt. If it could not get food below water, it would try its luck above.

The men were all talking at once. They could not agree on what they had seen rise out of the water. They were traditional Inuit hunters, and knew almost every animal and fish that lived below the sea or ran up the rivers, possessing knowledge that had been passed down through generations and sharpened on the grit of decades of firsthand experience and observation.

Now the only thing they could agree on was that

they did not know what had surfaced to take the seal. It was enormous, larger even than *arviq*, the bowheaded whale. And *arviq* did not eat seals, one of the men said.

"What else could it be?" Darm asked.

"*Arviq* cannot even break through the ice now!" another man shouted above the others. They were upset, their voices tinged with panic. "There is four feet outside the leads, and *arviq* can only break through half of that!"

It was true, Joe thought. The whales would not rely on leads for their air supply, and even though it was weakened by the spring sunshine, four feet of ice was a formidable barrier even for the reinforced skulls of *arviq*. No, *arviq* were still far to the south and east, where the ice was thinner.

He glanced back at the jumble of land-fast ice, several hundred yards to the west. He had one advantage over the other men: He had not seen the beast rise out of the water, and so his own panic was secondhand. He was able to think, and he was thinking about Danny Pakak's last words. Thinking about the safety of the shoreline.

"Let's go in," Joe said. "Whatever it was, we can talk about it on land as easily as we can out here."

"He's right," Darm said. "The hunting is ruined anyway." Joe watched as his brother-in-law walked over to pick up his rifle. He had never heard Darm sound quite so agreeable, so ready to quit hunting at midday. He began to feel his own panic rising, the staccato thump of his pulse in his throat.

The ice exploded around his brother-in-law.

The shattered ice flew in all directions, some of the pieces larger than a man. Joe ducked instinctively as a slab the size of a snowmobile whirred through the air next to his head. He fell to the ice, losing his grip on his grandfather's rifle. The carbine slid along the ice and disappeared into a newly formed fissure. He shouted for Darm and then fell silent, his words caught somewhere deep in his chest.

Something unimaginable was behind the spray of ice and seawater, suspended vertically in front of him. Its mouth was closed, the nostrils smashed back from breaking through the thick ice. Its striped hide was crusted with gray barnacles. It hung in the sky fifteen, twenty feet above him, eclipsing the low-riding sun.

And that's just the head, Joe thought. His mind spun around and around that single fact: What he was seeing was *only the head*.

It sank slowly, jaws still pointed toward the sky, and for a moment Joe thought perhaps it was a whale, some abomination of a whale, for nothing else could compare to the size of this monstrosity. Then the jaws parted slightly, revealing yellow teeth larger than a man could put his arms around. The eye on Joe's side opened, and he was amazed to see it was a brilliant green, a sharp emerald inside the hooded eye socket. The nostrils flared, sucking in fresh air. The abomination's eye seemed to fix on Joe, marking him, and then it submerged. A wave rolled over the fractured ice, the displaced water stopping just short of Joe's boots.

"Darm!" Joe shouted. "Nuqtak! Paarvu!"

He heard a garbled sound from the jumble of ice in front of him. He moved forward carefully, using the

chunks of ice to check his progress. There! Darm was
clinging tightly to a small floe. Joe knew he had only
moments to get his sister's husband out of the water.
Inuit were notoriously poor swimmers, and a wet floe
was impossible to hold on to for long. The other two
hunters had already disappeared.

He rummaged into the small hunting pack he carried and pulled out a long cord, which had a lead
weight and large treble hook at the end—the same tool
he used to retrieve his harvested seals. He glanced up,
estimated Darm was fifteen feet away, and peeled off
loops of cord. An old saying from the Sunday school
he had briefly attended flitted across his mind: *I will
become a fisher of men.*

He threw the weighted hook underhand. It passed
over Darm, the cord falling on his shoulder. Joe quickly
pulled in line, felt tension, and reared back hard on the
cord. Darm yelped in pain and Joe retreated backwards,
playing out line until he was behind a large block of
ice. He sat down and planted his boots against it.

He began to pull, ignoring Darm's cries of pain.
Joe's eyes were squeezed almost shut with exertion,
his muscles straining as he sluiced his brother-in-law
toward safety.

*The predator took a moment to savor its meal. It
liked this prey, the strange outer hide, the tender salti-
ness within. Once this prey had even tried to hunt the
predator, when it had been much younger. It still bore
the scars on the back of its neck, and it still remembered the pain.*

They made a small meal, but to the predator, none were more satisfying.

"Pull yourself up on the ice!"

Joe could feel the panic setting its claws in him now, climbing out of his throat, flooding his brain. Darm was at the edge of the shattered ice, still on the floe, unable to lift himself onto the main ice sheet. And Joe could not go to him—the wet ice was far too slippery.

Joe took a deep breath, wrapped his hand around the cord, and pulled as hard as he could. Something popped in his lower back, hot and painful. His vision began to swim and still he leaned back, knowing the cord might break. Part of him was actually wishing waiting it would break, because his desire to get away from this place was now almost as strong as his desire to save his best friend. Darm let out a strangled cry and suddenly the tension changed on the cord, becoming manageable. Joe kept pulling until Darm was on the other side of the ice chunk, moaning, half-drowned, but still alive.

Joe stood, blinking to clear the swimming black and green dots that filled his vision. "Come on," he said to Darm, pulling him to his feet. He pointed toward the land-fast ice, a realm where no creature that swam could penetrate. "We need to run, Darm. Can you run?"

Darm wiped a shaky hand across his face, where ice had already begun to form on his eyelashes. The hook was embedded into the big muscles of his shoulder, and a thin red stream of blood, diluted with seawater, ran from his clothes down to the ice. "Bet your ass I can run," he said.

They sprinted toward the distant ice ridges, boots thudding on the thick ice.

The predator moved underneath them, the water much darker away from the open leads. The huge serpentine shape passed underneath the two fleeing hunters, turned and came back. Strength was returning now, and with it memories, a series of sensations and calculations. It needed food, yes, but it lived for the hunt, the sense of closing in on the prey. The first ripping of flesh.

The water was getting shallower, and ahead the predator could feel the edge of its range, a solid obstruction. It dropped in the water column once again, then turned in a lazy arc. From a hundred and twenty feet above it, the signature sound of fleeing prey triggered the killer switch in the predator's mind. The predator shot upward, huge flippers powering its bulk through the water column.

One moment Joe was running, and the next he was half-submerged, draped over a small, triangular floe. The beast had exploded through the pack ice again, directly under their feet.

He looked around blearily, a warm trickle spreading from his head down the side of his face. Darm was nowhere in sight, and when Joe shifted position to look around there was a searing pain in his right leg. He could see the bulge of his broken femur through his leggings, pressing against the big muscles in his thigh.

Joe Inupiat floated alone in a smashed circle of ice,

thirty feet in diameter. So many times in these past few years he had lain in bed, thinking about what the elders said about this new life. Technology and constant streams of information could be good, they said. Such things could make life in this hard world a bit easier. But it could also make you nearsighted, turn you snow-blind in the soul. A man could lose his feel for the tundra, for the sea, would lose whatever magic was left in this life. And Joe had felt the magic ebbing these past years, unsure if it was changes in the world that brought it on, or changes from living through so many seasons here at the frozen top of the world. So he hunted and he waited for something unexplainable, something to strum that live wire deep in his chest, something to bring back the magic.

Now the sea had granted his wish. He turned over on the floe and crawled forward so he could peer down into the depths. He could see his damned magic down there, impossibly long and thick, only forty feet below him. It was tiger-striped along its back, the tail lined with sharp scutes that reminded him of the rough saws the elders used to carve blocks of snow for traditional *igluit*.

Joe fought for consciousness, for strength. There was no hope of reaching shore, no hope of even getting off this floe. Blood dripped steadily from his head into the water. He thought of his daughters, and for a moment he felt their soft hands in his own, could feel the weight of them in his arms as he carried them to their beds.

He pulled cold air deep into his lungs, warmed it, savored it. "Come on," he shouted, slapping at the water. "Come on and finish it!"

The predator turned its gaze upward, green eyes gleaming.

After it had finished with the last of the prey, the predator retreated to the ocean floor to rest. At two hundred and seventy feet, the pressure was incredible, but the predator had infrastructure built for such depths.

It had been a satisfying meal, but the predator was far from full. For a week it had been roaming its ancient hunting grounds, and the predator could feel the changes in the water, in the ice, could sense that some shift was occurring. There was a strong current here now, with less salt in the moving water. The predator watched the small plankton drift by, heading southeast.

After an hour's rest, the predator lifted itself off the ocean floor and surfaced for air. It would adapt, as it always had. Submerging once again, the predator dropped into the southbound current, big flippers rotating steadily, letting the movement of the water lead it to food.

It was still very hungry.

Chapter 1

Seven weeks later, five miles off the Gloucester coast

Something very large was suspended directly underneath the *Tangled Blue*.

Gilly Blanchard tapped the buttons on the Furuno sonar display, zooming in on the large half-moon arc just below their baits, which showed up as small fingernails on the sonar. The other two baits were positioned below bright orange floats, roughly thirty yards off each corner of the Grady-White's stern. The floats were barely visible in the thick fog.

He turned back to the console, glancing at the readout from the FishHawk sensor, suspended on a lead ball weight twelve fathoms deep. The temperature at seventy feet down was only forty-three degrees, with a subsurface current of just over three knots. Overhead, hundreds of shearwater petrels swooped low over the water, their black-edged wings the only relief in an otherwise gray universe.

"You believe this, Cap?" Gilly called over his shoulder. "We got another looker."

Brian Hawkins looked up from his chum board. He was cutting long strips of herring into chunks, using the side of the blade to carefully scrape away the long, bloody kidneys. Gilly liked to kid him about how careful he was with the bait, how fastidious he was in general, especially compared to how he could be the rest of the time. It didn't bother Brian; he knew what he knew. Blood brought in sharks, and sharks were a pain in the ass. And this day, so far, had been remarkably free of pains in the ass.

"She gonna?" Brian said, chopping the rest of the herring fillet into three-inch chunks. He was careful in his speed, timing his cuts with the motion of the boat. Blades, waves, and fingers, he thought. Mix those three for any length of time, and eventually your gloves are going to have empty spaces in them.

"Dunno," Gilly said. "Cruising for now. She's a big one."

Brian dropped a few more chunks overboard, then slid the rest of the chum into an ice cream bucket. He straightened, groaning at the pain in his lower back. He'd been meaning to build a little chumming station at chest level for years. He only seriously considered it after cutting bait, when his backbone felt like it had been pressed in a vise. By the time they got back to port, and the little workshop in the marina garage, his mind was nowhere close to bait cutting. It was set on that first drink—the best one of the day, as Hemingway used to say—or maybe just a warm bed.

"Getting old, Cap," Gilly said.

"Experienced," Brian said, rolling his shoulders. "Seasoned."

He was forty-two, still able to put in a full day in the

ship, and sometimes a full night in the bar. Maybe a little softer than he wanted to be around the middle, but
hell. It was always that way at the beginning of the season, all those long winter nights in front of the tube, or
parked in front of the bar at the Riff-Raff. The weight
would come off, it always did. His short beard was still
dark brown, with only a few rogue whites in the mix.

"You need a little pick-me-up?" Gilly asked.

Brian glanced at his first mate. When a man bought
a boat, part of the process was negotiating over the
gear included in the deal. Did the price include the out-
riggers? Fishing gear? Some men wanted to keep the
existing electronics; others were only interested in buy-
ing the hull and would add their own equipment later.
When Brian sat down with old Denny Blanchard that
day in the back booth of the Riff-Raff, he had been
prepared to haggle over all sorts of details, some he
was prepared to give in to, others that were absolutes.
He certainly sure hadn't been expecting to get a first
mate out of the deal, especially one with three DWIs,
two stints in county for distribution of a controlled
substance, and a gimpy leg from rolling his daddy's
diesel truck on I-95 at three in the morning.

"Prescriptions," Brian said. "For every damn pill
you have on board." He motioned out to the gray wall
of fog that encircled the boat. "I mean it, Gil. The
Coast Guard comes up on us in this crap and—"

Gilly held a hand up. "First," he said. "I'm keepin'
eyes on the radar, dude. I'm not blind. Ain't no pings
within ten miles."

"*Dude?*" Brian said. "Denny'd roll over in his grave
hearing you talk like that. You're forty-seven, not seventeen."

"Then I'm sure he's twisted up like a mummy by now," Gilly said. "If he cares enough to pay attention to me when he's dead. He sure didn't when he was still kicking." Gilly grinned. "Second, you know the lamedick Coasties are scattered all over hell and gone. There's been what, three sinkings up by Fundy, another down by—"

He was interrupted by the sound of the rod banging off the port side, followed by the scream of the drag on the big Penn reel. Brian slipped on his gloves and moved quickly to the corner rod, a nine-foot Fin-Nor, bent over nearly double. The 200-pound test monofilament was flying off the reel, the line counter flashing past a hundred, a hundred fifty, then over two hundred in the span of seconds.

"Big one," Brian said, wrapping his hands carefully around the rod handle. He needed to wait until the run was over before removing the rod from the rod holder. On smaller fish that wasn't always the case, but today the fish were running large. Running huge, actually. They didn't use stand-up gear on the *Tangled Blue*, and if one of these behemoths yanked the rod out of his grip Brian would be out close to two grand. It was better than being strapped to the bastard when it went over, but it still wasn't good. A different kind of hurt.

Gilly limped to the other corner of the boat, flipped the reel on the other rig to high gear ratio, and started cranking in line. He got the float in, unsnapped it, and rolled it toward the bow. By the time the float bounced down the stairs and into the cuddy he had the line out of the water, the live herring wiggling in the air with the big 11-ought hook through its nose. Gilly flipped the herring off the hook and stowed the rod, then moved on to the other two lines. Brian barely noticed. The first mate of the *Tangled Blue* had his faults, as did her captain. But there wasn't a man in Gloucester who could clear a deck as fast as Gilly Blanchard.

Two minutes later the gear was stowed and Gilly fired up the twin 350s, then activated the automatic retrieve on the windlass anchor. The fish had pulled out four hundred feet of line and was cutting hard to the port side, still pulling drag at a relentless pace. Brian shook his head and took a deep breath, waiting for the brief lull when he could pop the rod free.

A good day on the water was one fish. Two-fish days happened rarely. Three-fish days—a one-man limit— were epic, the kind of day where you almost cringed, thinking of the hangover that would result from that night's celebration. Many boats never raised three fish in a day, and more than half never saw two in the hold in a season.

The pitch of the drag changed, and the tip of the Fin-Nor rod came up a fraction of a degree. Brian slid the rod out of the holder and pulled back steadily. This would be their sixth hookup, perhaps their fifth fish of the day. And all of their fish had been caught off a little underwater hump at the edge of this icy, food-rich current streaming down from the north.

"Take it ten degrees starboard," he called out over his shoulder. The big 350s rumbled under his feet as Gilly positioned the boat so the line was straight out the back. Brian watched the spool grow steadily smaller. He was down to the backing now, braided Dacron line that made a slight sizzling sound as it coursed through the roller guides.

"Out four thirty," Brian said, just loud enough to hear over the rumble of the engines. "Five hundred, five twenty-five." He shook his head as the numbers on the counter whirred past. "She's out six and still going strong."

Gilly whistled, lit a cigarette. Six-fifty was the magic number.

"We chasing?" Gilly hollered.

The line counter went past six hundred and fifty feet, with no signs of slowing. "We're chasing," Brian yelled, and despite the sore muscles in his shoulders and back, despite the black thoughts that had once again begun to circle his mind, he offered up a tight-lipped smile to the foggy world, to the shearwaters who chirred and darted above them. Nothing in the world could compare to the thrill of hooking into something stronger than yourself and trying to make it your own.

It came up slowly, the rod quivering slightly from Brian's aching shoulders. He'd been fighting for a little over two hours, gaining a few inches here, a foot there. They were a half mile from the original hookup, and he had only started to gain serious amounts of line in the past ten minutes. The tendons in his left hand, which he used to pull in line while reeling with his right, were ready to cramp.

Gilly moved up next to him, held up a plastic water bottle to his mouth. Brian drank quickly, eyes trained on the line stretched tight in front of him. The fish was starting to cut to the side, and angling up and out. Moving slowly but surely, like the good ones inevitably did. The other fish they had caught that day were large—giants, by definition—but none of them were in this league. An epic fish for an epic day.

"She's coming in," Gilly said. "We're gonna be weighted down something fierce, we land this sow."

Bad luck, Brian thought. *Never talk about size until you wrap the damn rope around its tail.* "Stick ready?"

Gilly lifted the harpoon, checked the coil of rope. "She's ready. How long, you think?"

"Not long," he said. "But she'll have a hell of a boat run."

"Nope," Gilly said. "She'll turn on her side, I'll stick her, and then you and I ain't gonna see this side of sober for a week."

Brian had to grin. He hadn't been on a legitimate bender for a while, and partying with Gilly usually left him half-paralyzed and wondering about liver transplants. But if they did land this fish, a good old-fashioned drunk was obligatory. Even without it, they had close to thirty thousand dollars of catch in the hold. If the meat was especially fatty, they might get another ten or twenty percent. Add in this one, and—

The rod went suddenly limp in his hand and he reeled in furiously, flipping to high gear retrieve with the pad of his thumb. It was gone, the fish of his life-time was gone because he had let himself get distracted, had let the goddamn thought of money enter into the equation of man and fish—

Tension surged back into the line, and the drag screamed again. Brian watched as the fish stripped another hundred feet off the reel, reversing the past twenty minutes' worth of work. The fish had simply made a run toward the boat, something he hadn't expected at this point in the battle. He switched the gear ratio back to low, checked the drag. "She's a funny one," he said to Gilly, who had moved back to the wheel to reposition them. "Flipped direction like a skipjack."

"Something down there," Gilly said, tapping on the sonar screen. "Must've spooked it."

"Shark?"

"Nah, looks like a humpie or a blue. Weird hook for a whale, but that's all it can be. Gone now." He tapped the menu button, switching to a wider transducer angle, and pointed at a large orange arc at the very edge of the screen. "There it is, leaving the scene. Fuckin' blubberhead."

The last run seemed to have exhausted the fish. It came in steadily after the last surge. The braided line came back up the guides, and the mono began to fill the spool. Gilly picked up the harpoon and stood to Brian's left, looking over the side.

"Oh my Jesus Christ," Gilly said. "It's a half-tonner."

The giant bluefin tuna came in slowly, an indigo-and-silver behemoth. It was hooked well in the corner of the mouth, the barb of the big hook clearly visible below its softball-sized eyeball. Its rear dorsal and anterior fins curved back like scimitars, the large dark tail moving slowly through the water.

Easily a half-tonner, Brian thought, temporarily forgetting his own jinxes on guessing weights before the fish was in the boat. *Hell, it might beat Fraser's record.* He had been fishing for a living for six years, and catching fish regularly for the last four. He had never seen, nor heard of, a bluefin nearly this large.

"You miss this goddamn thing—"

"I miss that fish," Gilly said, hefting the harpoon, "you take me to the charity house for the blind and retarded. It's as big as a goddamn house."

The bluefin, only twenty yards from the boat, started to turn sideways. It was a long throw for even a good stick man, but Gilly was right—it would be hard to miss. Gilly brought the harpoon to his shoulder, and as he did the tuna seemed to see him, or sense his intentions. It turned away and swam hard down to the depths, pulling more drag off the reel, but slowed after only about seventy feet. Brian carefully applied pressure to turn it around.

He cranked down slowly, steadily. The hook had been in the fish for two hours now, long enough to wear a hole in the fish's mouth. Every turn, every run enlarged that hole, and made it easier for the hook to pull out. A fish like this was not only epic, it had the potential to be worth six figures—or more. A recent bluefin tuna of exceptional quality had just sold to a Japanese fish broker for $1.7 million. For a guy eighty grand in debt, they were numbers hard to put of mind.

"Hit it as soon as you can," Brian said. "Stick her hard."

"Yeah, Cap," Gilly said. "I got her." He was serious for once, Brian saw, even a bit nervous. Probably thinking of all the tail and blow he could score with his first mate's share of today's catch.

The tuna made another short, hard run just out of sight of the boat. The rod bounced hard twice, three times, then stopped, became deadweight. Brian pulled back on the tip slowly, feeling the fish out—was it dogging him, swimming away just hard enough to create a stalemate? It didn't feel like it was even moving. The weight on the other end was solid, unmovable.

"What's she doing?" Gilly said.

The line started to peel out again. It went slowly at first, then faster, stripping hard-won monofilament back out to sea. The number on the counter, which had been as low as fifty-two, slipped past a hundred. A hundred and fifty. Brian leaned back on the rod a bit, made a small adjustment to the drag.

"Don't break," he whispered. "Don't you break on me now."

The line picked up speed, hit three hundred. Gilly set the harpoon down and slowly backed to the wheelhouse. Brian looked back at him and nodded, and Gilly put the transmission in reverse. The big props churned, moving them backwards at two knots. Yet still the line stripped out, with no signs of slowing.

"Give it more!"

Gilly pushed down on the throttle and the *Tangled Blue* plowed stern-first into the four-foot waves, seawater splashing up and over Brian. The spool spun faster and faster, now well into the Dacron backing again. It didn't make any sense. He'd seen the fish, and large as it was he could have sworn he'd broken it. But he had never hooked anything this large, either. He held the rod tip high and reared back, trying to turn the massive fish one more time.

And still the line went out, the spool now half-gone.

At twelve hundred feet Brian yelled for Gilly to turn the boat. They should have spun at a thousand, but he had been so sure, so goddamn certain, that he could turn it.

Gilly turned the Grady-White in a tight circle, costing Brian another hundred and fifty feet on the one-eighty. By the time they were pointed at the fish, he could see metal on the inside of the Penn's spool. In a few more seconds it was over. There was a sharp snap as the backing popped off the spool, and then the line disappeared through the roller guides and into the sea.

Brian staggered back at the sudden loss of resistance, almost losing his footing on the wet floor of the boat. Gilly set him down on one of the yacht chairs, his eyes watching the seas to see if the massive fish might float to the surface, its heart burst after the long battle. But the seas were empty, even the shearwaters gone.

They looked at each other for a long moment, the exhaust from the engines wafting over them. Brian could not feel any distinct sensation in his arms except the sharp ache from his tendons. All else was a throbbing, burning pressure. He wondered if he was having a heart attack.

"Big fish," Gilly said.

"Yeah," Brian said. "Woulda been a keeper."

Gilly turned back to the wheel. He put the transmission in forward, and after a moment the deck cleared of exhaust fumes. They continued on in silence, moving at a slow troll through the fog-laden chop back to their original mooring. Sometimes at sea there was nothing to talk about. And sometimes, there was so much to talk about that a man couldn't say anything at all.

The call came in over the radio twenty-five minutes later.

"Mayday-Mayday-Mayday. This is the research vessel Archos. Mayday-Mayday-Mayday."

Gilly reached down and turned up the volume on the marine radio, then picked up the handheld transmitter. They had just finished stowing their gear and were having a rare onboard beer together when the marine radio started talking.

"Mayday-Mayday," the voice said again, the panic obvious through the crackle. *"We are a research vessel operating two miles off of Boon Island. We've struck an underwater object and are taking on water. The bilges cannot keep up, repeat, the bilges cannot keep up. We are going down fast. Mayday-Mayday-Mayday."*

They looked at each other. If the Coast Guard picked up, the *Tangled Blue* would wait for guidance, perhaps even offer assistance. But the amount of static on the transmission suggested the *Archos* had an undersized marine radio antenna, a common and deadly sin on the open ocean. The *Tangled Blue* had a thirty-foot marine antenna, good enough to transmit for fifty miles or more under the right conditions. After a moment, Brian reached over and took the handheld mike from Gilly's hand.

He clicked on the transmit key. *"Archos,* this is the fishing boat *Tangled Blue.* What are your numbers, over?"

There was a burst of static, and then the man's voice came on again, the panic now mixed with excitement. *"Thank God,"* he said, his voice booming and distorted. *"We don't know what happened, we were just anchored and all of a sudden—"*

"Sir, you need to settle down, and hold the mike farther away from your mouth. Give me your numbers, your GPS coordinates. Over."

"Right . . . Sarah! What are our coordinates?"

The man repeated them, and Gilly reached under the dash and scribbled down the numbers.

"Good," Brian said. "Now repeat the coordinates. Over."

"We're going down, for Christ's sake!"

"Repeat the numbers," Brian said. "Over."

The man swore, shouted at Sarah again, and spit the numbers out. Brian understood the man's frustration; he also knew more than one rescue attempt had been unsuccessful because of an incorrect latitude or longitude reading. Gilly wrote the repeated coordinates underneath the original numbers:

43.121096 N, 70.433092 W
43.121096 N, 70.433092 W

Gilly ran his index finger across the numbers to cross-check, and then punched the coordinates into the Furuno, which doubled as a chartplotter. The *Archos* appeared as a small blip on the screen, sixteen long miles away.

"We have a fix on your position," Brian said. "Hold for a second, over."

He handed the microphone back to Gilly and pointed at the numbers. "See if we can skip those to the Coast Guard."

Gilly repeated the distress call to the Coast Guard while Brian did the math in his head. Top speed was about twenty-seven knots in these seas if the *Tangled Blue* was unloaded, with their current half-full fuel tank. With well over a ton of ice and giant bluefin tuna in the hold, they would do no better than sixteen or seventeen knots, tops. It was the difference of a half hour to get there unloaded, versus an hour loaded.

Brian turned to Gilly. "Tell me good news."

Gilly shook his head, "Still up in Fundy, looking for floaters from the *Margaret Jane*." The *Jane* was one of the three ships that had gone down in the Bay of Fundy in the past week. "They're out ninety minutes, two hours. No chance of air assistance with this damn fog. Can't raise anybody on Boon, either."

Brian rubbed his forehead, then held out his hand for the mike. "*Archos, Archos, Archos,* this is *Tangled Blue*. Do you copy, over?*"

"We're here, Tangled Blue. Did the Coast Guard answer you?" The *Archos* could hear the transmissions from the *Tangled Blue*, but not any responses.

"We're coming to your assistance, *Archos*. But we need to know your *exact* situation. Do you understand, over?"

"We understand, over."

"How much water is in the boat? How long will you stay afloat, over?"

There was shouting from the other side, at least three or four different voices. All of them filled with panic. *"It won't be long,"* the man said. *"Ten minutes, maybe fifteen. We don't have a lifeboat."*

"Do you have life jackets, over?"

There was a pause. *"We do,"* the man responded slowly. *"But the water is very cold, Tangled Blue. We won't last long."*

"Hold on as best you can," Brian said. "We're on our way."

He tossed the microphone on the dash and walked back to the hold. He leaned down and popped the lid, uncovering four massive bluefin tuna, the first of the year for any boat in the region, the thick bodies covered in the ice from their onboard machine. That ice allowed them to achieve the top market price, well worth the extra costs for the machine and lower fuel mileage the weight of the ice caused. Each tuna was worth thousands of dollars, just one of them enough to cover his operating costs for most of the season. He reached over and pulled a stainless-steel hook from the gunnels.

He looked up at Gilly. "Come on, give me a hand."

Gilly stood, spit over the side of the boat. "They better be worth it."

Brian sunk the tip of the hook deep into the rich, red meat of the nearest bluefin. "They won't be."

Chapter 2

Captain Donald Moore stood on the deck of the *Nokomis*, watching passengers stream along the boarding dock, forty feet below him. It was a calm, gray day with a light west wind. He held the fax from his first mate in one liver-spotted hand, the paper fluttering in the light offshore breeze.

The passengers moved steadily on the boardwalk below him, mostly middle-aged couples, some younger people, even a few children. Some of the passengers carried their own luggage; others walked with bellmen pushing their carts behind them. Moore watched with interest. He liked to see the people he was going to spend the next week with, not the individuals but the general type. Sometimes you could tell they were all going to be assholes; sometimes it was just the vast majority. Now he saw the low ratio of people carrying their own bags and figured it was going to be a typical voyage, heavy on the assholes.

The complaints would be endless. *The sea is too wavy. It's too cold. Too hot. Captain, there's a lady on*

C-deck who is suffering from motion sickness and wants to return to port.

Moore leaned against the railing, the cool rounded brass pressing against his belly. Sheep, he thought. They go into a floating hunk of metal, head into one of the deadliest oceans in the world, then complain when it's bumpy.

Well, maybe this would be different than the cruise ships, where all anybody wanted to do on those trips was relax, get drunk, get laid. Plenty of time to bitch about what was wrong in the downtime. This was different, all the bells and whistles of the slot machines, the cards spinning out onto the felt, the chips coming and going. Maybe it would be different, maybe not.

He glanced back at the wheelhouse, at the Zeiss binoculars that had been a present from his first wife, Chanterelle, twenty-nine years ago. The glass was still unscratched, the optics superb. Sometimes, when he put the binoculars up to his eyes, he thought he caught a trace of the light perfume Chant used to wear.

Moore considered getting the binoculars, then dismissed it. He didn't need to look down there and see their faces. And he didn't need the ewes to look up—as they always seemed to do just before boarding—and see their captain peering down on them with binoculars. Some dirty old man in a clean white uniform.

Below him, a couple was arguing about something, probably the weight of the woman's luggage. He thought back to his inaugural captain gig, standing on the deck of the cruise ship *Santa Barbara*, watching and listening to a short, well-groomed passenger hurling abuses at one of the baggage carriers on the boardwalk below them.

Moore had been nervous, excited about the imminent voyage, the gravity of their charge. He had been a bit dismayed at the passenger's lack of couth, and said as much to his first mate.

Know what's the difference between a cruise ship and a cucumber, Captain? the first mate said.

What? Moore's voice was sharp. He was nervous, and when he was nervous he was snippy. He also felt the distinct urge to have a stiff drink.

On a cucumber, his first mate had said, *all the little pricks are on the outside.*

Now, aboard the 272-foot-long *Nokomis*, he heard footsteps along the gangway, followed by an exchange between Collins, his first mate, and another baritone voice. A wiry, dark-haired man of medium height emerged from the doorway, somewhat stoop-shouldered, chest hair pushing out of the unbuttoned collar of his white oxford shirt. Moore thought he looked like the kind of man who should be wearing a gold chain, tattoos on his forearms.

Another little prick.

The man looked at Moore, glanced back down the narrow aisle to his right, then strode over, hand outthrust. "Captain Moore? It's been a while."

Moore took his hand, paused, and readjusted his grip. He had forgotten; Rollins was missing two fingers on his right hand. "Nice to see you again, Mr. Rollins."

Rollins nodded. "Frank, Captain Moore. Or Frankie, like my friends call me. I don't mind." He reached into his jacket pocket, and Moore took a cautious half-step back.

Frankie withdrew his iPhone, pretending not to notice Moore's recoil. He tapped the screen a few times,

then peered down at the readout with the annoyed squint
of a man who needed bifocals. He held the screen out
for Moore. "We're in for some weather."

Moore glanced at the screen politely, then opened
the fax Collins had handed him earlier. He let out a
long, measured breath. Despite the calm conditions at
the marina, the NOAA marine forecast showed the offshore conditions were predicted to deteriorate quickly.
The current five- to seven-foot swells were forecast to
double or even triple in the next seventy-two hours, with
the potential for larger rogue waves in the mix. Dense
fog and intermittent rain would persist, and the twenty-
knot north wind was predicted to increase overnight.
The only thing missing, Moore thought, was a typhoon.
A small boat advisory was already in effect for offshore
waters, and a special note had been added to the bottom:

> *Due to ongoing rescue operations in the area
> in recent days, Coast Guard response time is
> considered inadequate to respond to any
> emergencies at this time.*

Moore blinked. There had been several capsized craft
in offshore waters recently, but this was the first time
he'd seen a disclaimer on a marine forecast. Goddamn
government.

Frankie leaned over the side of the *Nokomis*. "Well?"

"It'll be bumpy," Moore said.

Frankie looked at him. "You prepared for it?" He
spoke like he moved, a pause and then a burst.

Moore tapped the brass rail of the *Nokomis* on which
Frankie was leaning. "She's got a shallow dead rise, and
that means we'll ride the swells instead of breaking

through them. The passengers will notice it, but it won't be terribly uncomfortable. If we get fifteen-footers, or breakers on the swells, then it might get rough."

"And those big waves they keep talking about? If we run into those?"

"Then it'll be rough as hell."

"So the tables, they're gonna go sliding around? Spilled drinks, people hacking up their caviar?"

"I don't think so, Mr. Rol—Frankie. I'll run a heading of about forty degrees out to the Line, where . . ." He paused when he saw the frown on Frankie's face. "Sorry. I'll head northeast to the international boundary, what we call the Line. Then we'll ride the waves south, parallel to the coast. Our travels would be a lot rougher if we actually had to reach a specific destination."

"And the fog?"

"Fog is an old problem," Moore said. "It's a modern vessel, Frankie. We have GPS and radar, several redundant systems. We will ride high enough in the water to show up on other craft radar as well. Fog is the least of my worries."

Frankie pushed himself off the railing, took a step toward Moore. "And what worries you most, Captain?"

"I'm sure you can imagine."

"The game."

Moore looked out to the ocean. The seas were bright until they reached the eastern horizon, where they ended in a thin black line. The darkness from the shadows of the waves.

"I understand my obligations," Moore said. "The seas won't be ideal, but they're manageable. It's the combination I worry about, the game and the weather. When things are rough at sea, people begin to complain. When complaining doesn't work, some people—rich people, especially—often begin to pry into the matters of the ship. To see what might be done better."

Frankie turned away, moving in the same abrupt, bird-taking-flight motion. He walked jerkily down the gangway, his diminished right hand trailing along the glass of the wheelhouse. In the distance, the bell tower of Boston's Park Street Church chimed lightly above the distant hum of traffic, then was lost in the babble of excited voices on the deck below them. Moore glanced back at the wheelhouse, at the traditional steering wheel he only used at the beginning and end of the voyage, and felt the old familiar thrill, the urge to wrap his fingers around the polished felloe and cut into the waves. The ship, so regal and silent this morning, was coming alive.

Moore's gaze paused on the other casino ship in the marina. *The Have Knots* was moored a quarter mile away, devoid of any activity. *Old Becker knows better than to run out into this slop*, Moore thought. *I wonder what it's like to do only the things you want to.*

Frankie stood, watching the city until the bell tower ceased its chiming, then returned. "I'm a professional, Captain Moore. Like you. So . . ." he brought his hands together in an eight-fingered clap. "I will trust you to ensure that the *Nokomis* tracks along her course in a timely manner, stays there for a certain period of time, and then returns to dock. You'll trust me that I will take care of business belowdecks. Complaints and any other matters. Understood?"

"Of course," Moore said. "I only meant—"

"You understand. Good." Frankie took the facsimile from Moore's hand, crumpled it up, and dropped it over the side of the boat.

Moore bit his lower lip, hard enough to hurt. A ship full of sheep, and now this man dropping trash over the side of his ship. Twenty years ago he would have thrown the little prick overboard. But that would be bad, or at least bad for business, and . . . imprudent. Moore was sixty-seven, the *Nokomis* a second chance. And second chances were like pretty young wives: They wouldn't stick around long if you didn't take care of them.

"I understand."

"Then bring us out to sea, Captain," Frankie said, patting the railing. "I'll tell you if you got anything else to be worried about."

Frankie Rollins moved down to the gaming deck, fingernails digging into his palms. Remembering.

The stench of stale smoke, cheap coffee. Six years ago, sweating profusely in the lower level of the security center at Caesars, a memory so vivid he could taste the wintergreen gum he used to chew, the mint pushing against the rising taste of bile. His heart thumping its way up into his throat, watching the man on the far side of the table who would, in approximately seven minutes, send him out into the desert for a slow beating, followed by a quick maiming.

He had met Manny Amato once before, at the annual Christmas Eve dinner, when Coriolos had sold out to the new owners. Both Manny and Frankie had been new to Caesars, but not the business. Manny was polite, interested in Frankie's background, and drank cups of black coffee around the almost constant smile he wore. The old dago bastard, Frankie thought, he'd probably started the background check before the cocktail shrimp had been cleared away for the main course. Thirteen months later, in the basement, Manny was still polite, still drinking black coffee around his stained teeth, but he wasn't smiling. Neither was his security detail.

And what was it Manny had said?

It's a modern casino, Frank. You can't be surprised we knew about this.

Frankie paused on the stairwell of the *Nokomis*, fingers thrumming on the handrail. It wasn't that they had said the same words, it was how they said them. *It's a modern ship. It's a modern casino.* Like Frankie was some ignorant hillbilly, didn't know there were security cameras at the 7-Eleven, couldn't understand how the cops found him at his trailer the same night of the robbery.

He took a step and then paused, thinking about the analogy. No, even hillbillies knew about video surveillance.

That was the kind of thing you had to be careful of, dating yourself with a bad comparison, and then having one of the kids give you that weird look. And that was another thing to be careful of, calling them kids. Frank was forty-eight, and for twenty years he hadn't worked directly for anybody older than him. His paychecks had been signed by kids, the decisions made by kids. But you couldn't call them that, or the paychecks wouldn't get signed at all.

Of course, after the desert, there hadn't been any more paychecks of any kind.

He drew his three fingers of his right hand across

his forehead. No need to dwell on it. Hell, the Mojave had been a net positive. He'd healed strong, the way a broken bone knitted together and became more resilient. And now, shit, he was an independent, a major player in a captive market.

He smiled at that, a captive market.

Whatever you wanted to call it, it was lucrative enough that he was ready for retirement. After this he was going to take care of some personal business, trim up the loose ends that were always fluttering around the back of his mind. Then move someplace warm, one of those retiree backwaters where he would be the young guy in town. Manzanillo or Puerto Vallarta, pick up some side action with the trophy wives. And never fucking worry again.

Except . . .

Except that wouldn't really be the case. When you had people to take care of, people you cared about, you couldn't really just hand them a bag of money and wash your hands. His mom with her habits, his sister with her illnesses, both real and imagined . . . neither one was cut out to function alone. Not when they were poor, certainly, even after decades of practice. He had a suspicion rich might be worse. Maybe take them with him . . . no, better yet, figure out a way so the money would come in regular, like a paycheck. His mother would appreciate that after all those years married to an ironworker. His sister could maybe get off the witch doctor prescriptions she was on, herbal pills and supplements, and get some real medicine. Real therapy.

He'd visit, once or twice a year. Like a rich uncle instead of the disappointing son.

Frankie entered the south wing of the main gaming room, occupied by a bartender and a couple of maids

running vacuums over the laminate flooring, the head-
lights reflected in the mirrored ceiling tiles. He went to
a line of slot machines, old ones that allowed you to
choose between the button and the manual lever. He
felt himself calming, settling into the feel of the place.
You wouldn't find this kind of machine in a modern
casino. Some Vegas accountant had done the math
years ago, figured out the time it took to pull a lever
compared to pushing a button, and just like that the
one-armed bandits went extinct. But the *Nokomis*'s
slot machines were manufactured by Character, the old
hulls retrofitted with modern guts. Not as fancy as the
rest of the machines on the gambling floor, but solid,
dependable. A good place to hide behind if a gunfight
happened to break out.

Those were the kinds of things Frankie Rollins liked
to think about when walking through a place for the
first time.

He walked over to the tables, the blackjack and
Caribbean poker, and saw that the felt was fuzzy. No mat-
ted places where the schmucks sat, no burn marks or
blemishes from spilled drinks. That could be bad or
good—either they didn't have much card action on
these cruises, or Sefelis Industries took the time and
expense to replace the felt when it got natty. He hoped
it didn't mean the card tables had just been added to
the venue, which might mean inexperienced dealers
and lots of headaches. Not that he gave a shit about the
take, not on this level, but Moore was right about one
thing: Be it ships or casinos, when things went to shit,
the moneymen started headhunting.

The far wall was lined with flat-screens for the sports
book. The Sox played later tonight; Frankie would have

to remember to come up and see what the line was, maybe drop a twenty. He hadn't been in Boston long, but it was strange how little things could open you up to the right people. Little doorways, like becoming a Sox fan, usually led nowhere. Sometimes, though, a comment about the wisdom of the starting rotation, or why the manager was or was not a douche bag, led to a conversation. And once in a while that conversation became interesting.

He moved closer to the bank of screens. CNN was playing an aerial video of a rescue operation off the coast of Nova Scotia. A few people had washed up onto a bleak escarpment of brown rock, little yellow penguins waving at the chopper. The scrolling tagline underneath read: *ROGUE WAVES CONTINUE TO PLAGUE NORTHEAST COAST. SURVIVOR SAYS THE BOAT FELT LIKE IT "BROKE IN HALF" UNDERNEATH HIM. TWELVE STILL MISSING.*

Frankie waved at a nearby bartender, a young black guy who was wiping out wineglasses. "You wanna turn the station, friend?"

The bartender looked up, saw what was on the screen, and flipped the channel to a soap opera without saying a word. Frankie had seen the soap before; even the names were familiar. He watched for a second, seeing if anybody'd got their shit together in the past decade. No, same problems. He moved on, taking a moment to drop a twenty in the empty wineglass next to the bar's register. He glanced back as he opened the door to the lower levels, in time to see the bartender fold the twenty into the pocket of his white oxford shirt. He grinned at Frankie and Frankie nodded back, knowing he had made his first friend on the *Nokomis*.

* * *

The next level down, C, was lodging. Frankie strolled through the busy hallway, nodding and smiling to people who didn't seem to notice him. The air smelled of people, sweat and cologne and perfume, and under it was the constant saline odor of the harbor. There were smaller rooms near the bow and Rollins saw those were crammed with younger men and women, partiers, smuggled booze bottles already perched in places of honor on top of the faux teak dressers.

He turned the corner of the hallway and went down the port side of C-deck, where the small rooms gave way to onboard facilities. There was a small medical room, currently unstaffed, and next to it a large room labeled DAYCARE. There was a small deli-slash-pharmacy in the center of C-level, with a bloated, goateed man behind the counter. An attractive blonde was trying to find something to eat for the brat hanging on her leg, while studiously ignoring the eye-fucking Mr. Goatee was giving her.

"You want a sandwich?" the blonde said. The kid shook her head. "You've got to eat something. How about an apple?"

"Uh-uh."

Frankie could've told her, no kid who just boarded a big ship wants to eat a damned apple.

"M&M's," he said. "With vanilla ice cream. Ship special."

The woman glared at Frankie, and he waved an apology as he walked past, the kid now babbling about ice cream. He turned the corner in the hallway, feeling the woman's eyes burning into the back of his head. He didn't get it. All these parents, they spent a

couple grand to get away, brought the source of their
tiredness with them, didn't relax, couldn't take a joke.
He wondered if it was guilt or love. If there was even a
difference.

At the far corner of the port side was Room C85,
and Frankie withdrew the key card from his wallet and
passed it through the lock. He stepped inside, giving
the door an extra little shove to get it to latch behind
him. It was a newly constructed room, built around an
existing stairwell, and it had the feel of a rushed job.
Hell, the entire ship's construction seemed lightweight,
shoddy, a bad vibe for a gambling venue. In Vegas, in
AC, there was a distinct feeling of substance in the infrastructure, a connection. You started to lose your ass
at the table, you could lean down, grab hold of it, feel
yourself secured to seven, eight feet of concrete. Anchor yourself, even as your money was flying away.
Out here, you started losing money, the waves and the
bird's-nest construction would probably send you
straight to your room, make you tuck your credit cards
under the mattress.

"Who is this?"

There were two men in the room, a large man who
looked maybe Samoan and an even larger Scandina-
vian-looking guy with his long blond hair tied in the
back. Great big slabs for arms, his face flushed red. It
was the white guy who had spoken, in a clipped Nordic
accent. *Hue is tiss?* Frankie looked at the Samoan. The
guy in the chair—always talk to the guy who was sitting down.

"Frankie Rollins. You guys with Prower or Latham?"

"You got the wrong room, little Frank," the Scandinavian said, taking a step forward. "Nobody's here but me and Adrian."

"They're expecting me," Frankie said, nodding at the door in the back of the room. "I got business down-stairs."

"Is dead-end room," the man said. "Our room."

"Shit," Frankie said. "Here I thought I was going to go talk to my clients, and what I did was"—he looked directly at the big Swede, or Dane, or whatever the hell he was—"I went and barged into your love nest before you could assume the position. You're the submissive one, Thor?"

"Funny," Thor said, and placed a hand on Frankie's shoulder. "Outside, little guy. Before you get in an accident."

Frankie considered his options. It was a small room, and Thor's massive hand was clamped firmly on his shoulder. "Frankie Rollins," he said again, looking around Thor's mass to Adrian. "Check with them, friend. I had the key card to get into this room, didn't I?"

Adrian didn't move. The hand shifted from Frankie's shoulder to the back of his neck, and then he was being propelled back toward the door. His feet touched the floor only two out of every three steps.

Well, shit. He couldn't let it start out like this.

He lunged forward, out of Thor's grip, and dropped to the floor. The big man was on him quick and Frankie rolled away, pulling the five-inch Buck knife from the scabbard on his hip, swiveling low and fast. Thor's arm passed over him, grazing his back, and Frankie brought the knife down. The blade entered between Thor's metatarsal bones and passed all the way through the white sneaker, quivering to a stop deep in the wood floor.

Thor bellowed and Frankie rolled away again, the big fist slamming into the floorboards where he'd been a second earlier. Adrian was watching them, frowning, and Frankie saw he'd made a mistake. Adrian wasn't in charge; hell, Adrian's lightbulb wasn't even screwed all the way into the socket. No, if there was a boss in this room, he'd just stabbed him in the foot.

Frankie shook his head at Adrian, who was just now reaching under his jacket. "Nope," he said, showing him the 9mm Glock he already held in his hand. "Better go downstairs and tell them what happened. You remember my name?"

"Yeah," Adrian said. "I remember it."

"Go on, then," Frankie said, pointing to the door with the muzzle of his gun. "I'll take care of your buddy."

After Adrian went out the back door to D-level, Frankie moved closer to Thor, who was half-bent, not quite touching the hilt of the knife. His back heaving like a bellows.

Frankie had seen a documentary once, where this trapper up in Maine had caught a fisher, this big mean-ass weasel sort of thing. It was caught by the front paw in a leghold trap and there was a catch-circle around it, a black patch of frozen topsoil torn into the snowy ground. The trapper had stepped inside the circle to release it—fisher season wasn't open yet, the narrator said in a dry voice—and just like that the fisher had darted forward and ripped away a chunk of the guy's jeans, and a piece of the guy's calf, faster than you could blink. Blood spraying onto the frozen dirt, the guy hopping backwards, the fisher maybe not going to be so gently released now. Rollins had played the attack in slow motion a bunch of times, lying slouched on the recliner in his apartment with his bourbon-rocks resting on his belly, thinking there was some kind of lesson there. Not getting too close to a dangerous animal being first and foremost, especially if you had good intentions.

Bad intentions, that was okay, just knock it on the head.

"I understand you were doing your job," Frankie said. "You got responsibilities, yeah, nobody gets through to D-deck. Assholes should've let you know I was coming."

Thor breathed in deeply, his head turning slightly, looking at Frankie out of the corner of his eye. Frankie looked down the massive leg to the knife and sneaker now perfectly motionless. He had only started carrying a blade after the incident in the desert, a knife at first and then, because a blade seemed silly, almost archaic, he bought the Glock. At first the pistol felt strangely heavy when he slid it into the shoulder holster, too dense, like he was carrying some mercury-filled secret with him. Affected his mood, made him less friendly, and he wasn't full up in the friendly department to begin with. He got used to it, in time. He'd gotten used to lots of stuff.

Blood began to leak out the side of Thor's sneaker.

"That's gotta hurt."

"Is starting to," Thor said. "I've never been stabbed before this."

"I would have preferred we shake hands," Frankie said. "Listen, you're gonna be working for me on this show. I already cleared that with both the guys, Latham and Prower, both their lieutenants know the drill. Hornydog and the Russian."

"Hornaday," Thor said. "Hornaday and Kharkov."

"Sure," Frankie said. "They might act like they're in charge, but I'm boss."

"Yes, is fine." No doubt Thor was feeling it now, the building pain fraying the edge of his voice. "You pull this knife out, *chef*?"

"I'm not a cook, you big fucking dork."

"Is Swedish," Thor said, then groaned. "Means 'man in charge.'"

Frankie could hear voices below them, at the base of the stairwell, and saw Adrian had left the door slightly ajar. The gap between the door and the doorframe wasn't quite square. Surprise, surprise.

The voices grew louder, and now Frankie could hear somebody moving at the base of the stairs. In a few moments they would be up here, looking for the guy who was supposed to run the show, keep things smooth. Come up and find a wounded giant bleeding all over the floor, and Frankie backed into a corner.

"I'm going to get that knife out of your foot," Frankie said. "No reason we got to wait, right? But remember two things, Thor."

The big man took another deep breath. "Yes?"

"There is only one *chef*," Frankie said, kneeling forward and placing his hand around the hilt of the knife. Thor hissed at the pain and Frankie let him feel it for a second, wondering if the big man was going to reach down and turn him into a pretzel. "And if he has to stab you again, it ain't gonna be in the foot."

He pulled the knife up and out in one clean jerk, wiped the blade on the cuff of Thor's pants, and slid it back into his sheath. He looked up, held Thor's gaze for a second, then reached down and unlaced his bloody sneaker. He felt the giant shift his mass above him, the floorboards groaning, and pulled the shoe free.

"Jesus," Frankie said. "I bet there's goddamn mushrooms inside this thing. You heard of Dr. Scholl's?"

He tossed the shoe aside and scrolled Thor's sock down over a large, hairless ankle, and used the dry upper portion of the sock to wipe the blood off Thor's foot. After the blood was sopped up it didn't look like much of a wound, a tiny red mouth in a big foot. He grabbed a towel from the bathroom, wrapped it around Thor's foot, and helped him to a chair.

"It's starting to hurt."

Frankie nodded. "Couple minutes, we'll go find a doc. I'll get you on light duty the rest of the cruise, full paycheck. But no more misunderstandings between me and you. Got it, Thor?"

The massive head nodded. "My name is Christopher."

Frankie placed the heel of his shoe on top of Christopher's swaddled foot and pressed down. "I'll say it one more time," he said. "Won't be no more misunderstandings. Between me and you, between me and anybody. There is, you get off your light duty and clear it up. I got more important things to do than play knife games. Understand?"

Thor's upper lip quivered. "I understand, *chef.*"

"That's good," Frankie said, removing his heel. "We're going to get along fine, Thor."

Underneath them the ship shuddered, and Frankie put a hand against the wall as the directional props pushed the ship away from the dock.

The door creaked open. Frankie looked up to see a pale face staring at him from the darkness of the stairwell. A compact, powerfully built man moved into the light, his head and face covered with short bristles of hair, bloodshot eyes centered by pale irises. The man's eyes shifted from Frankie to Thor, and then back to Frankie. He took another step forward, his black leather boots silent on the floorboards. Not so much stepping as gliding.

Frankie's hand tightened on the Glock, and he made a conscious effort to put the gun back in its shoulder holster.

"You Latham's man?"

The man's nostrils flared. He took another step forward, his hands empty, no evidence of a weapon. It gave Frankie minimal comfort; the man was radiating coiled tension. His irises were so pale they appeared silver, swimming in the bloodshot sclera. His lips were bloodless in contrast.

"We're on the same team, friend."

The man took another step forward, then paused as Adrian came out the door behind him. Adrian's shirt was untucked and he was sweating, breathing hard from the climb up the stairs.

"Yeah, that's the g—" Adrian started to say, and then

the man with bloodshot eyes swiveled, his arm flickering out, the index and middle fingers jabbing Adrian just below his Adam's apple. Adrian fell backwards, his eyes blooming wide in surprise, his hands coming up to cover his throat. He coughed weakly, tried to draw in another breath, and his eyes opened wider when he realized he couldn't inhale.

"Jesus," Frankie said. "You didn't have to do that."

The man turned back to him, his expression unchanged. Behind him, Adrian wheezed out another weak cough and sank to his knees, his eyes bugging as he fought for breath.

"What the hell?" Frankie said. "Help him, Thor."

Thor went to Adrian and began prying his hands off his throat. Frankie made a conscious effort to check his anger. The man was Latham's head of security, probably cherry-picked from dozens of mercenary types.

"Tough guy," Frankie said, nodding. "Bet you were popular at recess when you were in grade school."

The man's lips peeled back slightly, revealing small and even teeth. "Go," he said in a slight Eastern European accent. "Or you will be hurt. Not like this." He jerked his head toward Adrian, who had finally managed to draw in a breath and was hacking it back out. "Hurt for real."

"When I said grade school," Frankie said. "I meant the one at the orphanage."

The man tensed, and Frankie started to duck, realizing his humor wasn't going over real well on the *Nokomis*.

"Kharkov."

The man froze, and then let his arm drop. A tanned, well-dressed man in his late forties stood in the doorway, his dark hair combed in a stylish wave, wearing an expensive-looking sport jacket over a white shirt open at the collar. His face was long and angular, the lips wormy. *Richard Latham*, Frankie thought. *My hero.*

Kharkov moved to the side and Latham stepped forward, surveying the room, batting his eyes once as Adrian drew in a choked breath, and turned his eyes to Frankie. Heavy eyebrows over dark and active eyes, a big, bent bird-of-prey nose, but there was a sagginess to his face, a slight hollowing-out to his frame. Eyes too small for the sockets, lips pulled back over his teeth. He looked, Frankie thought, like a starving eagle.

"What's the problem?" Latham said.

Thor spoke up. "No problem, Mr. Latham. I screw up, Mr. Frankie straighten out. We are good."

Latham glanced at Thor, then turned back to Frankie. "No problem?"

"Communications glitch," Frankie said. "Some asshole forgot to tell them I had clearance." He jerked his chin toward Thor. "Your boys better get his foot looked at. Terrible toenail clipping accident, you shoulda seen it."

Latham took a deep breath and steepled his fingers, rubbing the pads against each other, then laced them together and rested them against his chest.

"Kharkov?"

"Sir."

"Is this okay? This type of situation?"

"No, sir."

"This sort of . . . chaos?"

"It won't happen again."

Latham reversed his laced fingers, cracked his knuckles, and pointed at the floor. "Get Doc Perle down here to look at his foot, then mop that blood up off the floor. Make it shine, Kharkov. You know how I feel about cleanliness."

"I'll get the doctor down here right away. A janitor, too."

Latham cocked an eyebrow. "Did I say I wanted a janitor?"

Kharkov's lips tightened. "I'll take care of it personally, sir."

Latham nodded. "Wonderful, just wonderful." He started toward the back door, then turned to Frankie. "You coming, or you want to help swab the decks?"

Frankie followed him, patting Adrian on the shoulder as he went past. There was a slight hum of conversation below him, the tinkle of ice in glass. The sound of a girl's voice, bright and pleasant. He could already tell he was going to like D-Deck better than the rest of the ship.

Chapter 3

They saw it on the radar when they were ten minutes away, the single blip separating into two distinct marks on the Furuno's screen. Gilly pulled the throttle back, dropping down to twelve knots, just fast enough to keep them on plane. The fog had grown thicker as afternoon slipped into evening, the saturated air coalescing into raindrops on the windshield before being slicked away by the wipers. A hundred yards' visibility, maybe fifty; it was hard to tell. According to the radar, they were two miles east of Boon's Island, a little less than a mile from the *Archos*'s coordinates. They'd lost radio contact ten minutes earlier, and the Coast Guard reception was getting scratchy.

Gilly tapped the second mark, his jaw muscles clenched. "You see that shit?"

"Keep going," Brian said. "Might be another boat, might not. No reason to turn around now."

Gilly brought her back up to twenty knots, adjusting their bearing to account for the strong current sweeping the *Archos* south. "ETA is five minutes," he said.

"That other blip is right on 'em. If we dumped those fish for nothing . . ."

"Leave it," Brian said. "Concentrate."

"Aye, aye, grandmaster of the high seas. If it's okay with your eminence, I'm gonna swing southeast on one-thirty and then work back up. Might have a floater who lost hold of the ship."

"Good plan." Brian went down to the cuddy, bracing himself with one hand as *Tangled Blue* crashed through the waves. It was a noisy boat on big water, the big inboards growling, the hull creaking. He could just imagine the microfractures blooming in her ribs, the piston walls pitting and gouging at the higher RPMs. Smitty, the owner of the marina garage, would probably like those sounds. Like so many coins falling into his bank account.

Brian gathered up the two life rings and the extra life jackets from the cuddy, then opened up the emergency kit. The flare gun was a converted Ithaca single-shot twelve gauge, its retrofitted barrel modified to take a huge eight-inch Thompson flare. He took the shotgun out, thinking of long-ago autumn days of grouse hunting with his old man, a similar Ithaca held lightly in his father's hands.

The Meat-getter. The old man had missed with it, but not often. For Brian, who could shoot minute-of-angle groups with most rifles but shotguns with only a modicum of success, the Meat-getter had been a venerated, almost mystical weapon. Seven months after his father died he'd taken the Ithaca out, oiled it, and loaded it with seven-and-a-half shot low base, and proceeded to miss three grouse (except they weren't called grouse, they were partridge, or *pahh-tridge* in northern Vermont parlance) in a row, easy going-away shots, the partridge flying low and straight down the clover-filled tote road that bordered his parents' back forty. When he returned home, he oiled the shotgun and placed it in storage. There would be no more sullying of the Meatgetter's legacy.

Gilly hollered from above, and a moment later the *Tangled Blue* slowed again. Brian grabbed two flares from the box of eight, slipped them into the shell holder on the Ithaca's barrel, and snapped the shotgun into the clips alongside the stairwell. He unhooked a coil of floating rope from one of the pegs and looped it over his shoulder, shaking his head to clear it. It was the fish, he supposed, those big early-season bluefins. Anytime he had a good day on the water he wished his dad was there to see it, to nod and smile. To approve, he supposed, although on bad days he thought of his father even more, knowing he would have got the same nod, a bigger smile.

"Cap?"

He climbed the stairs. "What is it?"

"There she is," Gilly said, pointing toward the horizon. The swells were five- and six-footers, with an occasional eight mixed in. Big slow-moving rollers, and as Brian watched the next set appear out of the fog he saw a rainbow sheen from spilled fuel on the side of the swell. There was a section of hull riding the wave, ten feet across, double-walled with foam insulation sandwiched between the fiberglass. It drifted past them, a crimson streak of blood smeared across the shredded fiberglass.

Gilly said, "What the hell?"

"Nothing out here to break her up," Brian said. "An explosion?"

"You'd think. But no burn marks."

"And lots of fuel left on the water. Maybe one of those rogue waves."

"Hell of a wave."

They came down one of the bigger swells and the horizon closed in for a moment. Gilly gave the *Tangled Blue* throttle, and they powered up the next swell. As they came up the far side Gilly turned hard to port, narrowly missing another piece of hull, this one shredded along one edge, with bits of fiberglass trailing in the water.

Gilly nodded toward the radar. "Junk's too small to show up until we're on 'em. One of those hit the props, we're on a slow float to Bermuda."

Brian dropped the rescue gear on the floor of the boat and grabbed the binoculars off the dash. "I'm going up on the bridge. Keep this heading and speed." He paused. "And don't scratch my boat."

"Suck it, Captain."

Brian climbed up the aluminum ladder, pausing when they crested the top of the waves, continuing when they were in the valleys. He reached the flybridge and moved carefully to the control counter to flip on the inter-boat radio. Normally, he would be able to control the boat from the flybridge, but the hydraulic steering cables had been broken for the past two seasons. It was a pain, but flybridge controls weren't required by the Coast Guard. If he still had those tuna in the hold, he would have been able to fix the boat up, pay the rest of his loan down. Hell, maybe spring for some new rod and reels. . . .

If, if, if. His father's voice came to him, a dry, amused tone. *And if a frog had wings it wouldn't bump its ass when it hopped.*

He keyed the mike. "You got me, Gil?"

"Yeah. What you see?"

He swept the horizon left to right with the binoculars, went down five degrees and swept again. "There's more debris straight ahead. Take her ten degrees east on the back side of the next swell."

"Just tell me the heading. I know when to turn the damn thing."

Brian grinned, scanning the sea as Gilly maneuvered down the next swell. "Okay, she's clear for a bit, but lots of fuel on the surface. Better turn on the blower motors." He was thinking about an explosion on the seas that had happened two years earlier, due to a charter boat captain who had run his boat through a slick coming from a disabled merchant ship out in the shipping lanes. When the automatic bilge pump activated there were enough fumes in the engine housing to start a fire, and the charter had gone down like a Viking pyre.

"Blower's been on for five minutes," Gilly said. "When you were dicking around in the cuddy. You see anything?"

"Negative. You got a visual on that debris on the port side?"

"Little tiny pieces, yeah. She musta blew, Brian."

"Roger that," Brian said. "Surface temp?"

"Thirty-nine."

"They're going to be popsicles if they're in the water. Where're we at on their original coordinates?"

"Just hit them," Gilly said. "I'm coming around on a zero heading, and we'll run back south on a one-eighty. I got through to the Coasties, asked for a bird. Choppers are grounded, but they offered an SRB out of Gloucester."

Brian scanned the horizon. It would be a waste for the Coasties to send out one of their Small Response Boats. He knew it, Gilly knew it, and he was pretty sure the Coastie officer knew it. Well, hard to know on that last one. A lot of the Coastie officers were kids, smart young men who didn't always understand the ocean, didn't realize that sending out an SRB in this slop was a waste of fuel. Air support wasn't always a godsend, especially in this fog, but Coastie chopper pilots didn't go out on hopeless missions. Once dispatched, the MH-60 jockeys would fly in coordinated grids, using the surface search radar like a metal detector to sweep the ocean's surface.

They came up on top of a big swell and Gilly turned hard, cutting into a wave like a surfer. As they crested, Brian saw something dark to the southeast, sliding up and over one of the swells. A second later it disappeared behind the endless series of waves.

Brian keyed the radio. "Bring her to a one-twenty-five," he said. "We've got something in the water, could be the main part of the hull."

They powered forward, running in line with the waves. He didn't see the shape again as they crashed through one wave, then another, the bow climbing high into the sky and then crashing down. They crested another wave and Brian saw it again, a jagged piece of flotsam riding the waves hard to the south, farther ahead of them than he'd expected the wreckage would be. The current was strong, as powerful and fast as he'd ever seen on the open seas, running down the western boundary of Gulf current. The Kaala, they called it, a wildcard current rubbing up against the massive North Atlantic gyre.

He brought the binoculars up again, adjusted the focus. "You got anything left?"

"A bit," Gilly said. "Don't want to come down too hard on the back side of these swells and swamp her."

"Better give it to her. I think there's somebody out there," he said, waiting for the shape to reappear. It came up another wave and he saw it clearly, a truck-sized piece of hull with someone clinging to a piece of railing, one arm wrapped around it at an awkward angle. The man's feet swung loosely as the piece of hull slid down the next wave. Two hundred yards away, just to the east of their current bearing. The big Chrysler engines growled as Gilly powered up.

"I got a partial visual, top of the last wave," Gilly called up a few seconds later. They went down another swell and back up again. "Yeah, I got him, Bri. Come on down."

Brian slid down the flybridge ladder, pressing the side of his feet against the railings and dropping fast to the pitching deck.

"There," Gilly said, pointing through the windshield. They could see the man clearly now, his white hair plastered against the side of his face, his right arm twisted through a piece of railing. His body flopped from side to side as the hull rode up and down the waves.

"How's he hanging on?" Brian said.

"He's stuck to that fuckin thing."

Brian brought up the binoculars. "I think you're right."

"Dead?"

"Doesn't matter," Brian said. "We're gonna get him."

Gilly glanced at Brian, his Adam's apple bobbing once in his scrawny neck, and then he slid out of the captain's chair, keeping one hand on the wheel. "Bring me up alongside," he said. "I'll see if we can latch on without busting up the boat."

Brian shook his head. "I got it."

"Might hafta get wet," Gilly said, almost gently. "Take the wheel, Cap. I got him."

Brian hesitated for a moment, staring at the side of the boat, the spray of water splashing over the gunnels. Panic, sudden and frantic, clawed up inside him, threatening to break like the waves. He tried to push it down, but there was no edge to push. It was just there, growing and shapeless and wild. The boat shrank under him, and suddenly he could feel the careless power of the ocean all around him, crowding around the boat.

"C'mon," Gilly said gently. "Take the wheel."

Brian slid past him into the captain's chair. He took the wheel, his hands trembling. Twisted in the seat, checked the gauges. All was good, all was fine. He brought the throttle down and then powered forward at the same speed. He felt the hitch right away, the slight clunk in the drive. They had pushed her too hard coming out here. Smitty had warned him. No time to worry about it now. He was in control.

Gilly moved to the port side of the *Tangled Blue*, a coil of rope in his hand. The old man's forearm was wedged under a piece of the hull's railing; the stainless-steel railing had been crushed against the hull, pinning his arm. His face was pressed flat down the side of the fiberglass and his skin had a purplish cast, darker near his neck and around his eyes. Cold seawater splashed up and over his face without visible effect.

Brian sounded the air horn. The man looked like he twitched. Brian hit the horn again and the old man lifted his head a fraction of an inch, then let it drop back to the hull.

Gilly began to shrug on a life jacket. "That hull's got some wicked edges on her, Cap. Don't get too close."

"What are you doing?"

"I gotta get in there."

Brian started to protest, then fell silent. Gilly was right—the hull could easily puncture the side of the *Tangled Blue* if they didn't try to control it. He held up a hand. "Wait."

"Hurry," Gilly said.

Brian flipped on the Garmin autopilot and raced down into the cuddy. There was a large toolbox underneath the aft cabin's bed and he searched it quickly, throwing tools to the floor. He found the hacksaw on the very bottom, the handle inked with a faded DL HAWKINS. He took the cuddy stairs back up in two quick leaps. Gilly tied the rope around his waist, and then traded Brian the tag end of the rope for the hacksaw.

"Ready," Gilly shouted, and before Brian could answer, Gilly leaped over the side of the *Tangled Blue* and into the icy waters.

Chapter 4

The world had changed.

The predator moved slowly along the edge of the current, between the cold and warmer waters. It was in unfamiliar territory, filled with quick, darting prey. The ocean was still rich with food, as it had always been. Even now the predator could smell three different prey species, two upcurrent and another floating in the warmer waters to its side.

The predator worked its jaws slowly, its jagged fangs rubbing against each other, making a sound like a glacier moving across a field of rubble.

It was beyond famished. The hunger was alive, clawing its way out of the stomach, up through the nerves and into the brain. Urging a single directive, over and over, like a separate, frantic pulse.

Attack. Attack.

It had worked its way south along the food-rich current, first pursuing the maddening, twisting little seals. It had streaked after the dumb sharks that turned away at the last moment, lain in ambush for the large, too-fast fishes that streaked away and left it tasting only *their terror-streaked wake. In desperation, the predator had descended to the ocean floor where there was only the semblance of light and attacked the long pale serpents that dwelt among the trenches that reeked of sulfur and even these creatures were too fast for it.*

This last hibernation had been a long one. It could feel age in its bones, could sense the shift in its world, a curve of evolution it could not quite bend to. A sense it had been left behind.

It was not slower, not weaker. If anything, this last period of decades-long hibernation seemed to have rekindled the predator's body. But the world had moved on, and this was no longer the predator's predictable kingdom, filled with prey that relied on its mass to repel attacks rather than its speed to avoid them.

Yet even now it felt something stirring inside its mind, a feeling of awakening.

An awareness.

It turned in a slow circle, eyes trained up at the wrinkled ceiling of the ocean. Smelling, watching, processing. Hearing its body crying to go on the hunt, to attack, but not giving in. Not yet. It was reveling in this new process. A thought wending its way through the predator's bloodthirsty cortex like a single phosphorescent algae twisting through the night seas.

The predator had evolved to attack large prey, to gorge on massive amounts of flesh and then rest. So when it had finally seen large prey, sunning itself on the surface, it had risen out of the depths and attacked. It had gone for the tail flipper, which had been finning rapidly.

The predator had ripped away chunks of the helpless prey, but the exoskeleton yielded nothing but a mouthful of splinters. In anger, it had struck again, and again, and eventually the prey had started to sink and then, only then did the outer shell yield morsels of food, little bits of flesh falling into the ocean.

It had turned out the exoskeleton was filled with the predator's favorite food.

It had smashed other shells as it worked its way along the current. It was good food, but not enough; soon its snout was gashed and sore from attacking the tail fins, and its stomach was still too empty. After striking a half dozen of these interesting but unsatisfying prey, the predator had gone in search of something that was more meat, less splinters.

It had failed.

Now the predator moved down into colder, darker water, the habitat it preferred when not hunting. As it descended the water column, the thought grew brighter, took on substance. As the sea diminished to a uniform gray the thought joined another, formed into something more.

A plan.

For centuries the predator had dipped in and out of consciousness, hibernating in periods of leanness, awakening to gorge and reproduce. Its species' natural lifespan was long, longer than the sea turtles they sometimes hunted, and the hibernations extended that lifetime exponentially, allowing them to survive long after its contemporaries had been reduced to calcified mud. It was not a difficult existence: Each time it awoke, the Arctic sea life offered the twin blessing of abundance and unwariness, entirely unprepared for the presence of this new uber-predator. But now food species were gone, either permanently or temporarily, jettisoned throughout the great expanse of waters by new currents.

Yet it had found some success. The exoskeletons of the floating prey were hard, but they were not dangerous. The tailfins were an annoyance, but an easy target for disabling the prey. There was not always much meat inside, but then again the predator had only approached moderate-sized species. Perhaps larger shells would result in enough food to fill its belly.

Perhaps the predator had been too conservative in choosing its victims.

It blinked, green eyes regarding the dull slate of the ocean with a new intensity. The thought was primitive, beyond abstract, existing only in a series of sensations, both remembered and anticipated. But something else had just registered in its mind, an illumination, a thought of how things were, and . . . how they could be. And for the first time in the long, violent existence of its species, the predator became aware of itself as a being separate from the ocean, separate from the air it breathed and the seawater that bathed its rough hide.

It was distinct from the prey it chased, and fundamentally superior to it.

The predator started to rise back up through the water column. The water lightened, and soon its body began to cry once again for it to attack. The predator swam faster, its serpentine body powering towards the surface.

Chapter 5

Destiny Boudreaux stood near the corner of the *Nokomis*'s bar, staring at the three men sitting around a low table in the center of the room. Talking and gesturing, their movements and words slow and easy. Going over some contract or business deal, she supposed, acting all refined and gentlemanly now. She could hear the slight squeak as the bartender, Remy, dried out the brandy snifters with a dish towel behind her.

"That tension, I feel it building," Remy said softly, his Acadian accent a pleasant, familiar sound. "Building up right here in front of me, jus' like a storm cloud on a summer afternoon. You behave now, hear? Little ass-grab don't mean much, grand scheme of things."

Destiny turned slowly, careful to keep the easygoing smile on her face. Remy wasn't big, maybe five-eight and a buck-thirty, a few inches taller than her, ten pounds heavier. Skin the color of coffee with milk, his dark hair falling back around his ears. Big hands for the rest of his body, his long fingers reaching around the snifters and placing them in the overhead slots above the bar.

"A grab is one thing," Destiny said. "That asshole over there"—she nodded toward Richard Latham, who was lighting a thin cigarillo—"was digging right in."

Remy looked down at the snifter in his hands, twisted the towel in. "You serious?"

"Like a goddamn gopher."

"He—?"

She shook her head. "He didn't get where he was trying to go."

"I thought he just goose you, way you jump like that."

"I should kick his ass." She was still putting on a good face, but the smile felt heavier every second. "I really should."

"Oh yeah?" Remy looked up at her, his hands still doing their thing. He had kind eyes, but Destiny had seen lots of guys with kind eyes do nasty things. Kick a guy in the face, or a woman, then look at her with those pretty blues or browns or greens and say, *We gotta get the fuck outta here.*

"Yeah."

Remy spun his drying towel in a tight spiral, then flipped it over and around his wrist and began to rub the bar down. It was a nice oak bar, she thought, but the guy who had finished it had done a shitty job with the epoxy coat. There were little air bubbles stuck in the clear coat, trapped for eternity because the carpenter hadn't stuck around for an hour to pop them free with a hairdryer as the epoxy hardened. She had seen it done right before, at a small bar outside Reno, and she had been amazed at how the epoxy had given the long walnut bar a richness and depth that she would never have expected. Her first real job, the carpenter her first real boyfriend. And now, more than a decade later, how many little bubbles were cemented in her? More than a few.

This bubble now, though, it was still rising. Still ready to pop.

Remy caught her by the back of her shirt as she started toward the table.

She turned, angry, and Remy let her go, holding up one finger. She took a breath and he nodded, then looked to the men in front of them until she followed his gaze. They were talking softly, elbows on their knees. When she turned back to Remy, he raised his eyebrows.

"What?"

"You know *what*," he said. "You gonna kick ass, you do it then, his paw down your skirt. He expect it then, maybe let you get a couple licks in. You go after him now, one o' them big bastards just scoop you up, throw your pretty little butt overboard." He paused, considering. "'Sides, them boys look like they got hard heads. You jus' hurt your hand."

Destiny looked at the row of men standing along the far wall, seven of them in all. Four of them had come in with Latham and looked like crosses between NFL linebackers and mercenaries, close shaven and hard-faced, their pectoral slabs bulging through their black shirts. The other three had come on board with the older

dude, Hamilton Prower. Prower was, she thought, the
only man in the room who knew how to dress. He looked
to be in his late sixties, with a ruddy complexion and a
heavy New England accent, his portliness somewhat
concealed by his tailored suit. He seemed very cheerful
compared to Latham, his blue eyes watching and absorbing, his mouth ready to smile. He had a cane that he
used constantly, though he didn't seem to have much of
a limp. The cane, like the rest of Prower, was dressed
up nicely: burnished walnut shaft, with gold inlays
near the handle.

Prower's bodyguards were smaller, ordinary-looking
men, their eyes roaming the room constantly but always
coming back to the slick-looking dude talking now,
Frankie Rollins. One of Prower's men, Hornaday, seemed
to be the boss of the smaller bodyguards, just as the scary-
looking dude with bloodshot eyes seemed to be in charge
of Latham's men.

Another man stood apart from the guards and the
three men at the tables. Tall and thin, slightly cadaverous, he had the look of someone not used to standing
while others sat.

One thing all these guys had in common, she thought,
there wasn't one of them going to fool her with kind
eyes.

"Hard heads, huh? Better hand me a wine bottle."

Remy's face was impassive. "They doing business,
girl. Go on, see if they want a drink. This good money,
hon. You and me both."

She bit at her lower lip, closed her eyes for a moment, sealed in the anger. Another bubble, locked into

place, never to pop. She reached down, adjusted the short black skirt that was her uniform, along with a white silk blouse and high heels. Nice clothes, but uncomfortable as hell and part of the reason she felt less like a hostess, which was how Frankie had described this gig, and more like the kind of girl who would do whatever, whenever, as long as the price was right. The other reason she felt vaguely whorish was because when Latham slid his hand down her skirt—not the first time something like that had happened—she hadn't punched him. Which *was* a first.

She glanced back at Remy. "Why are they paying us so much?"

"How much you getting?" Remy asked.

She pursed her lips. Ten grand for four days' work, plus expenses. She knew working girls in Vegas, better looking than her, that would consider this a solid gig. And they'd damn sure be doing more than delivering drinks and picking up smelly ashtrays.

"More than the going rate, let's say."

He grinned. "My first thought? Your job, it be something kinky, but now I see kinky and"—he peered at the brass name tag on her white blouse—"Mizz Destiny, they don't go hand in hand. Least not on the job."

"No, Frankie would have picked a different crew for that." *I hope*, she added silently. "He's got a game set up."

"'Course he do. Frankie always got a game set up," Remy said, his voice dropping down until she had to lean closer, smelling rich coffee, dark rum, his light aftershave. "Always working something. This something maybe a bit more on the hush-hush. Word from the crew is we running out thirty-five mile, twenty past the Line." His eyes went thoughtful, then cleared and he straightened. "But we ain't gonna talk about all that crud. He paying us good, and I ain't asking nothing."

"How far are we out now?"

Remy shrugged. "Been moving for two hours, we out in it." He pointed with his chin toward the table. "Go on, girl, be nice. Them boys look like tippers, especially the old dude with the cane. You want, feel free to share with your Uncle Remy."

"Tell me again how it goes," Hamilton Prower said. "I want everything to be perfectly clear in my mind." He had his cane clasped between his knees and was leaning forward, his expression open and frank.

Frankie nodded, leaned forward. To his side, Latham's face flickered with annoyance.

Well, no wonder the bent-nosed prick was annoyed, Frankie thought. They had been over the rules several times before they boarded, even signed a contract that Frankie knew would never show up, much less hold up, in any court of law. The format and structure of the game was his design, tweaked by Latham and Prower, yes, but simple to the point of banality. He'd run other games other ways, depending on his clientele, sometimes with exotic stakes or conditions. This one was as straightforward as it got. Cash for chips, and they played until the chips were gone. The chips winner got the pot, and the loser . . .

That was always the question, what the loser was going to do.

"We'll cross the international line about five o'clock," Frankie said. "That's fifteen minutes from now. You'll hear the captain send a message over the intercom, hear the rubes cheering upstairs. After that the party gets going upstairs. It'll probably go on until two, three in the morning."

"And our game starts at seven," Prower said. *And ahh game stahts at seven.* Frankie wondered if the accent was real. It was the kind of Nor'eastern drawl you expected to hear in a backwater tavern, not from a partner in one of Boston's top legal firms.

"Seven sharp," Frankie said. "We'll be well out to sea, no Coast Guard to worry about. The game is five-card draw, no wild cards. I got both your antes in my account." He swallowed the last of his drink, jingling the ice cubes to signal he wanted another. He wanted another look at the girl he'd hired, too. "There's a thousand dollars in chips for your initial stake. You get one buy-in, at the same cash-to-chips ratio, a thousand-to-one. No minimum, but we set the max at two grand, got to vote it in. You can buy in a third time, but that's it."

"Agreed," Prower said. "And the dealer? You said there would be a dealer. Impartial."

"I did," Frankie said, leaning forward as if this were the best question yet. As if they had not already discussed it several times. "The man flaked out, didn't pass the background check. Of course, you get that money refunded." Frankie paused, set his glass down gently. "He lied to me, gentlemen," he said. "He didn't mention his stint at a certain casino that was shut down by the Nevada State Gaming Commission for fraud, or that he was indicted and pled down to conspiracy to commit. He wasted my time, and yours. He is resting uncomfortably at the moment."

Prower's eyes opened slightly at this, in consternation or admiration Frankie could not tell. Nor did he care. It was all bullshit; he had any number of dealers who would jump at the chance to make good money for dealing this child's game, but none he wanted to pay thousands to, and nobody whom Prower and Latham would both trust. The bartender and the cocktail waitress were necessary, both of them with a reputation of honest work and minimal gossip. The girl, Destiny Boudreaux, he might have to get to know better. She was built well, and the light green streak she wore in her dark amber hair did something to him. He'd worried a bit about the color in her hair, wondering if Prower—who seemed not only well on the road to dribbling insanity, but also a bit of a prude—would object. But the old bird, who obviously fancied himself some sort of East Coast aristocrat, had not spared her more than a passing glance.

"It's fine," Latham said. "I'm not a card shark, and I'm comfortable enough assuming Mr. Prower isn't, either. What say you, Hamilton?"

"Certainly," Prower said. "A fair enough resolution."

"Good," Frankie said, leaning forward. "Listen, it's an unusual solution to your problem, I get it. But the game itself is straightforward. And remember, it's just a game. Luck and skill, and you're playing for chips.

You don't have to worry about what happens after. That's what I'm here for."

Latham's lips peeled back in a thin-lipped smile. "You can stop selling now, Frankie. I already paid you my million bucks."

Frankie glanced back at the bar. Destiny and Remy were talking again, not paying any attention to them. He turned back to Latham. "I just want it clear, there's no turning back."

"We're a little far out to sea for a course correction," Prower said. "In more ways than one."

"You'll shake on that?"

Frankie put his hand out over the table, between the two men. Hamilton reached out first, his hand hot and dry in Frankie's. Latham shook next, his palm cooler and sweatier, the exact opposite of what Frankie had expected. Another minor surprise, and he needed to quit being surprised. These two guys, no matter what they looked like, were stinking rich. Men who would show the faces that worked best at the time, who might thrive on deceiving friends and enemies alike.

Then Latham and Hamilton shook, and to Frankie it seemed that Prower and Latham regarded each other as kings might, not enemies or friends, just a man who was not his to boss around and so somebody with no place in their own life. But a man who must be tolerated nonetheless. Frankie could feel the appraisal each took of the other, neither man minding the other's stare, so deep was he within his own calculations.

"A handshake means a drink," Destiny said from behind them. "Right?"

The three men turned slowly, all at once. And the moment was broken.

"Yes," Frankie said. "One more drink for these two gentlemen."

Destiny reached deep inside herself to control the eye roll. "Okay," she said. "Let happy hour begin."

Chapter 6

Brian watched Gilly trying to cut through the railing, dismay and self-disgust welling inside him.

I never learn, he thought.

I never, ever learn.

As a teenage boy growing up in the wilder regions of northern Vermont, with parents who had grown confident in his abilities and judgment, Brian had few limits on his activities. He had no curfew, save for sunset on moonless nights when his mother feared he might find the starlight insufficient for navigation and wander off into a river or cave—the former of which was unlikely, the latter of which there was a profound scarcity in northern Vermont—but he was sensitive to her fears and returned on those nights early to watch television or read.

There were similarly few restrictions on what items he might take with him on his travels, although his father's firearms were generally off limits unless it was hunting season, and lighters and matches were forbidden when the woods were droughty. Brian soon discarded the burdensome hatchets and axes he'd read about in his boyhood novels and went about armed only with a canteen and a slender Buck jackknife, a gift from his grandfather, the carbon steel blade thin and long. He took great pride in the knife, and always looked for opportunities to use it, especially in front of others.

One day when he was fifteen he helped his father hang a quarter-beef they had received in payment from a neighboring farmer. The beef, a massive purple-red slab, hung suspended from a block and tackle attached to the garage rafters. A length of rope was needed to secure the quarter to the rafter to release the block, but when his father slapped at his front pocket it was empty. Brian offered his knife with considerable pride and then watched with mounting dismay as his father strained to saw through the rope with the dull blade, the strands popping loose one by one as a steel cable might under great stress.

There had been no reprimand. Later, his father had shown him how to work the whetstone, grinding the invisible cutting teeth into the blade's edge and then straightening them with several swipes on the sharpening steel. A process Brian had already been shown but one he watched attentively now, the hot blood of youthful embarrassment still burning in his cheeks.

When he was done, his father took the knife, pressed it flat against the back of his forearm, and drew the knife forward. A small cloud of black hairs wafted to the concrete floor of the garage, leaving a bare patch of skin just above his father's wrist. Then he had spoken one sentence before handing the knife over.

Any tool worth carrying, his father had said, *should be ready all the time.*

Gilly had been on the piece of hull for several minutes. He was completely drenched, and there was a jerkiness to his motions, the slowing of articulation that indicated the first stages of hypothermia. The old man lay motionless at his feet, not moving now, even when Gilly slapped his face.

The hacksaw blade scraped against the stainless-steel railing, barely biting into the hardened metal.

Better to cut his arm off, Brian thought. *But I doubt the blade could make it through the bone. Jesus.*

Gilly continued to saw, his arm moving mechanically. The waves were still building, and occasionally the rope stretching from the cleat on the *Tangled Blue* to Gilly's waist would tighten abruptly when one of the swells caught the slack. Gilly seemed to sense this before the tension could jerk him loose, and would abandon his sawing to secure a grip on the railing until it passed.

The section of hull surged forward on a large wave and Brian chased it, powering up the large swell, the wind howling around the edges of the *Tangled Blue*'s cabin. The hull was five yards to port and above his eye level, and he could see something curved protruding from the underside of the fiberglass, its shape distorted by the water. The bottom of it was pronged, with a slight flaring around the circumference. It curved upward into the thick fiberglass of the *Archos* like a scimitar.

That's why the hull isn't flipping over, he thought. *Whatever it is, it's acting like a rudder and a counterweight.*

He checked his instruments, his grip tightening on the throttle. "Oh shit," he breathed.

There was a massive green line on the radar screen, half a mile behind them. He knew what it was immediately; the Kaala ran counter to the Gulf Stream's direction, and the opposing currents and sharp delta in water temperatures had created more than the thick fog. It had also spawned rogue waves, monsters that could swamp even the large merchant ships.

He took a second to watch the radar swing around again. The wave was moving in line with the smaller waves, coming up on the *Tangled Blue*'s stern. Coming on them fast. If they could get under power and cut behind Boon Island, the rocks would break the wave's power.

He set the engines back to autopilot and leaned over the side of the boat, hands cupped around his mouth. "Gilly!"

His first mate glanced up, long hair falling over his face.

"Rogue coming up behind us!" Brian shouted. "You close?"

"Not even halfway," Gilly said, his voice shrill. He held up the hacksaw. "This blade's for shit!"

"Hang on, you're coming in."

He hit autopilot and started pulling, the wet nylon rope piling on the floor at his feet. The section of hull was shaped like a triangle, with two rounded points and the third much sharper, with a steel base for the railing embedded in the fiberglass, sheared off in a bright wedge of metal. He paused as the hull neared the two men spinning in the uneven waves. Watching the deadly point of the fractured hull swing toward them, then away. Then back at them. Gilly stuck the hacksaw under the place in the railing where he had been cutting and tried to pry the old man's arm loose. The hacksaw frame flexed, then bent.

Gilly looked up at Brian and shook his head.

Brian glanced back at the radar. The wave had nearly halved the distance to them in the past minute.

"Stupid," he muttered, "Stupid, stupid, *stupid*."

He wrapped the rope around a cleat, then picked up another coil and ran it through the two life rings. He dropped the rope and floats overboard, the life rings bobbing at the waterline of the *Tangled Blue*. A thin protection against the spinning, jagged flotsam he was about to bring in.

He pulled the hull closer, timing its rotation, and when the jagged end spun outward, he yanked in the rest of the slack. The rounded side butted up against the *Tangled Blue* and he ran a half hitch over the cleat, then lunged forward and gathered in the rest of the slack from the rope tied to Gilly. The hull bumped lightly against their side.

"Cap?" Gilly said from below him. "The fuck you doing?"

"Hold on!" Brian shouted over the steady roar of the wind. "I'm sending down the tackle!"

He pulled a pin on the crane assembly, swiveled it over the side, and locked it into place. Denny had used the rig to haul bluefin over the side of the hull in the old days, before Brian had retrofitted the *Tangled Blue* with an aft hatch and an electric winch to haul fish through the back of the boat. The crane was unwieldy, a bit of an eyesore, and added extra weight. But Brian had left it in place, sometimes even using it to unload his catch when the marina's crane wasn't working. Mostly he just liked the look of it, a retrograde contraption that conjured images of men in oilskins, kerosene lanterns swaying above decks. Simpler times.

He lowered the rope and hook overboard. Gilly caught it, quickly looped it around the railing, and pounded the side of the boat three times. Brian leaned over the side and looked down at his first mate. "Ready?"

"It'll be a damn wrecking ball if a wave catches us wrong."

"Climb up."

Gilly looked from Brian to the old man.

"He's pinned," Brian said. "I need you up here."

Gilly pulled himself up the rope, hand over hand, and slid over the edge. He looked behind them, peering through the thick wall of fog. They could see nothing, hear nothing other than the wind and waves coupling and clashing, the creaks of the *Tangled Blue*'s hull. The dull throb of the Chryslers—Brian was sure that one or more cylinders were missing now—echoed back to them against the waves. Brian felt an urge to check the radar again and dismissed it. It was the same as seeing fish on the graph—you had to trust your electronics. Just because you couldn't see something with your naked eye didn't mean it wasn't there.

Then, as Gilly moved alongside him, they heard it. Not an amplification of sound but the absence of it, a muting of their world as the giant wall of water blocked out the sounds of the wind and the waves behind it.

He shoved Gilly toward the cabin. "Go," he said. "Get us in front of it."

Gilly stumbled to the captain's chair, leaving a trail of seawater on the boat's vinyl floor. Brian leaned over the side. The hook of the block and tackle had slid to one end of the railing. The old man was still motionless. Brian leaned back into the rope and began pulling. The crane tower creaked, straining as the hull lifted off the water and its full weight swung into open air.

The Chryslers powered up and the *Tangled Blue* surged forward. The *Archos*'s hull caught the top of a wave, and the crane bent hard, the wood fibers popping. "Back her down," Brian said, paying out more rope.

Gilly let off on the throttle just as the rogue wave emerged, its height lost in the fog above them. No more than sixty yards behind them, a wall of water that would not simply swamp the *Tangled Blue*—it would turn her into splinters.

The hull dipped into a wave, and more of the heavy marine rope burned through Brian's palms. The hull swung out from the side of the boat, skipping and then digging, the rope snapping and popping. Water sprayed over the old man, and Brian felt a moment of terrified hilarity; for a moment, the old man looked like he was bodysurfing behind the *Tangled Blue*.

Several large foothill waves reached the *Tangled Blue* and shoved it forward. Another of the waves caught the *Archos*'s hull, spinning it toward them, the jagged end rotating around like a knife spinning on the floor. Brian could see the gleam of shorn metal heading straight for the side of the *Tangled Blue*.

"Hard starboard!"

Gilly cut the boat to the right as Brian pulled his bait knife free of his belt sheath. The fractured hull surged toward the *Tangled Blue* atop another foothill wave, moving with a preternatural speed as the elasticity of the rope pulled it back in. Gilly turned the *Tangled Blue* away, not quite fast enough, and the hull smashed into the back corner. Brian went sprawling across the slick vinyl floor, holding the bait knife out away from his body, and crashed into the corner of the large tackle box on the other side of the boat. The thick plastic buckled under his weight and he spun off it, coming to a rest under the captain's chair.

Brian choked in a breath, the low slimy fish smell filling his nose as the boat swayed and surged under him.

Must be how the beached bluefins feel, he thought.

Gilly was calling his name, asking if he was okay, and Brian slapped him on the back of his calf. He was still holding the bait knife in his other hand, which was good. He intended to cut the damn hull loose as soon as he got could get up. He couldn't see the giant wave or the *Archos*'s hull, but he could tell by the angle of the rope on the block and tackle that Gilly had powered up again. They still weren't moving very fast; the hull and the old man were acting like a drift sock, keeping them to a maximum speed of six or seven knots. Fast enough to stay ahead of the giant wave, but not enough to pull away.

He felt the first relaxation of his solar plexus, and a thin trickle of air worked into his lungs.

Gilly prodded him with his foot.

Brian got to his knees, digging the point of the knife into the vinyl floor as an anchor point. The crane assembly was straining over the side of the boat, the marine rope popping beads of water out of its taut length.

Go ahead, he thought. *Cut him loose.*

No.

Too cold. The water's too cold and he's been in there too long. Already dead.

Yes. It is cold and he is still alive.

The rational voice, the one urging him to cut the line, was his. The other was different. It was not his dead wife's voice he heard, nor his dead son's. Nor his dead father's. It was his own voice he heard but it felt *of* them, of all of them, distilled into a separate entity. A voice he had heard before.

"I don't cut him loose we all die," he gasped.

There was no answer to this, not from Gilly who could not have heard him, nor from that disembodied voice that appeared unsummoned but never truly unexpected. Just his own conscience, with its self-righteous lisp. Most of the time he could believe that, knew he was a man haunted by regret and sorrow but nothing more. Perhaps slightly crazy as well, which he could live with, even appreciate.

He got to his feet and crossed the twelve feet to the starboard side. The back corner of the *Tangled Blue* was smashed in and he could hear the water shooting out the side of the boat from the bilge. They were taking on water, how much he couldn't be sure.

The shattered hull was fifteen feet behind them, as far as the rope would let it go. The hull was just about to be caught by the last foothill wave, which would undoubtedly push the damned thing into the same corner of his foundering boat. And behind that the rogue, the mountain that pursued them.

The old man was still motionless. Brian turned his gaze to the rope, ignoring Gilly's shouts. The rope quivered under the tremendous tension. All he would have to do was touch the edge of the bait knife to its length and the rope would part. They would live.

And the old man would die.

"Shit." He tucked the knife into his pocket and pulled on the pair of rawhide gloves he kept in his back pocket. They were Filsons, unoiled to improve their grip, his constant use the only thing that kept them from turning into salt-caked claws. Gilly and the others at the marina laughed at what they called his farmer's gloves, but there was nothing better for working with rope, or for handling fish if you didn't mind the mixed smell of rawhide and fish that would permeate your hands for days afterward.

"Drop her into neutral!"

"Do *what*?" Gilly shouted.

"Neutral! Do it now!"

The transmission clunked. The last foothill wave caught the hull and lifted it, the much larger wave behind it now seeming to rise straight out of the ocean's surface, casting the faintest of shadows on this dull day. The rope sagged at the sudden release of tension and the terminal knot, which was wedged against the upper block, finally loosened. Brian stripped in the slack, letting the wave do the heavy lifting. The hull surged closer, and as the wave crested next to the boat, he screamed at Gilly to give it juice. At the same time he pulled as hard as he could down on the rope, taking in every bit of slack.

The *Tangled Blue* moved forward as the wave shadow crept over her deck. Brian braced himself for impact, yelling for Gilly for more speed as he stripped in another foot of rope. There was a lull, then the boat shot forward, and Brian half-hitched the rope to the cleat a split second before it was ripped from his hands. Then the rope snapped tight with an audible pop, spraying his face with water, and the *Archos*'s hull jerked up and out of the water.

The crane bent over the side of the boat with a splintering sound. Brian gathered in more rope, grunting with effort. The hull was swinging crazily in the air, halfway up the side of the *Tangled Blue*. Gilly's wrecking ball.

The boat tipped to port as they climbed the side of a large wave and the hull swung outward. Brian played out the foot of slack he had just gained, letting it sizzle through his gloves. The hull dipped lower, and the curved protuberance under the hull brushed the water's surface, the old man's leg flopping over the side of the hull. It paused there, at the far end of its pendulum, and then swung back toward the *Tangled Blue*.

Brian heaved on the rope as the hull careened toward them. He caught a glimpse of the old man's face, his brown eyes lucid, arm still twisted under the steel rail, and then his vision blacked as he strained to pull the hull high enough to clear the *Tangled Blue*'s gunnels.

He was sixteen inches short. The hull smashed into the *Tangled Blue*'s gunnel and the stern skidded sideways. For a moment the man was right in front of him, almost within reach, but Brian could not let go of the rope. The hull swung out again, paused, and careened back toward the *Tangled Blue*.

No, he thought, leaning into the rope with all his strength, his shoulders and hips screaming in pain. The hull popped loose of the ocean for a second, then brushed across the top of the wave. At the contact, the protuberance on the bottom of the hull splashed into the ocean.

Brian felt the loss of weight immediately. He wrapped his hand in the rope and yanked on the rope, using every muscle he had earned in the past forty-odd years, his tendons taut as the rope. And then he gave it just a little bit more.

The hull came swinging in, scraping up and onto the gunnel. It balanced there, undecided on which gravity it would follow, then the boat tilted and the *Archos*'s hull crashed onto the deck of the *Tangled Blue*. It slid across the deck, pinning Brian's right foot and shin to the starboard side. He was vaguely aware that the old man was screaming, his voice a raspy creak only a few inches from Brian's ear.

"You okay?" Gilly's voice was tight with worry.

Brian pushed himself up and looked at the wall of

water. They were at the wave's base, stern down, the gray-green water just inches below the gunnels. He opened his mouth to yell at Gilly to power up when the boat surged underneath him and he fell back to the deck, the mountain of water curling above the boat.

Chapter 7

They had told her there was going to be a day care, and she was okay with that. Taylor Millicent knew all about day cares, and babysitters, and waiting out those long evenings with near-strangers. One summer, she had even learned firsthand about a snotty brand of babysitter called a nanny.

Her parents had also warned her there would be some grown-up card games, which she couldn't play. She didn't mind, but she felt a brush of irritation at their choice of words. Grown-up card games; she wanted to ask them if they were going to play blackjack or Caribbean poker, or that endless hold-'em game Taylor associated with her grandmother's game room at Crestview Homes. Maybe their eyes would widen, or narrow. Would *focus*. Anything besides that distracted, I'm-explaining-the-world-to-a-nine-year-old expression. But she didn't say it, because her parents liked to think she didn't know what they were really doing. That they were gambling.

Whatever. Her parents did not go to the reservation

casino for the buffets, and Taylor suspected those end-of-night fights when they came home from Atlantic City weren't because someone cut them off on the interstate.

No, she didn't care that they gambled, only that they were gone a lot and sometimes they fought (only sometimes; other times they came home all snuggly and touchy and that was better, but not much), and that she sometimes felt like she was more of a well-loved pet than a daughter. Like one of those little Yorkies with a ribbon in its curly hair. Which she wanted, really bad.

They had *also* told her they would eat dinner together on this vacation, every night, and they hadn't even *started* to follow through on that. It was the first night, and there had just been some sort of announcement about crossing the international line, and cheering she could hear from the other rooms, and then her mother had unwrapped a soggy croissant sandwich from the deli and held up some foil packets and asked her if she wanted mayo or mustard. Then they both watched her eat, not hiding their impatience very well, and told her the breakfast buffet would be really good. And then it was time to go see the other girls.

Which was the second part they hadn't been completely honest about.

She looked around the day care, the simple art and the primary colors, the blocks and big-lettered books. Six other kids, and she was the only one not in diapers. Her mother had promised there would be a kid room on the *Nokomis,* and here it was. What a crock.

The day-care lady was Amanda. She was nice enough, but there wasn't nearly enough of her for all the babies. Taylor had already changed two diapers herself—pees, not poops—and had read that book about race car dogs with funny hats to a curly-haired little boy named Xavier, who seemed to want to grow up and be either a wrestler or a boxer, or maybe one of those ultimate fighters her daddy liked to watch on television. Or perhaps a street criminal, like the ones her mother was afraid of. The book had settled Xavier down and he was sleeping in her arms now, hot and sweaty. He smelled like a race car dog himself.

Amanda, who was bent-shouldered and had a long face, sort of like a horse's, smiled at Taylor. "Nice job," she whispered. She was holding a chubby girl, not even a year old, who was swiping the air ineffectually with clenched baby fists. The baby's face was red and blotchy.

"Is she sick?" Taylor said.

"Just teething," Amanda said. "How come you're not in school, Miss Lucky?"

"We got out early this year," Taylor said, a small fib. The rest of her classmates at Harrison Elementary had to go to school for another two weeks, but her parents had asked the school if Taylor could be allowed an early start on summer vacation. Her parents had Important Jobs, and now it was time for Vacation. She'd spent time in summer camps the past few summers, but now it was easier (and cheaper, Taylor suspected) to just bring her along.

The school didn't mind. Her fourth-grade classroom was really full, and Taylor, who had just finished her end-of-year testing, was putting up scores indicating she should be in junior high. As her dad said, missing a few math assignments and the last chapters of *Where the Red Fern Grows* weren't going to screw her up too bad.

"I just finished with finals myself," Amanda said. "I'm exhausted." She nodded toward Xavier. "Want to lay him down?"

Taylor stood, feeling Xavier squirm and then go still, a line of spit running from his open mouth to her forearm. She walked carefully to one of the small rooms at the back, really no more than a closet, and settled Xavier softly onto the mattress. He tossed and turned for a moment, then rolled onto his belly and stuck his butt up in the air, elbows out to the side. A few seconds later, tiny snores issued from his lips. He was kind of cute when he wasn't awake.

Taylor wiped Xavier's drool off on her jeans and went back into the main room. "You're a big help," Amanda said. The girl was snuffling cries into the crook of her arm, and Amanda stated rocking her again. She nodded toward the small desk at the entrance. "There's a note on there for some Anbesol. Want to run down to the pharmacy and pick it up?"

Taylor walked to the desk. "Where do I go?"

"Just down the hall, to your right." Amanda shifted the girl from her right arm to her left. "If the store doesn't have it, go see Doc Perle in First Aid. He's short and round, looks like a pink bowling ball with glasses."

Taylor giggled.

Amanda gave her a weary smile. "I'm going to lay down with her. You can just hang out, okay?"

"Okay," Taylor said. The room smelled of sweat, of baby pee and baby poop. A trip down the hallway sounded like heaven. "I'll be right back."

* * *

The chubby guy with the goatee at the convenience counter didn't have the Anbesol. He directed Taylor down the hallway to the small medical clinic. She wondered if she was supposed to tell Amanda, then remembered her tired smile, that big yawn, and decided to just go. It wasn't like she was on a pirate ship or something, with danger all around her. No, the ship felt like a slightly unsteady motel.

It felt good to be alone, with a mission. She could handle being alone; she didn't get scared like other kids. She'd known that for a long time, at least a year. There was no reason for a babysitter, she realized as she padded down the hallway, no reason for day care. Their room on the *Nokomis* had satellite television and a mini-fridge, and she had brought four new books. Why come down here to help babysit strangers' kids? She liked Amanda and felt sorry for her, but Amanda was getting paid. Taylor was supposed to be on summer vacation.

She turned down the angled deck way and saw three men leaving the room marked FIRST AID, twenty feet from her. One man was tall and thin, the other guy thick and muscular, with close-shaven hair. She'd seen the shaven man earlier, when they had boarded, standing outside a door at the end of the hall, and for some reason had felt a trickle of fear when his bloodshot eyes had passed over her. The shaven man had winked at her, and she had turned away and forced herself to walk, not run, back to her room.

The third man was not much taller than she was but very fat, his bald head gleaming in the hallway lights.

Doc Perle. The shaven man's hand was clamped above the doctor's elbow. Doc Perle was protesting the grip but unable to break it. The shaven man didn't seem to pay the doctor's protests any mind, just kept steering him down the hallway.

There was something going on, something . . . urgent. Yes, that was the word. They had come for the doctor because something urgent was happening.

Maybe someone was hurt.

Maybe someone had been killed.

Or maybe . . . maybe the ship was being attacked, like that movie with the Somali pirates, and she would need to help free the captain and there would be—she wasn't sure—maybe there would be a boy, eleven or twelve, who would help her. A smart boy but strong, too, who was scared of the pirates but more scared they'd hurt Taylor and so they would do brave things together. . . .

She paused in the hallway. Ideas entered her mind and then split and ran in different directions, sometimes all at once, like lightning forking into the night sky. Her parents knew this, had her tested, and didn't find anything bad; her grandma diagnosed her as a scatterbrain, pure and simple. Grandma was always getting hushed by Taylor's mother, but Taylor figured she was right.

Still, she wasn't scatterbrained *all* the time.

The door to First Aid was locked, the room dark inside the rectangle of glass in the door. She could either wait here, go back to the stinky day-care room, or follow Doc Perle. Taylor shifted from one foot to the other, biting on her lower lip. Maybe they were just taking him to dinner, and they held his arm like that because he had a bad leg. The shaven man, maybe he wasn't as bad as he looked, he was one of those guys that was only scary on the outside. Maybe he had saved Doc Perle's life when a horse had fallen on his leg during a military raid, and now they were best friends, and ate dinner together every night while they plotted ways to avenge those who had wronged them. She would approach their dinner table and quietly ask for the Anbesol. They would question her, suspicious she might be a spy for the other side, but soon they would see her obvious intelligence and admit her into their circle. Later, they would take her to the horse farm in Kentucky where they raised Arabian stallions that were as smart as a person and tell her she was destined to be a Freedom Rider.

She took a deep breath. Okay, her mind was in overdrive, even worse than normal. The cause was simple: too much downtime, followed by the day care and three hours of immersion in First Reader books. Also, the realization, not quite formed or coherent, that she was done being Mommy and Daddy's perfect little girl.

She started after the men, thinking "Freedom Riders" would make a good story for next year's English class.

Frankie stood at the edge of the bar, nursing a whiskey-water, just enough booze to feel in the back of his throat. It was almost eleven o'clock, and Latham and Prower were deep into the poker game.

Latham handled his cards slowly, careful not to bend the edges. He was sweating, little streams running down his face. It obviously wasn't from the game, Frankie thought; Latham had been kicking Prower's ass all over the card table for the past four hours. Prower had made a strong run to begin with, but had lost a big hand to Latham forty-five minutes in and he had never recovered. Now Prower was on the defensive, and Frankie could see him taking inventory of his shrinking pile of chips after every losing hand.

Frankie's mind kept trying to do the math. If the game was over tonight, or even early tomorrow evening, he could be in Akron by Tuesday. Tuesday was good, a working day, and he would have the cash to get things moving. It wouldn't take more than a day or two to finish up business, and then he would shake Ohio dust from his clothes once and for all. Leave enough cash to get them set up for a while, not enough for them to act like Powerball hillbillies, but enough to take care of the big-ticket items, move out of that ratty little trailer. He'd go take a nice long break with a clear conscience, come back and get them set up with something like an annuity, regular as a paycheck. He was more and more convinced that was the way to do it.

Concentrate, he thought. You got plenty to do right here.

He pushed himself off the bar and walked behind Latham. He had a three of hearts, followed by a six, seven, and eight of mixed suits, and a suicide king on the end.

"Your bet," Latham said.

"Two hundred," Prower said, tossing half of his remaining chips into the center of the table. A tumbler of Glenmorangie was at Prower's elbow, the ice cubes catching the mellow light of the room. Against the wall, an iced tray filled with platters of shrimp, beluga caviar, and assorted salami and cheeses remained untouched. Adrian was standing on one side of the cart, stealing furtive glances at the food.

Prower's cheeks were bright red, the veins a darker purple, not nearly as sweaty as Latham's. Strange for a fleshy man like Prower to be so obviously nervous and still dry, Frankie thought. It reminded him of a boy he'd known in junior high, a butt plug of a kid who had weighed two hundred pounds at fourteen and was unable to perspire. The gym teacher made the entire class run until the kid, who would be gasping for air by then, either passed out or puked on his shoes. It had been a lot of fun, junior high in northern Ohio.

"Price of poker just went up," Latham said mildly.

Prower spun his cane in his hands. It was the same motion he'd performed early in the game, when he had bet the equivalent of eighty thousand on a pair of sixes. Latham had folded, and Prower had shown off his two sixes proudly, although he wasn't obliged to.

Frankie leaned forward, feeling his own pulse quicken. He'd been at tables where men had tens, even hundreds of thousands of dollars, had seen their expression twist and expand as fortunes were won and lost. He had never been party to stakes like this, and he was acutely conscious of his own self in that moment, could feel the air sliding in and out of his chest, the dizzying rush of adrenaline. There was nothing like a good game to get the juices flowing.

Latham wiped the sweat from his forehead. Then he slowly counted out his own stacks of chip next to Prower's bet, which was spread out across the center of the table in an uneven spray.

"See it," Latham said, then pushed out another column of chips. "And raise you another two hundred."

All right, Frankie thought. *Here we go.*

Captain Donald Moore was ready for bed.

He stood out on the deck of the *Nokomis*, the same location where he had met Frankie earlier that afternoon. The running lights of the *Nokomis* cast a yellow veil in the thick fog. Below him, the waves rode up along the sides of his ship and broke in a steady roar. The air was thick and cold, December air, heavy with the briny, minerally smell. The unmistakable odor of the North Atlantic, but with a twist, a hard, clean smell like cold metal. From the Kaala, no doubt, which was turning out to be a major bitch of a current.

In his fifty-plus years on the sea, Moore had never seen anything like the disruptions caused by the Kaala. Even the bitter North Sea or the East Indies, violent waters that did not suffer mistakes, were more predictable than this slop. Seas moved, yes, sometimes at deflecting angles to the weather patterns. All sailors knew this; the world above and the world below were just that, two different worlds. A tropical storm could be a fearsome presence, great cumulonimbus clouds stocked with enough energy to blow the all navies of the worlds to smithereens. Yet below the surface the tiniest fish floated along impervious to the energies above the surface. Likewise, the tides and currents and upwellings in the ocean decimated entire marine habitats or regions, while leaving those above unaffected by, and usually ignorant of, the changes below.

The Kaala was an exaggeration of these contrasts, a great ribbon of icy water flowing south against the warmer Gulf Stream. Already today the *Nokomis* had to endure two rogue waves, the latter a true monster, thirty feet tall if it was an inch. They had seen the wave on the radar in plenty of time, because NOAA was spitting out marine advisories left and right, and Moore had dedicated one of his junior officer to full-time radar watch. He took the wheel himself as the wave closed in on them, shutting off the autopilot and steering the *Nokomis* into the swell so they took it at a quartering angle. He warned the crew and passengers beforehand, and when they rode up the wave the bridge was quiet, almost churchlike. The *Nokomis* crested the massive wave and he powered up, his insides tingling as they tipped downward, and then there was the thrill of the descent, and he was in full control of the ship as the rogue wave lurched past them and was lost into the fog-shrouded world. Then there was cheering from the sheep below, and for a moment, Captain Donald Moore felt like a sailor again.

Now he glanced back into the bridge. He could see the radar through the glass, and the seas were clear. The GPS indicated they were twenty-seven miles out from the Massachusetts coastline, past the Stellwagen Bank. Sonar showed the floor of the ocean as a series of smooth humps, more than a hundred fathoms below them.

Too far out.

It was that prick Giuliani's fault, forcing the casino boats to go three miles out, minimum, before the gambling could begin. In the past year the local and state politicians, enthralled by the money flowing in from the land-based casinos, had taken it a step further and banned ship-based gambling inside the Line. The fuel bill for the big Allis Chalmers diesels was murderous even with a three-mile run—at twelve miles out, they had seen a steady decline in profits. Well, the offshore gambling industry was on a long downslide, a fact reflected in his paltry captain's pay . . . which was still more than he could make doing anything else.

He did not know his employers at Sefelis Industries. He was well aware of the rumors; Sefelis was mobbed up, and that the *Nokomis* and its gambling losses were a front. Moore did not particularly care if it was true. He suspected that, at the very least, Sefelis was not the most principled player in the marine entertainment world. That they had hired him, an unofficially blacklisted captain who had not piloted a ship for eight long years, loomed large in this suspicion.

None of that mattered now. He was back on the sea, and the *Nokomis* was a decent ship with a legitimate purpose. His tenure with Sefelis had gone smoothly for fourteen months—a paycheck every two weeks, a crew of officers who were competent if not stellar. And sometimes his unseen employers actually heeded his e-mails and provided what was needed to maintain, if not upgrade, the ship.

Then the phone had rung on a dreary Tuesday afternoon, a loud klaxon in the small office he maintained near the marina. He jumped, choking on his cigar smoke; the phone had been silent for weeks. When Moore answered, the voice on the other end asked him to meet for dinner to discuss a business proposition. When

Moore told the caller he needed to contact the Sefelis business manager, the caller just chuckled.

"No," Frankie Rollins said. "I don't think we want to discuss this with your employers. Best you and I meet in private. Maybe over a glass of brandy? You prefer Matador, if I'm not mistaken."

It wasn't just the name of the brandy. There was something in the man's laugh, the confidence in it that caused a cold sweat to break out on Moore's brow. The cold sweat continued, on and off, for the next few hours. By the time he met Rollins at the *Troquet* later that night and looked through the documents the hairy little weasel handed him, the sweats dried up.

"I don't have any money," he said.

"I know," Frankie said, then took a long drink of his cabernet. "You think I don't know that? I've looked at your finances. You ever hear of a prenup, Captain? Jesus."

Moore did not answer. His seared Muscovy duck breast, served with fresh morels and wild leeks, was untouched in front of him. He was thinking there could only be one other explanation if it was not blackmail.

"Which one of them did you know?"

Thinking of the names in the papers. *Gervais. McConnelly. Peterson. Rukavina. Pendleton.* Names he thought of each night as he lay in bed, names that burrowed through his brain. The faces, never in focus to begin with, faded with each year until only the names remained, wiggling through his brain, no less damning than a verdict read from a jury.

Frankie frowned, then laughed. "Those assholes that drowned?" he said. "I didn't know any of them. Never really hung out with the cruise ship crowd, Donald. I want something a lot more simple."

What he wanted was a venue for a game, a standard poker game with what Frankie called *somewhat unusual* stakes. A game set up between two powerful men, a game that required a location where both players could have peace of mind. A place where Frankie did not have to worry about outside interferences, about eavesdropping, about the local cops who had taken something of an interest in his goings-on in the greater Boston area. If possible, a venue where the United States might not have complete jurisdiction should the *somewhat unusual* game encounter difficulties.

Moore left the restaurant almost relieved. The nagging worry he had entertained for years had finally manifested itself, but what Frankie requested was not terribly difficult. Sefelis Corporation took little interest in his routes, and despite past transgressions, he was still a good sailor. If need be, he would take the *Nokomis* to Ireland's western shores to keep his past silent.

So here they were, well past the Line, immersed in a sodden, foggy world filled with shifting currents and waves that sprang out of the ocean like enormous blind Furies. The water was so cold he had told his radar man to watch for icebergs on the graph. Bergs were almost unheard of this far south in summer, typically occurring off the Newfoundland coast, but he didn't trust the International Ice Patrol to catch every iceberg that floated south, not with this current acting as midwife between the Arctic sea and the Atlantic.

Yet he was not overly worried. The other ships that had wrecked in the past weeks were much smaller craft, their radar arches not nearly as high as those of the *Nokomis*. A tall radar perch meant they could see the rogue waves miles off, and the powerful Allis Chalmers engines allowed them to position the *Nokomis* so the huge waves couldn't swamp them. The shifting currents made navigation more difficult, yes, and the clash of warm and cold waters kept the air filled with fog. But they were the standard problems.

No, he thought, there was nothing much out here to be worried about.

He turned to go to bed, sparing one final glance over the seas. The fog had lifted as the night cooled, and he could now see all the way back down along the side of the ship. The waves curled and splashed, rocking the ship. Above them, he could make out the faint glow of the full moon through the thinning fog banks, its reflection just barely grazing the tops of the waves.

Moore squinted, screwed his fists into his eyes, and stared into the black ocean. For a moment, he thought he had seen something off the flank of the *Nokomis*, a massive shape cutting just above the surface like a wide-hulled submarine. When he looked again, the seas were empty.

Nothing, he thought. An illusion.

He knew fog was a great catalyst for creating optical tricks on the open sea. Once, on a severely hungover morning off the Vancouver coast, he had altered the course of the cruise ship *Veritas* to avoid running into an armada of World War II–era battleships. The armada had turned out to be nothing more than a set of low clouds, scudding just above the horizon, curled into iron destroyers by the morning sun and his own brandy-soaked brain.

He was about to laugh at himself when he saw the

shape again. Closer this time, cutting though the waves cast by the ship's props. Seventy-five meters back, the faint moon glow just bright enough that he could see the surface was not smooth, like a submarine would be, but rough, absorbing the meager light rather than reflecting it. And it did not move in a straight line, but with a slight side-to-side gyration. It rose above the water's surface in three locations, front, a thick middle, and another, thinner spot, far behind the first two.

He spun back to the bridge and pounded on the glass. Collins looked up, startled, and rushed over to open the sliding window. "Captain?"

"Kill the running lights," Moore said. "And hand me my binoculars. Quickly."

He took the binoculars from Collins through the sliding window, ignoring his officer's quizzical look, and walked back to the railing. The shape was still there, keeping pace with the ship. Whatever this was, it needed to be identified, perhaps reported. Then he remembered Frankie's conditions, the mandate that there be no contact with the outside world. Well, it would still need to be reported. Eventually.

The banks of lights on the ship went out in three separate events as Collins flipped the switches. By the time Moore's eyes adjusted to the darkness, he had lost sight of the shape. He closed his eyes, filtering out the moonlight through his eyelids. When he opened his eyes again the shape was there, appearing in the darkness like one of those children's illusionary pictures. It was closer yet, the front of it only fifty meters off the starboard corner. Enormous, whatever it was. At least the same size as the giant whales, the big blues and the North Atlantic rights, but this was no whale. It did not move the same as the whales, did not have the same uniformly rounded back.

The Russians, his mind whispered. Twenty-five years since the end of the Cold War and his mind would not give up the threat. Could the Russians have deployed a unique submarine that . . . what?

Trailed a casino boat in the middle of the Atlantic?

He swept the ocean surface with his binoculars, found the dark blotch, and adjusted the focus. As he did the shape slid beneath the moon-tinged waves. Before it sank into the ocean Moore thought he saw two pale orbs reflecting a soft green in the moonlight.

He lowered the binoculars and waited for the shape to materialize again. Turn the ship's lights back on, perhaps? No, whatever it was, animal or machine, it seemed to be less shy in the dark. Whatever it might be, it was something he had never seen before in all his years at sea. He needed a witness. His own accounts of events that happened at sea had been called into question in the past, sometimes with very good reason. But now he was dry, lucid, and he wanted someone to verify what he was seeing. Cut the damn naysayers off at the pass.

He ran back to the window and shouted at Collins to come out. His first mate checked the *Nokomis* controls, then moved quickly to join Moore on the deck. His face was impassive. "Captain?"

"Watch," Moore said, pointing down the side of the boat.

"For what?"

"You'll know it when you see it," Moore said. "Just off the starboard side. Right at the waterline."

Collins peered dutifully into the ocean. He was thirty-five, perhaps forty, with eyesight that would be better than Moore's. Moore wondered if he should get the digital camera from the bridge. No, it was too dark. Even with the flash, all the photo would show was the black ocean, perhaps the long flank of the ship.

"I don't see anything, Captain."

"Keep looking," Moore said. They waited, listening to the big ship cut through the waves. The ocean remained empty. Perhaps whatever it was could not keep up with the ship. "What's our current speed?"

"Six knots," Collins said.

"Stay here," Moore said. "I'm going to drop her off a bit."

He ran back to the bridge, his heart thumping. The thrill of the unknown. It was the driver behind his obsession with the sea, his obsession with different seas, different ports. Different women. And when it felt as if he had seen what there was to see, when he had discovered Ecclesiastes was right—there was nothing new under this sun—he had turned inward. Had given up on finding enlightenment through the world and turned not to God, as Ecclesiastes suggested, but to booze. Which he had liked all along but found himself in a love affair with as he reached his early fifties.

And then, perhaps inevitably, the cruise ship. The typhoon, the marine advisories. His own drunken stubbornness to acknowledge them, although none knew he was drunk, not then and almost never. The reef crawling up out of the bottom of the ocean on the sonar screen, the depth alarm klaxons waking him from the half-slumber he was in.

He dropped the *Nokomis*'s throttle back until the GPS plotter showed they were at four knots. A bit slower than he would have liked in these seas, but it would only be for a moment. He punched the MARK button on the plotter, and their coordinates popped up on the screen. The cursor was blinking on the chart plotter screen, waiting for a label.

Moore considered for a moment, then punched in seven quick letters and ran back out onto the deck way.

As he crossed through the narrow doorway the ship shuddered, then lurched hard to the side. Moore crashed into the doorway, his shoulder and forehead hitting at the same time. He slumped to the ground, a trickle of blood running down the side of his face.

He got to his feet groggily, looked out through the glass at Collins, who was leaning over the deck way with the binoculars and shouting. Moore braced himself against the doorway with both hands, wondering if they were under attack, if the shape had indeed been a Russian sub. Then the ship tilted hard to port again and he staggered across the bridge, colliding with the control console this time. The ship rocked back to center, and Moore grabbed the edge of the console to keep from skidding across the deck.

The ship was still for a moment, and then two things happened at once: The alarms on the *Nokomis*'s engines and bilge started screaming, and the *Nokomis* seemed to lurch forward, as though someone had given her a giant push. Moore looked up through the glass, meaning to call Collins back into the bridge, when the ship lurched again. His first mate flipped over the side of the railing, Moore's binoculars still gripped firmly in one hand.

In front of him, the sonar screen showed a massive

serpentine shape just a few yards beneath the *Nokomis*.
On the chartplotter, Moore's label for their current coordinates flashed on and off, on and off.

UNKNOWN, the chartplotter flashed.

UNKNOWN.

Chapter 8

They lost all power just after midnight.

Brian had been nursing the *Tangled Blue* south-by-southeast, having long ago lost hope he could run back to Gloucester in the building seas. The *Archos*'s hull had punctured the side of the *Tangled Blue* below the waterline and in close proximity to the fuel tank. Either the lines or the tank itself had been damaged, maybe both, and the Chryslers were both missing, the port on one cylinder, the starboard engine spitting unburned diesel and smoke and backfiring, missing on two, perhaps three cylinders. Water in the diesel, Brian thought. Son of a bitch.

He stared out over the dark sea, taking stock of his situation. Gilly was mildly hypothermic and the old man was drifting in and out of consciousness, his arm broke, sick with shock. The current was pulling them ever farther south, and he could only get about six knots out of *Tangled Blue,* not enough to break free of the Kaala and reach shore. Above 3000 RPMs, the engines would misfire and threaten to stall.

He shifted his gaze from the endless dark waves to

the GPS screen. His original goal had been to head into Massachusetts Bay, get out of the worst of the waves and current, then limp his boat in to Quincy and see how much room was left on his Visa for the repairs. But the seas and the current had swept them far offshore, and when he tried cutting hard to the coastline the ocean smashed against the long sides of the *Tangled Blue,* causing more water to pour over the damaged hull.

Just before midnight he checked the GPS route projections again. At their current heading they would slide past Cape Cod, miss the last protuberance of North American rock by more than a mile, and drift off into open seas.

He closed his eyes, imagining the vast open seas off the coast, marked only by the underwater geology, the ridges and trenches, darker blue over light blue in his mental map. The *Tangled Blue* pitching and bobbing in the offshore seas, her engines too weak to make it back to shore, not powerful enough to navigate through the monstrous swells.

He opened his eyes, breathing shallowly. After a moment he nudged the throttle forward, ignoring the popping and backfires, and turned toward shore. Eight knots, then nine. The *Tangled Blue*'s engines labored as the icy water splashed against her starboard side, and the bilges hummed as they pushed seawater out of the hold. Brian spread his legs to absorb the pounding, gritting his teeth as his boat crashed into the huge swells.

After a few minutes Gilly came up from the cabin, wrapped in his thick sleeping bag.

"We could call for a tow," he hollered over the

noise of the Chryslers. He moved next to Brian and scanned the instrument panel.

"Not in this slop."

"We could just wait and—"

"No, Gilly." It wasn't just stubbornness; with the number of wrecks in the past week, and the heavy fog, the Coasties wouldn't respond unless they were in a life-threatening situation. That meant a private ship, which would demand a salvage fee, and if Brian gave up a piece of the *Tangled Blue*'s worth he would have to give her all up.

"Anybody know we're out here?"

"Doubt it," Brian said. "I sent in a disabled vessel alert a half hour ago and got static. You feeling better?"

Gilly nodded. "Still got the shivers, but I can think again."

"When did it start?"

"The shivers?"

"You thinking," Brian said.

"Stick it," Gilly said. He leaned over to peer at the GPS map and tapped the speed. Eight-point-three knots. "Won't win any races, will we?"

"No."

"Tank cracked? She got hit pretty hard down there."

"Maybe," Brian said, cutting the *Tangled Blue* into a twelve-foot-high roller.

They chugged eastward in the pitch-dark seas, picking up speed slowly, the engines lugging and hitching, the swirling air on the deck rich with the smell of unburned hydrocarbons. The waves were hitting them broadside now and the boat rolled from side to side, coming down with teeth-snapping impact on the bigger waves.

"Easy," Gilly said, tapping the RPM needle. "Starboard engine's gonna shit the bed."

Brian glanced at the course projection. If they could hold this heading for just five, ten more minutes it wouldn't matter. They could simply float south, and the big open mitt of Plymouth Harbor would catch them sometime around dawn.

"You're at five thousand," Gilly said. "And hotter than hell. Cracked something, Cap." Brian did not reduce speed and Gilly stared at him, eyes bleary behind the wet tendrils of hair spilling out of his knit cap. "Gonna burn her up."

"My boat," Brian said. "Go downstairs and warm up."

"What's got your panties in such a twist?"

Brian pressed down slightly on the throttle. The bottom had come up fifty feet, and the current was strengthening as the water became more shallow. The Kaala was like a massive river, and the current was stronger the closer they got to the coastline. Ahead of them, the spotlight of the *Tangled Blue* reflected against the surface of a towering blue-black wave. Without a word both men braced themselves for the impact.

The boat slewed sideways and then tipped hard to the port side, the massive roller lifting them on a twenty-degree angle. There were breakers on top of the rollers, the frothy water catching the running lights just before they hit. They went into the trough and water flooded over the gunwales. It surged across the deck as they descended the wave, surging around their ankles and cascading down the steps to the cuddy.

"Check the bilges," Brian said, hauling hard on the steering wheel. They had spun almost ninety degrees and were broadside to the waves. The ship pitched and rolled, more water splashing over her sides.

Gilly leaned over the side. "Still spitting," he shouted. "Couple more like those and they won't be able to keep up. We lose engine power—"

"I got her," Brian said, and gave both engines more throttle. The boat surged forward, engine sputtering, the bow swinging around so they quartered into the waves. The sea caught them, pushed them back where it wanted them. Brian swung the nose of the boat back around, zigzagging against the brute strength of the current, his face stony. They were close to the vectored route he was seeking; another half mile and they would be on the inside curve of the shoreline.

"Look," Gilly yelled, and Brian saw the bright green blotch on the radar. Land. They both grinned, and at that moment the starboard engine stalled. Brian twisted the ignition and the engine sputtered, started, and died. He turned the key again and again, but the engine would not catch. After a while he switched the key to the off position and turned the boat so they were running with the waves again.

"What's the port engine status?"

"Missing," Gilly said. "On one, maybe two cylinders." He looked up. "We lose power on both, we lose charge on the batteries. Don't got enough juice to run the bilge."

Brian took a deep breath, hand tensed on the throttle, and glanced at Gilly.

His first mate shook his head. "No, Brian."

Brian exhaled, then rubbed a hand across his face and turned to Gilly. "That was a stupid plan you had."

"Well," Gilly said. He reached into his pocket, withdrew a crumpled cigarette, the paper stained dark with moisture. He tossed it overboard. "I'm sorta impetuous at times. What now?"

"We'll leave her right here," he said, tapping the throttle. He glanced at the GPS, the thin green line of their course now headed back out to sea. "And call it in."

Gilly picked up the marine radio. "This is *Tangled Blue* transmitting in the blind," he said. "We are dead in the water, repeat dead in the water, and requesting assistance. Coordinates are 42.30 north, 70.29 west. Again, 42.30 north, 70.29 west and heading south-southeast at three-point-five knots. This is the *Tangled Blue* requesting assistance." He released the transmit key and listened to the reply of static. "You want a May-day, too?"

"No," Brian said. "Wells doesn't need a doctor, does he?"

Gilly waved it off. "I got plenty of cure for that old fart in my duffel. He's fine." Brian frowned and Gilly held up his palm. "All legit."

Another wave rocked the boat and they both grabbed onto the dash. Brian studied the seas for a moment, then opened one of the aft hatches and pulled out a drift sock, a large nylon cone with ropes attached at five points along the circumference. "We need to straighten out."

Gilly held out his hand. "I got it."

"Just steer the boat."

"You sure?"

Brian climbed onto the starboard gunnel, bracing himself against the side of the cabin. Feeling the motion of the sea, trying to find the rhythm in the sets of waves. He considered slipping on a life preserver and dismissed it. If he fell overboard, the *Tangled Blue* could not turn back into the waves to recover him. The cold water would kill him within minutes.

"At least tie on a rope," Gilly shouted. "Don't be an asshole."

Brian edged his way around the cabin toward the enclosed bow of the boat. He didn't believe in tying ropes to people while they were onboard; like most captains, he abhorred tripping hazards, and ropes made it difficult to swim. If he fell overboard, he would have to make it back onboard with his own strength, just like any other sailor.

He knew he was being reckless, even foolish. It felt good, and that was foolish, too.

He edged forward. It was quieter outside the cabin, the sound of the waves breaking against the *Tangled Blue*'s hull almost peaceful. The boat surged and rolled under him. He put a hand on the front corner of the cabin, working his way onto the enclosed bow. He swiveled his body around the corner, lost his grip on the cabin, and dropped to his knees, the railing pressed against his side. He licked his lips, tasting the salt.

Low and slow, that was the ticket.

He inched along the bow, staying inside the bow rails. The boat reared and bucked under him and he dropped to his stomach, worming toward the bow cleat. He fumbled in the darkness, hand groping, and finally looped the rope over the cleat. A quick clove hitch, yank it back to cinch the knot. Good, now double-check the knots. Still good. Now toss the bitch overboard.

The drift sock floated out to the end of the rope, sank a few inches, and flared open as it filled with water. The rope snapped tight, spinning the ship around in a half-circle so the bow was facing the waves.

He inched backwards to the front of the cabin, got to his feet, and worked his way back around the cabin enclosure. A wave splashed over him, the spotlight illuminating the cold water a second before it fell on him. He let it wash over him, concentrating on his feet and his hands, keeping three points of contact on the side of the cabin. The wave subsided, and he scuttled forward before the next one could hit and dropped back onto the floor of the boat.

Gilly grabbed him before he could fall. "Dumbass," he said, pushing him back to arm's length. "What are you grinning about?"

"Been a while since I've done anything right," Brian said. "Get an answer on the radio?"

"I got static," Gilly said. "I think we fucked up, partner."

Brian looked through the windshield. The spotlight was bright enough to see the endless sets of waves barreling down from the north, riding up on the bow of the *Tangled Blue* and breaking around her. He clicked it off to save the batteries.

"Well," he said. "Any other bright ideas?"

"One," Gilly said, heading toward the cabin. "Let's go get drunk."

Wells was huddled in a bunk, shivering under several blankets. Gilly had wrapped his broken arm in a bum sling, then draped several blankets over the old man. Wells shook and mumbled, a shrunken man with salt rimed on his ears and the edges of his nostrils. The hand on his broken arm was cold to the touch.

Brian wiped the seawater from his own face. He figured Gilly was right—Wells was in pain, but he wasn't in any immediate danger. Gilly held out a tumbler of Seagrams and Brian swallowed it in two gulps, the whiskey tracing a fiery path down his throat.

"Another?" Gilly said.

"In a minute." He ducked into the aft cabin while Gilly poured himself a drink. He put on dry clothes, taking a moment to revel in the feel of his shriveled toes inside his wool socks. Then he took his cell phone off the charger, saw the *no service* message, and went back into the cuddy. Just in time to catch Gilly with the bottle to his lips.

He held out his hand. Gilly passed him the bottle, and Brian took a long drink himself before setting the bottle on the table. "No more."

"Hypocrite," Gilly muttered.

Brian walked over to the old man and put a hand on his bony shoulder. "You doing okay?"

"Sleepy," Wells mumbled. "Arm hurts."

Brian helped Wells into a sitting position, then took the glass and poured it a quarter-full. "This'll cure what ails you."

Wells opened his cracked lips and Brian poured the whiskey in, noting with satisfaction when Wells's eyes widened, losing some of his dopey expression, and the old man spluttered and tossed his head.

"Whoa," Brian said. "Easy, big fella. Breathe in nice and slow."

Wells sniffed loudly several times, his mouth working. "Can I have another?"

"Hell yes," Gilly said. "That's the spirit." He had been watching the old man's contortions with a mixture of sympathy and amusement. "Hair of the dog, right, bro?"

"Where am I?" Wells said. He made as though to motion with his right arm and grimaced. "I think my arm's broken."

"You're on the *Tangled Blue*," Gilly said.

"How'd I get here?"

"We plucked you off a piece of your boat about three hours ago. What the hell happened?"

"We need to go back to shore," Wells said. "I need to tell . . . I need to call Sarah's parents, and Desmond's wife, and . . ."

"Here," Brian said, handing him the glass. He watched as the old man stared into the amber liquid, then drank. A bit more color had come back into his cheeks, and his eyes had cleared considerably. *He wasn't just hypothermic*, Brian thought. *Not this whole time. He was trying not to think about what happened.*

"Your boat," Brian prodded.

Wells shook his head. "We were working outside Boon. Sarah just dropped the sonde and she was logging the data into her laptop. Marcus had collected all his samples for the day and he was trying to run stats on it, a regression analysis I think, and he couldn't get the data—"

"The boat," Brian said. "What happened to your boat? Was it a wave?"

"No," Wells said, and convulsed in a great shiver. "No, it wasn't a wave. Something ate it."

"Oh," Gilly said, eyeing the bottle on the table. "Yeah. That happens."

Brian shot Gilly a look. "What do you mean, Mr. Wells?"

"It's Dr. Wells, actually." He squinted at Brian. "Something came out of the water and destroyed us. We had been gathering data for several hours, nothing strange except the weather, and then there was this tremendous lurch and I fell down. I got to my knees and I could see . . . something . . . tearing at the back of the boat. It had these huge curved teeth, like snake fangs or . . . I don't know. The outboards went dead and a moment later it ripped both of them—both outboards—completely off the back of the boat."

"And what's a sound?" Brian said. "You said she dropped a sound?"

"A sonde," Wells said. "It's a device for measuring water chemistry. We were traveling down the Kaala as part of Sarah's master's thesis."

"How old was your boat?" Gilly said.

"It was the university's boat," Wells said. "A twenty-four-foot Boston Whaler, a recent model." He looked up sharply. "The engines didn't fall off, if that's what you're implying, Mr . . . ?"

"Mr. Gilly, actually. He's Mr. Brian." He had poured himself another drink and now he tossed it back. "So what, exactly, ate your boat?"

"You think this is a joke?" Wells said. "My students are dead. I saw Sarah in the water, in a cloud of her own blood, and then that . . . thing . . . came out of the ocean and killed her. She screamed and then she was just gone. It swallowed her." Wells's voice faltered. "It swallowed her, and then it looked at me. It *saw* me."

Wells seemed about to say something, then clutched his bony shoulders and began to sob. After a minute, Brian put a hand on his shoulder. Wells's pulse was thumping rapidly on the side of his neck.

"Cap?"

Brian nodded, and Gilly began rummaging through his seabag, evaluating a half dozen orange medicine bottles before finally settling on a sample packet. He handed the foil package to Brian: two pills of Xanax, 500 milligrams each. Brian pressed them into Wells's hand.

"You've had a hell of a day, Dr. Wells," Brian said.

Wells stared at the pills, then popped them into his mouth. "Wash her down," Gilly said, holding out a glass of water. Wells gulped the water down noisily. Gilly held up his own glass, which had magically refilled with more Seagrams, and clinked it against Wells's empty glass. "You're safe now."

Wells leaned back and closed his eyes. After a moment he began to snore. Brian motioned Gilly toward the stairs. "Should he have booze with those pills?"

"Oh yeah," Gilly said. "It won't kill him."

"Just put him to sleep?" Brian took Gilly's glass, drained it, and set it on the counter upside down. He had not eaten since noon, and he could feel the heat of the whiskey, combining with the meager warmth of the cuddy. If he sat much longer he was going to fall asleep himself.

"Might," Gilly said. "But he won't have bad dreams, least not any he'll remember."

"No more," Brian said, taking the bottle. "For any of us. I mean it."

He pushed the cuddy door open and climbed back up

to the deck. The port engine rumbled unsteadily, but the gauges showed good temp and oil pressure. The GPS still had them floating right past the edge of Cape Cod, which at their current speed they wouldn't reach until first light. He would have to make the hard decision in the morning, either risk losing the port engine for a final run for the shoreline, or make the Mayday call.

Or what, he thought, staring at the engine hatch. *Float down the coast until you end up in the Caribbean?*

No. We go like this until dawn, and with any luck the wind swings around to the east, like it sometimes does after a strong northern blow, and you ride onshore breezes into Plymouth Harbor and anchor in twenty feet of water. Easy-peasey. One more story for the Riff-Raff.

See how good you're doing? You could have said one more story for the grandkids and then felt bad. Because you don't have kids, or a kid. But you didn't say that. You're doing good.

Okay, stick with the boat. Maybe you miss Plymouth and swing around Cape Cod. I can see that, see the fancy pricks standing on their lawns, staring at us through the fog. Then the wind swings around to the east and instead of a gentle harbor you've got the hard shoreline crashing in front of you. Not so good, but by then Gilly will have light to work with and we can throw the anchor. Gilly digs in, get his hands greasy. Maybe siphon off the pure fuel from the top of the tank, put it in a couple cans, then drain the water off the bottom?

Even he knew it wouldn't work. The water and fuel were too mixed up; it wouldn't separate until it had a chance to rest, and that wouldn't happen out here, not in these seas. Well, Gilly would think of something. All they needed was daylight, a little bit of luck.

Luck, the cold voice inside him said. *Yes, you've had so much of it. Now if it'll just hold.*

He walked over to the caved-in corner of the boat. The thick fog and the darkness closed around him and now, instead of feeling insignificant, he felt the universe constrained to the deck of his boat. He stood in its epicenter. Not its master but its lone prisoner.

And underneath him, the cold waters of the Kaala bore them to their new destination.

THE UNKNOWN

Chapter 9

The numbers weren't adding up.

Moore squinted at the two gauges on the *Nokomis*'s instrument panel. One was for a float valve on the lowest berth, which showed the level of seawater in the hold. The *Nokomis* was designed to carry several thousand gallons of bilge water in the ballast tanks, connected by a series of pipes that allowed him to move the water from side to side, from bow-side to aft. The gauge read six inches of water when they had left Boston Harbor, evenly distributed among the four tanks. Once they reached the open seas and he could tell they were in for a bumpy ride, Moore had added two more inches, making her sit down in the water, allowing the keel to bite into the ocean. That brought her up to eight inches, roughly two thousand gallons of water.

The other gauge was the on-off status of the four bilge pumps, located above the ballast tanks. Each of the pumps was rated at five hundred gallons per minute, and three of them had been running for the past twenty minutes. The fourth and largest one, the big emergency

pump, was located slightly higher than the other three.
It would not kick in unless the water breached the first
containment structure, when the bilge water was at fourteen inches.

They were at sixteen inches, over four thousands of
gallons of water, and the fourth bilge still wasn't running.

Actually, Moore thought, the numbers were adding
up right. If you wanted to show the equation for a ship
that was going to sink, slowly and steadily, these were
the numbers. Yes, these were the numbers you would
want.

He turned as Fred Wright entered the bridge. Wright
was a dark-haired man with a protruding brow and intense, dark eyes, dressed in navy blue overalls with the
knees and wrists stained with grease. He held an amp
meter in one hand, a coil of electrical wire in the other.

"The fuck happened to Collins?"

Damn, Moore thought. *That's right, they knew each
other. Friends or something like that.*

"He went overboard," Moore said. "I'm sorry, Fred, I
really am. We couldn't turn around, not without power."
He willed himself to take in Wright's furious gaze. "I
threw him an Illuminok ring," he said. Illuminoks were
the new life rings, complete with automatic distress
signal capabilities and strobe lights that activated when
it hit the water.

"So? Did he grab on?"

"I don't know," Moore said. "It was dark, and we
were still getting pushed around by the seas. He . . . he
may have."

"Better hope he did," Wright said. "Better goddamn

hope, Captain, that I don't have to call my sister and tell her that her favorite cousin is feeding the fuckin crabs off Stellwegan Banks." He moved forward, his face a foot from Moore's. Moore's nostrils filled with the smell of industrial lubricant soaked into Wright's clothes and skin, overlaid with his mechanic's oniony breath.

Cousin, Moore thought. *Wonderful.*

"You understand what I'm saying?"

Moore straightened. "Watch your tone, Fred."

"Have you radioed it in?"

Moore had moved back as Wright advanced, until his back was brushing the steering console. Now he pushed past Wright and returned to the instrument panel, tapping at the large GPS screen. "We haven't moved under power since he fell over. See? We're only a few hundred yards away. If he was still afloat, he would have seen us. We have spotters looking for him, and as soon as it's light—"

"He'll be frozen cock stiff by then," Wright said. "You gave up on him. Didn't even call it in, did you?"

"For what purpose? You think the Coast Guard could have got out here in time to do anything?"

Wright furrowed his brow, his lips twisting.

"Listen," Moore said, his voice gentle now. "We don't have power, we're taking on water, and you need to take care of the ship. We'll keep shining the seas, and if we see him, we'll get him on board." He motioned at the amp meter in Wright's hand. "Now. What's the status of the upper bilge?"

Wright opened his mouth, caught himself, then sighed. "It's still down," he said. "Bad electrical connection."

"So why aren't you working on it?"

Moore and Wright swiveled in unison. Frankie was standing in the doorway to the bridge, freshly shaved, his tone conversational.

Wright turned to Moore. "The hell's this?"

"Seems to me," Frankie said, taking a step forward, "you've already got the hard part figured out." He ambled to the instrument panel, glancing at the screen showing their location, and traced a finger along the 76th parallel. The GPS screens showed the ship about two miles southeast of the last GPS coordinates, still labeled UN-KNOWN. There were three other officers on the deck besides Moore and Wright, and all of them watched as Frankie ran the three fingers of his right hand down the navigation screen, tapped it, then ran a hand lightly along the steering wheel.

"Oh yeah?" Wright said. He was clenching the amp meter so hard the plastic cover was buckling. "What's the hard part?"

"Diagnostics. You said you got—quote—a bad connection." Frankie turned to Wright. "Now all you got to do is get down there and fix it. Make it a good connection."

Moore stepped between them before Wright could take another step. "Gentlemen," he said, placing a hand on Wright's chest. "Control yourselves." He turned to the rest of the crew. "We all have jobs to do, and none of them involve talking. Wade?"

"Yes, Captain," their duty officer said. Wade Vanders was young, a couple years out of college, trying to grow in a patchy beard.

"You logged the event?"

"Yes, sir." Vanders cleared his throat. "But we have another issue."

"Yes?"

"We just received a call from the onboard day care. It seems one of the children is missing."

Moore felt something drop in his chest. It was an actual physical sensation, as though a gallon of cold liquid had been poured into his stomach all at once. "When?"

"She wasn't sure. The girl's nine, name of Taylor Millicent. The day care sent her out to get some medicine from the onboard pharmacy last night and she didn't return."

"She's been missing all night and we hear about it now?"

"Sir," Vanders said. "The day-care lady fell asleep, and the kid was supposed to stay at the facility overnight, so her parents didn't know she was missing. This just came through. The parents are extremely upset, sir. We have all available men looking for the child."

Moore could feel his pulse throbbing in his temples. For the past year, the *Nokomis* had been able to hold together, to scrape in a modest profit, and yet deep down he'd known, goddamn *known*, the threads would unravel one day. He had hoped to be retired by that time. "How many passengers and crew do we have, total?"

"One-seventy-five," Vanders said. "One-seventy-six, counting Collins, sir."

Wright started to say something and Moore cut him off. "Wade, you're familiar with the Emergency Action Plan?"

"Yes, sir."

"What's your next step?"

Vanders looked at the screen, then back at Moore. "Sir? Have we declared an emergency situation?"

Moore paused. The kid was right; he needed to declare an emergency before the EAP kicked in. The three criteria for enacting the plan were clear: If the crew or passengers were in imminent danger; if the ship was disabled and subject to sinking; or if they were under attack. Two missing people didn't trigger it, but two missing people and a foundering ship . . . shit, it might. He had only had to enact a maritime EAP one other time in his life, a time he remembered vividly. Full investigations, with interviews with every member of the staff and the crew. . . .

"No," he said. "That's not what I meant."

"Sir?"

Moore glared at Vanders. "Don't be dense. What *would* be your next step? If we had to go to an emergency situation, how would you direct the boatswains?"

"Oh," Vanders said, his face darkening and then brightening as the answer came to him. "We would ask passengers to congregate near the lifeboats for drills. Since it's dark, and if we had time, I would probably wait until dawn. If the weather allowed it, and we were shallow enough, we would deploy anchor so that we would provide a reference point for search-and-rescues. After that—"

"That's fine," Moore said. "Deploy anchor. Graves, lead the search for the girl. She's around here somewhere." Hell, she had to be; the *Nokomis*'s deck was flanked by high guardrails in all of the passenger areas, another insurance requirement. "At oh-seven-hundred,

Wade will notify the passengers that we will be performing a drill. Practice it, make sure everyone knows what to do. One person in each group needs to know how to operate an outboard motor. Call them a captain, it should help."

"Wait a second," Frankie said, touching Moore's sleeve.

Moore shook him off. "After you deploy the anchor," he said to Graves, "get some men to help Wright with the bilge. Plug the damn breach if you can. If we have to put these people out on the open sea with those waves . . ." He paused, letting his mate think about it. Thinking about it himself. The lifeboats on the *Nokomis* were closed-hull, but not solid metal enclosures like they were on more modern ships. The hulls were aluminum, the enclosures canvas. A big wave could crush the enclosure frames, and the next one could fill it with water.

Graves frowned. "Cap, we're over a hundred fathoms. Six hundred feet. We only have a thousand foot of chain."

"It's not ideal," Moore said. "It'll slow us down, though. I want to stay near the place we lost power."

"That's plenty of chain," Frankie said. "I'm doing the math right, you got four hundred feet extra."

"The anchor chain should be five times the depth," Moore said patiently. "Less than that, you tend to bounce along the bottom." He looked at Wright. "Can you get the big bilge running?"

"It's not the pump," Wright said. "It's the wire. I gotta run ten, twelve feet of six-gauge from one of the big batteries, and I don't have enough onboard to snake it all the way around the bulkhead. It needs to go through a twelve-inch gap to reach the terminal, with about three right angles in the gap. I can't worm my way through, and besides that, it's half underwater."

"How about your crew? Any of them fit?"

"Danny might, but he's claustrophobic as hell. The other two are bigger than me."

"We'll find somebody," Moore said. "What about the props?"

Wright shook his head. "Hard to tell. I think they sheared right off."

Moore pinched his fingers against the bridge of his nose. "We'll think of something." He opened his eyes and turned to the rest of his crew. "Start looking for the girl. Talk to the day-care lady, talk to her parents. Keep them calm. Everything's going to be all right."

After Wright left, Moore motioned Frankie to his quarters. Once inside, he unbuttoned his collar and sat down on the small couch, motioning Frankie toward the single chair by the door. "Sit," Moore said when Frankie didn't move. "We better talk now, because I won't have time later."

Frankie lowered himself into the chair. "You can't be this stupid."

"No?" Moore said. "That's what I was going to say about you."

"How so?"

Moore rubbed his temples, pressing hard against the headache he felt forming there. "So far, nobody knows about the game, your cargo, any of that stuff. But let's talk worst case and the ship sinks. We're both screwed, even if we make it back to shore. Agreed?"

"I suppose."

"Of course we are. But we're not there yet, so let's talk about the other possibility."

"We don't sink."

"Very good. We don't sink," Moore said, tapping his fingers on the armrest. "Fred Wright is a temperamental man, but he's a damn good mechanic. He has to be, to keep a tub like this running, especially with what he has for a budget and crew. He'll get that bilge going. But now there's a little girl missing, and that's a whole new wrinkle, a whole new set of emotions. I don't know what we collided with—"

"You keep saying *we*," Frankie said. "Like all your pretty little sailors were standing there, each with a hand on the wheel?" He raised an eyebrow. "I won't ask what your other hand was doing."

"The ship was on autopilot," Moore said calmly. "In six hundred feet of water, with nothing on the sonar or radar to suggest a collision might occur."

Frankie leaned forward, elbows on his knees. "Then why'd we slow the boat down just before we hit, Captain?"

Moore paused, held Frankie's eyes for a moment, then looked away. "There was something in the water," he said, staring at the picture on the wall, Winslow Homer's *Fog Warning*. Look at that goddamn fisherman, he thought all calm and resolute. Looking up at those dark clouds on his horizon with austerity. "It was behind us, Frank. We didn't hit it—it hit us. Collins saw it, too, just before he went overboard."

Frankie frowned. "Say again."

"It hit us," Moore said, then waved it off. "Doesn't matter. It hasn't hit us again, and Wright will get the bilge running. That's the good news. But we're powerless, and we lost a man, and we probably won't get him back. Not good, no, but accidents happen at sea. Add in the missing girl . . . if I give the impression of *under*reacting . . ." He paused, waiting.

"Okay," Frankie said. "There'd be questions, no matter what happens. We get back to shore, the Coast Guard investigators are talking to your crew—"

"Asking them, 'Did Moore have you follow procedure?'"

Frankie nodded. "They start digging in, looking for dirt, wondering why your panties *weren't* in a bunch. So," Frankie said, "you're not actually planning on abandoning ship."

"Christ," Moore said. "Abandon ship? All we need is someone to fit through that gap and run power to the big pump."

"Through the bulkhead."

"Yes. We get that big bilge fixed, we're fine."

"But we're still dead in the water."

"We can always get a tow," Moore said. "It happens all the time. Gives us plenty of time to wrap up loose ends."

"This great mechanic," Frankie said, tapping a finger on his knee. "He can weld up the cracks in the bulkhead, too?"

"Yes, if he can find them."

"And how long we got, he can't fix it? Like none of it?"

"Worst case? Four to six hours."

Freddy looked down at his hands. "And if you find someone to worm their way through that twelve-inch gap?"

"Then we have all kinds of time." Moore said. "Why? You got somebody in mind?"

Frankie grinned. "You coulda just come right out and asked."

Chapter 10

First Officer Mason Collins had been treading water for several minutes when he saw the strobe light flicker as the life ring crested one of the dark swells, fifteen feet away.

He had plunged deep underwater after he'd been jarred loose of the *Nokomis*, and by the time he surfaced and got his bearings, the lights of the ship were a hundred meters away. He watched as the searchlight crisscrossed the sea, the beams passing over him three times without pausing. The swells blocked the light from reaching him, and he didn't have anything to signal the ship with—the strobe light on the life ring, powered by a nearly dead battery, was too weak. Still, he was certain the ship would turn around to get him. It had already seemed to stop; now it just needed to come around and pick him up.

The water was very cold, but he kicked off his shoes, then unbuckled his pants and let them float away. When the *Nokomis* came back around, he would have to swim to it, or maybe swim out of its way.

It took him fifteen minutes to realize that the *Nokomis*

was not coming back. Instead, it seemed to drifting farther and farther away.

He kicked forward, pushing the life ring out in front of him. He had to move slowly to keep the ring from diving, and as he swam he kept his eyes trained on the lights of his ship.

Three hours later, dawn had colored the horizon a soft peach color. Collins had long since stopped swimming, and for the past hour had merely floated at the mercy of the current. The water didn't feel nearly as cold; the storm must have pushed the warmer Gulf Stream waters into the edge of the Kaala. Yet his limbs were weak from holding onto the ring, his thoughts disjointed. The fog had returned, the *Nokomis* had long since disappeared into the grayness, and Collins's world had shrunk to a radius of a fifty meters.

He had slowly come to realize that in the darkness and the fog he had somehow floated past the *Nokomis*, and was now adrift and alone in the vast sea.

He tried to think about his wife, but his thoughts would not seem to stick. It was little wonder; their marriage was dull, perfunctory. No kids. Who, then? Most of his close friends were now scattered across the country, chasing careers, and the few that remained in town were busy with T-ball and dance and Cub Scouts. His wife, yes, he should think about her. She might miss him for a few weeks, even months. Then she'd concentrate on spending his generous life insurance policy on—

He chuffed mirthless laughter into the interior of his life ring. It would be dolls—his wife had a weakness for porcelain figurines. The lasting reminder of his time on earth would be a bunch of white and blue dolls staring blankly into the future in which they, like all others, must surely shatter.

His mother, though, alone in her apartment on the East Side . . . she would miss him. He remembered when he was a kid and she had decorated his room to resemble a treehouse, complete with a hammock in the corner of his room, after he had fallen in love with *The Jungle Book.* He slept there for more than a year, and some days she would snuggle in the hammock with him, and they would rock away a Sunday afternoon, talking and laughing. He could feel the security of the hammock now, a warm and gentle swaying, secure in the knowledge he would never be alone as long as he had his mother. . . .

Ahead of him, something broke the surface of the ocean.

Collins watched it with glazed eyes, the hammock forgotten. He felt no great fear as the creature swam toward him, no real concern even as it closed to within ten yards. It was the same beast he had seen on the *Nokomis.* Yes, those had been eyes he had seen. Green eyes, huge malevolent cat eyes, and yes, those were teeth as well.

Teeth everywhere, curved like sabers, the back sides marked with back-slanting extrusions, like repeating fishhook barbs. Teeth that were designed to seize prey and never, ever let go.

The thing blinked, and it was that simple movement that finally triggered Collins's sluggish nervous system. His heart began to thump harder in his chest, pushing warmer blood out to his extremities. The beast watched him, sucking in air, its foul exhale washing over Collins. Its snout, badly gashed, oozed blood into the ocean. Collins watched the blood mix with the seawater, a

thin red cloud ballooning around him. The water swirled
around his legs from the movement of the beast's fins.
His thoughts began to gain focus as he looked at the
wounds on the creature's snout, the way the blood
mixed with water. The flexing of enormous muscles as
it raised its head to gaze at something over Collins's
left shoulder.

Collins did not move. The beast was still looking
beyond him, its enormous jaws slightly open. It had
dismissed him for the moment. Yet he could feel the
tensed energy in the creature, a sense that any movement on his part would result in quick and violent reaction.

The creature breathed in, its jaws opening wider.
The curved fangs were cracked and pitted, and there
was an open and bloody socket where one had broken
away. Another tooth was cracked badly, and there was
a bright smear of metal or paint along the edge. Beyond the teeth was a huge gullet, rings of red cartilage
disappearing into darkness. He could smell its breath, a
fetid mix of salt and blood and digested meat.

The water swirled around him as the creature submerged, its tremendous displacement almost sucking
Collins and the life ring under the water. Collins kicked
weakly, moving away from the swirling vortex. He did
a short half-circle in the eddy and came to rest, waiting
for those teeth to rip into him. Nothing happened.

He kicked, slowly, and turned to look at the sea behind him.

For a moment there was nothing but waves and fog,
and then the shape of a fishing boat appeared, its out-
riggers upright, empty flagpoles disappearing into the
fog. It was silent, a ghost ship with its bow pointed into

the waves, floating backwards on a course that would pass a hundred yards from Collins.

He tried to yell and managed a weak, garbled noise. He cleared his throat and yelled louder, kicking his way toward the ship. Perhaps God, or Someone or Something, had sent the vision of the beast to him on purpose, waking him from his reverie. His feet kicked in the current and he yelled again, almost joyously now, pushing the life ring with one arm and waving with the other.

He had only made a few yards when the sea surged in front of him, a wall of water between two waves. The mound of water grew, then broke away to show a mottled green-black head, the enormous eyes squinted into thin green lines. In Collins's last thoughts he understood the look in the creature's eyes, what it meant. It was not evil, not hatred, not even contempt. It was just hunger.

Its jaws opened, and First Mate Mason Collins disappeared from the surface of the ocean.

Chapter 11

Frankie and Christie walked down Deck C's hallway, the doctor stealing an occasional glance at Frankie. They had just finished their early breakfast, and the hallways were still barren. It felt good to be out and about; D-deck was off limits to passengers and most of the crew, and it was easier for them to go up and eat on the main level instead of running every meal down to D-deck. A select few, including Prower and Latham, ate downstairs.

Frankie didn't mind going up. It was good to see the rest of the crew, feel the mood. Which was better than he had expected. Nobody was panicking, and he had a feeling the gaming deck might even see a bit of activity later on in the morning.

He felt refreshed after his little exercise in the bowels of the ship. He hadn't been able to worm all the way through the gap, but he had got far enough in to snake the electrical line through to Wright. Ten minutes later, the emergency bilge was running, and another thousand gallons of water was spitting out the side of the boat every minute. It was a mess down in the bilge, rank with a fishy, oily smell, and he'd taken two showers in a row to rid himself of the smell. It felt good, though, accomplishing something real. Now they needed to finish the rest of the morning's business.

"So you're an electrician now?" Christie asked.

Christie carried a blood pressure kit in one hand, and he moved with the loose shuffle of a man who had not been yelled at to hurry in a very long time. It wasn't like the walk a working man should have, Frankie thought. Hell, men *moved* when he was a kid, mill workers and construction guys always moving. Hard-faced men striding to the car or the bus stop, holding aluminum lunch pails, working with their feet and hands all day. Moving, always moving, and then in the late afternoon they'd walk or drive to the bar, finally sit down and their mouths would pick up where their feet left off. Sometimes the hands would come back into play later in the evening, completing the cycle that had started when they'd picked up their lunch pails in the morning.

Now he was in a white-collar world and shit just naturally moved slower. Still, he was tempted to plant a boot in Christie's bony ass, speed it back up.

"No," Frankie said. "Not an electrician. But I gotta slide through some nasty bilge, I'll do it. Just like you better be ready to do your part when the time comes."

Christie gave him a bland look. "I wouldn't be here otherwise."

"Good," Frankie said. "That's real good. And how are our clients, doc?"

"Don't call me that," Christie said. "How many times do I have to tell you? Somebody hears I'm a doctor, next thing you know I'm down in the First Aid room, treating strep throat."

"What's wrong with that?" Frankie said. "You could pick up a few extra bucks, maybe do an exam on some of the better looking girls."

"I don't think so," Christie said. He was thin and pale, with a spray of faded freckles the only distinguishing mark on his cadaverous face. He stopped now, turning to face Frankie. "The last thing I need is someone screaming for a doctor, and everybody starts looking at me."

Frankie passed a hand through the air. "Settle down. There's a real doc on board, board certified or whatever. I'm just screwing with ya."

"I don't appreciate it."

"Well," Frankie said. "It's a good thing I don't give a fuck about your feelings, isn't it?" He reached into his pocket and popped a stick of gum into his mouth. "We going to have a game today?"

Christie shrugged. "Prower's blood pressure is a bit high, and his leg is bothering him again. Latham's is better, but his circulation is very sluggish." He shrugged. "I don't see anything to suggest we should stop the game. Latham's request probably isn't the best idea."

"I'll see what she says. Unless you want to ask?"

Christie shook his head. "That's not my kind of thing."

"Fine," Frankie said, clapping Christie on the shoulder. It was, Frankie thought, like slapping one of those fake plaster skeletons. He almost expected to hear bones rattling.

"I'm gonna split," Frankie said. "You all right? Look like you gotta go take a shit or something."

"The ship," Christie said. "Is it . . . ?"

"Oh, hell," Frankie said. "It's fine. Besides, we

planned for this." He motioned Christie down the hallway, deserted at this early hour. "Well, not exactly this, but we can get off the rig fast if we need to."

"But the fog—"

"Fog is an old problem," Frankie said. "We're modern men, right, doc?"

"I suppose," Christie said. "I just never thought we would—"

"Hold on," Frankie said, taking a step back. The door to one of the service closets was opened slightly. He opened it all the way, let his eyes adjust to the darkness. A young girl sat on a bunch of folded towels in the back of the closet, arms crossed over her knees, looking up at Frankie with red-rimmed eyes. It took him a minute to realize why her teary face caught him off guard. Then it came to him—it had been years since he'd seen a girl crying who didn't have mascara tracks running down her cheeks.

"You okay, Taylor?"

"How do you know who I am?"

"We been looking all over for you," Frankie said. "What're you doing in a closet?"

"I . . . I went to go get some medicine," Taylor said. "I was supposed to find Doc Perle, but then the boat started shaking, and then it stopped. I heard someone yelling, and this guy with a shaved head came running back up the hallway and . . . I thought maybe we were being attacked, so I hid. I heard people calling out for me, but I didn't recognize their voices, and I thought it might be the scary guy."

"This scary guy, did he have bloodshot eyes?"

She nodded.

"Kharkov," Frankie said. "Don't worry about him, he only looks scary."

She bit her lip. "I fell asleep."

"It's not a bad plan," Frankie said, nodding. "Sometimes, shit starts going down, hiding's the best thing a person can do." He stepped into the closet and helped the girl to her feet. "You know what room you're in?"

"C-12." She looked up at him. "You swore."

"Yeah, it's a bad habit. Don't start, 'cause quitting can be a bitch."

Taylor wiped her eyes with the back of her forearm and snuffled. Frankie waited, and decided the snuffle was actually a tired sort of giggle, and led her out into the hallway. "Let's go see your folks," he said, then turned to Christie. "Go ahead and do that last checkup. He should be awake by now."

"Right," Christie said, then patted his portable radio. "Want me to let Moore know you found her?"

"Hold off on that," Frankie said. "I want to be a hero about as much as you want to be a doctor. Go see our *renunciar,* then meet me down in the bar." He watched the doctor amble away, then called out his name before he rounded the corner of the hallway.

Christie turned. "Yeah?"

"I went by your cabin last night, heard you listening to Marley."

"You got some kind of rule against that?"

"What I'm saying," Frankie said, "is you should listen to the words, not just the music. Like, you know, 'every little thing, it gonna be all right'?"

Christie considered this, exhaled through his nose. "Not for everyone it won't be."

Frankie shrugged. "It will for the people that matter."

Taylor's room was at the far end of the ship, a walk of a couple minutes. They moved slowly, Taylor trailing a hand along the wall. Frankie wasn't in a big hurry, either, happy at his little piece of luck. Kids went missing and people just went bat shit, lost all perspective. One time in Henderson, years ago, he'd been watching this house, just watching it with no orders to do anything to anybody, which meant the pay was for shit. But work was work and he'd still liked to get high regularly then, an expensive habit. He didn't even know whose house it was, just that he was supposed to mark down how many vehicles stopped in, how long they stayed, et cetera, et cetera. Typical druggie surveillance.

Around two in the morning the streets lit up with cherries and then the spotlights popped up and then they were all running at him, half-bent over with long shadows trailing, holding rifles and shotguns, all kinds of shit. Frankie put his hands on the steering wheel real quick, and the next thing he knew he was being dragged from the car and his face was pressed against the asphalt, still hot even in the early morning hours. He could smell the tar, could feel the pressure of the swarm of men standing over him, and when they found the knife on his belt his face was smashed even deeper into the asphalt.

He was grilled for several hours, no lawyer. He was pretty sure he wasn't the guy they wanted. Also sure that his employer, a low-class hustler named Jimmy Twos, wasn't who they wanted, either. Turned out he was right; some little kid had been snatched the street over from him around midnight, and the mother had said the guy had come crashing into the bedroom, took the kid at knifepoint. The first detective was wound up, all the way up, kept yelling in Frankie's face; he wasn't happy with Frankie's story that he had pulled over to take a nap. After a while, Frankie was pulled from that room into another, where a different detective started talking at him, and this detective was scarred badly along one side of his face and his words came out slowly, somewhat mangled-sounding, and he scared Frankie more than a little. He was thinking of just calling one of the low-price lawyers he knew when the scarred detective was called from the room.

They had found the kid, safe with his father, who had not been brandishing a knife but the kid's favorite toy, some sort of Transformer fighter jet. The mother was a tweaker, had taken the kid from the father earlier in the night, and so everything was not what it had seemed, which the cops seemed not at all surprised about. Frankie was let go at dawn, and decided, right then and there, it was time to quit working the residential areas. Working around kids was like throwing cherry bombs onto a bonfire.

"Why is the tall man worried?" Tayler asked him now. She had stopped, obviously reluctant to go back to her room. Maybe her folks would beat on her, Frankie thought, though he'd heard that wasn't in style anymore. Probably not on a thin-walled ship full of suburban liberals, anyway. An old-school parent could end up in jail pretty quick.

"He's one of those people who worry too much," Frankie said. "You know what I mean?"

"Like my mom."

"She's a worrier, huh? I bet she's sick to her stomach right now."

"I suppose," Taylor said, looking down at her shoes. "What's a *renunciar*?"

"Come on," Frankie said, taking her hand and pulling her down the hallway. "This it?" He knocked on the door and it opened a split second later, a wild-eyed woman in his face. She looked down at Taylor, who was crying again, and a flash of something—anger, or maybe annoyance—flashed across her face. Then relief flooded over that other emotion, and she bent down to grab Taylor.

It was an odd reaction, Frankie thought. Being pissed off first, and then she acts like Ma Ingalls. He was reflecting on this when someone barreled into him and sent him reeling, pinning him against the far wall. A fist came up under his arms and hit him low, right in the liver, and his legs buckled. He sank down to the floor, trying to catch his breath.

"Why's she crying?" a man demanded. He leaned over Frankie, lips peeled into a snarl. He had a short beard that parted around his sour expression. "What'd you do?"

Frankie tried to speak, ended up with a weak cough. It had been a hell of a good punch.

"Found . . . found her."

"Bullshit."

"No, Daddy!" Taylor shouted.

The guy's boot whistled in underneath Frankie's arm, connecting low in his ribs. He slipped down the wall. When he looked up, Taylor was in front of him, her hands planted on her father's chest.

Kids, Frankie thought, trying not to moan. *Like goddamn cherry bombs.*

"He found me!" Taylor yelled, and down the hall several other doors opened. "He found me while you and Mom were here, in your room. He didn't do *anything!*"

The guy paused, his foot halfway back for another kick. People were moving into Frankie's peripheral vision. One of them was Thor, who placed his forearm against Taylor's father's chest and pushed him back, slowly but forcefully, into his room.

Frankie took a couple breaths. Thor was blocking his vision of the guy, which was good, because as his strength was coming back so was his anger. He'd be pissing red for a week.

He struggled to his feet. Nobody offered to help him and he noticed that, too. He looked around, saw the grim faces and narrowed eyes of several other parents in the hallway—the booking agent had placed the young families together in the same wing, it seemed.

He stood with his back against the wall, breathing slowly. There was a metallic taste in his mouth, sweat running down the sides of his ribs.

Taylor squirmed out of her mother's grip and pushed herself between Thor and her father, talking to her father but, Frankie thought, also addressing the crowd. "I went to get medicine," she said. "Then something hit the ship, and I got scared. And I hid in a closet, underneath a bunch of towels, and I fell asleep. When I woke up I was still scared. I opened the door a crack, just to watch and see what had happened. Mr. Frankie found me, him and another guy."

Her father was straining to look at Frankie around Thor's arm. Taylor frowned, seeing she wasn't getting through, or her words weren't right. "Dad, he just found me like, two *minutes* ago."

The kid was smart, Frankie thought. She had seen the thing twisting up her dad's mind—all that time she had been gone, the things that might have happened to her in those long, unaccounted-for hours.

"Somebody better call the ship's security," one of the parents said. "Just to make sure."

Thor turned to her, favoring his hurt foot a little. "I am ship security," he said, then gestured toward Frankie. "So is he. We are looking for the girl for hours now."

The eyes turned back to Frankie, not quite believing, and he could feel his face burning into their brains, the last thing he wanted. No, he supposed, the last thing he wanted was to be here a minute longer, trapped in this domestic drama when he had work to do. They would remember him now, for better or worse. He pulled his radio from his belt and turned it to the command center channel. "Captain Moore, this is Frankie. Taylor's been found and delivered to her room. She seems fine, but I want you to send Dr. Perle down to take a look. Copy?"

There was a long pause, and Frankie was pretty sure everyone was thinking the same thing: *if the captain doesn't respond . . .*

Hell, he was thinking it, too.

The radio crackled. "That's great news, Frank."

Frankie had never cared for the captain's tone; dry and deep, it had a commanding tone that made Frankie feel like a working stiff, instead of the guy in charge. But the parents visibly relaxed, and a moment later, when Moore announced over the intercom that the girl had been found, people started moving again, disregarding Frankie as they tried to make their way into the room to see Taylor, not touching her but smiling at her, talking in soft tones about how happy they were to see her. Thor was leaning down to whisper into her father's ear, and whatever he was saying finally drained the anger out of the man's face, replacing it with a confused sort of apprehension. Then Thor turned the man to face Taylor, who was still looking up at him, and father and daughter embraced. The people in the room smiled, the women holding their hands to their mouths. A few people actually clapped.

Thor worked his way back out of the small room. "You ready, *chef*?"

"No," Frankie said. "We wait until Perle gets here."

It was a good five minutes until the doctor arrived, his fringe of hair rumpled. He nodded at Frankie as he went past, leaving a scent trail of cologne over the top of cheap gin. Perle went into the room, gave Taylor a tight smile, and made a shooing gesture at the crowd. "Everyone out, except the girl and her mother. Back to your rooms." He turned to Frank. "The captain says thank you, and that you should get some rest. If I see anything of concern, I'll let you know."

That did it. The last remaining tension in the room deflated and the people went back to their rooms. He looked straight at them, remembering the old trick he had heard, that it was harder to remember a face that looked you straight in the eyes than it was to remember a face you saw at a quartering angle. He wasn't sure if it was good advice—the guy he heard it from eventually got picked out of a lineup for a carjacking, spent seven years inside before getting killed in the yard. No, probably it was bullshit, but it did make the people look down right away, so there was some benefit to it.

The father exited last, not looking at anyone. Frankie thought it would be a good time to punch the guy in the kidney, send him down to smell the carpet.

"Come on," Thor said, putting a heavy hand on Frankie's shoulder. "Leave him."

"I ain't gonna do nothing."

"Swedes can smell evil thoughts. Come on."

Frankie watched as Taylor's father walked down the hall. "What'd you tell him?"

"The truth," Thor said. "You were good guy, but sometimes with the bad temper." He glanced down the hallway, saw that Taylor's father had disappeared, and let his hand drop from Frankie's shoulder. "And that I, personally, did not care for what he had done."

Frankie looked up at Thor's face, which was without a shred of humor. "Sweden is one of those neutral nations, right? Full of level-headed people?"

Thor shook his head. "Only to a certain point. Then Svear go Viking, chop down people who get in the way." He shifted his weight from his good foot to the bad, then back again. "Sometimes is easier to chop."

"I got your name right after all," Frankie said. "Good old fuckin' Thor. Listen, you stay by my side from now on. We got some work to do, it might need some chopping. How's your foot?"

"It's a little sore."

"Sorry we had that misunderstanding," Frankie said. "There's a couple other guys I shoulda stabbed in the foot before you."

Thor waved it off. "It's nothing. Do we go to the deck at seven, for the drill?"

"That's for the civilians," Frankie said. "We're gonna go downstairs, get the boys to play some cards."

Chapter 12

Gilly bent over the doghouse, his tools placed carefully on a piece of canvas on the deck. The deck was dim and wet, the rising sun hidden behind the fogbank. The two cordless lights planted inside the doghouse created huge hand shadows as Gilly maneuvered the Dewalt cordless drill with one hand, backing out the long anchor bolts on the fuel pump.

Brian was quiet. He'd learned at age six that offering advice to a guy with bloody knuckles, especially one forced to work at an odd angle, wasn't a good idea.

The wind had not swung around to the east. It had stayed north until dawn, and when dawn arrived, the *Tangled Blue*'s wind vane edged to the northwest. For some time their drift remained parallel with the coast, and then they had slowly started to slide out into the open ocean. Overhead, the fog rolled over them in an endless gray curtain, blowing apart and then coming back together.

"There she is," Gilly said, sliding the pump off its mounting posts. He ran his fingers down the intake fuel line, pinched it, and cut it free. He repeated the process on the other side of the pump and climbed out of the doghouse, holding the pump by the flexible fuel lines. Brian handed him a coffee can and Gilly drained the lines into it, the milky diesel swirling across the bottom of the can.

"Shit," Gilly said, staring at the bottom of the coffee can. "Look at all that water."

"Surprised we're still running," Brian said. "She looks like half-and-half."

"That's a good old American engine for ya," Gilly said. "But there ain't a lot we can do about the fuel. I bet most of the water's floating on top of the fuel. We rev her up, pound into the waves, we'll just mix it back up."

Brian stared into the fog, thinking. Gilly was almost always right when it came to matters of the ship. Now that it was daylight they could see the ragged gash in the side of the *Tangled Blue* where the *Archos*'s hull had smashed into them last evening, fracturing the tank. Their entire fuel supply was compromised, and the auxiliary tank had been cracked when Brian had bought the ship six years earlier.

"So we try a Mayday."

"I guess so," Gilly said, digging in his shirt pocket for a cigarette. "Shit, Brian. I don't know what else we can do."

Brian reached for the radio, then paused. There was a green mark on the radar; it had crept in while they were dismantling the fuel pump. It was about a half mile to their south, somewhere in the thick fog. Gilly stepped up next to him and they both watched as the radar painted its picture on the screen. They were drawing closer to the object, which appeared to be moving slowly south.

"Fishing boat?" Gilly said. "Drifting off a kelp bed?"

"In this?" Brian gestured at the roiling sea around them. "Too big for a trawler, at any rate."

Brian picked up the radio, confirmed it was on Channel 16, and spoke into the mike. "This is a private American fishing vessel *Tangled Blue* calling the unnamed ship located near—" He paused, and read the coordinates off the GPS. "Do you read me, over?"

Gilly leaned close, studying the shape on the radar screen. "Merchant ship, maybe."

"I don't know. It might be a—"

"Copy that, *Tangled Blue*. This is the *Nokomis*, an American entertainment ship operating in international waters. Captain Donald Moore speaking."

Brian closed his eyes and exhaled softly. "This is Captain Brian Hawkins from the *Tangled Blue*," he said. "We're having a bit of engine trouble, Captain Moore. Seek permission to dock alongside *Nokomis* to make repairs." The large ship would have fuel transfer pumps, and they could suck the bad fuel out, drum it, and probably buy enough fresh diesel to make their way back in. No need for a tow, or even the potential salvage fee.

He waited for Captain Moore to grant permission. After a minute, Brian shot Gilly a quizzical look. "Captain Moore? Did you receive my last transmission, over?"

"Roger, Captain Hawkins. Please stand by, over."

There was silence, followed by a long burst of static as the *Nokomis*'s captain keyed the mike. "*Tangled Blue*, be advised the *Nokomis* is operating in a disabled state. Docking of your vessel is not recommended in

light of the current conditions. Repeat, sideboard docking is not recommended at this time. Over."

"What is the nature of your mechanical issues?"

Another long pause. "We have lost power to our
outdrive." Moore's tone was clipped. "We are taking
on a small amount of water and have deployed the anchor. We have very limited maneuverability, *Tangled
Blue*."

Brian glanced at Gilly. His first mate gave him a
shrug and Brian pressed down on the mike as he turned
the rudder of the *Tangled Blue* toward the *Nokomis*.
"Thank you for your advisement, Captain. We'll be on
your western flank in fifteen minutes."

They pulled in the drift sock and Brian brought the
boat up to four knots, nursing the port engine toward
the green demarcation on the radar. In a few minutes,
the ship appeared, a darker shape amid the gloom. He
approached slowly, taking the waves at a quartering
angle. The ship was bigger than he'd thought, and they
were running crossways into the seas.

"Lost its outdrive?" Gilly mused. "And what'd he
say it was, an entertainment ship?"

"Yeah."

"Like a floating brothel?"

"You wish," Brian said. The glimmer of hope was
growing by the minute. He wouldn't lose his ship, he
wouldn't lose his profession. And they had not returned
empty-handed; they had saved a life. At the very least
it would make a good story to tell at the Riff-Raff.
"Pretty high-flanked."

"Yup," Gilly said. "We're gonna scratch her pretty paint, we don't come in just right."

"I can't come up aft," Brian said. "We'll smash right into her in these waves. I'll run alongside, nestle right in." He glanced at Gilly. "They don't offer a tender, you throw a grapple up there. Don't snag a hooker."

"If I do, I get to keep her," Gilly said. He checked the inflatable life vest on his belt. It was the only kind Brian liked; just yank on the cord, it inflated, and all you had to do was slip it over your head. "You serious about the grapple?"

"They don't offer a rope," Brian said, "You hook on to her. We aren't going to float away with our good manners." They could see the ship's lettering now, could see a crowd of people standing on the deck. He handed Gilly the binoculars. "What're they doing up there?"

Gilly raised the binoculars. There were large groups of people standing in knots along the length of the *Nokomis*, listening to several men, one of whom was gesturing with his arms. The rising sun was somewhere behind them, a brighter area in the fog. "Looks like he's showing them how the lifeboats are launched."

"Great," Brian said. He picked up the mike and hailed the *Nokomis*. "We're coming alongside, *Nokomis*. Send down a rope."

Brian nosed the *Tangled Blue* forward, and now some of the people on the deck had seen him and were gesturing their way. It was hard to tell in the fog and low light, but the *Nokomis* looked like it was noticeable lower in the stern, the bilges spraying out steady streams of water. *Taking on a bit of water*, Moore had said. Well, it was a big ship, and big ships didn't go down easily. As long as he had a few hours for Gilly to work his magic, the *Tangled Blue* would be fine, too.

Brian swung the bow around so it was facing into the waves, then put the transmission in reverse to feather them alongside the *Nokomis*. The deck way was about five feet above the flybridge. Gilly moved to the starboard side and dropped down a line of inflatable bumpers to keep the two hulls from touching. They were on the leeward side, the water as calm as he'd been in since leaving the marina.

"*Tangled Blue* is on your starboard," he called out on the loudspeaker. "Toss a rope over and we'll hook up."

They were more than halfway down the flank of the ship when a rope thumped onto the deck. Gilly dropped his grapple and quickly looped the rope around the cleat aft of the captain's chair, then walked to the stern cleat and repeated the process. When he was done, he had twenty feet of rope left, which he threw back up to the *Nokomis*'s deck way. A moment later the rope was pulled tight, the *Tangled Blue* bumping lightly alongside the *Nokomis*.

Brian let out a long breath. It was the same feeling he'd had when he first started fishing, back when he would run out into the building storms, setting lines as the barometer plunged. The fish would often be extremely aggressive just before the storms, but the best action happened well offshore and he would have to battle his way home, white-knuckled, the lightning cracking the sky open above them. Everything inside clenched and puckered—*we're all watertight now*, Gilly would say—the fish slopping in the hold, waves crashing against the pier heads. And then, finally, entry into the calmer waters of the harbor, everything loosening up in him that had been clenched. The sudden relaxation that washed his mind of everything.

We're going to make it.

He turned to Gilly, who was shrugging on his backpack, and nodded. His first mate grinned back at him and had just opened his mouth to say something when the back of the *Tangled Blue* exploded.

A wall of water washed over Gilly, sending him against the gunnels. Underneath the water was a huge head with massive jaws. Brian watched, paralyzed, as the head swung from side to side like a battering ram, smashing into the hull and then thrashing from side to side, ripping the boat apart from the inside out. The back half of the *Tangled Blue* went under, sending water rushing up the tilted deck, flooding over his boots and pouring into the cuddy.

The creature bulled its way forward, halfway hidden in the water and fragments of the disintegrating boat. Gilly was cornered, the boat disassembling in front of him, the high flanks of the *Nokomis* blocking his retreat. The creature surged forward and the boat crinkled, structural runners snapping like toothpicks. Brian could see a tail lashing at the surface, many yards away. His first thought was that there must be two of them, whatever they were, and then he realized that, no, it was just the one.

"The rope!" he shouted to Gilly as the boat tipped backwards, porpoising, the bow pointing to the sky. "Climb the rope!"

Gilly leaped for the stern mooring rope, which had broken loose under the impact. He caught it and clenched his feet around it, beginning to worm his way upward, curling his body around the thick rope.

My fat ass will never do that, Brian thought, and then the beast smashed into the hull again and the back half of the *Tangled Blue* was ripped free. Released from the weight of the engines, the front of the boat slapped back down onto the water. Almost immediately it filled with water and began to list to one side, held in place only by the stern mooring line. Brian saw instantly that the rope wouldn't last. Once the boat filled with water, the rope would snap or the cleat would pull free.

"Wells! Get up here!"

Wells let out a strangled cry from the cuddy, which was already almost submerged. Brian clambered down the stairs into chest-deep water and saw Wells struggling to get out of his sleeping bag. His eyes were wide with panic, his left arm clawing at the zipper. He unzipped him, grabbed Wells in a loose headlock, and pulled him toward the stairs, which had turned into a surging waterfall. Something barred his path and he looked down in the water. The old Ithaca flare gun had fallen loose from its clips and was leaning across the stairwell. He grabbed it in his free hand, slung the strap over his shoulder, and pushed Wells onto the deck.

The *Tangled Blue* was nearly swamped, held afloat only by one strained rope. The foam insulation blown into its cavity had been shredded under the assault, and the water was covered with the sheen of fuel and smashed pieces of fiberglass. The top of the flybridge was almost level with the deck on the *Nokomis*; they could jump from the flybridge to the safety of the larger ship.

He pushed Wells up the first couple rungs and was about to follow when he heard the water boil behind him. The creature was just off the stern, partially hidden by the distortion of the rainbow-colored sheen. Then two huge nostrils broke the surface, followed by the eyes. Brilliant green, and containing an awareness Brian had never seen in a fish or sea creature before. It was striped, Brian saw, long jagged lines that looked like the sea's surface on days when the clouds raced across the sun.

And for a moment, as the jaws began to open, he thought it was not only colored like the ocean—it *was* the ocean, the savage embodiment of it.

Above him, Wells stumbled across the *Tangled Blue*'s flybridge to where she was butted up against the larger ship. Wells held up his arms, and Gilly and another deckhand yanked him over the railing and onto the *Nokomis*. Brian was still only a quarter way up the flybridge ladder.

"Climb!" Gilly shouted from what seemed like an incredible distance. "Jesus, Brian, *climb*!"

Brian shrugged the shotgun off his shoulder, broke it open, and slapped in two flares from the elastic shell carrier that was fitted over the stock. He heard the creature suck in air, heard the slither as water passed over its hide, and forced himself not to look up until the breech snapped closed.

He hooked an ankle around the ladder. It was close now, its jaws open in a parody of a grin. It was enormous, like nothing Brian had ever seen before, like nothing anybody had ever seen before. The teeth were enormous and curved obscenely, the back sides cruelly barbed.

It gets hold of you, he thought, *it'll never let go.*

Above him, Gilly and Wells were yelling for him to climb. He watched the beast move closer, pushing a wall of water in front of it. A crazy thought was running through him, repeating over and over in his mind. The idea that this creature wanted to sink those barbed teeth into the last member of the Hawkinses. Wanted to drag him down to join his wife and child.

It came out of the water in a surge, jaws opening wide.

"Here," Brian said, holding the shotgun to his shoulder, and fired both barrels as the creature exploded out of the sea.

The flares shot out in phosphorescent streaks, burning so brightly that his vision was instantly reduced to black with green tracers. One of the flares veered off into the sky like an errant firework, deflecting off the creature's hide. The other lodged in the corner of its eye, burning and spitting as the creature continued toward him, massive jaws opening and opening and opening, and then he was inside their shadow and they began to close, and he was falling, falling away even as the jaws closed above him, blocking out the dim light of the morning sky.

Chapter 13

Destiny sat at the small table in the lounge of D-deck, drinking coffee and watching Remy play a game of solitaire at the bar. It was a little after seven, several hours before she had to squeeze into her hostess uniform, and she was dressed in blue jeans and an Arizona State sweatshirt. It was her favorite shirt, slightly frayed at the cuffs. Sometimes, when she wore it, she wondered if people thought she was an ASU alumni, an ex-sorority girl. It was a comforting thought, being mistaken for something she could have been.

She said, "You ever go to school?"

Remy looked up from his cards, eyebrows furrowed. "What you mean? 'Course I did, got a diploma and everything. All twelve grades, baby."

"I mean college." She took a sip of her coffee. Remy had made it in a French press and it was good, better than she was used to. He wouldn't let her put in any cream, though, said it would be like adding Sprite to good wine.

"Nooo," Remy said, looking back down at his cards. "See, my senior year high school, I got in a bit of trouble. Wouldn't been a big deal, 'cept that I was born in

October, trouble happened in February, so I was eighteen. Had to finish my education inside, took two years, but the diploma's real. Stamped and everything. Got it in a file cabinet, somewhere back home."

"Were you any good at it?"

"School?" Remy laughed. "Better than I was at stealing cars, anyway. I liked math and history; the rest wasn't worth much."

She smiled. "You ever wish you had?"

"And what," Remy said. "Be a math teacher?"

"Sure, why not?"

"No," he said. "I like the life I got. There's rough spots, sure, but mostly good. I got a bit of walking-around money, a couple ladies happy to see me when I come visit. Lots of freedom, which I 'spect most math teachers think you get on summer vacation. Me, I got a little shack up near Thibodeaux, right there in the delta, go there anytime. Eat big old shrimp for dinner, have a drink, and watch the sun slide down."

She took another drink of coffee and nibbled at the edge of the croissant Remy had brought her from upstairs. "Aren't you going to ask me if I went to college?"

Remy laughed again. "College and Mizz Destiny? No girl, don't believe I will."

"I could have went to college."

Her tone had been sharper than she'd meant. Remy moved several cards around the bar slowly, very deliberately, and she knew if he was going to answer, he would answer carefully.

"It's all right," she said. "I didn't know it was that obvious."

Remy sighed, scooped the cards into a pile. He

shuffled and began to lay out a new game. "How long you been outta high school? Five, ten years?"

"Five years? Come on."

"Okay, say ten. In those ten year, how many college-educated people you work with, side by side, any given year? Not counting managers. Not many, right?" He peered down, chuckled. "Them old suicide kings, they always get me. Man king of the world, stick a knife in his own ear. Where was we?"

"We weren't anywhere," Destiny said. "I'm going to go back to my room, take a nap."

"That might be a good idea. Yeah, now I remember what I was saying. We don't work with those kinda people, not usually. After a while, you get a feel for the people you do work with. Not saying we non-college folk dumb, not that. Fact, I think maybe some people go to college just so they get a piece of paper they can show people, say to them look, I ain't dumb at all. No, whatever it is, they got a different way of looking at the world, like they done something a monkey couldn't do."

He looked up, and she was right: He had kind eyes, but they weren't always that way. He was looking at her intensely now, not with malice but with a seriousness that was unsettling. "Lotta us, we *know* our work could be done by a monkey. Way we move, way we look at things. Jus' a job, ain't our life."

She brought the cup and saucer over to the bar. "Sorry I brought it up."

"What I mean is you pick up on that, right away. Way people speak, way they—"

"You don't have to spell it out for me."

He took the cup from her, pressing his hand against hers. "How long you been looking to break out?" he asked, almost like he was talking to himself. "Never mind, it don't matter. One thing, though, you should quit asking questions if the answer already built up in your mind. 'Cuz, Destiny girl? The answers you want gotta be your answers."

She went back to her room, rubbing at the corners of her eyes. She felt like an idiot, surprised a little Creole bartender could see how transparent her fantasy world was, how she longed for something more than this smoky, cramped world, for being someone more than an afterthought in this dull existence. A world peopled by savants. Pull a lever, get a few chips, hope for a draw card. Win, lose, drink, smoke, maybe tip the drink girl. Look at her ass, if it's nice take a minute and stare. Above all: Forget the real world, lose it in the numbers and lights and chips.

And she was the one supposed to be a monkey?

She tried to feel indignant, but it wouldn't come. That wasn't what Remy was saying. She and Remy had jobs, not careers, and the distinction was reflected in their postures, their expressions. She did an adequate job, moving fast in a world where speed was expected, never forgot a drink order, almost always smiled, hardly ever had to fake it. If she had some talent in her job it was knowing how to read a customer, whether they wanted her involved in their world or not. If not, she stayed out of the way, made sure they didn't wait for anything. Otherwise, she made sure to smile, to ask about them, to not only *act* interested but to actually *be* interested. People could tell the difference, and she was lucky; she found a lot of people genuinely interesting.

She'd made a base salary of thirty-two thousand the year before, and with tips had tripled that. Most of the tips were cash, or chips she cashed out, and was mostly tax-free. Two hundred dollars a day, average, though sometimes as low as thirty or forty bucks. Once she'd received a thousand-dollar tip, but that was a fluke, happened only once every couple years from what she'd heard, and she'd split it with another cocktail waitress.

Almost a hundred grand a year. It sounded like a lot of money, even to herself sometimes. More than her parents had made combined, outside Savannah on the old estate. Difference was they had been happy, or at least they had been before that sweltering August day in the garden. But she was getting closer to her goal, even after paying the ridiculous four-grand-a-month rent so she could live in a small condo in a gated community between Vegas and Henderson.

She had to get going . . . how would Remy put it? Shit or get off the pot. Good old Remy, he might have been trying to flatter her, he might not. She was thirty-four, but could pass for twenty-four . . . on a good day in the right light, she thought wryly. On a bad day she could see that old bitch Forty peeking around the edges of the mirror, lurking in the small crow's-feet of her laugh lines. Soon the tips would start shrinking, and then she would be moved to another job, away from the high-stakes tables.

Or she could move on to her career. There was

$53,412 in her savings account, another eight grand in her checking. With this payday—another cash job—she could finally do it, make the plunge. And to hell with trying to look like she was still in her twenties.

She leaned back into the pillows, knowing sleep was unlikely between the coffee and the jar of her emotions. And her daydream, which seemed to be taking on flesh every day.

There was a way to do it, she was pretty sure, where it would be like she'd always been part of the community. Start slow, set up the greenhouse first. Make gifts of flowers, donate to ladies' clubs, combine a grand opening with a wine tasting, whatever. Keep the prices as low as possible without looking desperate. They'd show up, she knew they would, and if she set up somewhere where the locals and the winter tourists could keep her busy year-round, so much the better. The backyard garden, that was the important part. Make it a tour, or set up the greenhouse behind it so people had to walk through. A pool, a fountain, some trees . . . she had it all set in her mind, though she knew it would change when she saw the land, saw what the native plants were. That's the way it worked, you had to use what you were given, enhance it instead of transforming it. She could see the ladies now, two or three of them. Standing, talking, pointing out the features with their wineglasses in their hands. Saying, I wish I could make my backyard look like this. The air heavy with the scent of chlorophyll, of blossoms.

And then she was there, saying, maybe I could come take a look? I might have some ideas.

She never heard the ladies answer in this vision,

never knew what happened. But that point, getting to that exact point, she saw a path as clear as the green-edged gravel road that had led to her parents' house.

Despite the coffee she managed to drift off into a light sleep, and in her dreams she was on her knees, kneeling in the rich black dirt of a garden. The sun was beating on the back of her neck, and the light breeze touched her hair, pulling it away from her head, letting her scalp breathe. It was just her, alone and happy with a basket full of seeds, and as she leaned forward to cut into the earth she saw the snake, inches away from her hand. It was jet black, curled up on a hill she had made for some red potatoes, long looping coils of scaly muscle. Its eyes were trained on the blue veins on the inside of her wrist.

There it is, she thought. As though part of her had been waiting for it, the snake a leading actor and she just support. The rest of it, the good parts, were just for contrast. This was the way it was. Every garden had a serpent, every dream had an end.

She woke, heart pounding. For a moment she thought her heart was going to hammer right through her chest, it was that loud, and then she realized someone was at the door. She sat up, trying to clear the cobwebs. The person at the door continued to knock, a steady rhythm like they weren't planning to go away. Remy, no doubt, come to apologize. The little peckerhead, she thought, I bet he brought me another cup of coffee.

She went to the door. Frankie Rollins stood across the hallway, head slightly bowed, looking up at her with a serious expression on his face. His white silk shirt was one button too loose, especially for this early in the morning. To his side was a squat, close-shaven man with red eyes.

"Sorry," Frankie said. "You sleeping?"

She nodded, running a hand through her hair. She could still feel that breeze from her dream lifting the damp tendrils of hair from the back of her head.

"Bartender said you were up," Frankie said. "How you doing? Everything okay?"

"Fine," Destiny said, stepping out into the hallway. It felt rude to talk across the threshold, make her employer stand out there like he was a Jehovah's Witness or maybe a vacuum cleaner salesman. At the same time, there was no way she was going to invite these guys into her room, where the only place to sit was the bed.

"Everything working out okay with Remy?"

"He's great," Destiny said. "Is there something wrong, Mr. Rollins? They said we didn't need to do the drill this morning, so I stayed below."

"Really? Mister?" Frankie said, then smiled. "You heard right, no drills."

The ship lurched slightly underneath them, and she stumbled a little, still groggy from her nap.

Frankie reached to steady her, holding her shoulder for a moment and then letting go. "I explained about the tips, before," he said. "This is one of those jobs, the tips are included with the check?"

"You did."

He motioned to the other man. "This is Kharkov. He works for Mr. Latham."

Kharkov watched her, his eyes roaming across her body, then pulled an envelope out of his pocket. "From

Mr. Latham. He was impressed with you, especially after we had ship problems last night. He said you were quite helpful."

Destiny tried not to look at the envelope, thick enough that the flap wouldn't quite close. "I just did what I was supposed to do," she said.

Kharkov was impassive. "If Mr. Latham says you were helpful, be thankful. You should not contradict him."

"I didn't mean—"

Frankie held up a hand. "It's fine. Mr. Kharkov here is a very literal man. Take the money, Destiny."

She looked at the envelope. "Is that all right with you?"

Frankie smiled. "I like to see money moving around. It's good for the circulation."

Destiny reached for the envelope, but Kharkov held on to his end. "Mr. Latham was impressed. He said there could be even more of these, if you do a few other tasks. Very simple tasks."

Slowly, so slowly she could feel her fingertips breaking contact with the envelope one by one, Destiny released her grip. She took a step backwards, the doorway to her room framing her.

"Hey," Frankie said. "Hey, don't get the wrong idea. Nobody's forcing anybody to do anything." He turned. "Give us a minute, Kharkov."

Kharkov took a few steps away, and Frankie leaned a bit closer. "You might want to think about it some more. You know what I mean? Don't say no right away, even if you're gonna say no later." He went to Kharkov, took the envelope from him and tossed it to her. "That can't come back with us."

"Was this part of the plan all along?"

"No," Frankie said. "You're a nice-looking girl, that was on purpose. Get a game going with a pretty girl watching, sometimes a guy will show off, build the pot a little. But that was it. Latham just took a shine to you. And he's not afraid to ask for what he likes."

She glanced down at the envelope. She could see the top two bills, both fifties.

"Don't worry about that," Frankie said. "Keeping it don't mean nothing, no obligations. You really are doing a nice job."

"Latham looks sick," Destiny said, shooting Kharkov a nervous glance. "He's sweating all the time, and his hands tremble. I don't think he could even . . ." she paused. "That sounded wrong, like I was considering it. I'm not. At all."

Frankie waved a hand. "I'll check back with you later. Can I tell him you said thank you, at least? It'll help me and Mr. Friendly here when we talk to him later."

She bit her lip. Thinking of how Latham had stuck his hand down the back of her skirt, the ways his fingers had been probing, burrowing. Frankie might be one of those guys, you didn't help him out he'd forget the amount he'd offered to pay when they'd set up the contract. He wouldn't make her play the game Latham wanted, but he might insist everybody at least play along. She nodded, the briefest inclination of her head.

And almost instantly that same feeling she'd had the day before returned, when she should have punched Latham. Destiny Boudreaux, the only prostitute in the world who'd never been paid for it.

"What's wrong?" Frankie asked. "You worried about the boat?"

Destiny shook her head. "Should I be?"

"We snagged on something last night, something floating in the water. Busted up the boat a little, nothing too serious. Might need a tow in."

"I knew about that. I'm not worried about the ship."

"No," Frankie said. "You seem nice and calm, level-headed. I think the other people down here, they kinda look to you, see what you're feeling. Like a bombinator, you know, tells the pressure of the air? Way everyone looks at a stewardess when the plane starts to shake. She gets nervous, they get nervous. She keeps smiling . . ."

"I understand."

"We get towed in, things change a bit. Nothing to get worried about, long as everyone does what I say. People start acting scared, running around? Whole different ball game."

"Really," Destiny said. "I don't get worked up over little stuff."

"Yeah." Frankie smiled. "I knew that before I hired you." His radio crackled, and Frankie pulled it free. A voice was asking for him to come up to the deck immediately, the man somewhat panicky.

"Got to go," Frankie said. "C'mon, Kharkov. Heel, boy."

He walked down the hallway, moving like every casino executive she'd ever seen, but Frankie wasn't an executive. *Bombinator.* That was cute, almost, except the way he'd said it, it was like he said the wrong word on purpose. Bombinator, not barometer. Seeing if she would correct him. Why, though? No reason to try and sound dumb in front of the cocktail girl, or in front of the help. Well, she wasn't sure if Kharkov was the help; he looked like the enforcer, yes, but his gaze held nothing but contempt for Frankie. As for her . . . well, Kharkov was the kind of man that gave her, and every other girl at the casino, the shivers. Emotionless, apparently lacking libido or the pull of any addiction, he would simply do what he wanted to do. To anyone.

Frankie was different. She'd heard about what had happened to him. It was the sort of thing people liked to talk about, the sort of thing certain people liked to advertise, help keep the troops in line. Frankie had taken a long hiatus after he'd been caught, and nobody seemed surprised when he disappeared. He was different when he came back, quieter, more thoughtful. He wasn't working the casinos anymore, but he had something going, hiring service people for short-term gigs. Private games, low-key, good money. Over the past few years he'd become a player, even a man of some respect. Now she was on one of his gigs, and the paycheck she'd been promised was starting to make more sense.

But for some reason, Frankie wanted to know if she would call him out on a wrong word. He might have been testing her out, seeing where her loyalties were. Or he might just be dumb, same as when he tried to scam the Coriolos. Either way, she had a feeling she and Frankie Rollins would have more words before the *Nokomis* threw out her dock lines in Boston Harbor.

She could only hope that when those words were spoken, the man named Kharkov was busy doing something else.

And, in her mind, she kept seeing the black snake glistening in the sun.

Chapter 14

There was pressure but no pain. He wasn't sure what had happened, how it had missed him, only that the world had seemed to drop away even as the creature had appeared over the top of him. Falling and tilting and then the pressure of the ocean had wrapped around him and he was going down, slowly, the world growing darker.

He exhaled a stream of bubbles. There was other fluid moving in the water, darker. He followed the movement of the bubbles, light and dark, and saw them racing toward the dim ceiling of light above him. Globs of oil, liberated from severed lines in his destroyed boat, losing the race to the bubbles of air.

He was fifteen feet under the surface, and something was dragging him deeper.

He looked down at the pressure on his foot, saw his ankle was twisted in the ladder of the flybridge. The *Tangled Blue* was sinking, leaking hydraulic fluid and diesel into the ocean as it descended, trailing the severed mooring ropes behind it. His boot was trapped between the rungs of the ladder, which had been crushed against the cabin. Another trail of bubbles escaped his mouth, involuntarily this time. And just like that he felt the aching hollowness in his lungs.

He yanked his leg upward and felt a wrenching pain in his knee. He blinked, trying to see through the water. The flared rubber sole of his work boot was wedged between the rung and the cabin wall. He leaned down, trying to peel back the cuff of his jeans to loosen his boot, which was laced all the way to the top eyelet. The double knot was tight, swollen by the water, and his fingers dug ineffectually against the waterlogged laces.

He caught a flash of movement, and more bubbles raced out of his mouth. The creature was fifty yards away, just at the edge of his vision. It thrashed and writhed, and when it spun its massive bulk around he saw the bright speck of light from the flare, still burning in its eye socket. Its head had an odd shape, distorted, and Brian saw that it had a section of the *Tangled Blue* lodged in its mouth, the fiberglass and steel infrastructure caught in those massive barbed fangs. It swung its head wildly, trying to free the remains of his ship from its mouth.

He looked down at his wedged boot and braced both hands on the railing, pushing upward as hard as he could. Pain exploded in his knee and his ankle, but the boot only wedged itself tighter between the rung and the cabin. He slapped at his pocket, feeling for his pocketknife. It was there, but wedged deep in his front pocket. He was trying to worm it free when he caught another flicker of movement, much closer this time.

Something was coming for him.

The shadow was a small circle at first, then details

appeared, arms and legs, scissoring toward him. The silver glint of a knife in one hand. Gilly moved past him and Brian clutched at him, lost in his panic, trying to pull himself up. He was rewarded with a hard blow to his cheek and more bubbles escaped his mouth.

Gilly dropped lower, bent over Brian's foot. There was more pain, and then release.

He thrashed for the surface, thirty feet away now, the last bit of air in his lungs pushing up in his throat. Gravity pulled him down. His wet jeans limited his movements, the heavy mackinaw flaring around him. His vision started to close in, blackness circling the edges, until all that remained was the light of the surface, distorted by the globs of petroleum in the water.

He breathed in his first mouthful of seawater when he was ten feet from the surface.

He thrashed in the water, trying to claw the water back out of his throat. It came retching out and there was more behind it, all the water in the world pouring into him. The light of the surface dimmed as he somersaulted slowly in the water, neither sinking nor floating.

Then he was being propelled upward, steadily pushed toward the light, finally breaking through the rolling waves. He managed a quick, greedy breath and immediately vomited seawater. He hacked, gagging as a fist pounded on his back, another hand holding his collar to keep his head above water. He managed another breath, coughed only half of it back out, and wiped the water and oil from his eyes.

They were twenty yards from the *Nokomis*, floating in a sea of debris, the air reeking of oil. He vomited

more seawater, teetering on the edge of unconscious-
ness as he retched, his vision fading in and out.

"Come on," Gilly panted, steering him toward the
ship. They chopped toward the ship, and when they
reached its side, Gilly plucked a rope out of the water,
looping it under Brian's armpits. Gilly's inflatable life
belt floated behind him like a fanny pack. Gilly must
have inflated it after he'd freed him from the flybridge
ladder, using the buoyancy of the life vest to propel
both of them out of the water.

"Ready, old man?"

Brian nodded, unable to speak. He could still feel the
pressure of the ocean inside his lungs, bulging against
his ears.

"Bring him up!" Gilly shouted, pounding the side of
the *Nokomis*.

The rope tightened, cutting into his ribs, his face
sliding against the hull of the *Nokomis* as he ascended.
He turned in a half-circle as he was pulled, his back
against the ship's hull. The remains of the *Tangled
Blue* still floating were spread out over a fifty-yard circle,
a ring of rainbow-colored sheen littered with small
pieces of fiberglass, foam, and clots of hydraulic oil.
Gilly treaded water next to the *Nokomis*, watching
Brian being hauled upward.

The smoothness of the hull was replaced by three
thuds as he scraped across the railing. Several hands
grabbed him and pulled him onto the deck, where he
collapsed. He started coughing again and put out a
hand to steady himself, clutching the railing.

Several men were leaning over the side of the railing, dropping the rope back down to Gilly. Wells was

huddled on the deck, back against the bulwark, a wool blanket over his shoulders. Farther down the deck way, a few other men were holding out their arms to keep back a small group of spectators.

Brian gasped, "What happened?"

One of the men turned back to him. "Your buddy cut the rope right before that thing hit you. Boat went down, and it went right over the top of you."

"I hit it with the flare gun."

"I saw that," the man said. "Might have driven it off."

"What is it?"

"Shit," the guy said. "Who knows?"

Brian leaned over the railing and saw Gilly slap aside a piece of hull to get at the rope. Gilly was like an otter in the water, had even been a diver for a few years, until his overtaxed liver revolted at having to process both alcohol and the dive toxins.

He saved my life, Brian thought. *Gilly Blanchard saved my life. Now he'll probably want a raise.*

"What is that?" one of the men said, pointing out beyond Gilly.

"Dunno," another said. "Part of their boat?"

Brian followed their gaze and saw a shadow at the edge of the debris circle. It was motionless, or nearly so, and for a moment he wondered if it was indeed the back half of his boat, held aloft by the intrahull insulation, or perhaps even the aft section that had been lodged in the creature's mouth. Then the shadow turned and started toward the *Nokomis*, simultaneously rising up toward the surface.

"Grab the rope!" the man shouted at Gilly.

Gilly clutched it to his chest, throwing a look over

his shoulder. A second later they were hauling him upward, Gilly not so much lifted as jerked out of the water. He skidded up the side of the *Nokomis*, his boots scrambling for purchase. Brian grabbed onto the rope, pulling as best he could in his confused state.

The sea broke open.

It was visible for just a moment. Its left eye was a smoking ruin and at the corner of the socket Brian could see where the spent casing of the flare was still lodged. It lunged upward, its tremendous flippers powering it straight out of the water. Mouth like a cave lined with slanting yellow stalagmites.

Gilly turned toward the creature at the last moment, one hand pushing off the *Nokomis*. His other hand splayed in front of him—*stop*. The jaws clamped down on Gilly's waist, at the exact apex of the creature's leap. They went down, then the men on the rope lurched forward, crashing into the railing and then falling back as the rope broke. There was a large splash below them, the spray arching over the *Nokomis*'s deck.

Brian rushed forward, bellowing.

Gilly bobbed to the surface, his life jacket inflated, still conscious, still aware. Brian turned, yelled at the men to throw him another rope. Then Gilly rolled slightly and Brian saw his legs were gone, his stumps jetting dark blood into the sea. Brian gripped the railing, planting his foot onto the middle railing, and the two men hauled him back from the edge. He strained forward, howling, and dragged them forward.

Gilly's face paled as the blood poured from him. The stumps of his legs moved in an awful parody of a man kicking his legs, blood blooming around him. Brian shouted his name, and Gilly reached up a hand, his hair dark against his forehead, his eyes wide. Then, slowly, the shadow moved beneath him, grew darker, partially obscured by the cloud of blood, and pulled Gilly underwater.

He grew smaller and less distinct, his image hidden by the debris and the plume of blood, melding into the blue-gray depths, until he was gone.

Chapter 15

Pain coursed through the predator.

It knew the ache of hunger, the sear of teeth in its flesh, the blow of a rival's tail. Once, many years earlier, the hot slice of a lance along its snout had sent it below the thick ice to sulk for days. But this fiery abomination lodged in the corner of its eye socket was a new experience entirely.

If anything, it had made the beast more aware of its body than any other event in its long lifetime, a fluctuating existence of hibernation and consciousness. It enraged the predator's synapses, burned deep into its neurons. It thrashed to free its mouth of the obstruction, then spun in pain-riddled circles; it could not stop the pain. There was no fighting back; there was only enduring. So it endured, waiting as the pain intensified. As its vision in that eye blurred, became watery and weak. Finally gray and featureless.

Now it swam through a watery world with no depth, with altered dimensions. It understood there would be occasional sacrifices when taking life. At the same time, something had hurt it; prey had hurt it. The predator *could kill, yes, and it would kill. But it could also hurt back.*

It had observed how the smaller shell had approached the larger, nestling up to it like a cub to its mother. How the prey would go to each other's aid. It had heard the anguished cries the prey had made when the predator had leaped out of the water and pulled its littermate into the ocean.

It could also hurt back, yes. And it could also be sly, like the large female that had raised it, over a century earlier. Roaming the depths, calculating, smelling. Hunting. Occasionally pulling one of the prey from the group.

Because, if you pulled the right one, sometimes the others would follow.

Chapter 16

Destiny stood with her hip braced against the corner of the bar, listening to the men's ice cubes tinkling against their glasses as the ship pitched back and forth. She shifted her weight from one foot to the other, sighed, and twirled a finger through her hair. It was only mid-afternoon.

"What they playing for?" Remy asked, his voice a murmur.

"I don't know," Destiny said. "Maybe they have a side bet, see if they can bore us to death."

Latham was down to a small pile of chips, perhaps fifty or a hundred dollars' worth. Prower, his blotchy face serious rather than triumphant, was playing it safe, letting Latham take the antes when his cards weren't quite right, betting high when he had a strong hand. Squeezing Latham out, slowly but surely. The whole time he twirled and tapped his cane, which seemed to be driving Latham bugshit.

"Now she's bored." Remy pushed a coffee cup across the bar to her. "This'll perk you up."

"Thanks." She took a sip, the brandy warming her

throat, radiating in her belly. "Aren't you the one said it didn't pay to ask questions?"

"That's before this whole thing turned weird," Remy said. He twisted the bar towel in his hands. "I never been on a ship, sits out in the water like one a them little red bobbers, don't do nothing. They coulda played cards in my backyard, had the whole place to ourselves. No, we gotta go out, middle of the goddamn Atlantic, screw around with whales and sharks."

"I think we're going to be out here until someone wins."

"Wins what?"

"Exactly." She took another drink. "Look at them, they're miserable. Sick. But they keep playing."

"Playing for each other's business, something like that?"

She shook her head. "Prower's a lawyer, and Latham owns properties all over the world. Some in Vegas, mostly timeshares. His people used to come around, ask some of us girls to go on the tours. You know the ones, little dog-and-pony shows, they get the tourists to buy a shitty room they can use for two weeks out of the year for thirty grand? They'd find some old goat, point to us, say you want to go on an air-conditioned bus with those girls? Have a drink, maybe look at a room or two?"

Remy smiled. "You ask my first wife about them timeshares. It end up a good deal for her, free and clear after we signed papers."

"Sorry," Destiny said. "Hope I wasn't one of the girls on the bus."

"You do that?"

"If I needed extra cash. What I'm saying is, could

you see Prower doing that? Or even being the kind of guy who owned something like that?"

The ship rolled with a large wave, and water sloshed somewhere below them. Remy stared at the floor, which was not wet but seemed to be growing more and more damp. "This is not good, girl. We gotta go up a level, get out of the bottom of the damn boat."

"You could talk to Frankie," she said. "Or the captain. But you do that, the payday goes away."

"I been happy poor, lotsa times. Don't think I'd be a happy dead man."

She took another drink of coffee. She didn't think they were going to die. If the men in charge weren't worried about the structural stuff, she wasn't going to get wound up about it, either. If they were worried, then . . . well, shit. Guys were always worked up about something.

Remy leaned closer. "They's a room, back down the hallway behind the bodyguards."

"I'm flattered, Remy, but we don't have the time."

"Be serious, now. Look over there, jus' don't make it obvious."

Destiny glanced at the two guards standing on either side of the doorway, their hands crossed in front of them. The men guarding the hallway had changed shifts every hour or two, but it was always one of each. Kharkov was ever-present, as was Prower's number one man, a fit man with a chiseled face by the name of Hornaday. Nobody had told her not to go down that hallway, and they didn't have to. When you worked for Frankie the rules were pretty apparent. As were the doors that were closed to you.

She turned back to Remy and cocked an eyebrow.

"Got somebody in there, I bet," he said.

"Probably a girl," Destiny said. Thinking of Latham's offer of cash, the way his hand had slithered down the back of her skirt. The kind of guy who felt a constant urge to press his flesh against another, whether the other person wanted it or not.

"I don't know," Remy said. "They made me go back there. Clean up some puke."

"When was this?"

"You remember the first evening, we had those big waves coming up and over? Everything banging around?"

"Sure."

"I went back there, cleaned up the mess. The room smelled, not just like puke. It smelled kinda rank, like some dude ain't showered in a while. And there were these zip ties in the garbage, all of them snipped. You know what they use those big zip ties for?"

"Tying garbage bags?"

"Sure, and people's hands, too."

She was listening to Remy, watching the game. She wanted to get off this ship, and the best way to do that was to do her job. Watch their drinks, and when they reached that quarter-full mark, quickly and unobtrusively replace it. That was how both Latham and Prower liked it, for some reason, for her to take the drink away before they were finished with the last one. They didn't have to tell her—she picked up on it right away. Why? Who knew? Whatever it was, it was. She drank on occasion, usually beer or wine. Sometimes, after a hard day, she would have a whiskey or a rum and Coke. Lots of ice. What she liked the most was the last little bit of the drink, ice cubes against her teeth and lips, liquid trickling through them as her air conditioner hummed and she knew that outside it was still over a hundred degrees, the hot dry wind blowing across the desert, and there she was, cool on the inside and outside.

Latham held his cards low, curling them tight, a habit any Vegas dealer would have broken him of immediately. They would have thought he was trying to mark the card, give them a little bend, a dog-ear to mark them. But Latham wasn't trying to cheat, Destiny thought, he was afraid others were cheating him. Prower held his cards out as he had from the beginning, country rube style, and he was drinking steadily. He took a long drink now, draining his glass for the first time, and when she turned back, Remy had a fresh one sitting on a napkin on the bar.

She brought it over. Prower appraised her, and she smiled dutifully. His face was an uneven red, but he had that look to him, the kind of guy who knows what he's doing. Cards or business or women, he might not actually *know* everything, but he had a strategy, a game plan. She found it an attractive virtue. Now, if Prower only looked like Hornaday . . .

She knew girls who had gone that route, hitched onto a rich guy. When they stopped back to see their former co-workers, the girls were often happy, or seemed to be, and usually dressed like they were trying not to show how much money they had. It had never appealed to her, not in any real way, though she'd had a few chances and knew it wasn't a terrible option. She blamed her imagination. It always put her underneath a guy like Prower, maybe one with even more of a gut. In her imagination she could feel the pressure of his belly, the smell of the liquor-soaked breath puffing against the side of her face, his mouth on her. . . .

An arm wrapped around her waist, and she found herself sitting on Latham's lap. He felt clammy even through his clothes, the arm around her waist radiating heat.

"Well, hello there," Latham said, his breath in her ear.

Destiny tried to push herself up and Latham's arm cinched tighter. "Mr. Latham, really—"

"Easy," he said. "Just sit for a second, huh? I need something to turn my luck around."

"I don't think this is—"

"Oh, quit. You accepted my money, now you can earn some of it. You don't like that, I can have Kharkov escort you back to your room. You hear that, Kharkov?"

Kharkov moved slightly closer, his eyes half-lidded. "Yes, boss."

"Would you like to take Destiny back to her room?"

"Yes, boss."

Destiny glanced around the room. Frankie was upstairs; he would only stay in the room for fifteen or twenty minutes before flitting off somewhere else. Prower was watching her with a neutral expression, though she noticed he was gripping the head of his cane tighter than normal. Behind her, Latham's breaths came rapidly, each exhale marked with a phlegmy little rasp. She didn't bother looking at Remy. If it came down to it, he was the one most likely to try to help, and the one least likely to actually be able to do anything.

"One hand," Latham said, moving his legs so Destiny was squarely centered in his lap. "You can sit here for one hand."

She remained very still as Prower dealt the cards. Her face was burning, equal parts rage and humiliation. Latham's body gave off a tremendous amount of heat, and he smelled sick, the low and cloying odor of someone with a chronic disease. At the same time he was obviously still strong, and the arm around her waist was creeping up, so that the top of his forearm brushed against the underside of her breasts.

It's a sad day when I can't wait to see Frankie Rollins, she thought. And on the heels of that was another thought, almost vicious: *Bullshit. You don't need Frankie to take care of you.*

Latham picked up his cards, fanning them in front of her.

"Wow," she said, letting a girly gush creep into her voice. "Do you have to throw some queens away when you have that many?"

Across the table, Prower smiled and discarded his hand, ceding the hand to Latham. Latham's hold grew painfully tight for a moment, cutting off her breath, and then he was reaching for the ante and she twisted up and away, grabbing the empty glasses before joining Remy at the bar.

She handed the empty glass to Remy. He dunked the glass in the underbar sink, ran it under the water, then began to dry it. Soap bubbles clung to the hair of his wrists. She was certain he was going to apologize, or tell her it was no big deal.

Remy didn't look at her. He was watching the game, and after a moment she joined him.

Prower had raised Latham fifty dollars on the opening round. Latham considered his cards, considered Prower. His shoulders hunched in tighter and then he expanded,

disgusted, and tossed his cards. He reminded Destiny
of an eagle she had seen a few weeks ago, up near
Tahoe, perched atop a road-killed deer. The way it burrowed into the meat, beak twisting, then would lean
back, ruffle its feathers as it looked around like it was
only surveying the countryside. As though it were
ashamed at the concentration it gave to the rotting
flesh.

Prower took the next hand, too, raising the pot to a
hundred after Latham checked, forcing him to fold.
Then it was Latham's turn to deal again. He shuffled
poorly, the cards sticking out of the bridge. He pushed
them back in with his fingers, tapped the deck against
the table. There were only a few chips left in front of
him.

Prower let his cards lie facedown until Latham was
done dealing, then picked them up. He sighed, tossed in
twenty in chips to match the ante. Latham pushed in another twenty, the minimum bet, and Prower matched it.

"How many?" Latham said. His voice was gravelly.
It was now three in the afternoon, and they had been
playing for about five hours, with minimal breaks.

Prower dropped four cards into the discard pile.
Latham raised his eyebrows and Prower showed him
the remaining card, the ace of clubs. You could only
draw four cards if you had an ace in the hole. Until now
neither one of them had asked the other to prove it.

Latham flipped four cards to Prower, took three for
himself.

"He's paired up," Remy whispered. "Probably low."

Prower stared at his cards, then checked by rapping
the table. Latham pushed his remaining chips into the

center of the table and leaned back, looking relieved to
be free of them.

Prower set his cards down, took a drink of brandy,
picked them back up. Latham had started to reach for
the pile, but pulled back, his face twisting into a scowl.
He had thought Prower was folding.

"What we got?" Prower said, tapping the head of his
cane lightly on the table. "You put in eighty?"

"Yes," Latham said. "Pot's at one-forty"

Prower glanced around the room. "Where'd Frankie
go? He's supposed to be down here."

"Upstairs," Latham said. "You need him to explain
something, Prower? Or can we finish out this hand?"

Prower shrugged, pushed eight ten-dollar chips into
the circle. "Let's see your cards, Richard."

Destiny leaned forward, heard Remy moving behind her as he tried for a better vantage point. Latham
turned over the two cards he had kept, a pair of jacks.
A blackjack hand, Destiny thought. Then he flipped
over the three draw cards and she saw the third jack, a
one-eyed spade nestled between a three and a five.
Knaves, that's what some of the Brits called jacks at
the blackjack table.

"Nice draw," Prower said, and by the tone of his
voice Destiny knew the game was over. Prower flipped
his cards over quickly, the lone ace and the two others
he had drawn, along with a king and a ten.

Prower made no move to collect his winnings. He
looked at Latham, who was leaning back in his chair,
then surveyed the room, eyeing Kharkov with special
attention. Nobody moved. Half the men were his, half
Latham's. And Destiny could see the calculations going

on behind his light blue eyes, could almost hear his thoughts.

"We need Frankie," Prower said.

"Go ahead," Latham said. "Send one of your men to go get him."

"No," Prower said. "You send yours."

"One of each, perhaps?"

Prower looked around the room, saw that he had three guards to Latham's four, and jerked his head toward Destiny. "Let's send her. Our people stay where they are."

She found Frankie in the wheelhouse, talking to Wells, the old man that had been rescued from the fishing boat. Wells was speaking softly but very earnestly, leaning forward, jabbing at the palm of his hand with a finger. Frankie and Captain Moore were listening, Moore with a somber expression, Frankie slightly amused. The old man was saying something about the currents, about cold water, and about predatory instincts. Behind him, one officer was monitoring the control panel, another was scanning the foggy seas with a pair of binoculars. She could tell both of them were also listening to Wells, the way they stopped moving when he spoke.

Frankie looked at her, held up a finger.

"If a tug comes out here," Wells said. "It will attack again. Do you understand? It attacked this ship but could not take it down, so now it will attack whatever comes near us. Just like it did the fishing boat."

"*Whatever* it is," Frankie said, in a tone that suggested they had already discussed what it might be for a good length of time. "It's probably gone."

"No," Wells said. "It killed that man who rescued me, Gilly. It attacked, and it was successful, and it will want more. That's how these kinds of predators function, whether it's a lion or a shark. Once they smell blood in the water, they don't leave."

Moore tugged at his short beard. "Dr. Wells, I fully appreciate your concerns. But we are taking on water, our propellers are compromised, and our bilge, which was repaired just this morning, is now malfunctioning again. We need to return to dock, and to do that we need a tug."

Wells turned to face the window. "I am not advising we should stay out here. What I'm saying is a standard tug is too small. It will attack it. We need to be airlifted, or transferred to a large ship. The Coast Guard—"

"We've already warned the tug," Moore said. "They were not overly concerned."

"What kind of warnings?" Wells said. "Did you tell them something ripped your propellers off and destroyed that fishing boat?"

"Listen," Frankie said. "Listen, I get where you're coming from. Is it pretty cool, being a research scientist? I bet it is. I bet the more theories you got, the more grant money comes in. But we got a lot of people on this ship don't give two farts about your ideas. They want to get back to dock before they take an ice bath." He turned to Moore. "And this man has a ship he's responsible for. We can take care of both with a tug."

"The other man," Wells said. "Hawkins. He saw it, too. He was leaning right over the railing when it killed his first mate. He saw the whole thing."

"Captain Hawkins?" Frankie said. "The man who boarded us without our permission?"

"Listen," Wells said, jabbing a finger at Moore. "I know what I saw. It's not a whale or a giant shark. It's something much more dangerous, and if you send that tug out here alone it'll be just plain murder. And I'll let people know, when it happens, that I warned you."

Frankie started forward. "We saved your ass, you ungrateful little sh—"

Moore grabbed his sleeve, tugging on it until Frankie followed him to the far corner.

"The forecast is bad," Moore said. "NOAA is predicting fifteen- to twenty-foot waves by this time tomorrow, and we're looking at a long haul in. This guy isn't some punk. He's a university scientist. He'll raise a hell of a stink."

"Not if I throw his ass overboard."

"Don't even kid about that," Moore said. "I have enough explaining to do about Collins, and now this fishing boat." He patted Frankie's shoulder. "Play nice, Frankie. Let me lead on this. I can handle Wells."

"What about that other asshole, Hawkins? He might raise a stink, too. His buddy got killed."

"The pirate? I've come too far to let a guy like him complicate manners. I have it covered, Frankie. Your man Kharkov already helped me with the specifics."

"Kharkov? He's not my man."

"We're all on the same team, though. Right?"

"Supposed to be."

"Good." They returned to Wells, who was going through his pockets, taking inventory. "Would it make you more comfortable, Dr. Wells," Moore said, "if I requested a cutter to accompany the tug?"

Wells looked up, suspicious. "Is that a Coast Guard ship? How big?"

"Twenty meters, minimum," Moore said. "Standard Coast Guard assistance vessel. I cannot ask for it based solely on what you saw, please understand. But I will ask for it to accompany us based on the weather conditions, and the disabled status of my ship. We're much heavier with all the water we've taken on, and that puts her hull under structural strain."

"This cutter," Wells said. "Is it armed?"

"Armed?" Moore said. "I don't know. I tend to avoid firefights while piloting my cruise ships. I imagine it has some weaponry aboard."

Wells was silent. Instead of waiting for his answer, both Moore and Frankie moved away, Moore toward the control panel array, Frankie toward Destiny. He rolled his eyes as he approached her, a rueful smile on his lips. He touched the back of her arm, steering her out onto the deck way.

"Come on," he said. "Time for some fresh air."

She breathed in the cold air, letting it saturate her lungs. So many years of breathing in stale smoke, the reek of ozone and cologne and perfume. In just a few weeks, no more than a couple months, she could choose what smells she was around. Sun-warmed dirt, the super-oxygenated greenhouse, blossoms on the fruit trees. She didn't like the way something smelled, she could get rid of it, or move away. Nobody would be able to tell her to stay there, to endure it.

Well, that was a bit in the future. For now, she would take the smell of the sea, Frankie's aftershave crowding in at the edges.

"Prower won," she said.

Frankie nodded, looked out at the sea. "It's too bad about the weather," he said. "You come out here, on a nice day? There's dolphins, sailboats, shit like that."

"I suppose." The wind gusted around them, sending her hair over her face. She tucked it back behind her ears. "They were kinda tense, downstairs. I think they wanted you to come down."

"What I like is when the sun starts going down," Frankie said. "The light turns soft, sorta pink and orange? My gramps, he used to call that his favorite color, sky-blue pink. I like it, too, when the sun isn't beating down on you. Not as much pressure." He thrummed his hands against the railing, the stubs of his fingers moving with the rest. "I wouldn't mind seeing the sun right now, tell you the truth."

Destiny was quiet. She wasn't sure if he was trying to be romantic, or if he was the kind of guy who liked to talk. Either way, the pay was the same.

He turned to her. "Are you tense?"

"Excuse me?"

"You said they were tense downstairs. I wanna know, are you tense, too?"

She shrugged. "The floor's getting wet, I'd feel better if we were moving. But I'm not going to freak out or something."

"Good," Frankie said. "That's good."

They were quiet for a moment. Destiny's thoughts strayed a bit, wondering what it would be like to go on a cruise like this, standing at a railing with the sky turning sky-blue pink, and talking with someone you liked. Or even loved. Not Frankie, he was too hairy and too . . . she couldn't quite put her hand on it. He was like a medium-sized guy that had little man's syndrome. But someone like her old carpenter boyfriend, a plain, good-looking guy who cared about her, cared about his work . . . yeah, that might be something worth experiencing. She'd had opportunities since then, but most of the time they felt like potential contracts. They would spend money on her and she would return the favor. No, she wanted something free and clean, something given without any strings—

Out on the sea, hidden behind the fog, something big broke the surface of the ocean.

She fell back a step, noticing that Frankie didn't so much as flinch, and caught herself before she fled back into the cabin. The noise came again, a loud sloshing that was different from the endless rolling of the waves. She stood where she was, subconsciously opening her mouth to hear the sounds better. Whatever was making the splashing noise wasn't far off, less than a hundred yards away.

"There's all kinds of stuff, follows a boat this big," Frankie said, not turning from the railing. "Dolphins and whales and whatevers. That's what our good Captain Moore told me."

She took a tentative step back to the rail. "Is that it? The same thing that attacked us?"

Frankie watched the ocean. When he didn't speak Destiny took a step forward, then another, until she was back at the railing with him. It was hard to focus, looking into the fog. Her eyes wanted to return to something concrete, something she could focus on. The brass railing, slick with condensation; her fingernails, in need of a fresh paint job; even the shoulder of Frankie's sports coat, sprouting random nylon tendrils that quivered in the wind.

"It can't get to us," he said softly, without turning. "The ship's too big."

"Good," she said, not entirely sure he was talking to her. "Did you see it, Frankie? When it came out of the water?"

There were more sloshing sounds out on the ocean. It sounded farther away from them now. Or maybe not. The fog muffled the noises, making it difficult to gauge distance.

"Frankie?"

He turned to her. "Yeah, I saw it, part of it. Biggest damn whale I ever saw. Then again, it's the only one I ever saw." He pursed his mouth as though about to spit over the railing and caught himself. "My guess is, those assholes pissed it off. They were hunting it, and it started hunting them back."

"Hunting a whale?"

He nodded. "Big money in stuff like that, whale fin soup, whatever."

"I thought it was shark fin soup."

"Yeah, that's what I mean. Think how much more you'd get, a big old whale fin instead." The wind blew her hair across her face and Frankie reached out, moved it aside, the stumps of his fingers right there in front of her. The stumps had healed inward, she saw, the wedges of skin puckered together. "The fisherman that made it onto the ship?" Frankie said. "He was still shooting at the friggin' thing, even as he was being pulled up the side."

She curled her lip in distaste, knowing that was the reaction Frankie wanted. Feeling the light but steady beat of her bullshit radar going off as he leaned forward, eyes measuring her response.

"As long as don't make it angry," she said. "It shouldn't bother us again, right?"

He patted her shoulder. "There might be a bit more to do, downstairs. Okay? You're a good person, Destiny, you've done a good job. We're almost done, you'll come out of this with a great story, a real nice check." He moved past her. "Come on down whenever you want. Take a minute, enjoy the breeze."

He was almost to the door when she called out to him. "You mean cash, right?"

"Yeah, of course," he said, without turning back. "Of course."

Chapter 17

It was supposed to be their first real family vacation.

He was on a salvage job outside Baia de Todos os Santos harbor in Salvador, Brazil, working on a faltering BP oil tanker that had run aground after a monstrous storm. A big job, three weeks, but the tanker was wedged fast into the mud and the work was not nearly as dangerous or technical as most of his gigs. The money on the big corporate salvage jobs was fantastic, even for a welder, and he had flown Sienna and Mason down as soon as his son's preschool graduation was over. Brian had missed the graduation, but he wouldn't miss his son's first days of summer vacation. He could still remember his old man picking him up after he'd finished kindergarten, down at the end of that long gravel road on a warm late spring day. No kindergarten graduation back in those days, but his father had let him know he'd done well, shaking his hand and then offering him a bottle of Coca-Cola, dripping ice water from the old green Igloo cooler in the box of the GMC farm truck.

Mason slept soundly the first night in the apartment

the company had rented for him, a nice place on the western edge of Salvador's Barra neighborhood, Mason's room adjoining theirs so they had a bit of privacy. He and Sienna did not sleep, not until the morning light began to trickle in through their open windows. The city normally carried with it the faint odor common to most South American cities on the Atlantic, a combination of sewage and slaughterhouse reek, mingled with the fetid odor of the overfertilized fields outside town, but this morning the winds blew in off the ocean and it smelled of salt and the rosewood trees planted in the garden and along the causeway. And lodged in his mind was the sweet realization the job was done, money was in the bank, and he had nine days to spend with his family before the next job.

"It's beautiful," Sienna had said. She was standing at the window with a light robe around her, watching the ship traffic in the bay. "What's the harbor called? In English, I mean."

"The Bay of All Saints." He and his coworkers in Borealis Salvage had come up with all sorts of alternate names in the past few weeks. The Bay of All Shit. The Bay of Ball Sweat. It had once been beautiful, no doubt, but the untreated sewage and effluents gave the water a brown, frothy appearance, especially at low tide. The Barra neighborhood had also undoubtedly once been beautiful, at least conceptually, with its whitewashed Portuguese buildings with clay tile roofs, but the streets were dirty and turned vicious at night. So he'd heard. The streets were dirty, certainly, but he ate and drank and traveled with the other welders, surly-looking men with slag burns tattooed on their forearms. Nobody bothered them.

But this morning it was beautiful, the wind blowing steady but softly off the ocean, and the name of the bay rolled off his tongue like a prayer of thanks. He rolled over in bed, thinking of Mason in the adjoining room, his first trip outside Vermont, his first summer vacation. His mind would be wide open, taking it all in, absorbing. How would he remember it? Brian could not hand his son a cold bottle of Coke, could not make him feel the way he'd felt as a boy, but then again repeats of what had worked for you were rarely as sweet for another.

"What do you have in mind?" Sienna asked, smiling. She was like that, could look at him and see where his mind was tending.

He reached out and pulled her into him, letting his hands run over the soft swell of her hip. "You know what?" he said. "Mason's never been sailing."

Brian sat in Moore's quarters, his face buried in his hands. Thinking of Brazil, of winds that switched directions suddenly. Not trying to push away the memories, which was impossible. At this point, he was content with blocking out the finer details. The way she had turned and looked at him, for example, the clean smooth line of her face catching the morning sun. How his wrists and hands looked against her skin, his skin flecked with tiny burns from hot slag, her own skin soft, cream colored. Ogre hands on the fair maiden, he'd said, and she'd replied that it had been a long time since she was a maiden. Nor wanted to be.

Then Mason wandering into their room, rubbing at

his eyes, trailing a thin *The Incredibles* sleeping bag he insisted on taking everywhere. The way he grinned and said *Daddy, you got sunburned*.

Details, like knives in his heart.

He ground his palms into his eyes. He could handle it, the way it had happened, but for the details. The goddamned details. Taking him by surprise, the pain still fresh after all these years. He knew it was a stupid trick of his own mind, a way to keep them alive, to keep them fresh. But at times, late on a winter night—or now, his last true friend killed before his eyes—the fine cutting edge of the details felt sourced from outside, from some malevolent being intent on torment.

Gilly's hand open to the sky, beseeching Brian or God or both to help him.

His severed legs, kicking in the water as he tried to swim in a cloud of his own blood.

The shadow below him, pulling him under the surface.

The door opened. Captain Moore stepped inside, followed by a squat man Brian had not seen before. Moore set an urn of coffee on the end table, poured Brian a cup, and added a shot of brandy when Brian nodded. He did not offer a drink to the other man, whom he introduced as Kharkov. No first name, no rank.

Moore poured himself a cup, without brandy, and sat down on the other side of the end table. Kharkov stood near the door, arms crossed.

"Sorry about your man," Moore said. "Your boat, too."

Brian nodded dully.

"I've sent a preliminary report to the Coast Guard," Moore said. "They've had other ships attacked in the same manner over the past week. In fact, it sounds like some of the wrecks may have been caused by the same phenomenon."

Brian looked up. "Phenomenon?"

"They believe it's a sperm whale," Moore said. "Like Moby-Dick, I guess. Or, more likely, a pod of them. There's some consensus that they've been irritated by ship traffic in their migratory routes. I understand there have been documented cases of—"

"You believe that thing was a *whale*?"

Moore frowned, took a drink of his coffee. "I'm not taking it as the gospel, no. But it seems a reasonable enough explanation. What I saw earlier seemed to fit with the description of a very large sperm whale."

"Listen," Brian said, speaking very slowly. "I don't know what that . . . thing . . . was that attacked us and killed my first mate. But I know it wasn't a goddamn whale. It had *teeth*, for Chrissake."

"Sperm whales have teeth, Captain Hawkins."

Brian stood. "Not the size of my goddamn leg they don't. Is that what you actually told the Coast Guard? That we were attacked by a whale?"

"Please sit down. We have serious mechanical issues to resolve on this ship, the weather is deteriorating, and I would like to record your statement. Kharkov will be the witness." He took a sip of coffee, motioned toward the chair. "Please, Captain."

Brian sat back, gripping the armrests, watching Kharkov in his peripheral vision. He was a big man, impassive, his crossed forearms knotted with muscle. Kharkov took a step closer, his fingers wriggling at his sides.

"Now," Moore said. "If you could recount—"

Brian held up a hand. "Just a second." He turned to Kharkov, who had crept closer. "You don't look like an officer of the boat. What's your role here?"

Kharkov's eyelids dropped a fraction of an inch and his chin came up. "I'm here to make sure you behave."

"Yeah? I'm going to make sure you drink your meals out of a straw, you don't quit breathing down my neck."

Kharkov nodded. "When I was with *militsiya* and we get jokes instead of answers, we break the funny bone."

"Could you find it?"

Kharkov nodded. "Was always the first bone."

"Enough," Moore said. "I'm understaffed, and Mr. Kharkov here is currently acting as my assistant. Now, Captain Hawkins, I understand your distress. If you could just give me your account—briefly—we'll let you get some rest. We also have a physician on board who could give you a sedative."

"I'll make my report directly to the Coast Guard," Brian said. "I don't need a sedative."

Moore set his cup down and leaned forward. "We really would prefer your statement now, Mr. Hawkins."

Brian noticed the demotion Moore had given him and gave him a tight smile. His mind, which had felt cobwebby, was beginning to grind away at the details of Moore's words, his chickenshit, paramilitary method of talking down. The goon at the entrance creeping in closer. The initial refusal to help a foundering ship on the open seas.

"I am requesting use of your ship's radio," he said. He turned to look at Kharkov, who was standing near the door. Could he fight his way through those scarred knuckles? "You're witness to that request, whoever the hell you are."

"That's not going to happen," Moore said calmly. "We are in critical communications with the tugboat *Santa Maria*." Moore set his cup down. "Listen, I have three different eyewitnesses that confirmed a whale destroyed your boat. You were in the water, Captain, under extreme duress. Please think of your reputation before you make any statements."

"Why?" Brian said. "Why in the world do you want to underplay this?"

Moore said, "The death of two men at sea will raise numerous questions, and it's my duty to record all pertinent facts until we dock. There is no *underplaying*, as you say."

"I commend you on protocol," Brian said. "But it was my ship, and my friend. I don't need my story filtered through you."

Moore flushed. "There won't be any filtering, either. As captain of this vessel it is my duty to record the facts of the incident, and to discover—"

"Oh, bullshit." Brian waved him off. "I'm not making statements to a man who thinks a whale could do this. You got a serious situation out here, Captain Moore. Your passengers—"

"I'm well aware of my responsibilities to my passengers."

"—your passengers deserve to know the danger they're in, the real danger. This thing is still out there, probably ready to attack anything that moves. I saw the damn thing, Hawkins, saw its teeth. It's built to grab on to something and not let go."

"Now you sound like Wells," Moore said, sighing.

"I'd have thought you might be more reasonable. At least acknowledge that you did not have time to get a clear look at the creature."

"I shot it in the eye with a flare," Brian said. "At a range of about six feet. How close were you?"

Moore sighed. "You can wait outside, Mr. Kharkov. Thank you for your assistance, but it appears our friend here is not ready for a statement."

Kharkov cut his eyes toward Brian, then grunted and exited. The door shut, but Kharkov's shadow continued to fill the door's opaque window on the far side, the wide shoulders blocking out most of the light.

Moore stood, walked behind his desk, and picked up a backpack. It dripped water as he carried it across the room and set it at his feet. "Your man, Giles Blanchard, was briefly aboard my ship before returning to rescue you. I believe you called him Gilly?"

Brian said nothing.

Moore said, "He dropped this on our deck before he dove back in. That was an awfully brave thing to do, I have to say. One of the bravest acts I've ever seen." He flipped open the backpack. "He has an interesting mix of materials in here."

"You went through his stuff?"

"Of course. We're a disabled vessel that has been attacked by something, most likely a whale, but as you say . . . it could be a more deliberate hostile act, perhaps with a human element? You were, and remain, a stranger to us. You boarded us without our consent." He held up a hand as Brian started to protest. "These are all facts, our communications logged and verified. You committed an act of piracy, Captain Hawkins, and as such anything you have is mine by maritime law.

That includes the backpack your mate dropped. It even includes you, Captain."

Son of a bitch, Brian thought. You finally landed us in it, Gilly, and you're not even around for me to say I told you so.

"Possession of narcotics on land by a friend is one thing, Captain," Moore said. "Having controlled substances on your ship in international waters? That falls squarely on the captain and owner of the vessel."

"Well," Brian said. "A few Xanax in my buddy's backpack."

Moore reached down and pulled a small Baggie from the backpack. It was secured with the same rubber bands they used to rig the releases on the *Tangled Blue*'s outrigger lines. "Sedatives are one thing, Mr. Hawkins. This does not appear to be sleeping pills."

Brian peered at the bag. "What is that supposed to be?"

Moore raised his eyebrows. "I asked Mr. Kharkov the same thing. Apparently, heroin usage is quite rampant in his home country."

"Bullshit," Brian said. "Gilly wasn't into junk."

"Be that as it may, it was in his backpack. Before that it was on your ship." Moore leaned forward. "You and I both know ignorance of the law is not a defense, Captain. When we return to dock, I will turn you and the backpack over to the proper authorities. Until then, the contents of the backpack will remain in the custody of our security man, Officer Vanders. We will have affidavits signed that the contents were not disturbed."

"You piece of shit."

Moore went on. "You can make a statement any time you wish, but it will be recorded here, by me, with one of my men as witness. After we have your statement and you have established yourself as cooperative, we can discuss the custody of your materials. In the meantime, you will remain under our—"

His words were cut off by a sharp rap on the door.

"What?" Moore called out.

Kharkov opened the door and ushered in one of Moore's officers, who was holding a pair of binoculars. "Sir? It's back."

"It?"

"You know, sir. The, ah, whale."

"You saw it, Graves?" Moore said.

Graves shook his head. "Not clearly, sir. It's been mostly submerged, and the fog is getting worse. But it has . . . something. It's . . ." He swallowed. "You have to come see for yourself."

"I don't see anything," Moore said, scanning the seas with the binoculars. "Did it show up on the radar?"

They stood on the deck way, twenty feet above the main deck, the bow of the boat curving out thirty feet in front of them. No passengers were up on the observation deck; Moore had restricted access, referencing the weather and the rough seas. Wells was there, though, plucking at Moore's sleeve, telling him he knew what the creature was. There was a waitress standing at the stairwell, watching Brian with a mixture of sympathy and distrust. She was dressed in a white blouse and a short black skirt, holding a pair of heels and alternating glances between his group and the sea. She had a light green streak in her auburn hair, a pretty face with clear skin.

"I didn't notice," Graves said. "But it was there, Captain, too big to be anything else. And I saw what it had in its . . . what it had with it."

In front of them, the waves rolled into the bank of fog. Crazy weather, Brian thought. Usually, the wind would scatter the fog, drive it into tatters. But the low-hanging clouds were persistent, scudding all around them, creating a shifting seascape where you could see fifty yards one minute, a hundred the next. He could hear the bilges pumping jets of water back into the ocean, going for two or three minutes, stopping for a few seconds, then starting up again.

"There!" Graves shouted. "Twenty degrees off the bow, right at the edge of the fog. It's . . . shit. It's gone again."

They could hear a splashing sound, not unlike the sounds dolphins would make as they leaped ahead of the ship. Two splashes, the first softer and smooth as it emerged from the water; the second a moment later, louder and sloppier. It sounded smaller than it had appeared, Brian thought. Maybe they were hearing a flipper, or a tail fin.

Slooop. Splash.

Slooop. Splash.

Slooop. The cloud of fog began to peel apart, and he caught a glimpse of something falling into the ocean, fifty yards away.

Splash.

Whatever had fallen bobbed on the surface, riding the rolling waves, then disappeared. Moore, looking through his binoculars, seemed about to say something when the water boiled and the object launched from the water. Something dark and massive swirled under the surface where the smaller object had been.

"It's a person," Moore said. His voice sounded dead. "A child."

"No, sir," Graves said. "We just did a passenger check. Nobody's missing that we know of."

"I saw it," Moore said. "It's a person."

"Yes," Graves replied, glancing at Brian. "But it's not a child."

Brian felt a wave of nausea as he moved forward, understanding. Graves tried to hold him back, and Brian brushed him aside as he bulled toward the captain. Kharkov stepped in front of him and Brian reacted instinctively, not with malice but only impatience, his arm flicking out, knuckles connecting squarely with soft cartilage. Kharkov fell back, holding his nose and cursing. Moore found himself suddenly cornered against the rail, his mouth half-opened, Brian advancing toward him. He glanced behind him, at the long fall he would have, and held up a hand.

"I didn't—"

Brian's hand went out, moving with the same speed that had surprised Kharkov, and yanked the binoculars from Moore's hand.

The others had fallen away, creating a pod of free space around him. Graves was holding Kharkov back, the latter of whom had bright streams of blood running over his mouth. Brian fumbled with the focus on the binoculars, trained it on the edge of the fog banks. The lenses were spotted with condensation, creating tiny circular prisms that distorted his view. But there was enough clear space for him to see the water, to find the disturbance just below the surface.

Gilly's corpse was thrown high into the air, cartwheeling over a wave. His legs were gone at the knees, and tendons trailed him like pale tentacles. His shirt had been ripped, and there was a long gash along the side of his face, but otherwise he had not been mutilated. One side of his inflatable life belt had been punctured, but the other flotation cells still held air.

His body slapped face-first into the sea. A moment later, the water swirled again, and his body disappeared. Brian caught a glimpse of the creature, swimming just under the surface, Gilly's body in the side of its mouth. Then it shot upward, the massive neck coming forward with a snap, and the corpse was launched into the air again. This time his body went straight up, his long hair covering his face and then falling away to reveal his waxy skin, the lifeless, staring eyes. No blood left in him.

"What's it doing?"

He lowered the binoculars and turned. The woman with the streak of green hair had crossed through the wheelhouse and joined them. Destiny, according to her brass nameplate. She was the only one within three feet of Brian; the rest of the men had fallen back. He could hear something pattering on the deck behind them and saw Kharkov's nose was bleeding into his cupped palm, dripping onto the deck through his fingers.

The woman was looking at him, waiting for an answer.

He held the binoculars to her. She held them up and Brian showed her how to fold them in to fit her eyes and adjust the focus. She swept the binoculars back and forth, then steadied them. Gilly's body went into the air again, rotating slightly in a horrible pantomime of a dancer's pirouette, then fell limply back into the ocean. She sucked in breath, and a low sound came from her that Brian had not heard in a long time. Not quite pity, not exactly despair. A combination of the two, distinctly feminine.

She lowered the binoculars, hands trembling. "It's playing with him."

Brian nodded, not trusting his voice, and took the binoculars from her.

"Don't," she said, putting her hand on his forearm. "Don't watch it anymore."

He lowered the binoculars and studied the creature with his naked eye, trying to ignore what it was doing to his best friend. It stayed just out of sight, working at the edge of the fog bank, submerging a few feet when it approached the ship. Occasionally, part of it would emerge, a sliver of dark green-black hide. Toying with the body, the mindless cruelty of a cat with a mouse . . . or something more?

"It doesn't want to be seen," Graves said, joining them at the rail. He was snapping pictures with his phone. "It comes right to the surface but no further."

It rolled then, displacing enough water that they were able to get a sense of how long it was, how truly massive. Graves's phone clicked and clicked, but when Brian glanced at the screen there was nothing to see but water and fog, with a faint shadow beneath the surface.

"That's not a whale," Destiny said, so softly only Brian heard her.

Gilly's body went cartwheeling toward them. It

landed just in front of the bow, disappearing from their sight under the curve of the ship's hull.

Then nothing, just the monotonous sound of waves rolling past them.

"This is horrible," Destiny said. "My God. *It's* horrible."

Brian barely heard her. He was thinking of a night several years ago, he and Gilly hunched over their drinks in the dim yellow light of the Riff-Raff's back booth. Drunk and getting drunker, at the point in the night where things could be said and perhaps not remembered. He had been talking about Sienna and Mason, wondering whether he should put up a marker for them, as her family had just done back in Wisconsin. A slab of granite over empty ground. The bile was there, always there, and when it needed to come out Gilly was the only person he could talk to.

They just want a place to visit, Gilly said. *Someplace specific, you know?*

They blame me.

Gilly had nodded. *You blame yourself. Can't expect them to feel any different.*

That part doesn't bother me, Brian had said. *Where they ended up. The ocean is no different than a cemetery.*

Sure, Gilly had said. A long pause. *Over deep water, that's about the best way there is. Right back to where we come from.*

That's where I'm going to end up, too, Brian had said. He was quite drunk by then and the morbidity he often entertained was coming out.

Maybe, Gilly said. *But not for a while, okay, buddy?*

No. No, I guess not.

They drank in silence. Then Gilly had set his glass down, hard. *Listen, don't go getting any ideas about a sailor's funeral for me. The old man had me on the sea since I was just a little shit, and I never cared for it that much. When I go, plant me somewhere dry.*

It was the kind of conversation that seemed, in retrospect, to have stumbled into a sacred place and then back out. Now, thinking back to Gilly's words, which at the time he had thought were perhaps an attempt to lighten the mood, he realized that it was the only request Gilly had ever asked of him.

When I go, plant me somewhere dry.

"I'm going down there," he said, pointing at the bow. He turned to face Moore and the rest of them, and something in his face made them retreat. Even Kharkov, with his bloody hand still clamped over the middle of his face, took a cautious half-step backwards. "And I'm pulling him onboard."

Chapter 18

Frankie wasn't sure, but he thought the odds were pretty good he would hear the guy's neck break.

Thor had one forearm wrapped around Prower's lieutenant's neck, his free hand pressed against the man's forehead. Hornaday, a clean-cut, slab-muscled, ex-military mercenary sort, looked scared shitless. He had been scuffling with one of Latham's men when Frankie and Thor entered the room, Hornaday all over the smaller man, then stepping back to pull a knife from somewhere on his body. Frankie couldn't tell where. The man was fast, the move practiced, and Frankie was already wondering how to dump the body when Thor moved forward.

He came in from Hornady's blind side, chopped the knife from his hand, and spun him around in a blur of his huge arms. Two maybe three seconds. Now Hornaday's knife lay on the floor in front of him, and the wrist that had been waving it around was bent at an awkward angle. Thor's long blond hair had come undone from his ponytail, the only sign he'd exerted himself.

Some of his hair lay over Hornaday's pain-reddened face. It was one of those images Frankie knew he'd never forget, the red-faced mercenary with the golden locks.

Now Thor was looking at Frankie, waiting for the command. Hornaday's neck would make a sound like a walnut breaking under a boot. Just one nod, and he'd have a sound to remember along with the image.

It would also, Frankie thought, result in a lot of cleanup. An immutable fact in his line of work; the more interesting something was to watch, or hear, the more cleanup was involved afterward.

"Let him go," Frankie said.

Thor shoved Hornaday away from him, then leaned forward and placed his boot on the knife blade. He lifted up on the handle, and the blade snapped off just above the hilt. Thor kicked the handle away, locking eyes with the other bodyguards one by one. Nobody would hold his gaze.

"This is silly," Frankie said. "Fighting with knives? Over what?" He turned to Latham. "I don't want nobody going home feeling like they got a bum deal."

"They didn't do that on my account."

"Really?"

"Really."

"You look upset, though," Frankie said.

"You know why?" Latham said. "Twenty-four out of twenty-seven hands, that's how many he won. Twenty-four out of twenty-seven. Seventeen straight at one point."

Even from across the room Frankie could see the big vein in the side of Latham's neck throbbing away. Dude was going to have a coronary, he didn't calm down. Or stroke out, right there in front of them. In a way, it would solve a lot of problems.

"Seventeen?" Frankie said, deciding to let it go. Latham had instigated the fight, of course, tried to spark a little chaos, maybe put himself in a better bargaining position. Rock the boat, so to speak. Not so many years ago, Frankie would have tried to push Latham on it, make him admit what he'd done. "That's a hell of a run."

"More than just a good run. Seventeen winning hands in a row doesn't happen."

Frankie held up a palm. "I was in Vegas long enough to disagree. It happens more than you might think."

"Not to me," Latham said. "Not like that."

Prower sniffed, took a drink, and looked around the room, his cane on his lap. Hornaday was watching him, nursing his hand but still waiting for a cue. A tough man, as was Kharkov, and no surprise there: They could afford the best. Men like Latham and Prower had contingency plans for every situation. Hell, they had contingency plans for their contingency plans.

"What we have here," Frankie said, "is a misunderstanding. The deck was straight, the dealers were, well, you two. The way you were hunched over your cards, Richard? Wasn't no way anybody could get a peek. Even if there was, Hamilton won half of his hands on draw cards."

"Lady Luck," Prower said. "She smiled on me, friend. That's all."

"That's all," Latham snarled. "'That's all,' he says. Shove your false sympathy up your Yankee ass, Prower. You don't fool me."

Frankie went to the table and sat down, breathing in the heavy smell of the two men's sweat, the aftershave that enhanced the BO rather than covering it, all of it overlaid with the Scotch and the coffee and the bitter odor of spent cigars. He glanced at Prower's pile of chips, then at the empty green felt in front of Latham. "You remember there was a buy-in option."

Prower frowned, started to speak, and was interrupted by Latham.

"Buy-in? He's not going to agree to a buy-in. This is the kind of purse you buy lottery tickets for, and now it's—" Latham was suddenly overwhelmed by a coughing jag, his face turning red as he hacked, flecks of spit spraying the table. He drew in a deep breath, coughed wetly, and then swiped his sleeve across his mouth. "Don't blow smoke up my ass."

"No smoke," Frankie said. To his side, he sensed rather than saw Thor tense, reacting to some movement in either Latham's or Prower's ranks. He waited, but whoever had moved must have stopped. "And I never said it had to be unanimous."

There was silence for a moment. Frankie watched Thor out of the corner of his eye, waiting for a bum rush.

But the only movement was Prower's lips, puckering to let out a low whistle. "You son of a bitch," he said to Frankie, not without a trace of admiration. "Let me guess, you're going to vote yes."

"How long you been working for Latham?"

They were in the small cabin that passed for Frankie's office, Frankie tapping away at his laptop. The rooms were tiny, too small for more than a couple of regular-sized people, and Frankie was starting to feel claustrophobic sharing the room with Thor. At the same time, he liked having the big man around. A wall of humanity between him and the rest of the world.

"Is my first job with him," Thor said. "And my last, I think."

"He was a little pissy after you grabbed one of your own guys," Frankie said. "You want to start fresh?"

"For you?" he asked.

Frankie nodded. "Just for the rest of this trip. After that, I got some private business I need to take care of."

Thor looked at him steadily. "I have a contract. The check comes after we get off the ship."

Frankie glanced at the screen and tapped refresh. He liked the way it looked, all those digits in his account, the way the cents at the end of the balance made it look even bigger. He could remember back when he was starting out, everything he wanted had a price tag with more digits in it than what he had available. Sometimes one place more, usually two or three. It was his philosophy, occasionally vocalized: *I need more digits.*

They had thought it was a funny line to repeat to him, sitting there in the desert holding his bloody hand. *There're yer digits, Frankie. Scoop 'em up.*

Now, though. Now he had enough to do the stuff he needed to do, the things he wanted to do, too.

He tapped refresh on the browser window, and the leading digit on his account went from a two to a three.

"And there we go," he said. There were eight digits, counting the thirty-seven cents. Somewhere in the past, not long ago, those thirty-seven cents would have mattered to him, would have been part of his inventory. "Let's check the others."

"It's not like I want to," Thor said as Frankie logged out, ran a security scan, and began typing in his passwords into the Deutchsbank log-in screen. "But I have family, back in old country. Mr. Latham, there is still a chance he will pay."

"That goddamn family thing," Frankie said. "Gets you every time, don't it? I hear ya, bro. I hear ya." He plucked a napkin out of the coffee tray, pulled a pen from his jacket pocket, and set it on the desk in front of Thor. "If Mr. Latham was going to write you that check, what would it look like? Say if he was real happy with you, put in a big fat tip?"

Thor frowned for a moment, not in confusion, then scribbled down a number and pushed the napkin back to Frankie. Frankie brought the napkin up, raising his eyebrows at the number, pretending to think about it. How the hell did Latham succeed in the business world? Paying peanuts, when anybody could see Thor was good, fast and efficient and about the right amount of smart. Like a well-trained bear.

Frankie opened his wallet and counted out hundreds until he reached Thor's number, then added five more. "You really will have a tip at the end, things go like they have been. Understand? And I been known to tip real good. Ask the bartender, Remy. He'll vouch."

Thor took the bills, folding them into a money clip. "I believe you, *chef*."

"Don't get too trusting, big guy. This is business, not just . . ." He squinted at the screen, and then his face relaxed. "Ah, there we go," Frankie said. He closed out the Deutschbank account, running the numbers in his head, adding up the cash he had already taken custody of. Even after he was done in Ohio, there was enough that he could buy a place, get the boat, drink the good stuff until his liver didn't know anything else existed. "We good, Thor?"

"Yes," Thor said.

"Latham doesn't have to know about our deal. No need to cut ties, you understand?"

"Of course, *chef*."

"All right, then," Frankie said. "Apologize to him, say whatever you big men say when you have to grovel. Let him abuse you, he wants to. If it still needs to be cleared up, I'll take care of it. But get the game started." He rapped on the wall of the room. "I got a feeling, this old piece of shit is going to be headed to harbor sooner rather than later."

After Thor left, Frankie closed down his laptop and put it in his locked briefcase. Then he opened the duffel bag in the closet, cleared away the dirty socks and underwear on top, and felt for the hidden zipper on the bottom.

The bottom of the duffel bag was lined with bands of hundred-dollar bills. The modern way to do business was online banking and offshore accounts, sure, but it was old school to distrust those little electronic numbers. He'd been clear on his payment terms: seventy-five percent deposited in offshore accounts, the remaining quarter cash on the barrelhead.

He stowed the duffel and the laptop back in the closet, then went into the bathroom and splashed water on his face. He looked into the mirror, checked his teeth, ran a hand back through his hair. "It's a whale," he said to his reflection, seeing how it looked, coming out of his mouth.

Good enough for the rubes on this ship, maybe. He wouldn't want to say it to the Coast Guard, or a cop.

He filled his cupped hands with water and brought it over his face, slowly, letting the chemical-scented water cool his skin. It was all still under control. Thor was one of those rare gifts, an underappreciated man easily bought. Prower was a better cardplayer than Frankie had anticipated, one of those guys that made it look easy, like it really was luck. Now Latham was ready to throw away another million, convinced he could make the comeback of the century. Well, shit, anything was possible.

He let the water fall into the sink and looked up at the mirror again. Anything was possible, he'd heard that so many times, but . . .

"But I wouldn't bet on it," he said.

He straightened, patted his face dry, sniffed an armpit. Still pretty good. He exited the room, locked it, and waited for a moment to see if there were any sounds coming from the game room. Nothing he could hear, just the soft voice of Remy, his voice nice and calm. The game must have already started.

He turned down the hallway, past the rows of empty rooms, the doors open, per his direction. He took a left and saw Christie was in his chair, head nodding a bit over some medical journal, his face loose and drawn with fatigue.

"I didn't sign on for this," he said. "Sit around all day . . ."

Frankie ignored him, reaching into his pocket for the key card. He unlocked the door, turned the knob, and cocked an eyebrow at Christie.

"Go ahead," Christie said. "He's sedated."

The room passed for a master suite on this level, maybe twelve feet square, a desk and dresser on one side, a twin bed on the other. There was a thin shape on the bed, blankets pulled partway over the torso. Frankie flipped on the main lights and the shape stirred, legs twitching. The room smelled like piss.

"Wake up, Cesar," Frankie said softly.

The shape stirred again, rolled over. *"¿Que?"*

"Go on, clear out the cobwebs. *Comprendes?* I want you to hear me clearly."

The man sat up and immediately bent over, hands pressed to his temples. He was Hispanic and thin, medium height, faded tattoos along his forearms and on the inside of his wrists. His black hair was close cut, running back thick and heavy from a clear, high brow. His eyes, somewhat clouded by the opiates Christie had administered, looked up from between his hands, trying to focus on Frankie. His wrists were bound by thick plastic zip ties.

"You like the sea life, Cesar?"

Cesar rubbed his temples. He had a large bruise along his swollen left jawbone, and his knuckles were scraped red, his right ring finger swollen like a sausage.

"You're a guest, think of it that way. Okay? Good. Hey, I got some news for you."

"Yes?" Cesar's voice was low, pleasant. "We on a ship, that the news?"

"He talks," Frankie said. "Listen, I saved your ass, Cesar. If Cappero had his way, you'd be pushing out the asshole of one of his Rottweilers about now. They'd be chewing on your bones in the backyard of his little estate, *hombre*, and when the dogs were done chewing, Cappero would have a bonfire. Pile up the bones, add some kerosene. Then puff, up in smoke, no more Cesar, like you never been. That sound about right?"

Cesar's face sagged a little. "You know Cappy?"

"That's what you used to do, wasn't it?" Frankie asked. "Take care of his dirty work, let the dogs do their thing? Don't look surprised, everyone knew you were Cappy's dog man. I ain't judging, I was born south of the border maybe I'd of ended up a dog man, too." Frankie shook his head. "Your buddy Mariana, he already met the dogs."

"Why am I still alive?"

Frankie sighed. "See, Cesar, that's the question. And I've got a great answer for you. A way for you to get out of this free and clean."

"Yeah? I don't think so."

"True," Frankie said. "I need a man, Cesar, someone who'll do what I need without question. The kind of man who understands that if he doesn't listen, doesn't do as I ask, then he's dead. Fish bait rather than dog food, but just as dead."

"Cappy gave me to you?"

"Not your concern. What I come in here to say was you got a chance. Do what I say, when I say it, and you got a chance."

Cesar's eyes seemed to gain focus. "This chance, I think is pretty small."

Frankie shrugged. "We're in international waters right now, on a real nice ship." He motioned to the desk, at the plate of cold food set there. "You got food, water.

Compare where you're at, the chance you might have, to where you might be." Frankie leaned forward and abruptly gave a short, sharp bark.

Cesar flinched.

Frankie laughed and stood. "Better than dog food, *hombre*. Better than dog food."

Chapter 19

Brian was halfway down the stairs to the main deck before he heard footsteps behind him. He took the remaining stairs two at a time, different scenarios running through his mind. The life belt inflated into a series of plastic-lined compartments, and when they were all deflated Gilly's body would sink. In this deep, cold water, his body might never float back up.

The stairwell ended in a hallway and he paused, unsure of which way to go. The footsteps were louder now, and a shadow fell across him. He spun around, fist cocked.

"Go left," Destiny said, stopping five steps above him. "Then another left."

He didn't move.

"Go," she said. "If you can get your friend's body somehow, go do it. A left and then another left."

He turned and ran down the hallway, shoved a door open, and was greeted by the open air of the front deck. He sprinted toward the bow, then detoured to the railing. The rope that Gilly had tossed to the *Nokomis*'s crew was coiled on the deck and he gathered it up, leaning over the side and looked up and down the length of the ship. He could see nothing but water; if Gilly's body was still afloat, it had either floated down the ship farther, or it was on the other side of the ship.

Or it had already been pulled back under.

"Hey! Stop right there!"

Three men emerged from the stairwell and started toward him. Kharkov, plus two others he didn't recognize, a huge blond man and a guy in a white shirt and sport jacket. The guy in the jacket held up a hand, his face bemused, and for a second Brian almost believed what this gesture implied, that he should hold on a sec. That they might just want to talk.

Then he sprinted toward the far deck, the man's face losing its benign look as they veered off at an angle, meaning to cut him off. He cast his eyes about the deck as he ran, looking something he could swing, a piece of pipe or a wrench. The deck was barren.

He reached the port side railing and craned his head over. For a moment he saw only the endless gray-green of the sea, then caught a glimpse the orange cell of the life vest, disappearing around the curve of the ship, over a hundred feet down the side of the ship. No way to reach it from the lower decks.

"Hey!" the big man shouted in a thick Scandinavian accent. "You stop now!"

Brian turned as the huge man leaped over one of the hatches on the deck, felt the thud of his landing. Brian made a quick loop in the rope he still held, then pushed the free end of the rope through to form a crude lasso. He hitched the free end of the rope over the railing and tied it in a quick clinch knot.

"Stop!"

The huge man was only fifteen feet away, too close. Brian reached for the small of his back, pretending to reach for a weapon. The big man skidded to a stop, as did Kharkov and the other man, and Brian used the few seconds of extra time to shrug the lasso over his shoulders. If he let these men detain him, Gilly's body would be lost forever.

"He won't," Kharkov said. None of them had moved, even when they realized Brian wasn't armed. "Not enough balls."

"How's the nose?" Brian said, swinging a foot onto the railing. He jumped as both Kharkov and the big man lunged forward, one of their hands brushing against his back as he dropped over the side. Then he was freefalling, the ocean rushing up to meet him.

It was like hitting skim ice, his body slamming into the top of a wave so hard his shoulder and hip went numb. His momentum drove him deep into the water, in the shadow of the *Nokomis*. Finally, his rate of descent slowed, and he paused for a moment, surveying the ship. He could see large furrows in the hull, and further back a thin trial of oil leaking from the gaping hole where the propellers should have been. He started toward the surface, climbing the rope rather than swimming. He could already feel his muscles contracting, growing stiff.

He broke through the surface and spat out a mouthful of water, paddling clumsily. The rope was caught in the slack, pulling on him with each wave. He turned in a slow circle and saw Gilly's body thirty feet away, bumping facedown along the hull, and started splashing toward it.

His corpse was caught in a seam created by the hull's displacement, not subject to the full force of the waves or current. Brian reached out and snagged the back of his collar.

"Gotcha," he said. "Gotcha, bud."

He looked around. The air pocket in Gilly's vest was enough to keep them both afloat. A good thing, Brian thought, because he probably couldn't tread water much longer. His jeans and boots restricted his movements, and his body was trembling with the cold. There was nothing here to grab on to, the hull rising up slick and featureless above them.

He let the current carry them down the length of the ship, letting the rope play out behind him, maneuvering Gilly's head above water. A silly gesture; he knew Gilly was dead, because his flesh was the same temperature as the water. Finally the rope pulled tight and they came to a stop, just aft of the wheelhouse. There was a row of portholes a few yards farther down, and the tops of the swells brushed the bottoms of the rounded glass. Above them was a deck way, ten feet above the portholes, a recessed hallway decorated with electric lanterns.

Another large roller washed over them. He peered into the wind. Nothing but endless sets of waves, coming out of the fog bank like rows of dull gray mountains.

He began banging on the side of the ship. It made almost no sound.

"Pull me back up!" he shouted, then coughed as water splashed down his throat. "Pull us up!"

The tension on the rope remained the same, periods of slack and then a hard pull as it caught a wave. He took a deep breath, waited until a wave broke over them, and yelled again, so loud his throat ached. The sound was swallowed in the roar and crash of the waves.

He felt the water swirl as something passed underneath him, dragging an immense wake. He went very still, pressing his body against the hull. The creature was only fifteen feet down, just low enough to pass under the hull of the *Nokomis*. It passed slowly, growing thicker until it seemed as wide as a two-lane highway, then began to narrow into a thick tail. Then the tail curved to the left as it banked into a wide circle.

Coming back.

Gilly's severed legs were still leaching a thin trickle of blood into the water. Brian watched the blood swirl and spin in the water. It didn't matter. Whatever had passed below them did not want Gilly.

Brian wormed a hand into his pocket, withdrew his pocketknife, and flipped it open. It had missed them as they huddled tight against the hull. It didn't matter. Their scent was thick in the water. Gilly's blood and his terror.

It would return, and when it did, he was going to cut out its other eye.

He treaded water. He waited for the monster to return.

He remembered.

The bodies had never been recovered. They had not been that far offshore when the sailboat capsized, perhaps two hundred yards from the harbor entrance. Sierra and Mason were both good swimmers. He had seen them go under and come back up and had gone inside for a moment to grab the life ring and then . . .

He hadn't been able to free the ring for a moment and by the time he freed it and jumped overboard they were gone. He had called and then screamed their names as the sailboat turned on its side and drifted away and he had swum after it, thinking perhaps they were clinging to the far side, and by the time the fishing boat found him forty-five minutes later he had screamed for them so long and so hard he could not even speak his own name.

Gone. The water was warm and they should have washed ashore but they never did.

It took a very long time to accept the fact they were dead. A period of denial punctuated by a startling sudden despair, more acute than even the grief-drenched days after the capsizing.

Then, more than a year later, the phone call in the middle of the night. Months after he had started to accept the idea he would never see them again. He did not have caller ID but could tell the call was from some great distance, the line scratchy, the voice a faint echo. He had been still quite drunk from a night at the Riff-Raff and he shouted into the phone. *What?*

A thin crackle of static. And then the voice, the sound of a young boy. Perhaps ten or twelve. *¿Hola?* The rustle of the phone being switched to the other ear. *¿Hola, padre?*

Who is this? Brian asked. There was a moment of

silence and then the phone clicked and there was only the vacuum of the empty line.

In the morning he had been quite sure it was a dream. That lasted for half of his breakfast—oatmeal, all he could stomach after the previous night's tap beer and mid-shelf whiskey—and then he had called the phone company and requested his records. The lady from AT&T e-mailed the records and ten minutes later he had printed it out and was looking at the phone number, tracing his finger along it over and over again. It had come at 2:47 A.M., a phone call from Juliaca, in the Puno region of Peru. Almost completely across the continent from where their boat had capsized. Across the breadth and width of a huge continent of almost half a billion people.

But the boy had said *padre*. The boy had been ten or twelve.

His mind seized upon the potential immediately and fiercely. A boy with amnesia. Washed ashore. Wandering aimlessly through the vile dirt roads and streets and then finally, after months of begging, discovering the number tucked in the back of his mind and knowing that it was a link to the home he sometimes remembered. Brian did not so much see this sequence of events as feel it, a dizzying rush of horror and desperate protectiveness and in that moment what had been dead in him sprung once again to life and he started making phone calls to the local travel agent, his oatmeal congealing on the kitchen table.

Two days later he stepped into the scorching tarmac of the Inco Manco Capac airport and for the next three months endured dysentery and corrupt civil service men who offered useless information for Brian's dwindling supply of *sol*. Many of the police and census takers and civil servants saw him at once, saw his purpose and took an air of familiarity with him. *Sí*, there was a foreign boy who had moved here. How long ago? It was hard to remember, *señor*. He spoke English, yes. Of course, he was with a woman. Or no, I do not remember if he was with a woman, *amigo*. It was possible. *Sí*, it was very possible.

Where was the boy staying? I do not know but there are records that are sometimes taken, along with photos. During registration for housing and other events. *Sí*, they are available but only to officials, to citizens, to me.

Always the conduit to the information he sought ran through the person he was speaking to at that moment, in that village or city or just a collection of miserable shacks. The conversations taking place in the slanting shadows of houses and shacks and trees, the men there squatting and smoking as the blistering heat baked into the dust of the streets.

He preferred to deal with the ones who held out for more *sol*. It cost him more, twice as much at least, but if they were shrewd enough to bargain he thought they might be shrewd enough to at least do some research, understanding this *nortamericano* would spend more money the harder they worked. Those who refused his money and cautioned against the frantic hope they saw in his eyes he despised, hating them more than even the cops who took his money without offering even a pretense of services actually being rendered. In these cautious, pitying people he saw the reflection of who he was, of what he clung to as the village children clung to their grimy homemade dolls.

When he returned home, he was broke, thirty pounds lighter, hollow-eyed. When he looked in the mirror he saw a man still lost, his hopelessness stamped on his face like ink. *My tattoo*, he had thought. *One that will never go away*.

Someone was yelling. He stirred himself as the water boiled and swirled near the bow. Another muffled yell from a man on the deck way, then an order from another man to get back from the edge. Then another shout behind him, sharper and much closer, and when he turned he saw the girl, Destiny, standing on the recessed deck way above the row of portholes. She was leaning over the guardrail, waving. Her neat white dress shirt had become untucked and was flapping in the wind.

"Hurry!" she said. "It's coming back!"

A wave rolled over him and the rope dug cruelly into his waist. He paused, thinking, and then released Gilly's body and swam against the current, the rope curling back behind him. After he had battled the current for twenty feet, he reached down and pulled in the slack he had managed to create and cut himself free.

He was swept back, riding the waves. Gilly's body was swirling in the slack current next to the ship and he grabbed Gilly's shirt collar, taking the main force of the waves on his right shoulder. Destiny leaned over the railing, her eyes flitting from them to the water near the front of the ship.

Once they were underneath her, he tucked back into the slower, shipside water and slid the rope around his stomach free. Then he worked the noose down and over Gilly's shoulders and heaved the remainder over the railing for Destiny. A moment later, the rope tightened. He banged on the hull, and to his surprise the body began to jerk upward, pausing for only a moment when it cleared the water and the full weight hit the rope. He heard a sharp word by Destiny, and then the body continued upward, moving steadily. Someone helping her, he thought. Frankie's men?

He glanced behind him. He could hear shouting from the bow, but there was nothing to see.

Above him, Gilly's body went over the railing and thumped to the deck. After a moment the rope splashed back down. He looped it around his waist, cinched it tight, and tugged it. The rope tightened, then paused. He was two hundred and twenty pounds, fifteen more than he should be after a long winter of too many beers and frozen pizzas.

"Tie it off!" he shouted.

The rope loosened and he went back into the water. A moment later it tightened, then jerked three times in his grip. He began to climb the rope, relying on the strength of his forearms and shoulders, the rope burning against his palms. He cleared the water and placed his boots against the hull, trying to walk himself up the side and take some of the pressure off his upper body. He managed two steps, and then his boots slipped on the wet surface and he thudded against the hull, sliding almost all the way back down to the water.

Destiny's face appeared above him, tight with panic. "It's right here," she whispered. "Don't move."

He turned, slowly rotating his body to face the ocean.

The creature was fifteen yards out, swimming parallel with them. It looked roughly half as long as the ship, a creature so immense his brain struggled to process the sight. For a moment his terror was overwhelmed with amazement as he watched it slither through the current, the trough of a wave occasionally exposing a green-black section of hide. It continued past, intent, the shadow of the massive head casting back and forth like a dog trying to catch a lost scent trail.

He turned a bit to watch it pass, and at his movement the creature banked hard. Even underwater he could see the lone green eye fix on him, the long and hideously barbed fangs growing as it opened its mouth. The rest of its body curled back behind it, the huge flippers positioning it so it was parallel to the ship.

"Shit," he breathed, and went hand over hand up the rope, not bothering with his feet. In seconds he was at the railing and trying to pull himself over, Destiny's hands wrapped in his drenched shirt as the water erupted behind him. The there was a moment of silence, the air murmuring unsteadily as it does prior to the passing of a train. Then the air became darker behind him, and the creature smashed into the ship.

The impact drove him over the railing, Destiny tumbling alongside him as they rolled to the opposite side of the deck way, thudding against the outside wall of the cabin rooms. The ship tilted back under the impact, pinning them there, and he waited for the pressure of teeth in his back.

Behind them, the boat sounded like it was coming apart. After a moment, he lifted his head and turned.

It had bit into the ship just to the right of the rope, missing him by several feet. It had crushed the railing in its massive jaws, smashing through them so its teeth were now embedded into the deck, caught in the fiber-glass and wood. The creature was trying to swing its head to the side, the neck muscles bunching as it tried to free itself. Only its nostrils and the top part of its head were visible, black-green hide stretched over two massive humps that anchored its jaw muscles.

Slowly, his legs numb, Brian got to his feet. He moved toward the trapped creature, pulling the jack-knife out of his pocket. The deck was covered in sea-water and was tilting hard back toward the creature, which was halfway out of the water.

He grabbed a mangled section of railing and leaned over, the floorboards shaking under his feet. The creature was stuck, yes, but he saw instantly that it would not be for long; already its shaking had opened up the hole in which its tooth was embedded, and the creature's own weight was working for it, pulling the tooth back to create a long furrow. The ship dipped down again, tilting dangerously, and from inside the ship he heard a chorus of faint screams.

He leaned down. It was not as big as it had looked in the water but it was still enormous, the body thick, swelling with powerful musculature where it entered the water twenty feet below them. The tail was whipping through the water, creating a rocking motion, adding to the momentum of the creature's head shakes. He felt a strong urge to reach out and touch the wet hide, to feel the texture of it.

It had not yet seen him. And whatever else it might be, however intelligent it might be, it was now in the same frenzied and single-minded mode of any animal caught in a trap.

In front of him the nostrils flared and he moved without thinking, leaping from the deck onto its upper jaw, the flat, upturned surface just above its teeth. He hooked his free hand in one of the massive nostrils and felt a warm wash of air over his hand. The creature thrashed underneath him, and he slipped, saved from falling only by his grip on the edge of the nostril. The creature's head twisted away and Brian slid over the top of the snout, now only two feet away from its good eye.

Its pupil contracted into a slit, and he could see himself reflected in the green eye, a hairy creature clinging to it like a louse. It did not move, did not do anything but watch him, and for a second he felt quite sure he would do nothing himself, that he would remain here affixed to it until it deigned to shrug him off.

Then he remembered Gilly, his hand spread open to the sky, stumps spurting blood. He brought the knife around in a short, vicious arc.

It jerked at the movement, breaking out of its reverie at the same moment Brian broke from his. The knife hit it on the bony protuberance under the eye socket, sliced through the hide to hit bone. It was jerked from his hand as the creature reared back, roaring in pain and fury. He felt its teeth come free of the deck way. He lunged as the creature fell away, grasping a section of railing that hung off the side of the deck.

He caught it, the brass slick under his hands. Underneath him he heard the creature fall into the ocean, and a second later the spray rose up to drench him. He was starting to slide down the severed railing, his palms sliding down the wet brass, when a hand closed over his wrist.

He looked up. Wells was lying on the deck, his bad arm folded under him. Destiny was holding onto his knees to keep him from sliding.

"Come on," he said. "Get up here before it comes back for you."

They huddled against the far wall, not wanting to move for fear it would hear them. Brian was shivering but did not feel cold; his body felt dislocated from his mind, his legs and torso were numb. Destiny stood slightly apart from them, breathing very deliberately. Brian wondered if she was going to hyperventilate.

He wondered if he was going to hyperventilate.

"Is it going to attack again?" she whispered

Wells shook his head. "I don't know." He turned to Brian. "That was an incredibly stupid thing to do," he said. "At the same time, I think you frightened it a little. It may think twice before it attacks us again."

"Oh, yeah," Brian said. "I bet it's pissing its pants. What the hell is that thing?"

Before Wells could answer they heard a man shout from somewhere in the bow, the deep Scandinavian accent from the man called Thor. Wells moved forward, peeking down the side of the ship. He ducked back, and they heard the man shout again. "They know we're here," Wells said.

"Well," Brian said. "We did have a fucking sea monster hanging from the side of the boat."

"It's a plesiosaur," Wells said. "Some species of it, a *Liopleurodon* or a kronosaur. Probably the latter. But it's evolved significantly. It's much larger, and the short-necked plesiosaurs had smooth teeth. This one has teeth that look like . . ."

"Ice saws." Brian regarded Wells for a long moment. "It's a dinosaur?"

Wells held up his hands. "Christ, man, I don't know. What'd it look like to you?"

"I don't know," Brian said. "All I know is that it missed me somehow."

"It's lost its depth perception," Wells said. "It's very visual. It hasn't figured out how to focus with only one eye."

"Bullshit," Brian said. "It saw Gilly's body just fine. It was playing with it like a dolphin playing with a ball."

"That was in the open sea," Wells whispered. "Here, alongside the ship, things are more difficult. There's a backdrop, conflicting images. It is an open sea predator, meant to attack and kill in the voids."

"How do you know so much about it?" Destiny asked.

"I don't," Well said, frowning. "I know ancient sea life, though, and I saw it when it attacked my research vessel, not so clearly as just now, just a glimpse. But I suspected what it might be even then." He laughed humorlessly. "More than a thousand years we've been sailing the seas, with tales of sea monsters around that entire time. And modern man never gave them a serious thought."

"It can't be a dinosaur," Destiny said. "Can it? They've been gone for millions of years."

"The ones on land, yes," Wells said. He turned and studied the fog-shrouded seas. "The life under the Arctic has never been fully catalogued, and I suspect that's where it comes from."

"Why is that?" Brian asked.

"Two reasons. You've heard of Bergmann's Rule?

No? It says that body mass increases with latitude. This is much larger than known fossil records."

"So it's been alive for millions of years?" Destiny asked. "I thought that was impossible."

"It is," Wells said. "Its life span would be no more than a hundred years, perhaps double that. Its species would likely spend considerable time in hibernation."

"And what's the second reason?"

Well pointed at the water. "The Kaala current. It's spawned a massive migration, a flux of movement from the Arctic waters to the south. The invertebrates came first, the plankton. Then the others, the next benthic level and the next, getting bigger and bigger. This species is the apex predator."

The breeze freshened and on it were more voices, men moving toward their location. Wells's voice dropped and Destiny moved closer, until she was at brushing against Brian. He could feel the warmth of her body and realized he was cold, very cold, probably pre-hypothermic. The adrenaline rush had chased the worst of the effects away, but if Destiny hadn't thrown the rope down to him, he'd likely be unconscious by now.

"You talk like there's more than one," Destiny said.

"We've only seen one," Wells said. "But it didn't melt out of an iceberg. The only way it could have survived this long is through reproduction, likely with long periods of hibernation in between periods of activity. Dinosaurs weren't, *aren't* the same as reptiles, but they're believed to have similar biology. Cold-dormancy is one of their traits they may share."

"Its breath was warm," Brian said. "It's not cold-blooded."

"Yes," Wells said. "Once it emerges from hiberna-

tion its body temperature would elevate to a level close
to ours. And that means it will have more energy than
a cold-blooded creature, that it can attack night or day."

"Listen," Brian said. "Whatever it is, it has flippers
instead of feet. That means the minute we get on land,
the less time I'm going to spend worrying about end-
ing up as its chew toy."

"Yes," Wells said. "Captain Moore might not have
seen it yet, but he can look at this"—Wells gestured toward the ruined deck way and crumpled railings—
"and understand it's time for some serious help."

"He mentioned a tug," Brian said.

"We need a large vessel," Wells said. "Or an airlift.
We have to make sure Captain Moore sends for one or
the other, and warn them of the danger. A tugboat is
too small."

"There might be a problem with that," Destiny said.

They turned to look at her.

"My boss," Destiny said, looking down as she
pushed out the wrinkles in her sleeves, then up at them.
"He has a game going downstairs, separate from the
regular casino stuff, supposed to be secret. High powered." She considered for a moment. "The captain might
listen to him. I doubt he'll listen to either of you."

"She's probably right," Wells said. "This guy,
Frankie? He seems to have a lot of clout. Perhaps we
can convince him to come up here, see what happened, and then he'll understand."

"He'll understand," Destiny said. "He'll understand, all right."

"Then we go directly to the captain?"

"I'm not so sure he's the right guy," Brian said. He
quickly told them the story of the heroin Kharkov had

planted in Gilly's bag. "Moore is doing whatever he can to stay out here. He either doesn't believe that this thing is . . . whatever it is . . . or he doesn't care."

"Then who do we talk to?" Wells asked. "We're too far out for cell phone range."

Brian went to Gilly's waist and opened the water-proof seabag clipped to his belt. He pushed aside the flare pistol, the flares, the wire cutters, and the space blanket. At the bottom, inside a plastic baggie for extra protection, was a small handheld marine radio. He un-zipped the baggie and turned the knob. The radio came on with a squelch of static, tuned to Channel 16. He stared at it for a moment and then flipped it off.

"Not working?" Wells asked.

He tapped the short antennae. "The only people sure to hear this are up there," he said, motioning to the con-trol tower of the *Nokomis*. The radar spun slowly, the top of the antennae lost in the fog. Next to it was the large marine radio antennae, the highest point on the *Nokomis*. "Even if I get through, they'll just contradict me with their own message."

"So?" Wells asked. "How do we proceed?"

"We split up," Brian said. "You try the captain again, tell him what we saw. Try to sound . . . reasonable. I'll give you fifteen minutes, then I'm going to go up there, see if I can make us heard some other way."

"And if he agrees?"

"I'll have this on," Brian said, holding up the radio. "I'll keep it on scan, so I'll hear any communications he makes. If he makes the call for help, good. If not, I do my thing."

"Your thing?" Destiny said.

"I'll take away their ability to contradict me." Brian

pointed to the control tower, thinking out the approach in his mind. It wouldn't be easy; he needed to get up one level, cross over the relatively open space that was the outdoor recreation area on B-deck, which was basically a couple rows of beach loungers, green plastic stretched over metal frames surrounding a shuffleboard area. Then he would have to climb up the back side of the control tower without being noticed, get up on top, then repeat the whole thing coming back down. . . .

"Go," he said to Wells. "I'll hang out for a bit, see if you can get him to see reason. Good luck."

"Same to you," Wells said. "And don't do anything stupid."

Wells went down the deck way, scanned the interior hallway, and then disappeared around the corner. Brian clutched his arms tight to his chest, starting to shiver, as he tried to figure out the best route. Destiny was watching him, and he noticed her forearms were covered in goosebumps.

He glanced at her. "Maybe you should get back to your job. I don't want to get you in any trouble."

She stepped forward, her eyes tracing the same route he was navigating in his mind. "You'll never make it. They're watching the ocean, mostly, but they aren't that blind. You're lucky, they'll just knock you around some and throw you in a room."

"If I'm not lucky?"

She shrugged. "I don't see any of them too upset about their buddies getting killed. You happen to fall overboard, nobody watching? Oops."

"Nice guys you work for."

"It's a one-off," she said absently. "You can't tap into the line, why do you want to get up there?"

*   *   *

It had been a lot of mistakes, especially for a man who didn't make them very often.

Frankie leaned over the side of the *Nokomis*, peering into the gray water as Adrian tried to climb a rope back up to the deck. The rope was one of four currently holding a lifeboat halfway between the deck and the water. Adrian had volunteered to captain the lifeboat on a little reconnoiter mission, see if he could pick up Hawkins and get back in the good graces of his bosses. That, of course, was before the creature had attacked Hawkins forty yards down the flank of the ship. After that, Adrian didn't want to go down anymore.

Frankie didn't blame him. He watched as Adrian climbed hand over hand back up to the main deck, hauling his bulk up an inch at a time. The lifeboat went down easily on the pulley system, but it wouldn't come back up. They hadn't known that, couldn't have known it, but it had still been a mistake.

The first mistake, though, even before agreeing to let Adrian be a lifeboat captain, was letting Moore handle Hawkins. That kinda shit worked on punks, applying pressure until you saw a crack appear. That was your way in, that crack, and once it appeared the rest of it opened up. But this guy, Hawkins, out here in the middle of the fuckin' ocean with a little boat that Frankie wouldn't have used to cross Boston Harbor, he wasn't a punk. Even when his little boat gets ripped to shreds by, well, goddamn *something*, instead of curling into a ball Hawkins shoots it with a flare gun. And actually hits the, well . . . the goddamn *something*.

And in the eye? Hawkins was either a deadeye, or

he had a horseshoe up his ass. Either way, you apply pressure to a guy like that, he's gonna apply it right back.

So that was mistake number one, applying pressure to Hawkins. They might have been able to cool him down if it had been done the right way, if you knew the right sorta pressure, but he had let Moore do the work, and Moore was, well. He was goddamn something, too, and Frankie thought he could probably put his finger on Moore a lot easier than he could describe what was swimming below them. Moore was soft, rotten somewhere in the middle like an old peach. Moore was, well, a goddamned pussy.

"*Chef?*"

Frankie ignored Thor for the moment. Okay, mistake number two was his, too, and it was as simple as letting Latham buy back in. It was a lot more money, but now that he'd seen the creature clearly, it wasn't nearly enough. He should just cut the game off right now, but then Latham would . . . Frankie snorted. Not *protest*. Latham would *erupt*.

"Frankie?" Thor's big fingers plucked at Frankie's sleeve.

And mistake number three?

He wasn't sure, maybe it was ignoring the hint of panic in Thor's voice right now. Frankie turned slowly to the big man. His brain was working over the mistakes but there weren't any fixes coming out, no product at all, just the feeling of a big smooth wheel turning over and over, not catching, not grinding.

"It's here."

He turned to follow Thor's gaze. At first he didn't

see it and then he did, a darker shape beneath the swells. One of the ends was pointed toward them. Not an end. A head. He could see fins behind the massive head, two pectoral fins moving languidly. Then it shifted, a slight bend in the bulk of it. A subtle movement he equated with the tremble that passed through a cat before it pounced.

"Jesus," he said to Thor. "It's going to—"

Thor yanked him back and then they were backpedaling, tripping over an access hatch and crashing to the deck, Thor's body smashing into him. Frankie rolled out from under him and saw that Brimson and Culver, Prower's other two men who had been lowering the lifeboat, were still near the railing. At that moment there was a single human cry below them and then the rope snapped tight and jerked Brimson into the guardrail; he had wrapped the rope around his hands to improve his grip, and the rope was cinched fast around his wrist.

Brimson uttered a gargled scream as the rope pulled his arm straight down. His shoulder popped, and his scream deepened, took on a rougher edge.

Frankie pulled the knife from his belt, took a single step forward, but before he could move toward Brimson the rope made a whipping motion, a millisecond of slack followed by a tremendous lurch. Brimson's arm pulled free in a cloud of red mist, settling over him. Blood began to pour from his shoulder in thick red torrents as he tipped over the railing.

From somewhere down the length of the boat a woman screamed. She had been screaming for a while, Frankie realized. There was a pause as she took a breath, and then the screaming resumed. He thought about joining her.

"Get back!" Thor bellowed. Culver had gone to Brimson's aid and was staring over the side.

Culver's head turned, his mouth open. One hand pointing vaguely to the ocean: *Did you see that?*

Then Culver disappeared. There was a moment when the empty space behind him was blotted out, filled with a massive head, with teeth, not so much puncturing Culver as crushing him, jellying his upper body. Then Culver flipped over the side, his knee ticking against the railing. By the time they heard the splash below them, Frankie and Thor were already running, sprinting back toward the center of the ship.

Moore met them at the entry door to the main deck. He opened his mouth to say something and Thor hit him in the chest with his forearm, sending the shocked captain flying. Frankie followed his fullback through the doorway, down the dimly lit hallway, and up the stairs to the wheelhouse. Graves was there, peering down at the deck with a pair of binoculars shaking in his hands.

Frankie and Thor came to a stop, hands on their knees. The ship shook as something struck it on the port side. A pause, and then another deep shiver ran through the hull. Alarms were klaxoning, three or four different ones.

Frankie was trying hard to get his breath. He hadn't run like that in years. Decades, maybe.

Thor looked at him, something in the huge man's eyes changed now. Not threatening, perhaps, but not as loyal as they had been.

"I didn't know," Frankie said.

The ship shuddered harder, listing to the starboard side. There was a pause of ten seconds when they all waited, watching the deck roll back, and then it hit again, colliding so hard that Graves lost his footing and Thor and Frankie clutched each other to keep afoot. The ship bucked again, and they heard a series of thuds and curses as Moore fell down the stairs.

"There," Graves said. It was circling off to the starboard side, just below the surface. It turned hard, the wake from its passage sending up two foot waves, and came barreling back at the side of the ship. "Brace yourself!"

It crashed into them again. The ship shuddered, and another set of alarms sounded. Graves shut them off with the side of his hand.

"We're breached," he said. "Again."

"How bad?" Moore asked from the wheelhouse entry. He had a gash on his forehead, blood running down the side of his face, soaking into the fabric of his collar. Frankie felt an odd sort of relief. Moore looked like a captain for the first time.

Graves studied the bank of screens. "It's contained to cells P3 and P4."

"How many in total?"

"Too many. We're two or three cells away from neutral buoyancy."

Moore walked unsteadily toward them, supporting himself along the wall and then reaching out for the control console. The ship shuddered again. Graves watched the instrument readings, scanning them, and entering in some of the numbers into the keyboard.

"It keeps hitting the same spot," Graves said at last. "It's concentrating on that one area."

Frankie gripped Moore's upper arm. "Any weaponry on board?"

"Nothing," he said. "We don't even have deck mounts for firehoses."

"Small arms?"

"There's a .38 snub nose in my safe," Moore said. "It's all yours."

They waited for the next impact. The ship moved slowly with the waves, rocking as the swells broke around her bow. "It stopped," Frankie said after a few minutes. "It gave up."

Behind them, Vanders was busy answering calls from passengers, logging entries, nodding as he said the same message, over and over: *Please remain calm. Everything is under control.*

Moore turned to Graves. "How far off is the *Santa Maria*?"

Graves consulted the radar screen. "Approximately twelve kilometers, sir. Anticipated arrival time is one hour, give or take fifteen minutes. Seas are real sloppy."

Moore tapped the screen that showed the water level in the hold. "Can we stay afloat for another hour or two?"

"Maybe," Graves said. "There's six inches of water on D-deck. It's coming up fast."

"The extra submersibles we requested?"

Graves nodded. "Onboard the *Santa Maria*. They might help a little, but the end result—"

Moore held up hand. "Easy on that. How are the passengers, Vanders?"

"Freaked out," Vanders said. "We're also logging outgoing calls at very high rates, Captain. We're still well out of range, but I'm still tracking very high cellular usage."

"No satellite phones?"

"We can't track that, but I doubt it. We'd have heard something from somebody by now."

Moore turned to Frankie. "The tug isn't going to be enough. We've got to call in for a passenger transfer, there's no way around it. I'm not putting the passengers into lifeboats unless we have no other choice. There is no debate on this, Frankie—go make your arrangements."

"What kind of transfer ship? You're not going to call in the damn Coast Guard—"

"I'm going to call whatever is available," Moore said. "But I'll keep it as low key as I can." He picked up the marine radio and turned it to Channel 16, then jerked his head toward the door. "Go, Frankie. You've got no more than an hour."

They watched as the creature rose up out of the ocean, first destroying the lifeboat, then plucking the men off the railing. Wells was right; it was learning, adjusting to its lack of depth perception, not making the same mistake twice. He knew now, for the first time, that it would never let them leave the ship alive.

"Destiny? You've got to relax."

She was breathing rapidly, so fast he couldn't see how she had time to inhale. Watching her, he realized he was breathing fast himself

"Inhale three times in one breath, ah, ah, ah," he said, demonstrating. "Yeah, that's it. Now let it out slow in one long one, then do it again. No slower, three big breaths in, one out. There you go. Ah, ah, ah."

She sucked in a long draught of air, held it, and let it out. "It's . . . *hunting* us."

"I know. Breathe, Destiny."

"We need to get off the boat."

Brian reached down and pulled Gilly's body back against the wall. Safe and sound and . . . what? Hell, just as dead as he had been. There was nothing left to save, just a waterlogged corpse . . . and Brian knew that if he could go back in time he would have done the exact same thing. But from now on, it was time to concentrate on the living.

"Listen," he said. "They aren't ever going to be more distracted than they are now. Find a place on the ship, high up as you can go, in the middle somewhere. You'll be fine."

"But he made the call," she said. "He asked for help. He asked for the Coast Guard."

"I know," Brian said. "But it wasn't a Mayday, and he didn't say ship was being attacked. Whatever shows up, if anything does, won't know what hit them."

"Then why did he—"

He hesitated, then put a hand on her shoulder, feeling her muscles trembling. "They don't want any authorities, the Coast Guard, nothing. They've seen the creature, seen what it can do. I'm pretty stubborn myself, and I would have been calling for the Coast Guard a long time ago." He watched her breathing. "Slow down."

"I'm trying," she said, her breath still coming in hitches. "Jesus, it's so damned *big*."

"Destiny? What kind of deal does your boss have going on?"

"I don't know," she said. "And quit calling him that."

"Who?"

"Frankie. He's not my boss," she said. "Not anymore."

Chapter 20

It was more like a foot of water, Frankie saw when he got down to D-deck, not the six inches Graves had seen on his digital readout. Well, the electronics were soaked, the sensors waterlogged. There were probably lots of things that weren't what they were supposed to be.

Latham was sitting on the lone couch, his feet on the cushions and his bony ass perched on the backrest. Remy was still behind the bar. He looked taller, and when Frankie splashed his way over he saw the little swamp monkey had found an empty milk cart to stand on, the bottles of booze stacked in front of him for easy access. Probably used to getting flooded out, Frankie thought. Maybe a man to watch if things got any wetter.

"They're calling in a transport ship," Frankie said to Latham. "We're going to have to cut this one short. Go make your call."

Latham was already shaking his head. "The money went into your account, Frankie. We're finishing."

"Look at the goddamn water. We only got an hour, tops. Not enough time to finish a second game."

"It's more than enough," Latham said. "My chopper is already scrambled and ready to go. Ten, fifteen minutes for it to touch down, fuck the waves and fuck the fog. Prower's arrangements are similar. We're going to play this one out."

Frankie smoothed the front of his jacket. His cowboy boots were holding back most of the water, but his slacks were wicking the moisture up his pants legs. "We'll finish the game back in Boston."

"No-ooo," Latham said. "We're going to finish it here, the winner is going to take his prize here. Your job, Frankie, is to give your clients as much time as possible. When time runs out, fine. We'll get in the chopper, discuss next steps."

"The passengers aren't going to be able to get on a chopper."

"Fuck the passengers, too."

"No."

Latham looked up sharply. Frankie heard the whisper of movement from Latham's bodyguard, Kharkov cocking his head to the side like a dog hearing the sound of a rabbit in a brush pile. Prower's remaining two men, Hornaday and the one called Stillson, did not move.

"Did you say something?" Latham asked.

"Listen," Frankie said. "You gotta realize, something's out in the water, and it keeps ramming—"

"I don't give a shit!" Latham screamed, the spit spraying out of his mouth. "I'm not leaving this ship until the game is over." He took a breath, and his eyes narrowed. "Go get me some time."

Frankie stared at him, feeling the coldness working into him, colder than the water. Latham sitting there with his prissy little feet up on the cushions barking his orders. Frankie could see him tipping backwards, his shiny shoes showing the scuffed soles, could hear the splash he'd make, the squawking—

"*Chef?*"

Thor's hand was on his shoulder, shaking him, breaking up Frankie's stare. Probably a good thing, because after Latham splashed down it would be two of them against five. And Thor was still technically on the other side; after the look he'd given Frankie on the deck, when he had seen creature in the water, Frankie had to wonder what was going through that big old Scandinavian brain.

"What, Thor?"

"You want me to move the . . . materials?"

Frankie thought about it. "Keep him down here, for now. Go upstairs and secure a couple rooms, one big enough for the game, another one for the rest of our guys. Bring the cards up, the chips. Grab a few bottles and glasses, we don't need the bartender anymore. Where's the girl?"

"Girl?"

"Destiny. She ever come back down here?"

"I was with you, *chef.*"

"Yeah, that's right." He turned to the bartender. "You seen her?"

Remy shook his head. "She went up to find you, boss. You sure she didn't fall over, the ship bouncing around like that?"

"Fall over?" Frankie said. "No, I'm pretty sure she can stick when she wants to. You see her, tell her to find me."

He walked past Latham, past the little bar, and down to Prower's room. His bodyguards were standing at the door, still at attention with water halfway up their shins. Good men, Frankie thought. I could use a couple more, maybe just Hornaday.

Frankie glanced at him, the impassive face starting to show a bit of stubble. "You doing okay?"

"He wants to see you," Hornaday said. "Later, I want to see you. Talk about your idea, sending my men over the side of the boat."

"You can talk now," Thor said. "You got something you need to say."

"Later," Hornaday promised, opening the door. "Go on in."

Prower was sitting in his office chair, his feet up on the bed. The room smelled of seawater and diesel.

"Mr. Rollins," Prower said. "I'm glad you—"

"Yeah," Frankie said. "Pleased as punch myself. Listen, looks like we're going to have to play this one out. You got your chopper dialed in?"

"Of course," Prower said, holding up a canary yellow satellite phone. "He's on speed dial, could be here in twenty minutes."

"What's his name?"

"Malvick Dierkes. Why?"

"I haven't heard of him. He reliable?"

"For what I had to pay for him," Prower said, shaking his head. "Yeah, he's reliable."

"Just make sure he's ready to go. This ship is going to sink, and when it goes down the last place either you or me want to be is in the water in one of those little lifeboats. There's something in the water, I don't know what the hell it is, but it thinks we're dinner."

"The thing that's been hitting the ship," Prower said. "The, ah, creature."

"You don't believe me, go take a swim," Frankie said. "The, ah, creature, is out there, sticking by us like one of those sharks on Discovery Channel follows a whale, takes bites out of it now and then? And we just gave it another three meals."

"What kind of meals?"

"The bodyguard kind," Frankie said. "Your numbers are going down a lot faster than Latham's. You lost three men to that thing, and Latham is still full strength. You're pretty good at cards, so you understand the odds, right?"

"You don't think he would—"

Frankie raised his eyebrows. "We have to play this game out for the next sixty minutes. Then we're getting the hell out of here—you, me, and Malvick."

"Latham can't win in an hour. He probably can't win if he had eight hours."

"No," Frankie said. "Not if he plays by the rules."

He held Prower's gaze for a moment and then turned to go. The water seemed deeper than it was just minutes ago, and he was starting to feel a bit claustrophobic, the ceiling starting to shrink on them.

Prower called out before he could open the door. "The Mexican. Is he still . . . ?"

"Yes," Frankie said. "Until the very last."

"Ah." Frankie turned, reevaluated Prower. His skin was mottled, his collar riding high over the ample double chin resting on the base of his neck. His cane was across his knees and Prower rolled it back and forth along his thighs, running it along his palms, then reversing course. A cane, Frankie thought. Mr. Hamilton Prower the old-fashioned gentleman, all he needs is a cigar and a fedora, replace the Yankee drawl with a dago accent, and he'd fit right in with the Coriolos.

"What's his name?" Prower asked.

"It don't matter."

"I asked, didn't I?"

"And I said it don't matter."

Prower looked up sharply, the cane coming around to point at him. "Really, that tone? You think those funds can't come out of your account? Think I can't find that little bit of cash you stored away? Come on, Frankie. I ask a question, you answer me, nice and polite."

Yeah, he could be a Coriolos, Frankie thought. One of those old-timer mafioso types, he talked so nice and smooth, you barely felt the knife going in.

"His name is Cesar," Frankie said.

Cesar Hierra, a minor player in a major cartel, a man of great ambition and modest talent. Like Frankie, he had been caught wetting his beak. Unlike Frankie, his punishment extended beyond a beating and some finger snipping.

But his boss, Alejandros Cappero, was a businessman, and through certain circles he knew Frankie Rollins
was a man who might pay for a carcass before it cooled.
Frankie paid for the blood typing, the tissue typing, all of
it out of pocket. When it came back as a match, he
knew his payday had come in. He made an offer, a high
one, one that would be hard to refuse.

Cappero balked, Cappero contemplated, he talked
about the dignity of human life, of his brother who had
fallen from grace, and finally he spoke of another bid-
der. A bid the Sonoran had scoffed at but, at the same
time, an offer he said he must give consideration to. A
family offer, yes, but the amount not insignificant in
that region. A place where a man's life was often less
than that of a dirt bike, of a Toyota truck with rusted
quarter panels. Of a horse or dog who might place in
one race out of twenty.

You must understand, Cappero said. I am a local
man, with local reputations.

So Frankie had tacked that price onto that of his
original offer, plus a small premium. Cappero accepted.

"Frankie?" Prower asked.

"He was supposed to die a month ago," Frankie
said. "The way these guys do it when you cross them,
they put you in a cage. Let their dogs pull you apart,
piece by piece. Then they leave you in there until the
dogs are full, or the stink gets too bad."

Prower's face was very still.

"Cesar used to do the work himself," Frankie said.
"It was his job for five years, he musta liked it."

Prower pursed his lips. "You think it's in his blood?
The ability to do something like that?"

"I think it's the result of living in a fucked-up place," Frankie said. "Listen, I gotta walk a pretty fine line to turn this out right. You want to reconsider, tell me now." He paused. "Please."

"It might not be that fine of a line," Prower said. "The men I have left are good, twice as good as Latham's. Hornaday is ex-CIA, you know. The very best."

Frankie rubbed at the corner of his mouth, feeling the stubble growing. "Just make sure old Malvick is ready to fly."

Frankie had to laugh. The new room fit his clients perfectly, but he wished they could have kept the furniture, made the men scrunch up on the tiny chairs, knees drawn up, the row of cribs along the far wall a perfect backdrop. Maybe he coulda stood up front, lectured them on fairness and kindness and respect before they started playing.

"It is okay?" Thor asked.

He had set up a folding table in the day care, two chairs on either side, a deck of cards in the middle, a bottle of scotch on the changing table next to it. In the hallway a few of the remaining passengers were talking in urgent tones, lugging suitcases toward the stairwells to B-deck.

"You didn't have to kick any kids out of here, did you?" Frankie asked.

"No," Thor said. "Was already closed."

"Okay," Frankie said. "Get Latham up first, humor any bullshit requests he has, within reason. Then get

Prower in here and start the game. You see an opportunity, you know, where he's distracted? Shove that cane up his ass."

"*Chef?*"

Frankie sighed. "Just start the game, Thor."

"And the other?"

"I'll take care of that," Frankie said. Cesar was used to his little room, his habitat. He could stay down there for a while. The original plan was to transport him to the chopper, after the game was over. It would look like a med-evac for any passengers who happened to be watching, or wondering why a helicopter had landed on the ship. Maybe that was still the best way, or maybe they would just let him go down with the *Nokomis* in six hundred feet of water, let the crabs do their magic.

Frankie shouldered his way down the hall, getting wedged in the masses moving toward the stairwell. They didn't want to let him through; everybody was jammed into the hallway, nobody wanting to give an inch. Hell, Frankie thought, it's not even wet on this level yet.

The ship lurched under them, the passengers yelling and jostling as they surged forward, Frankie caught in their wake. He dropped his arms and threw a couple medium-hard elbows, catching a young punk in the ribs and a chubby woman with long dark hair in the upper arm. She squawked, turning to glare at him, but it gave him enough space to slide forward and duck into the stairwell.

He got out on B-deck with a surge of passengers. The gaming floor was filling fast, the card tables stacked with suitcases and duffel bags. Everybody was on their phones, trying to place calls and texts, but nobody seemed to be getting through.

Oh, it was going to be a big old shit sandwich, no doubt about it, and Moore was gonna have his mouth full. He turned and went back to the stairwell. One of Latham's men, a fierce-looking man with a scar running diagonally across his forehead, was stationed in front of the stairs.

"Anybody get past?"

"Past?" Scar asked. "Me?"

"Okay, good man."

Wright was in the wheelhouse, jabbing a finger at Graves as he spoke. Vanders had a pair of earphones clamped on his head, and as data came onto the screen, he scribbled furiously on scratch paper. He was trying to make eye contact with Moore, who was slumped behind the wheel. The old man from the fishing boat, Wells, was being escorted into Moore's cabin by Kharkov. He was sputtering a protest.

Welcome to the loony bin, Frankie thought. *I fit right in.*

"What's going on?"

Moore looked up, his eyes rimmed with dark purple circles Frankie hadn't noticed before. His face had gone slack, and the liver spots seemed to have darkened on his hands. "He wanted me to send out a Mayday. Said we needed to warn the rescue ships."

"And you said?"

"I told him to take a rest," Moore said. "I think we all need one."

"You do look tired."

"There was an emergency call made to the Coast Guard," Moore said.

"You been downstairs lately?" Frankie said. "Half the damn passengers are calling in to the mainland, someone musta got through. You should go down there, tell 'em they're gonna be fine." He paused, studied Moore's pallid face. "On second thought, send one of your crew members instead. Vanders, maybe."

"The call," Moore said. "You know what it means?"

"I don't think a civilian call means much of anything," he said. "Pull yourself together, Donny. You already made a distress call, the authorities know about it, and as long as it isn't a pure-D emergency . . . they gotta be used to people getting panicky, making their own calls. Right?"

"It was more than that," Moore said. "Somebody radioed in that we were under attack by an underwater vessel. They said the crew was compromised. That the captain and his crew might even be complicit in the attacks. They called in from a marine radio, not a cell phone."

Frankie cocked his head. "Complicit?"

"That was the word he used."

"Hawkins?"

"Who else?"

Frankie closed his eyes. "He say anything about the thing out in the ocean?"

"He said it was an underwater vessel. You know, like a submarine?"

Frankie ran a hand through his hair. Until now, as far as the rest of the world was concerned, they were just a casino ship experiencing mechanical problems on the open seas. With the Coast Guard resources stretched thin from all the issues, they had received only a moderate amount of attention. A deliberate attack on an American ship from a sub, though . . . shit, that would trigger a massive response. Air support, too, he supposed, a total lockdown of the air and seas. There would be no chopper to rescue them, nowhere to flee.

"You're starting to understand," Moore said. "The light finally comes on. Amen."

"Jesus Christ," Frankie said. "How'd he commandeer your radio?"

"He didn't. He disabled our system, and used a portable radio to make the call."

"You still heard him, though?"

"Oh," Moore said. "We all did, didn't we folks?" None of the crew responded, but Moore nodded nonetheless. "Yes, our good friend Mr. Hawkins was perfectly loud and clear."

Frankie took a deep breath, inhaling until he could feel his lungs stretching. There it was, that damned scratchy feeling, the one of being trapped inside his own devices, caught inside his own skin. Made him want to do something violent. Not chew off his own leg, no, not that. Chew off someone else's leg, maybe.

"What was the Coast Guard's response?"

Moore smiled slowly. "That's the question, isn't it? It's what the rest of the world does that matters."

"Snap out of it," Frankie said, clicking his fingers in front of Moore's eyes. "Are they sending that cutter? Choppers? What?" In his mind he could see them launching everything they had, scrambling aircraft, contacting submarines, a fleet of gunships headed their way. The loss of American life might get them interested, but an attack *on* Americans? Frankie wasn't a military man, but figured that would get the whole world moving against them. Goddamn Hawkins. It was a pretty nice move.

"What'd you say?" Frankie asked.

"I said, they're not sending *anything*," Moore repeated. "He broadcasted on an open channel, and *we* heard him just fine. The Coast Guard didn't respond, and the only reason for that is—"

"They didn't hear him," Frankie said, leaning over the top of Moore. "You could have told me that first."

Moore looked up. "Does it matter? He keeps hailing them every few minutes. The transmission is weak, but it's not that weak. Sooner or later the *Santa Maria* is going to hear him, and they are going to radio in his message to the Coast Guard."

"So call the fuckin' tug!" Frankie shouted. "Tell them you have a rogue man on board, that we just bumped up against a whale and this Hawkins guy is just wigging out. Jesus, man, do something!"

"Hawkins snipped our transmit line," Moore said. "The receive line runs on a separate cable on this ship, and he missed it. We can't radio out, just receive."

"You can't fix it?"

"I sent Wright up there to check. Hawkins snipped off a ten-foot piece of wire, probably threw it in the ocean. We don't carry spares for those types of things."

"Call in to the mainland, then," Frankie said. "You got a satellite phone."

"I considered that," Moore said, his words coming slow, deliberate. "But if we call in on the satellite phone, we're going to have to explain what happened to our radio wire. They'll know things are out of control. The end result . . ."

"Is somebody all up in our business," Frankie said softly. Moore had a point; as soon as they acknowledged they had a rogue man on board, someone who had commandeered the radio, any semblance of things being under control was gone. Piracy would get them plenty of attention, too.

"Does he know we heard him?"

"Probably not."

"You don't carry handhelds?"

Moore shrugged. "Not on a ship like this. Unless there's sabotage, the main radio is bulletproof."

"And how far off is the *Santa Maria*?"

"Ten kilometers," Moore replied. Then, speaking carefully, he added: "Most handheld marine radios have a range of less than five kilometers. In these seas, at the rate the *Santa Maria* is approaching, that gives you maybe a half hour."

Frankie started for the door. Thirty minutes. It would be tight but there was time. Finish the game, let Christie do his thing, then hop onto the chopper. From the Atlantic Ocean to Boston Harbor to Ohio to Mexico. In three days, this would be a good story, nothing more. This one time, I was out on the ocean, and this damn thing kept attacking us, busted a hole in the side of the ship, and then these other assholes show up. . . .

Well, he'd have to set it up better than that. He had never been real good at storytelling.

"What are you going to do?" Moore called out.

Frankie pushed through the door and kept walking, eyes already shifting to the shadows in the hallway.

The *Nokomis* was a big ship, and finding a rat was going to take all the resources he had. He would need pushers, and posters. Drive Hawkins out into the light. And then, well, shit. He had hadn't spent all those summers of his youth at the Summit County Landfill with a .22 rifle for nothing. Settling crosshairs between those itty bitty evil eyes and *pop*, one less menace in the world.

Frankie broke into a trot.

THE DARKNESS
BETWEEN THE WAVES

Chapter 21

The world had changed.

The predator circled, keeping the shadow of the prey on the inside, on the good side of its vision. The pain in its ruined eye had faded to a dull throb, and even its hunger had faded. It had not fed well, but it would not starve, and hunger was not the only sensation driving it now.

The world had given it new prey, one that fought back. One that could hurt the predator. The predator had drawn the smaller prey out into the sea, as planned, yet it had escaped, it had prevailed, this insignificant creature that had then dared to attack the predator again.

Yes, this prey was different. It would have to die in a different way altogether.

The predator finned slowly through the depths, the cold waters washing over it, bringing with it the scent of other creatures, fat prey that blew jets of air up through the water's surface when it breathed. To the north, up current, another old and familiar scent was woven into the water, getting stronger each passing hour. Normally, this approaching presence would trigger the predator, would cause it to be simultaneously excited and nervous.

The predator was only vaguely interested. It was committed to this prey, which did not understand that the only purpose it could have, the only worthwhile destiny, was to be consumed by the greatest of all creatures. For its proteins to be digested and reassembled into the body of the predator. Instead, it fought: It sent out streaking lights that burned and robbed the world of depth, it climbed on the predator and tried to bite back.

The predator would not allow the world to change that much.

Predators killed. Prey fled, and died, and became part of the predator.

So it had always been, and so it would be again.

Chapter 22

Taylor shot up straight out of bed, the blankets falling down to her lap. She had been dreaming she was on a rowboat, pulling on the oars as she headed toward a little island marked by a coconut tree and a pink bicycle, when the rowboat shuddered hard under her.

She looked across the room to her parents' bed and almost called out for them, then realized the tangle of blankets was just that—blankets, with nobody inside. She glanced toward the bathroom, a tiny room decorated with plastic seashells that smelled of Lysol. The door was open, the interior dim.

The ship rocked again, and she grabbed the headboard, stifling a shout. Or maybe a sob, she wasn't sure. The clock on the bed stand read 3:18, and the light trickling through the porthole meant it was afternoon, not the middle of the night. Other than that, she didn't know what was going on.

"Mom?"

She waited a moment, then swung her legs over the side of the bed. She was still dressed in the same clothes she'd worn the night before; dimly, she remembered

falling asleep to the sound of her mother and father arguing. They were trying to decide whose fault it had
been that she'd got lost—whose fault besides Taylor's,
that was—and she wanted to tell them to stop, that it
was all okay now. That they could blame everything
on her, she didn't care. After all, she was the one who
had disappeared, who had panicked when the ship had
been . . .

She rubbed her eyes. Had been what? Nobody had
told her, but whatever had happened wasn't normal.
When things were normal, her parents would talk about
what they were going to do, what their plans were for
the evening or the weekend, same boring old stuff.
When things weren't normal, like when there was bad
news on the television news, or the time somebody in
their neighborhood had been attacked, their parents
talked about what they *weren't* going to do.

Before she'd fallen asleep, she'd heard her mother's
words very clearly: *We are never, ever going on another cruise in my lifetime.*

Which was more than okay with Taylor. It would've
been nice, though, if her mom also would never ever
leave Taylor alone again. Yet here she was, the only company her rumpled blankets, and now the ship was . . .
tilted. And smelly, like the boatyard where her Uncle
Cameron kept his old Chris-Craft, the watery reek of
diesel and old seaweed. It was too quiet, too dark. She
tried the lamp, then the remote. Nothing.

She stood and walked to the door, twisted the lock,
and peered down the darkened hallway, still clutching
her blankets.

"Mom? Dad?"

The boat shuddered again and she banged into the

doorjamb. She looked back inside the room, rubbing her shoulder. She couldn't just sit there and wait. Not in the darkness, not without knowing if her parents were okay. The problem, though, was that they had taken the key cards with them. She would have to leave the room unlocked.

"Their fault," she said softly as she glanced around the room. "It's not like there's anything here to steal. . . ."

Even as she said it she realized it was true. Her mom's purse, her dad's wallet, even their phones were gone. That meant they had either gone to get something to eat, or they were gambling. Probably gambling. It was their way to blow off steam, they often said, and after the way her father had attacked that man, the way they were arguing . . . they were like a couple of teapots hissing and shaking on the stove.

One quick look into the gaming area, just enough to make sure they were okay, and she would come back to the room. They wouldn't even know she was gone.

She was halfway up the stairs to B-Deck when she heard the door open above her. For a moment she felt a strong desire to turn around, run straight back to her room, and wrap herself in the blankets.

Don't be silly. It might be Mom and Dad.

The thought was not entirely comforting. If it was her parents, they would be angry with her for leaving the room, perhaps even angrier than before. But they would also be *there* in front of her, where she could grab on to them the next time the ship shuddered.

The shadow of a man appeared above her on the dark stairwell. They regarded each other for a moment, their eyes adjusting to the gloom. He was the close-shaven man with the strange red eyes, except the upper ridge of his eye sockets were jutting out so all she could see were dark circles where his eyes should have been. He studied her back, lacing his fingers together and popping the joints slowly.

He took a step down. "You are lost?"

He took another step down, the dim light reflecting on his teeth in what she supposed was a smile. She wanted to turn around and run, but knew it would be silly.

"Little girls," he said, "shouldn't be alone."

She watched, unable to move, as he drew closer to her. She started to say something and he grabbed her arm above the elbow, his fingers digging into her skin. "Where are your parents?"

"I . . . I think they're gambling."

"No," he said, pulling her with him. "No one is gambling. Is no fun happening anywhere, this ship. Come."

She pulled back. "I don't want to go with you."

He nodded. "But you will come." He traced one finger down the side of her nose, ignoring her recoil. "Little girls should not be alone."

They went down to D-deck, the man named Kharkov pulling her close to his body, digging his knees into the back of her thighs when she slowed. The room was flooded up to her knees, and there was only one other person down here, a little rat-faced guy behind a bar stacking bottles into a duffel bag.

She tried to call out for help and barely got a sound out before Kharkov clamped his hand over her mouth.

The bartender looked up.

"Is a troublemaker," Kharkov said. "She goes into the holding cell."

"That little girl's trouble?" the bartender said. "She looks like a long-tailed cat in a room full of rocking chairs. Where're her folks?"

"You will be little girl," Kharkov said. "You say any more words."

The bartender raised a single eyebrow, then leveled a finger at them. "Kharkov, right? Bring her to me, Kharkov. She doesn't go anywhere until we talk to Frankie."

Kharkov paused, and she felt his breath blowing over the top of her hair, fetid, and suddenly she could taste the sweat on the palm clamped over her mouth. She thought of biting, knew it would taste worse on the inside, knew it would cause retaliation that would be even more painful. Then they were moving toward the bartender, the cold water pushing against her shins. Kharkov shoved her onto a stool and faced the other man, giving her a look that seemed to shrivel up her insides.

"What is your name?"

The bartender ran a hand through his hair. "Where were you bringing her?"

"I told you this already. What is your name?"

"Remy. Why? I don't care you wanna report me, asshole."

"No," Kharkov said, staring down at the water. "Is just I like to know the names, not just the number."

"What're you talking about—"

Kharkov leaped forward, encircling one hand behind Remy's head and smashing it down on the bar. Remy's forehead made a splat sound on the polished wood, his nose breaking with a sound like a popsicle stick bridge crunched underfoot. Kharkov wrapped his fingers through Remy's hair, pushed it back up. Taylor caught a brief glimpse of Remy's face, the nose pushed almost to the edge of his cheek, the left eyebrow split open to reveal the pink gleam of bone.

Then Kharkov slammed it down again.

And again.

By the fourth time, Taylor could tell there was no resistance left in Remy's neck muscles, no control anywhere, just the strumming of his shoe against the interior of the bar. Finally, Kharkov quit slamming Remy's head and just held it there, fingers twined through Remy's long hair, Kharkov's head cocked slightly to the side. After a moment he lifted the now-unrecognizable face up, popped his thumb out of his other hand, and jammed it into Remy's trachea, smashing it flat. Remy didn't resist. Remy didn't move.

Remy, she realized, was dead.

"Come," he said. "Or we do same thing with you."

He pulled her off the stool and started toward the back hallway. "What?

"Why?" she asked, her voice little more than a croak. "Why did you do that?"

He looked at her and then shook his head. "Little girls," he said, a new inflection in his voice, something she thought might be bemusement. Or, perhaps, some awful species of affection. "Little girls and their silly questions."

He dragged her down the hallway, flung open a door, and pushed her onto the bed. She scrambled to the far corner, pulling a pillow up and over her chest. He watched her with that bemused expression on his face, then sat down on the edge of the bed. He ran the edge of his thumbnail under his other fingernails one by one, inspecting the detritus before wiping it on the sheets.

"Ever since I was little, girls would do this," he said. "Act scared. Is silly game, I think, but one that is played often enough."

Taylor swallowed hard. "I want my parents. Right now."

"I don't mind games," Kharkov said. "There were no games when I was child except those I made myself. Is still this way. And a man must have . . . entertainment. Yes?"

"Mister, I don't want to play a game. I just want—"

He nodded slowly. "A man must have something to take his mind off thoughts about what was done, of games others played with him. Without that, life would be . . ."

He turned to her, suddenly and completely focused. "It would not be fun at all."

He moved forward, his presence seeming to fill the room, enveloping around her. She opened her mouth to scream, realizing that the only person on this entire level was likely poor dead Remy, that Kharkov was a full-grown man who did not care if she was hurt, much less upset. She would need to go for his eyes, but she was paralyzed with fear, filled with the terrible desire to do whatever he wanted, to not disappoint him. Because to disappoint a man such as Kharkov would mean her face would look just like Remy's.

He reached out a hand, then paused as a voice said his name. The static-filled voice crackled again, and his hand, inches from her, drifted down to the radio on his belt. He turned down the volume knob until the radio clicked off, lifted his hand, and then sighed. He flipped the radio back on.

"Yes?"

"Get your ass up here, Kharkov. We got a man to find."

"Five minutes, I will be there."

A slight pause. "I don't see your ugly mug at the roulette table in thirty seconds, Thor's throwing your ass in the ocean and keeping your money as a bonus."

The radio went silent. Kharkov stared at it for a moment, his head cocked to the side, and she waited to see if he would smash it against the wall. Instead, he carefully replaced it in his belt holster and gave her a conspiratorial wink. "A short break," he said. "You will wait for me, yes?"

He unbuckled his belt and slid it out of the loops, then slid it around her wrists. "Yes, you will wait for me."

Chapter 23

The way she saw it, there was really only one thing a smart woman would do. Get up, not too fast. Brush her hands along her hips, frown at the wetness on her clothes, the blood, and the seawater. Take in the tiny utility closet they had crammed themselves into, lit by dim twelve-volt lights. Look at Brian, say something like *I got to get out of these clothes*. Let it hang there until he nodded. Then she would walk off, get to her room, lock the door, and text Frankie.

Smart, easy, and not even *wrong*.

The not-so-smart thing to do would be to continue to crouch here, in this tiny little room with a guy she'd just met, a guy who was talking into the marine radio, trying to bring in the authorities. Which of course was the last thing her employer wanted, something he might kill both of them for. No, he was her former employer. Well, whatever. If Frankie found them, they were both going in the drink.

"You okay?" Brian said. "You look like you want to say something."

"I was thinking of turning you in to Frankie," she said.

"Not a bad idea," he said, nodding. "Get a little bonus."

"Why did you go in after him? Your friend's body? And don't say because he would of done it for you."

Brian shook his head. "Gilly wouldn't have gone in for my corpse. Maybe if there was a big fat wallet in my back pocket."

"So why?"

"Because," Brian said, "I don't like to lose things."

He had settled down, Destiny noticed, and he was pretty good at following through on his plans. Climbing up high on the ship, avoiding the eyes of the crew, clipping the antennae wires and tossing it into the ocean before scampering back down, grinning a little as he pulled her into the closet. Crazy . . . but practical. So that, maybe, was part of the reason she was still crouched here. Things were fraying at the edges, but maybe he could hold shit together, at least long enough for them to get off this ship.

"You think Wells made any progress?"

"With his swimming dinosaur theory?" Brian said. "Yeah, I bet they've got him on the lecture circuit."

"Nobody likes a smartass."

"Sorry."

She leaned closer to him. "Is that what it is?"

"I don't know," he said. "I've seen it twice, and all I know is it's not something I've ever seen before, or even heard about."

And that was the other part keeping her here, Destiny thought. This experience, as terrifying as it was, was also, well . . . *interesting*. Maybe the most interesting thing she'd been involved with for years, and Brian was real, very much a man who thought and moved, in that order.

Brian keyed the marine radio. He repeated the same message as before, the same exact words. Even the sound and speed of his voice was the same, and she realized he was being repetitive in case someone had only picked up part of the message before; this time they might be able to fill in the missing words. Practical, she thought. I doubt that's going to be enough to save him.

Brian clicked the radio back to receive mode. They waited, breathing quietly with their mouths open.

Brian glanced at his watch. "We'll try again in five minutes," he said. "No answer, I'm going to get higher up on the ship, get a line of sight to the horizon." He seemed about to say something else when the ship tipped hard to the side, sending her skidding into him. Below them, a long screech of stressed metal reverberated through the infrastructure.

"Feels like the boat's flexing," Destiny said. She'd seen reenactments of shipwrecks on television, the way they would tear in half once they took on enough water, the waves breaking the ships right in half. It was how the *Edmund Fitzgerald* had sunk, the ship in the Gordon Lightfoot song. Broke itself in half on a massive wave, sent her crew into the cold seas of Lake Superior, where they had died quickly of hypothermia. The water in that vast inland sea was not much colder than the Kaala was now.

"'That good ship and true was a bone to be chewed,'" she said under her breath. "'When the gales of November came early.'"

"Huh?"

"Old song. I think we're the bone to be chewed on this trip."

"Oh." The ship shook again. "Whatever's chewing on us," he said, "it's pissed."

She planted her palms on the floor, intending to move back to her original spot, when he touched her arm. "Listen, thanks for helping me. I'm going to have to try and get somewhere where the signal can travel farther. You want to stay here, that's fine, but if I were you I'd just go back to work. That way, whatever happens, you'll be okay."

"As long as we don't end up in that thing's gullet."

"You know what I mean."

"I do," she said, coming to a decision. "But you have a better chance with my help."

"Don't be silly—"

From down the hallway they heard the opening and closing of a door. Then another door opened, a voice called out something, and the door shut. Someone was searching the hallway, opening the other rooms. Brian reached up and grasped the doorknob, looking around the utility room. "Look for a weapon. Anything."

"Brian," Destiny whispered. "They'll have guns."

He pointed behind her. "Unscrew that broom handle, quick."

She started to object, saw the look in his eyes, and quickly twisted the wooden handle off the push broom in the corner. He released the door handle and took the broomstick in both hands, holding it like a jouster's

lance. It wasn't much of a weapon, not for a close space
like this. He'd have to jab, to poke instead of swing.
Maybe they'd be unaware, wouldn't be paying attention, and it would be like in the movies, where the
good guy . . .

She paused, wondering when she began thinking of
Brian as the good guy. Maybe he wasn't. But he was op-
posed to Frankie, and while Frankie was lots of things, a
good guy was not at the top of the list.

"Brian?" Destiny said. "They have guns. You have
a goddamn *stick*."

He turned to her. "Go," he said. "Quick. Go out there,
tell them you were hiding. Try to lead them away."

She stood, thinking, *Okay, it might work*, then paused
with her hand on the door handle. It wouldn't work.
Frankie and his men were too methodical, too smart to
just follow her blindly away from their search area.
They had no idea what she'd been up to. They'd look,
and although it would be a surprise for them to see
her in the company of Brian, a guy she had no alle-
giances to. . . .

Yeah, it would be a surprise. For all they knew, he'd
taken her hostage.

"What are you doing?"

She moved in front of Brian, pressing her back
against his chest, and wrapped one of his arms around
her waist. She took other hand, the one still holding
the broomstick, and positioned it so the wooden dowel
was pressed across her throat. "I'm going to scream," she
said. "I'm your hostage, understand? When I break free,
you get your distraction."

She touched his arm, felt the corded muscles, pressed lightly but firmly. "I know what I'm doing."

"You sure?" he breathed into her ear.

"I'm loud," she said. "Be forewarned."

She began to scream for help.

They pushed out into the hallway, the broom handle banging against the side of the door, Destiny screaming. He was happy to get out of the closet, because she was right about being loud; she had a clear, alto scream that sounded like an opera singer's. It wasn't an unpleasant sound, but the sheer volume was like knitting needles in his eardrums.

They crashed out into the hallway, squirming, Brian struggling to hold her tight. She was muscular, her upper body twisting, leveraging her butt and hips against his waist. For a moment he wondered if it was a ruse, if she was really trying to free herself, and then one of her elbows smashed into his ribs and his grip loosened, not much, but enough for her to squirm away if she wanted. Instead, she elbowed him again, a deliberately glancing blow, giving him time to recover. He squeezed tighter. It was like holding on to bag full of pythons, all those muscles twisting and constricting.

It wasn't a bad feeling, he thought as they twisted around. Wrong time for it but hell's bells. How did that old Waylon Jennings song go? "The only two things in life that make it worth living, a guitar in tune and a good, firm-feeling woman"?

Good firm-feeling woman. Be better if she wasn't trying to knock the wind out of him and screaming at him to let go. But better than any of the women he'd picked up at the Riff-Raff.

All of this flashing through his mind in the seconds it took for them to clear the doorway.

He spun around, trying to focus on the people in the hallway through the spray of Destiny's hair. They were only ten feet away.

Destiny sagged in his arms.

A man and a woman, middle-aged, stood watching them with open mouths. The woman's eyes were red rimmed and the man's bearded face was pinched, somewhere between angry and bewildered.

"Not what you think," Destiny said, shrugging Brian's arms off her. "Seriously," she said. "We were, uhh, play-acting." The couple was still staring at them, incredulous, the man cocking his head to the side. Destiny turned and pressed herself against Brian, then kissed him on the mouth and put an arm around his waist. "I have a thing about, uh, bondage," she said. "We both do."

The woman's mouth was open. She blinked twice. "You scared us."

"Sorry," Destiny said, pinching Brian's back.

"Yeah," Brian said. "Sorry. I'm, uh, embarrassed."

"You haven't seen a little girl, have you?" the man asked. "Nine years old, blond? Her name is Taylor."

"Oh, God," Destiny said. "Not the same one that went missing earlier?"

"It wasn't our fault," the woman said. "We got in an argument, she was acting snotty and, well, we thought the argument was over. When we got back to the room, she was gone."

"When you got back?" Destiny asked.

The woman's face constricted. "What are you, a

waitress? Screwing off on the job with your little friend? Nobody doing their job. No wonder our little girl is . . . is . . ." She started to sob and when her husband didn't react Destiny went to her, fighting off the woman's hands and holding her, looking back at Brian once with a look that said, *What can you do?* Destiny led her down the hallway, talking softly, asking where they had looked.

Brian motioned for the man to walk with him.

"Playacting, huh?"

He could hear other men talking on the deck above them; they must have heard Destiny scream. The whole ship might have. "Yeah," Brian said. "What's your daughter's name again?"

"Taylor."

"And how long has she been gone?"

The man shook his head. "I don't know, maybe an hour. We haven't told anyone." He paused, and jabbed a finger at his wife's back. "*She* wouldn't let me, not after what happened earlier. We feel terrible. I know Taylor's safe, she has to be, but Ashley's upset."

"Where have you looked?"

"This was the last of C-level. We already checked B-level, the gaming area. There's an arcade on one end, we thought she might be there."

"She likes video games."

He shrugged. "That's the kind of place she might go, right? The kinda place kids would hang out. She's been such a little shit this trip. Typical woman, right?" He looked to Brian for a reaction, got nothing, and sighed. "We stepped out for a minute, just to get our breath."

Brian stole a glance at the guy's face. Yeah, the guy was the real deal, calling his missing girl a little shit, a typical little woman. All of this in a bored tone. The ship was sinking, a creature was circling them and attacking anything that ventured close to a railing, and this asshole figured it was just a typical little woman thing. He felt his blood begin to heat and pushed it aside. There was no time for it.

"We'll look below," Brian said. "Okay? We'll meet you back here, this exact spot, in twenty minutes. You go up to the top, talk to the captain. Have them put out an alert."

The man swallowed. "It's just that, with what already happened—"

"That's the least of your worries," Brian said. He stepped closer, close enough to smell liquor on the man's breath, to see the way his short beard was turning gray. "There's a chance we're going to have to evacuate this ship. It's taking on water, and there's something down there waiting for us to go into the water. You want your little girl to face that alone?"

"There's some talk about launching a couple lifeboats. Get away from the ship, head toward shore, get some help."

"Yeah?"

"Listen, I think it's a good idea. Send some help back for the entire ship. You find Taylor, maybe you and your girlfriend could hang on to her. That way Ashley and I could go for help, but she wouldn't have to be out there on the ocean."

"You're kidding, right? Your daughter—"

"She's adopted," the man said. "Doesn't mean I don't

love her like my own, you understand? We had her since she was little, and the whole time she's been full of sass, always—"

"Go talk to the captain, damn it." He raised his voice enough for Destiny to hear. "We'll meet you back here in twenty minutes, no later. Get the captain to put out an alert."

The woman looked back, wiping at her face. "Marcus?"

"It's fine, Ashley. He's right, we need some help." He wrinkled his nose. "And no more cruises, ever again."

They left, moving staidly down the hallway, the woman fumbling in her purse. They watched, expecting her to pull out a phone, and instead watched as she opened a compact mirror to check her makeup. Destiny looked at Brian, her color high. "Jesus, they're parents?"

"I know."

"We're going to help, aren't we? They don't know about D-deck, and maybe she snuck down there." Her eyes were very intent. "You are going to help, aren't you?"

"Yes," Brian said, looking above him as footsteps thudded across the deck above them. "I think we better find a place to hide while we're at it."

They heard the men inside the day care as they went past, Prower's voice booming about something with his cards. There was no guard outside the door and they went past silently, padding down the hallway to the corner room. The lights had begun to flicker, and the air felt stagnant and damp. The HVAC system wasn't working, and Brian supposed it had either shorted out or they were trying to conserve as much power as possible.

Destiny led him to C-85 and pressed her ear against the door. She had only listened for a moment when they heard the day-care door open behind them. Brian twisted the knob and they slid inside the room, which was deserted.

"Now what?" Brian whispered.

She pointed to the back door. "That's the batcave entrance," she said. "It sounds like they moved up here, but we need to be careful."

Destiny pressed her ear to the flimsy hollow-core door, her hand splayed out for silence. "Okay," she said after minute. "I thought I heard a voice. Must have been from someplace else on the ship."

He allowed her to drag him into the stairwell. The *Nokomis* felt different, sluggish in the big rollers, and the way it was tipping suggested a new hole must have been opened in its hull. The bilges had been losing the battle inch by inch before; now he suspected the battle was turning into a rout, the water pouring into the hold. The room below was dark, and he could hear water sloshing back and forth as the ship rolled with the waves.

"Is that someone walking?" he asked. His voice was magnified in the hallway and Destiny winced at the noise.

"Shhh. It's probably just the water slopping back and forth."

"This is like going into the lion's den," he whispered.

"They're gone," she said. "Come on."

They descended the stairs. The water was up to their

waists by the time they reached the bottom, and the room was littered with playing cards and liquor bottles. Several wooden chairs bobbed in the water, which was covered with a rainbow-colored sheen. The air smelled like low tide in summer, a rank and oily odor that wasn't the sea; it was the smell of flooded toilets, of men who had been cramped in a small space for too long, the sour reek of tension and fear. The only light was from the exit signs, which cast a baleful red light over the water.

"Who's that?" he said, pointing toward the bar.

Destiny followed his gaze and sucked in her breath, then let go of his arm and waded toward the bar. The body was facedown, the shoulders hunched out of the water, dressed in a white shirt, stained pink around the collar.

"No," she whispered. "Oh, Remy, no."

She could only turn him over halfway. Brian knelt beside her, feeling the coldness of the flesh as he sought purchase in the bartender's clothes, the unmoving limpness of the body already starting to harden. It was the coldness that unnerved him; he had never realized how quickly the human body lost its warmth.

"On three," he said.

Remy's face was a pulpy mess when they flipped him over, the lips split and his two front teeth broken off at angles. His left eye was blood filled, the pupil milky, and a thin serum of watery blood oozed from a laceration that split his eyebrow in half lengthwise. His throat looked strangely concave.

"Jesus," Brian said. "Was he one of Frankie's guys?"

She looked at him, her eyes wide. "He was like me," she said. "Hired help."

"Not a bodyguard."

"For who, a fucking Pomeranian? He was just a bartender."

He pulled her to her feet. "Whatever this was about," he said, gesturing around the room, "it's gone sour. I don't know what's worse, the thing in the water—the kronosaur—or Frankie's guys, but I don't think either group would think twice about slitting our throats."

"You're wrong," a thick voice said from behind them. He whirled around to face Kharkov, standing between them and the back doorway. He was pointing a pistol at them, his thin lips revealing a wedge of small, even teeth. "I have been thinking about it a lot."

"Easy," Frankie said from behind them, stepping out of the stairwell. He was flanked by Thor and Hornaday, the latter with his own pistol drawn. Frankie slid his radio back into his belt holster and gave Destiny a reproachful look. "You coming back to work?"

Brian cast his eyes from Frankie to Kharkov, then back to Frankie.

"You got a gun?" Frankie said.

"I'm not a gunfighter," Brian said. "I catch fish for a living."

"Yeah, and now you're gonna feed them, you don't watch yourself." His eyes flickered to Kharkov. "He screws around, shoot him in the belly." Frankie holstered his pistol. "What're you doing down here, Destiny?"

Before she could answer, Kharkov stepped forward, then nudged Remy's corpse with the toe of his boot. "They were murdering this poor little man," Kharkov said.

Chapter 24

It was one of those situations, things had gone bad for so long Frankie supposed he was due for a stroke of luck. First the weather, then the . . . .well, the fucking creature . . . and then Brian Hawkins jumping onto the boat, off the boat, then back on, morphing from a rescuee into a saboteur. Latham playing cards like an old drunk bully, so used to things going this own way that he allowed a bad hand to turn into a bad game. But that run of bad luck finally turned when Kharkov, already on his way to meet them in the manhunt, had seen the very people they wanted coming down the stairwell. He had radioed Frankie, and they had caught the two neatly between them. Now they had Hawkins in custody, which was good, and they had the girl, which was, well, not as easy to define.

Frankie sat in Moore's cabin, scratching his face and thinking.

She didn't seem to be real happy with the situation, either. Nice little jab on her, too, her fist raising a mouse on Hornaday's cheek when they took them into custody. Hawkins hadn't resisted, he knew the game was up. Had simply looked at Frankie, his eyes framed by those thick black eyebrows, a cold fire there that Frankie knew wasn't going out anytime soon. The decision on Hawkins wasn't easy, but it wasn't that hard, either. You didn't want a guy like that around, burning holes in things with his eyes.

Hawkins had to go, but they couldn't just drop him over the side. The time had come to be sure, and Christie had everything they needed for that in his little hypodermic case. All Frankie had to do was pay the fee.

Frankie pretended to think about it. Putting out Hawkins's fire for the price of a cheap imported car? Shit. That was a bargain, pure and simple.

The girl, though, Frankie could almost explain her actions. Could feel where she was coming from, how she had ended up where she was. Caught up in the current, unable to swim against it, and now it had turned into a riptide. Frankie had done the same thing once, had ended up in the desert with the stumps of his fingers shooting jets of blood into the sand.

Funny the way things turned out. Not just for her, but for him as well, sitting here, considering fates. For the first time in a long time with some degree of, what was it called? Latitude, that was it. Like the lines on a globe, the ones that showed you where you were, where you might wanna go.

He knew what Christie's advice would be regarding the girl. And it would be good advice, the kind that both Latham and Prower would expect he follow. A couple quick injections, one for Hawkins and one for her, then over the side, let the sea wash away their troubles. Or let the bigmouthed critter circling them take care of it.

Frankie had paid Christie already, digging out the bills from the duffel bag now stashed in Moore's desk drawer. The captain was in the first mate's room along with Wells, the two of them locked up for their own good. Now Frankie went over to the desk and opened the bag, running his fingers across the packets of bills. Plenty of money here, even after he had paid Christie for the needles.

Twenty grand per needle. Forty grand for both, and Frankie wasn't sure he wanted to pay that kind of money to get rid of Destiny Boudreaux. Some of that was affection; some portion, he had to admit, was his reluctance to pay for something he saw no benefit in. But he couldn't just let her go, either.

And that gave Frankie an idea.

He stood, a few hairs he had rubbed off his scalp drifting down onto his pants. Thor was standing a few paces from the doorway, keeping guard like the good soldier he was. He turned when he heard Frankie, his expression calm, but there was a tightness to his features now, an edginess to his eyes.

"Yes, *chef*?"

"Bring the girl up here," he said. "Untie her first, case anybody sees you. Hawkins gives you any trouble, tap him on the head."

Frankie watched in admiration as Thor left without another word. He moved quietly for a big man, listened to instructions, and then, more important, followed through. Probably the only man Frankie had met that he could remotely imagine having for a partner. He was going to have to get rid of the big Swede, of course, but he didn't like that idea, either. It would be like putting down a faithful Labrador.

He sighed. That was the thing about caring about people; it was like a contagion. Pretty soon you were caring about people who weren't your immediate family, people who didn't even technically work for you, and the symptoms were painful. Short-term side effects included getting screwed over, usually by the people you cared about, the assholes not reciprocating your feelings. Keep going down that path, keep caring, and eventually you ended up with things like wars, trying to save whole nations of people from being miserable.

He knew better, damn it. There were only a few people you allowed in, and those people were ideally both *a*, ignorant of what you did, and *b*, located somewhere far, far away from where you did your business. Like Ohio, for instance, in a little trailer park outside Akron. A dusty place where the air smelled of burn barrel smoke on Saturday evenings, a cement pad where mobile homes mass-produced in the 1970s sat slumped and peeling. Inside, dim interiors with blocky nineteen-inch televisions streaming out local talk shows and soaps, the air inside smelling of cat food and moldy insulation.

You could get people out of those places, even if they had set down roots. But only if you were smart, if you limited the rest of your caring to the bare minimum.

Thor arrived a few minutes later, pulling Destiny with him. He had one hand on the back of her neck— typical Thor-hold—his other hand hanging at his side, red and swollen.

"Trouble?"

Thor pushed Destiny into the captain's cabin.

"Hawkins tried to stand up, I tell him sit. Hard head, that one."

"Lotsa hard heads on this ship," Frankie said, turning to Destiny. "You gonna behave?"

She stared at Frankie and he motioned Thor away and closed the door. Okay, go ahead and be a shit, he thought; it would make his decision easier. It was uncharted territory for him anyway, and he could feel the sweat starting on his forehead, under his arms. The same discomfort he always struggled with, whether it was jokes or jobs or the few relationships that didn't include a toll-free number and a tip for good service at the end of the night: How to get started?

"You want to die?" he asked.

She studied his face, hers still defiant, but after a minute she must have seen something in his eyes or the set of his mouth, and realized the question wasn't rhetorical.

"No."

"I thought so," he said. "Others have. Died."

"From that thing in the water, right?"

He held up a hand. "Let's go easy. Listen, you know there's something a little . . . heavy . . . going on, don't you? We got people getting killed left and right, and the ship ain't in the best of shape."

She nodded. "We didn't kill Remy."

"Don't worry about that," he said. "I'm not. At the same time, there is absolutely no way I can just let you go on your way, you see? You've seen . . . things. And don't even start with the 'I'll never say a word' thing. Even if I believed you, and I don't, my business partners wouldn't."

She breathed slowly, her eyes never leaving his face.

"We have a situation on board," Frankie said. "And we also got a planned set of actions, which still gotta occur. You might be able to help me out. If you can, I might be able to help you out."

She looked away, toward the windows, and Frankie studied the lines on her face. She couldn't be much more than thirty, but there was something about the way she talked, or didn't talk when a younger woman might have, that made him wonder if she wasn't older. Then there was that little streak of green hair. Most of the girls he knew, they had color in their hair it meant there was a piercing in some sensitive area, maybe a few tattoos. Trying to create an aura of what, independence? Jesus. With Destiny, though, it was different.

Fuck, he thought. *I'm not thinking about her the right way at all.*

"Destiny?"

She turned back to him, her voice calm. "Yes, Frankie?"

"What do you want? I mean, outta life? It's a weird question, I know. But it matters."

She pushed a lock of hair out of her face and leaned forward. "One, I don't ever want to be on a boat again," she said. "Or stuck in a casino, or even in a restaurant where I have to put a little number sign up on my table so they know where to bring my food. Two, I want to be outside, make my own food, or have someone make it that cares about it. Three, I want to work my muscles, get dirty, and then take a long bath at the end of the day. Four, look at beautiful paintings and pictures and places and drink cold white wine on a warm spring night."

He nodded. "That sounds pretty good," he said. "You been waiting for someone to ask, I can tell. Anything else?" He was thinking about her in a clawfoot tub now, bathroom windows open with the curtains blowing with a nice spring breeze.

"I want to deal with my own trouble, not everyone else's."

"Yeah," he said. "That's kinda where my own mind is. I got a proposition for you. I think it matches up okay with what you're thinking. But it ain't gonna be a free ride, Destiny. Not even close."

She looked at him again, eyebrows arching a bit. He could almost see what she was thinking, Frankie wants to get laid . . . no, wait, that doesn't solve anything.

And that was the funny part, because what he wanted was, well, to help her. And to do it, he was going to have to ruin her.

"Listen close," he said. "I'm going to be perfectly honest about what you need to do, and you better give me a perfectly honest answer whether you're gonna do it. Got it?"

She nodded, concentrating now.

"Good. I'm going start with a guy, a real piece of shit, who's on this boat right now. A guy named Cesar Hierra, who used to train dogs to eat human flesh."

Twenty minutes later he was on his way back to the wheelhouse, thinking that of all the promises he'd ever heard, the ones that were kept and the ones that weren't, hers had been the most convincing.

She got it, he could tell by the way her expression changed about halfway through. Right about the time he brought Latham and Prower into the picture, what they wanted, it was like she saw how the last few pieces of a jigsaw puzzle fit together. She started weighing it in her mind, long before he came down to brass tacks, so he gave her some time, rambling on about his own reasons, his mother and sister back in Ohio struggling with a tiny Social Security payment and some welfare. Both of them sick, his sister with a degenerative arthritis the doctors thought had been caused by a tick bite years earlier. How he was going to help them, how he wasn't in this just so he could be another rich asshole.

Framing himself as an example, how even a good person needed to get their hands dirty sometimes.

"So what do you say?" he'd asked. "You game?"

A single tear rolled down her cheek, and she nodded, causing it to fall off her cheek and land on her knee. And that tear was good, that was fine; it hurt him a little, drawing it out of her, but it was better than the alternative, shooting her full of whatever colorless poison Collins had in his bag and turning that lovely little body into chum.

It was sort of a lovely little mind, too, he thought as he went into the wheelhouse. Or at least it had been.

He shook Moore's shoulder. "Wake up, Captain. You need to make some decisions."

Moore roused himself. He was falling apart, Frankie knew, and that was a good thing in a way. A strong captain would have done all sorts of things that would have compromised this fucked-up cruise, would have sent different directives and communications, would have planned for not only emergencies but also . . . shit. Another word he loved, could never remember. Contingencies, that was it. He loved the sound of it; it was what he had planning for his whole life, without ever remembering the word.

"Been a long night?"

Moore rubbed his eyes, twisted around to see who was talking, then glanced at his watch.

"What's the situation with the ship?" Frankie asked. "If you don't know, point me to the person who does."

"I was just resting my eyes."

Frankie spotted Graves at the console and walked away from Moore. "How we doing, Captain?"

Graves looked up, the dark smudges under his eyes the only signs of trouble. "We're taking on water in a serious way," he said. "The tug isn't going to have the juice to pull us in."

"Then how are you going to get back to shore?"

"How are we getting back to shore?"

"That's what I said."

Graves glanced over to Moore, who appeared to be listening to them. "His call, technically. But I think we're going to need to transfer everyone to a transport vehicle. If we can get a cutter out here, we'd be fine."

"Sounds reasonable."

"We can't radio them with the cable cut."

"So what happens now?"

"I think we offload the kids onto the tug," Graves said. "Pack in as many people as we can. We'll have the tug call for a cutter, and get the rest of them off when it shows up."

"And the *Nokomis*?"

Graves held his index finger out and made a descending see-sawing motion. "Down she goes."

Frankie closed his eyes and tilted his head back. Best thing, from a pure logistical standpoint, was to maintain radio silence. "I got a guy on board," he said, "who has a satellite phone we might be able to use. Think you could get in contact with a transport ship?"

"You're telling me this now?"

"You want it or not?"

"Christ, yes."

"I'll be back," Frankie said. Another complication, and Latham and Prower wouldn't like it. But he would fall asleep a lot easier at night, listening to the waves pounding the Mexican beach, if he wasn't carrying the weight of sending all these people to the bottom of the sea. Hell, he could end up looking like Moore, nodding off in his recliner and missing all those pretty sunsets.

Chapter 25

Brian sat on the wooden chair, feeling his pulse beating against the top of his skull where Thor had struck him. The big bastard had one coming back to him. Forget the fists; he was going to pick up a chair, maybe the one he was tied to, and smash the backrest right across that wide face, feel the wood and teeth splinter.

Good idea, but it probably wasn't in the cards. The two zip ties around his wrists and ankles meant he wasn't going anywhere, except over the side of the ship. A couple strips of plastic, a few bad decisions, and here he was. Four decades, give or take. The first couple of decades floating by in a blur of sunshine and wide-open, bursting life; the third and beginning of the fourth decades where it began to take on a sweetness, a ripeness, Sienna and then Mason. Fourth decade just started and now almost over.

He didn't want to go out like this, and he guessed the Mexican sitting across the room didn't, either. They had exchanged glances a couple of times, but so what? The Mexican was zip tied, same as Brian. There was only one guard in the room, a guy named Hornaday, but he was alert, staying back, good protocol.

The Mexican was rolling his wrists. He was doing it slowly, trying to hide his movements from the guard. Brian almost told the Mexican not to bother. He'd used these industrial-strength zip ties on his boat, and there was no way a man could escape them if they were tight, which they were. Sometimes if you left them out in the sun they would turn brittle, but their days of sunlight were over.

The ship lurched underneath him, and the infrastructure gave an almost human shriek. It lurched again, and he leaned against the momentum as the ship rocked to the side. The *Nokomis* started to come back to center, and then the creature hammered them again. They lurched hard to port, the alarm clock sliding off the little bedside table.

The Mexican was looking at him with raised eyebrows. Brian blinked three times. Why not?

They started to rock back to the center and the creature smashed into them again. The Mexican tumbled awkwardly to the floor, rolling down the carpet toward the guard, who was bracing himself against the door frame. The Mexican rolled in a tight ball toward the guard, a turn and half, traveling at a good clip toward Hornaday's ankles. Brian watched with interest, impressed with the move.

Hornaday saw him at the last second and sidestepped, letting the Mexican slam into the wall.

"Nice try, Cesar."

Brian hit the floor at angle, using his shoulders and elbows to start his own roll. He was taller than Cesar and his feet tangled in the other bunk before he could tuck into his own somersault. At the same time the ship began to level out, slowing his progress before it had barely begun He heard the Mexican grunt somewhere behind him, and a moment later felt a boot pin him to the floor.

"Stop this bullshit," Hornaday said, and then his words broke off in a high-pitched scream, and the boot on Brian's back was gone. Brian pushed himself over. Cesar's teeth were buried in Hornaday's other ankle, and he was shaking his head from side to side, ripping into the Achilles tendon. Hornaday swung his other boot back for a kick and Brian pushed himself forward. The boot meant for Cesar's face hit Brian high on the shoulder and Hornaday, suddenly unbalanced, went sprawling.

Brian fought through the snarl of arms and legs and struggled to a kneeling position. He brought his hands up over his head just as Hornaday looked up, and Brian's clenched fists caught him just above the hairline. The blow sent Hornaday back to the floor, where he screamed again; Cesar was pulling the stringy flesh away from his ankle, a scene straight from a zombie movie. Brian brought his clenched hands down again, getting his upper body into it this time, and hit Hornaday just above the corner of his left eyebrow.

Hornaday's scream trailed off, his glazed eyes rolling back in his head.

After a moment Cesar released Hornaday's ankle. For a moment the two men regarded each other warily, and then the Mexican's face broke open in a bloody grin.

"Taste like T-bone," he said in perfect English. "Rare."

"Jesus," Brian said. "Wipe your face off."

He went through Hornaday's pockets, forgetting about the pistol until he saw the Mexican pull it from under Hornaday's shoulder holster. Hornaday's pants pockets were empty, not even loose change. A pack of cigarettes inside his jacket pocket, a couple smokes rattling around inside. No knife, no clippers.

"We have to get out of these," Brian said, holding up his wrists. "The whole damn ship probably heard him scream."

Cesar held up the pistol. "I have this."

"They've got them, too," Brian said. "Come on, help me look."

He hopped to the far side of the room. It was sparsely furnished; no medicine kit in the bathroom, no nail clippers or razors, just a bed stand with a Gideon Bible and a small plastic-wrapped container of facial tissues inside the drawer. There wasn't even a sharp edge to rub the plastic against. No hard corners on cruise ships, Brian thought. That makes sense.

"Hey," Cesar said.

Brian turned, for some reason expecting the gun to be pointed at him. But Cesar was holding up Hornaday's cigarettes, a little book of matches tucked inside the cellophane.

"Damn right," Brian said, hopping back over to him.

Cesar was a few inches shorter than Brian, well-muscled, and his eyes were very intense. He peeled a match free, then twisted the book around to expose the scratch pad. "You hold the book," Cesar said. "I have the match."

It took several tries until the match popped into flame. Brian held out his wrists, palms bent backwards. The heat was sudden and intense, the whiff of sulfur over-whelmed by the stench of burning wrist hair. He struggled to keep his wrists steady, fighting every natural instinct in his body. His skin burned along with the plastic, crackling under the heat from the tiny flame. He groaned.

The ship lurched under them and the flame moved away for the briefest moment, then back to his skin. Fresh pain, still a surprise after its second-long absence. He mumbled something about taking a break.

"Almost there," Cesar said. "It doesn't look as bad as it feels."

Then his wrists were free. His first instinct was to punch Cesar and he took a breath instead, looking at his wrists, now covered in strands of scorched plastic caught in hair. Closer to the zip tie, his wrist hairs were burnt into brittle brown ghosts. The skin itself was smudged and charred, but Cesar was right, it wasn't as bad as it felt.

"Now me," Cesar said.

"In a minute." Brian dropped to the floor and pulled another match. He popped it on the scratchpad and held it to the zip tie around his ankle. "It's better this way," Brian said. "They come in that door, one of us better be able to move."

"I'm the one with the gun. Come on, it's my turn."

"Two seconds," Brian said. The flame ate into the plastic around his ankles, softened it, and a moment later he was free. He stood, looked at the pistol in Cesar's clenched hands. Not pointed at him, but close enough. "I'm not leaving you tied up on a sinking ship," he said. "Long as you don't point that gun in my direction."

"The match."

"Put the gun down."

Cesar pursed his mouth, glanced at the door, and set the gun down on the bed. *"Darse prisa,"* he said. "Hurry up."

Brian struck the match and leaned close, noticing Cesar's fingertips were blackened from where he had held the match. He held the flame just under the plastic, watched as the white turned a light brown and began to bubble. The skin behind turned from light to a darker brown, then began to blacken. Cesar did not move, did not make a sound. In what seemed a fraction of the time it had taken for Brian's ties to melt, Cesar was free, rolling his wrists and nodding. Brian handed him the matchbook and watched as Cesar quickly freed his ankles.

Cesar stood. "So. You're Frankie's man?"

"No," Brian said. "I'm a castaway. Fishing boat captain." Cesar frowned, and Brian shrugged. "I had bad luck, lost my fishing boat. Washed up on this ship."

"Ahh." Cesar racked the pistol, saw the gleam of brass, and pushed it forward. "I'm a bad luck man, too. You said the ship is sinking?"

"Yeah," Brian said. "There's something in the water trying to get us all the way sunk. You hear that thudding? That's it."

"Yes," Cesar said. "I heard the thudding. Listen, how does a man get off of this ship?"

"I've been working on that. In the meantime, I'm guessing you don't want to run into Frankie Rollins."

"No me importaria."

"Huh?"

"I wouldn't mind."

"We're outgunned," Brian said, shaking his head. "Way I see it, you find a place to lay low until the rescue ships show up. Then you sneak on board the other ship—"

Cesar smiled, his upper lip still smeared with blood. "Us *inmigrantes*, we're real good at that."

"Good. What do Frankie's people want with you?"

"Nothing good," Cesar said. "I bet they don't want nothing good for you, either."

"Yeah, we're two peas in a pod," Brian said. "Wipe the rest of that blood off your mouth, will you?"

Cesar drew his forearm across his mouth. "We stay together," he said, inspecting the smear. "They shoot at you, less bullets for me. You ready?"

"I have to find a woman," he said. "And an old man." He paused, thinking *Steady, steady*. What else was he forgetting? Push the panic down, think. Where did his responsibilities end? "Maybe a little girl, too."

"Yes," Cesar said. "Yes. How about a boy, an old lady? Transvestites, too. Get them all, *hombre*. Get them all."

"These are friends of mine," Brian said.

"And after you save these people, we're supposed to meet somewhere so you can help sneak me onto this rescue ship?" Before Brian could answer Cesar shook his head and wagged the muzzle of the pistol at him. "No, you come with me."

"I'm going to get them," Brian said. "Flap that gun around all you want. You shoot, Frankie's men are damn sure going to hear it."

"Ah, a stubborn bad luck man." Cesar let the pistol fall to his side and inspected Brian again. "Okay, we stay together. Like a team, *sí*? Come on."

He opened the door and went out, no hesitation, holding the pistol tight against his hip. Brian followed him, stepping over Hornaday. The bodyguard was not quite unconscious, his glazed eyes following the movement. He made to grab Brian's ankle, his hand coming up in a slow, dreamlike motion. Brian sent a boot into his ribs and closed the door behind him, shutting out the sounds of Hornaday's groans. The floor was slick with his blood.

"Where now?" Cesar said.

Brian looked down the hallway. To the right was the day care. Was Destiny in there? Maybe. Open the door and find out, get your ass shot off. To the left of them were passenger cabins, doors closed. They could hide out in one of those for a while, maybe, watch the door . . .

Brian thought of the ship in his mind, a cross section. The *Nokomis,* half-full of water, steadily slipping into the sea. Soon enough it would roll. The impacts from the creature had stopped for the moment, but if they started up again, the extra momentum would nudge the ship over the balancing point. If she was in there with a bunch of armed men, there was little to be gained by going in after her. Once the ship started to fill with water, though, they would all be forced to move.

"Ship is going down." He touched Cesar on the shoulder and pointed to the exit sign above the next door. "We go up."

Cesar went through the hallway door fast, something about the way he moved suggesting experience with these kinds of situations. The stairwell was deserted, so dark all they could see were the edges of the individual treads. They took the stairs two at a time, pausing briefly at the landing at B-deck, listening to the beehive buzz of the crowd.

"No," Brian said, catching hold of Cesar's arm before he could open the door. "One more level. Let's go find *el capitan*."

Cesar frowned. "I don't trust him, neither."

"We aren't going to have tea with the man."

The door to A was locked. Cesar pointed the pistol at the lock and Brian caught his arm once again, waved him back. He lowered his shoulder, tucking his arm in tight against his body, and hit the door. It rattled in its frame and he heard splintering near the lock. He backed off a few steps, rubbing his shoulder.

"Ready?" Brian said.

"They ready for us, too. You just warned them."

"They might be expecting somebody," Brian said. "It sure as hell ain't the two of us."

He hit the door hard, keeping his feet moving after the impact, feeling the frame of the hollow core door splinter around the handle. He kept going, following the arc of the door around, clearing a lane for Cesar to come through.

The deck way was abandoned, although he could hear people screaming again, somewhere below them. Ahead of him, in the wheelhouse, a lone officer was watching something out the far window. There was a knot of men at the bow of the boat, the same location where Brian had jumped overboard to retrieve Gilly's body. Some were dressed in ship whites, others the quasi-professional jumpsuits of Latham's and Prower's bodyguards. They were all looking over the side of the ship.

Brian padded softly along the backside of the wheelhouse, crossing over to the port-side deck way. They could hear the people on B-level deck way more clearly now, shouting at each other, some of them sobbing. Brian leaned over the edge and sucked in his breath. The water fifty yards off the *Nokomis* was covered in wreckage. Several people were trying to swim back toward the ship, battling the large waves in their bulky orange life preservers. Another lifeboat was motoring away from the *Nokomis*, the Honda outboard whining.

"Their lifeboat," Cesar said. "It exploded."

Brian scanned the surface. One of the survivors swimming toward the *Nokomis* suddenly disappeared, sucked below the surface, a massive swirl marking his location. A moment later another survivor disappeared, this one giving a strangled cry before disappearing behind a wave. When the wave passed, all that remained was half of a life jacket, ripped into shreds.

"What is this?" Cesar said.

Only two people were left in the water. One was swimming toward a piece of the lifeboat's hull; the other bobbed in his life jacket, head down, unconscious. The remaining lifeboat was still motoring away from the *Nokomis*, battling the waves. It was grossly overloaded, the small Honda outboard pushing the boat forward at only a few knots.

"Look," Cesar said, pointing. "What the hell?"

A massive green-black back broke through a wave twenty yards behind the boat, water shearing off its hide. There was a fresh chorus of screams from B-deck, men and women alike. Water frothed along its sides as it plowed through the waves, the long body moving sinuously. Then it disappeared underwater, its tail breaking the surface far behind the rest of it.

The skipper on the lifeboat heard the commotion and glanced behind him, just before the kronosaur disappeared. He turned hard to starboard, nearly tipping the small boat, then overcorrected, whipsawing the tiller back toward port and causing the people in the lifeboat to throw their hands out in an attempt to regain balance. The lifeboat rocked hard, one gunnel nearly dipping underwater, and rocked back to center.

There was time for everyone to take a breath, then a curtain of saltwater erupted behind them. Inside the spray of water was a wedge-shaped head, the width of it roughly the same length as the lifeboat. Its jaws opened, and the neck bent as it dove in on the lifeboat.

Someone tried to stand, perhaps meaning to dive, and he was still standing when the entire lifeboat disappeared into the creature's mouth, the curved teeth clamped firmly around the aluminum.

The deck of the *Nokomis* was silent except for a few sobbing women. Brian could hear Cesar mumbling Hail Marys.

A moment later, part of the lifeboat bobbed up to the surface, the outboard prop spinning in a high-pitched whine. Then the engine coughed, spluttered, and died. After a few more seconds, a person broke the surface, then another. In a moment, there were a half dozen people around the lifeboat, two of them apparently unconscious. A middle-aged man with a short beard flapped weakly at the surface, his face pale. In a few seconds he slumped over, rolling in the water, and Brian saw the stump of his arm spurting blood into the water.

Two others started to splash toward the *Nokomis*, battling the swells and the cheap life jackets that had been stocked aboard the lifeboat.

"Life rings!" someone shouted below them. "Throw the life rings!"

The two swimmers were halfway back to the *Nokomis* when the creature emerged again. It had moved off a short distance and was whipping its great head back and forth. After a moment, the remains of the aluminum boat went flying, shook loose from its curved fangs. It landed with a splash, bobbed on the surface for a moment, and slowly sank.

The kronosaur slid back into the water, already turning toward the *Nokomis*.

It was headed toward the swimmers, who were close together. One of its flippers broke the surface and made a tremendous splash, sending water thirty feet into the air. The rearmost swimmer had turned to look behind him and went stiff as he saw what was coming, his upper body bent back away, one hand splayed out in front of him. The other swimmer was still flailing at the water, head turned sideways, eyes squinted nearly closed.

There was the tinny pop of a handgun from the deck, and a divot appeared in the water in front of the creature. The pistol fired again, and this time Brian could clearly hear the thwack of lead hitting flesh, a sound he remembered from deer hunting, a sound unlike any other. The creature disappeared.

Below and aft, Frankie stood at the edge of the ship's railing, his pistol smoking, the slide locked back.

"He hit it," Cesar said. "He drove it—"

It came out of the water teeth first, jaws agape, enormous nostrils flared like manholes. The two swimmers, only five feet apart, tumbled into its maw at the same time. The kronosaur continued out of the water for twenty feet, its jaws crunching shut, the massive teeth closing like an enormous bear trap. It surveyed the *Nokomis* with its good eye, even as its gullet contracted and expanded, and hit the water with a huge splash, leaving the *Nokomis* completely silent.

"Look," Cesar said. "There is still one left." A woman was still clinging to the side of the lifeboat.

It looks like death, Brian thought. Death incarnate. But it has weaknesses. It bleeds, it's missing an eye. It had missed him as he swam alongside the *Nokomis* to retrieve Gilly's body, it had missed him again when it had lunged at him on the deck way after Destiny and Wells had pulled him to safety. It might miss the woman, whom he now recognized as Ashley, as long as her body blended into the hull section of the ruined lifeboat.

"Don't move!" he shouted down to her. "It can't see you if you don't move! Not a muscle!"

His was the only voice in the silence, carrying well above the wind and waves. The woman looked up at him. He sensed rather than saw the rest of the people following her gaze, and he felt Cesar stiffen beside him. Frankie Rollins stepped out from behind his men, his pistol at his side, and nodded in their direction.

"Stupido!" Cesar hissed.

"Shit," Brian said. "No!"

The woman let go of the lifeboat and swam toward the *Nokomis*. She had gone only a few yards when a wake appeared behind her. The mound of water built, the wall of water surging higher and then flattening out, spreading over the waves. The woman did not turn but she must have sensed it, and she broke left at the last moment, just as the gaping mouth of the kronosaur emerged out of the water. She fell into it with a rush of seawater, and the kronosaur's jaws flexed and shifted, pushing its prey to the side of its mouth where it could be broken down. Then it slid back below the surface.

They waited, still silent. The sea was empty of life, the wreckage from the two ships quickly scattering downwind and then disappearing.

Brian looked down at Frankie, who was shoving in a fresh clip and barking orders. Thor and Kharkov were nearby, but their blank faces were still watching the seas. Frankie slapped them, each in turn, the sound of his palm on their cheeks carrying up to Brian and Cesar. Which was where Frankie was now pointing, his words indecipherable but the meaning clear enough.

Cesar tapped the barrel of his pistol against the side of his leg. "No more rescuing, *hombre*. We just *go*."

They turned and ran as Thor and Kharkov started toward them from the front of the ship.

Chapter 26

Frankie suspected he could have been a Patton, maybe a MacArthur or a Doolittle. In a situation where critical thinking mattered, where logic triumphed over chance, he knew how to handle shit. He wasn't a bookish guy by nature, but he wasn't afraid to put in research, to develop Plans B through ZZZ. He could see the different outcomes, could develop strategies through or around them. He could adapt. What he wasn't good at, what he was afraid of, were the wild cards in the deck, the things outside his control.

And the fuckin' thing beating hell out of this ship sure wasn't going to take any orders from him. Neither was that goddamned Yankee fisherman yelling down at them like he was Moses come down from the mountain, with the Mexican—the one guarantee Frankie held as the most important, absolutely-can't-fuck-it-up piece of the equation, his get out-of-an-early-grave-free card—now standing next to the goddamned Yankee fisherman.

Frankie's only advantage was that Hawkins didn't know the value of the card he held.

He wiped the sweat from his forehead and turned to Thor and Kharkov. "Kill the fisherman," he said. "Shoot him and throw him overboard. The Mexican you *don't* shoot, or I throw you overboard. Understood?"

"Yes," Thor said. "And what do we do about the creature?"

"Not a goddamn thing," Frankie said. "Tug should be here any minute, and that'll keep everyone occupied. We get the Mexican back in a room, finish the card game, and after that, things go smooth. Or smoother." He turned and saw the ship's engineer standing at the railing, still looking down at the sea. "Wright! Get over here."

Wright walked over to them at once. Frankie was glad he came; he'd entertained a brief, vicious urge to shoot Wright full of holes. Make a point about obeying orders in a timely goddamn manner.

"You know the ship best," he said to Wright. "We seal the stairwell, they're stuck up there. Right?"

Wright closed his eyes. "There aren't many places to go," he said. "A few rooms, but no exits. If they had a rope, I suppose they could swing over the side and down to B-deck or C-deck. D-deck is damn near underwater by now."

"Is there rope up there?"

"A ship this size, there usually isn't a lot of extra stuff lying around. They'll probably either go into one of those rooms and wait for us, or they'll try to go over the side."

"Okay. What do you think, Thor?"

"I think," he said. "This guy gets backed into a corner, he comes out like the *grävling*. The badger."

"Teeth and claws first," Frankie said. "You're probably right. And our little Mexican might get scratched up in the process. We need to take them clean."

"There is one other way off that level," Wright said. He paused, scratching the whiskers on his chin. "Hell, it's even possible they'll see it. We push them to it, they'll see it for sure."

He sent Thor and his Kharkov as pushers, letting them advance slowly along the top level of the *Nokomis* toward the starboard corner of the stern. Frankie patted Thor on the shoulder before he left.

"Keep an eye on Kharkov. I don't trust that bullet-headed prick."

Thor nodded. He was no killer, Frankie thought, but he would obey, and would become a killer if Frankie told him he had to be.

"*Chef?* You are okay?"

"Fine," Frankie said, shaking his head. "Go on, get them moving. They've likely got Hornaday's pistol, so push them nice and light." He turned to Wright. "You ready?"

He followed Wright back down to B-deck, then ran down the tilted deck way toward the starboard corner. They were on side of the ship that had tilted up, and he had to push himself away from the wall as they ran. Wright, with his steel-toed leather boots, seemed to be getting better purchase on the canted deck than Frankie was with his oxfords.

"There," Wright said, panting.

Frankie nodded. Two vertical sheet metal ducts rose vertically to the top of the ship, the long rectangles recessed into the side of the ship. There were two pipes alongside the HVAC ducts, a waterline for fire suppression and the electrical conduit. The space between the pipes and ductwork was a bit wider than a man. Frankie could see at once how appealing it would be if you were trapped; simply press your back against the ductwork, walk your feet down the pipes, and slide down to B-deck.

Wright looked out to sea. "That goddamn thing. Just waiting for us to launch another boat."

Frankie watched the shadow shift and flex under the water. A long dark cloud, right at the edge of the fog, moving in a slow gyre under the water. Coiling and uncoiling its massive body. Occasionally, some part of it would break through the trough of a wave, but for the most part it kept submerged. Too far away for the Glock, which he suspected would be useless at all but point-blank range.

"What's it waiting for?" he asked. "It could sink us if it wanted."

"I don't know," Wright said, touching the sidewall. "This old bitch is tougher than she looks."

"Can she stay upright?"

Wright peered over the edge, glanced at the shadow a hundred yards off the ship. "We're sitting too low. A few more collisions . . ." He held a hand out, turned it sideways, and flipped it upside down. "I been there before, in a little fishing boat off the Banks."

"It flipped?"

Wright nodded. "Total clusterfuck. First mate hit his head on the wall, and the captain broke his arm. Then she spun back around topside and I ended up with the wheel in my face." He touched his nose along the slight curvature. "Bled everywhere."

"But you didn't sink?"

"No, she was full of air, and when we rolled back upright, whatever water we took on we pumped back out through the bilges. Our dear *Nokomis*, on the other hand, doesn't have much air left in her lungs."

Frankie scratched the back of his neck. Only a half hour until the chopper took off. Out of reach of the ocean, away from this shadow with teeth. Just lift off and leave the fog behind, then back on land, money in his account, not too many regrets.

Above them they heard the soft pad of footfalls, then muted conversation. A moment later they heard scraping noises. "Son of a bitch," Wright said, stepping back away from the railing. "Here they come."

They backed away from the ductwork, the soft squeak of shoes pressing against metal coming from above. Frankie pressed himself against the wall, rubbing his finger over the safety on the Glock. He could see boots now, pressed against the pipes, coming down slowly. Galoshes, not boots.

Frankie raised his Glock. Hawkins's legs dropped down, then his waist. Frankie slipped the safety off. One of Hawkins's hands came down, gripped the water pipe. The other hand appeared and took hold of the pipe, a foot lower. Hawkins's galoshes wavered a couple feet above B-deck, then dropped to the deck, facing away from them.

Frankie took a step back, moving into the alcove space that led back into B-deck, pulling Wright with him. A few seconds later, Cesar dropped onto the floor next to Hawkins, holding Hornaday's pistol in one hand, his eyes looking everywhere at once; the space above them, the deck way, the ocean to their right. Turning around now, seeing their shapes out of the corner of his eye, the pistol coming up.

"Don't," Frankie said, stepping out of the alcove. Cesar's gun hand continued on its arc, and without having made a conscious decision to fire, Frankie's finger twitched. The Glock jerked in Frankie's hand. Cesar flew backwards, his pistol clattering across the deck way, and came to a rest against the railing.

"Shit," Frankie said.

Hawkins didn't move, his eyes trained on the Glock. Frankie stepped onto the deck way, leaving Wright inside the alcove. Cesar was trying to pull himself up the guardrail.

"Turn around, Cesar," Frankie said.

Cesar rotated his head around, his breath ragged. His right shoulder was leaking blood onto the railing, and through the hole in his shirt Frankie could see the splinter of shattered bones. Shit, he hadn't expected the Glock to make that big a mess. The slug must have hit a bone, blown up an artery or something.

"Jesus Christ," Wright said from behind him.

"Come on," Frankie said. "We gotta get him to Christie." He glanced at Hawkins, who was also staring at Cesar. The blood was bubbling out, spreading across his shirt. It looked like a grenade had blown up in his armpit.

"On second thought," Frankie said to Wright. "Go get Dr. Christie. Hurry."

"You mean Dr. Perle?"

"Christie," Frankie snapped. "He's my personal physician. Tall, skinny, looks like a mortician." Wright took off.

"Your shirt," Frankie said, pointing the gun at Hawkins. "Use it as a compress."

Cesar had slid down, his unhurt arm still hooked over the side of the railing. "Easy," Brian said, kneeling beside him. "We have to stop the bleeding."

Cesar muttered something as Brian placed his folded shirt over the worst of the blood stream, the cotton fabric quickly turning red. Cesar's mouth was moving, his dry lips moving next to Brian's ear.

"What's he saying?" Frankie said.

Brian didn't look up. "That you're an asshole."

"You remember that," Frankie said. "You start feeling like a hero, remember that assholes and heroes don't mix."

"He also," Brian said, "says it sucks getting shot."

"Remember that, too."

He stood watching Brian's shirt turn red until he heard footsteps behind him. Christie was hustling down the deck way, the doctor's bag bouncing against the side of his leg as he ran. He nodded at Frankie and hunkered next to Cesar, asked a couple questions Frankie couldn't hear, and lifted the compress. He placed the compress back on his shoulder. "Get him up," Christie said to Brian. "We need to get him back to my room."

"How bad?" Frankie said.

"Bad enough," Christie said. "It's the big arteries

going into the arm. We need to work quick, before he goes into arrest."

"Is the girl there?"

"Yes. I showed her how to do it, no problem. We've gotta move."

Christie got under Cesar's unhurt shoulder, leaving Brian alone. Without thinking too hard about it Frankie brought the pistol up, squaring the sights in the middle of the fisherman's chest.

Chapter 27

Taylor sat in the middle of the bed as it floated across the tiny cabin, her very own lifeboat. She was wet, the mattress soaked through but still buoyant. Water continued to come through the door, first just seeping under the sill, then starting to pour in around the edges as well. When the water was at the second hinge the bed tipped suddenly to the side, and she shifted her weight to keep from sliding off. The bed immediately tipped the other way, spilling her into three feet of icy water.

She hit the floor, trying to scream and only managing a few bubbles through the towel Kharkov had taped around her mouth. The mattress and box spring, suddenly free of her weight, drifted over her. She shoved it away and scooched along the floor, pushing her head above water as soon as she was clear of the mattress. The bed drifted away, coming to rest against the nightstand table.

She sucked in as much air as she could through her nose, then screamed, the sound only a muffled whine by the time it got through the towel. If someone had their ear pressed against the door they might have heard her, but nobody was out there. She didn't think anybody was going to be out there, either, because in another few minutes D-deck was going to be completely underwater.

There's no way they'll forget about me, she thought, trying to fight off the panic. *I'm missing and they* will *come looking for me.*

But the night before, she had also been missing. The only people looking for her at this point would be her parents, and she held out no great hope that they could track her down, that either one had the wits and resolve to find the hidden stairwell in C-85. And if they ran into Kharkov . . .

She didn't want to think about it.

She started to hop toward the bed, half-swimming through the rising water. She reached the edge of the bed, thought about Kharkov's warning, and went past it to the door. The water was above the second hinge now, halfway up to her chest. She turned around and held the doorknob between her tied hands and twisted it open. A small wave of water surged over her and into the room.

She continued hopping down the hallway, then paused to survey D-deck. Across the room, the water was up to the third stair, and everything that floated was pressed against the far wall—several bottles, two chairs, and a long shape that she knew had to be the body of the man who had tried to help her.

Kharkov's words came to her again: *If you leave room, I will turn you inside out.*

She moved cautiously into the main room. The deck was tilted toward the wall where the debris and the bartender's body were floating, and as she hopped toward the stairwell she began slipping toward that end. She forced herself to slow down, fighting against the temptation to break for the stairs in a mad scramble. If she fell down, there was nothing to pull herself up with, and she would end up under the chairs. Under the dead body.

Her progress was agonizingly slow. At one point, footsteps pounded over her head and she stopped, rabbit-still; she was sure the heavy thuds were from Kharkov. But the footsteps kept on pounding, and after a moment she started toward the stairwell again. Her clothes were soaked through, further constricting her movements, and she could feel claustrophobia working its way inside of her.

Finally, she reached the stairs, narrow and steep. They looked impossible.

She turned around and sat down with a splash, her butt landing on the third tread. She brought her feet up onto the floor and pushed up, then slid her butt onto the fourth tread. From above her she heard faint screaming, the sound of gunfire. She put her feet on the next set of stairs and kept pushing.

Chapter 28

Brian tried to keep his eyes off the muzzle of the gun, instead focusing on Frankie's forearm. He thought it might bunch a little before Frankie shot, just a twitch, and that was going to be his split-second chance to do something. Jump over the railing, he supposed. Or bum rush the little weasel.

As Christie escorted Cesar past Frankie, Cesar roared something in Spanish and lunged, breaking free of Christie's grip and charging toward Frankie. Frankie swiveled as Cesar rammed into him, but his shoes slipped on the deck and Cesar rammed his shoulder into his midsection. Cesar's feet kept driving, bending Frankie's upper torso over the railing.

Brian charged forward, lowering his own shoulder like a linebacker. It would only take one good shove to finish the job Cesar had started and send Frankie tipping over the railing.

Then he slipped and sprawled onto the deck, flat on his stomach. Before he could pick himself up, Christie was on him, fingers digging at Brian's neck. Brian rolled to the side, catching a light blow on the back of his neck, then another on his shoulder. The latter sent a sharp pain racing down his arm, as if he'd been stung by a hornet.

He got to his knees, parried another punch. Christie's face was red, his eyes frantic. Brian brought his fist halfway back and jabbed it straight out, clipping Christie neatly on the jaw. He tried to stand and only made it halfway up before Brian hit him again and he fell back onto the deck, his eyelids quivering.

Cesar was losing his struggle with Frankie, his one good arm slowly being forced back, blood splattering on the deck from his wounded shoulder. Frankie's Glock was coming around by degrees, almost to Cesar's forehead, Frankie's finger white on the trigger.

Brian got to his feet, and wobbled. He took a step forward and went back instead, his hands out for balance, and stumbled against the railing. The deck was giving way under his feet. He looked up at the two men locked together just ten feet in front of him. Cesar's teeth were bared, trying to bite Frankie's neck, a growl bubbling from his mouth.

Brian slid down to the deck and looked at Christie's hands. Long and pale fingers, no wedding ring, no watch. There was a small syringe in his palm, the plunger was fully depressed, a drop of liquid at the end of the short needle.

He looked up. Frankie had worked a thumb into the gunshot wound in Cesar's shoulder and was grinding it in. Cesar snarled something and disengaged, pushing Frankie's gun hand back and retreating two steps. Frankie brought his gun around, hollering for Cesar to stop, but he was too late; Cesar was already charging him. Frankie stepped to the right and brought the gun around in a short arc as Cesar passed, hitting him just behind the ear. Cesar slumped over the top of the railing, arms hanging limply over the side.

"Gaa," Brian said, trying to stand and only falling back onto his butt. "Gaadaa yoo."

"Little bastard is strong," Frankie said, breathing hard. He looked down at Brian. "What the hell did you do to him?"

"Just a little poke," Christie said, and to Brian his voice sounded like it was coming from miles above. "A lot quieter than firing off that goddamned pistol. Jesus, they could probably hear you clear across the ship."

Frankie peered down at Brian. "He's absolutely stoned."

Christie struggled to a standing position. "Let's toss him over the side and get working."

Brian listened, feeling concern trying to spike through the chemical stupor. Everything had taken on a dreamlike air, but once they dropped him over the side . . . twenty feet through the air, then six hundred feet of water . . . he'd probably wake up just in time to die. His face had slid down to the deck and his cheek was pressed against the cold wood, giving him a clear view of Cesar. The blood dripping from his shoulder seemed to be the brightest color in the world, the scarlet backset by the gray-blue of the rolling seas. Then his vision filled with the head of the kronosaur, the massive jaws clamping down on Cesar's head and shoulders. Cesar's feet jerked up and over the railing and his entire body disappeared.

Frankie rushed to the railing and emptied his pistol into the sea, screaming. The pistol clicked empty and he stood there, shoulders hunched, neck corded. Then he backed slowly away from the railing and joined Christie, who had pressed himself against the inside wall of the deck way.

"What?" Christie mumbled. "Jesus. That . . ."

Frankie turned around, his nostrils flared. "That fucker just ate a three-million-dollar meal." He pressed a hand to his forehead, bringing it down slowly over his eyes. "Lord, oh, Lord, what a sense of humor you must have."

After a little while Christie said, "Three—million— dollars?"

Frankie laughed. "Never knew how much money a healthy O-positive heart could bring, didja? Even with fifty-fifty odds of rejection, I had all kinds of buyers lined up."

Christie rubbed at his temples. "A hundred grand for the surgeon, for the *skill*, and you're a millionaire?"

"Not anymore," Frankie said. "They'll pull those reserve funds back the second they find out. Don't look so cheated, doc. Any asshole with a scalpel can cut the thing out. They had a real doctor hired to put it in. Jesus, I don't know if I should laugh or eat a goddamn bullet."

"We did it over, would you go half and half?"

Frankie flapped his hand. "Let it go."

Christie stepped closer. "You think you got everything figured out, huh? And the whole time the solution is right here, staring you in the face." He moved forward and kicked Brian in the small of the back. Brian coughed, feeling the pain spike "You still got a donor, dummie."

Frankie frowned. "The odds of him being O-positive are what, one in three? And all the other work with Cesar, mixing the blood together . . ."

"The antigens," Christie said. "Tissue typing. The blood mixing, cross-matching. You're right. The odds he'll match up as well as our departed little Mexican are very, very low."

Frankie started to speak, to object, and then fell silent.

"There you go," Christie said. "It gets rejected, well, we already knew there was a fifty percent chance that would happen." He stepped forward, stretched out his skinny arm. "Right, partner?"

Frankie opened the door to the room next to the day care. Thor was on one bed, Destiny on the other. She glanced up when he entered, then looked away. She was very still, her only movement her fingers, digging into her thighs. Frankie looked down, saw the blood streaks on his jacket and white shirt. He should change clothes.

"I need you to do a transport," he said to Thor. "B-deck, back corner. I'm gonna take Destiny to the gaming room. They still playing?"

Thor nodded. "Latham came back, but is still down. Prower is playing poorly."

"Because Prower's an asshole," Frankie said. "Both of them are, just like me." He walked over to Destiny and waited until she looked up. Her upper lip was trembling, her face pale.

"What?" she said. "You waiting for me to disagree?"

"Just making sure you're still okay with the plan."

"I'm here, aren't I?" she said.

"You'd be here," he said slowly, "in this room, regardless. Understand? I been nice to you, I wanna keep being nice to you, but I'm not in the mood for attitude. Are you okay with the plan?"

"Yes."

"Good." He turned to Thor, who was on his way out the door. "Any news on the rescue ships?"

"I heard nothing," Thor said. "Graves said you were going to make a call, with the satellite phone."

"Shit," Frankie said. "That's right, I got distracted." He paused, thinking. "Go help Christie with that passenger transport, then meet us back in this room. Anyone asks about the passenger, he fell and hit his head."

He took Destiny's hand and followed Thor out the door, then knocked on the day-care room door. The door opened a crack, a bloodshot eye appeared, and then the door swung open. Kharkov ushered him inside, his large body giving off a smell of mildew and cabbage. Hornaday stood behind and slightly to the side of Prower, his face bruised and his ankle wrapped in a bloody towel. Prower looked up. His pile of chips was considerably diminished.

Frankie sighed. "The game's over, gentlemen."

Latham spoke in a low, unhurried voice. "We heard a lot of shooting."

"Target practice," Frankie said, directing Destiny into the small couch. There were two bottles of single-malt

Scotch on the table next to the couch and he poured a healthy dollop into one of the glasses. He drank half, breathed, then finished the rest. "Call your transports. Prower, I need to borrow your phone when you're done."

Latham turned, his movement as measured as his voice. "I'm still in this game."

"The ship is going down." Frankie set the tumbler on the table. "The game is over."

"We agreed it would continue," Latham said, and beside him he felt Kharkov turn slightly. He breathed in through his nostrils, trying not to look at Kharkov. Thor wouldn't return for several minutes, and for now it was just him and a room full of people who didn't like him.

"The tug will be here in minutes," Frankie said. "We need to get everybody off the ship before they arrive."

"No." Latham's voice was mild, without anger.

Frankie took a deep breath. "We're all going to end up—"

"Bet it all," Prower said. "I haven't looked at my cards. We play this out, no draw. Straight-up stud poker."

Frankie considered, then nodded. He'd seen this done before, mostly in garage games, usually when everyone was too tired or too drunk to keep dragging the game out. Just shove your chips in, flip the cards over, and see what happened. At this point, he would have endorsed a game of slapjack just to get it over with.

"Okay," he said. "We finish this out, but no more draws, no more bets. You each have five cards, just turn 'em over."

Latham glanced at Kharkov, who shrugged, and then Latham turned back to his pile of chips. Sweat dripped down from his scalp to the collar of his shirt. He hesitated, and then pushed his chips into the middle with the side of his hand. Prower glanced at the pile, separated out an equivalent amount, and slid it next to Latham's.

"Flip 'em," Prower said.

Latham turned his cards over. A pair of sixes, with a king high.

Prower tilted his head to the side, squinting at Latham's pair, then began to turn his cards over, one by one, slapping them on the wooden table. A four of clubs, *slap*. A five of hearts, *slap*. Then a seven of clubs, followed quickly by a six of diamonds. *Slap, slap*, and Prower was flirting with his inside straight. "An eight would be nice," Prower smiled grimly. "Or a three. Or a seven. I'm not picky."

"You looked," Latham growled.

"No, boss," Kharkov said. "I was watching him the whole time."

Prower flipped over his final card and the room seemed to deflate. Jack of spades. A shit hand. Latham reached forward and started to pull in the stacks of chips.

Frankie stopped him. "No," he said. "You guys are close to even. Leave them in. One last hand." He put out a hand as the ship shuddered, a deep, ratcheting vibration running through the room. "Winner takes everything."

Frankie watched closely as Latham shuffled, looking for any of the dozen ways to manipulate a deck. It looked clean, though, three shuffles and a split, followed by another shuffle. Latham held out the deck for Prower to cut. Prower tapped the top of the deck and said, "We'll play these."

Latham dealt the cards faceup, one at a time. Prower drew a four and a five, and Latham drew a king and a jack. On the third card Prower drew a queen, Latham a deuce.

"Want to trade those last cards?" Prower said. "No? Okay, king is boss."

"King is boss," Latham said, then flipped Prower's fourth card on the table. It was a four of hearts. Prower pursed his lips, nodded slightly. He now had a pair of fours, with a queen high.

Latham dealt himself another king.

"Cowboys," Prower said. "Son of a bitch."

Latham flipped Prower his last card. He was already thumbing his own back when he realized what he had dealt Prower. The four of diamonds, Prower's third four of the hand.

Latham's final card dropped to the table. It was the ace of spades, the one-eyed snake. His pair of kings with an ace high had lost to a small three of a kind. His color began to build, working its way up from the neck. His hand was still clutched around the deck, his eyes still on the three fours he'd dealt Prower.

"You son of a bitch," Latham said.

"Sorry about that," Prower said. He pushed himself out of his chair, leaning heavily on his cane, and then walked around the table, his hand out. "Fine game, though. You certainly rallied."

Latham, still seated, looked up at Prower. From somewhere above them they could hear an alarm sounding. "You wouldn't be interested in selling the prize to me?" he said. "Cash, stocks, perhaps some property? Anything is possible."

"No," Prower said. "The cards have spoken, and rather clearly. I'm going to listen to them."

"Yes, I guess they have." Latham said. "Kharkov? Plan B."

"Huh?" Prower said, and at the same time there was a soft whoosh, like a jet passing by very high and very fast, and a round hole appeared in the middle of Prower's belly. The hole grew, darkening and spreading over Prower's silk shirt. He took a step forward, his face still fixed in an expression of befuddlement, and the whooshing sound came again. Another hole appeared in Prower's shirt, less than an inch from the first one. Prower stumbled, fell against the side of the makeshift card table, and dropped to the floor.

On the other side of the table Hornaday was leveling his pistol, trying to shift his weight on his good leg. Frankie started to duck when the noise came again, this time much louder, and Hornaday's left eye imploded, a spray of pink emerging from the back of his head. He stood upright for a moment, his pistol still pointed in Frankie's direction. His swollen lips opened a fraction of an inch as though he might say something, then he fell over backwards. Destiny screamed in the background, the noise barely registering. Frankie's ears seemed to be suddenly full of cotton.

Latham walked over and toed Prower's corpse. "I had to listen to him much longer," he said, "I would have done it with my bare hands."

Frankie could barely hear him. He was careful not to move. He was thinking very hard and very fast.

"You should have told me you wanted this earlier," Kharkov said from behind Frankie. "Is a very easy thing to do."

Latham's face twitched. "I would have beat him if he'd dealt me a few decent cards."

Kharkov took a step closer to Frankie and shoved him in the back of the neck with something small and round. His smell washed over Frankie, and he could feel his knees unhinging, his bowels wanting to un-clench. "And this one?" Kharkov said. "This one *I* am sick of listening to."

Latham turned to face them. "Don't be rude, Kharkov. Mr. Rollins is our partner. Put that gun away—you're scaring him." The pressure in the back of Frankie's neck went away.

"The girl?" Kharkov asked.

Latham frowned. "What the hell is she doing in here? Christ, Frankie, you're getting sloppy." He turned back to Kharkov and motioned towards the bodies. "Drop her over the side with these two. Let the goddamn lizard swallow them."

Frankie adjusted the lapels on his sport jacket. "She's with me."

Latham turned back to Frankie. "Come again?"

"I'll take care of her later," Frankie said. "For now, I need her."

Latham stared at him. "You on your game, Frankie?"

"Yeah," he said. "You want the prize, you want it smooth? Let me run it my way."

Latham watched him, started to say something to Kharkov, and the ship shuddered again, this time accompanied by a bass metallic groan, the sound of steel slowly crumpling from underneath their feet. "Smooth, huh?" He pulled a satellite phone from the inside pocket on his sports jacket and tossed it to Kharkov. "Give Remmie notice, and tell him he better bust his ass getting out here."

Chapter 29

Captain Donald Moore stood at the railing, a Padrón cigar smoldering in his hand.

Below him, a tugboat had emerged from the fog, crashing through the swells. The sea itself was empty, with no sign of the creature. The remnants of the lifeboats had washed away, as well as the bodies of the passengers who had died in front of him. Because of him.

He raised the cigar and inhaled. The ember had gone out as he gazed at the sea. He held the cigar over the side of the railing and let it drop, a thin trail of ashes following it down to the ocean.

Behind him, the loudspeakers announced it was time for the passengers to ready themselves for transfer, to make sure only their lightweight valuables were with them. Put on life jackets, make sure the children and any elderly were near the front of the line. How many passengers were left? Moore wondered. At least fifteen had died in the ill-fated attempt to launch the lifeboats. Another half dozen had gone over the edge, either drowned or devoured.

Twenty people dead. Almost three times the number that had died off the coast of Florida.

The creature broke the surface directly below him. It was looking at him, not the tugboat; it must have sensed the cigar entering the water, had cued in on the tiny splash. Moore stared back, curious. Perhaps this creature was some agglomeration of those people whom he had inadvertently killed, all those years ago. A medley of haunted souls, recombined into this creature. *Gervais. McConnelly. Peterson. Rukavina. Pendleton.*

The creature finned itself just below the surface. Its good eye was canted upward, waiting to see if anything else might fall into its world.

The tug was getting closer. It would not be able to pull the *Nokomis* back to shore, he supposed; there was too much water in the hold. They could transfer thirty or forty people onto her, perhaps. The rest . . . well. Perhaps there would be a transport ship, perhaps the Coast Guard would send that cutter.

His own days on the sea were over. It was all over: The bright hard afternoons with the blue chop spraying along the sides, the calm evenings when the ship was running smooth and the crew was in good spirits, nights when he could stand in a spot like this and see the river of stars overhead, snaking across the black sky. Knowing it was as close to heaven as he would ever be.

He stared into the water. Even if everyone who remained on the ship lived, there would be so many questions. Families seeking answers, insurance companies looking for facts. There would also be a courtroom full of questions, with an old sailor just left of center stage slumped in a chair, wearing a cheap sport jacket or an orange jumpsuit, the sea to which all questions flowed. How did it happen? When did it happen?

How did he, the captain of the ship, *let* it happen?

He looked back at the wheelhouse, his neck creaking. Graves and Vanders were working diligently, arranging the details of the tug's approach, probably trying to figure out what to do with the rest of the crew and passengers. They took no notice of him, and he wondered if they had gone through the formal mutiny motions, had voted him off the island, or were just rolling with it.

He looked down. The creature was still staring at him. Its green eye seemed to suggest an invitation, or perhaps a question. That was a crazy thought, except . . .

Except that it *was* looking at him, and it seemed to understand there was a decision to be made. That it might partake in that decision.

In the distance, the tug hit its air horn. It would be at their side in a minute, perhaps two.

Moore put his foot on the rail and pushed himself up, straddling the railing and then swinging his other foot over, until his heels were planted against the outside of the railing. Below him the creature's tail moved back and forth, setting little whirlpools to spin off in all directions. The railing vibrated under him, the ship moving in tiny jerking movements, like a vehicle traveling down a corduroy gravel road.

What is it you're supposed to say, Moore thought. *Good-bye, cruel world?*

He pushed himself off the edge, landing cleanly in the water just a few yards in front of the creature. He sank several feet, caught himself instinctively, and pushed back up to the surface. The cold water was a shock to his body and his heart was thudding in his throat, racing as it hadn't in years.

The creature moved closer, just under the surface. Its eyes, one a ruined mess and the other a sharp, intensely alive green, were framed above the enormous snout. The stained teeth curving out of its black gums, the serrated backsides clotted with bits of flesh and fabric from life jackets. It rose in the water column without seeming to move, the water cascading off its barnacled hide.

"Go ahead," Moore croaked.

The creature flared its nostrils, its good eye still holding that same question Moore had seen from above, breathing in his scent. Then it exhaled, and the intense scrutiny of its gaze relaxed. It sank back down in the water and turned away without touching him, sliding underneath the canted bulk of the *Nokomis*.

Moore treaded water for a few more moments. His arms grew heavy, his legs weak. Eventually, he went under, the old biology kicking in as he descended, the need for air, the need for light. He opened his mouth and breathed out his last air, watching the bubbles race for the surface. Then he gathered the last strands of his will and inhaled deeply, inhaled the seawater he had loved for so long, letting it fill his lungs.

He thrashed, jerking in the water for some time. Then he fell still and sank, lifeless, beneath the shadow of the *Nokomis*. From the darkened water under the ship a green eye watched him sink, then turned upward, to the shadow of the approaching tug. The long tail began to lash back and forth again, sending underwater dervishes through the water.

Chapter 30

Brian lay flat on the couch, his wrists and ankles bound once again by zip ties, a plastic sheet spread underneath him. He was dressed only in his boxers, his body lit in bright detail from a portable fluorescent light Christie had rigged up. They were keeping him doped, enough to render him motionless but fully conscious.

"Listen," Frankie said across the room, speaking into a satellite phone. "You don't need my name, I'm just a passenger, happened to find this phone. I'm on the cruise ship *Nokomis*. It's sinking, our radio communications are down. No, no cell phone, either." He paused, rolled his eyes at Thor. "I already gave you the coordinates, you don't gotta talk to the captain to confirm them."

Christie looked up from his row of instruments to Thor. "He's getting soft."

"Shhh," Thor said.

"No, I understood you the first time," Frankie said. "But you don't get someone out here, people are gonna die. The ship was hit by something, you understand? Hit on purpose. Send whatever you can."

He clicked off the phone and shook his head. "Government employees, Jesus Christ. I told her people gonna die, she gives me a lecture on protocol. That's why I don't pay taxes." He looked over to Thor. "Go get the girl."

He knelt next to Brian as Thor exited the room. "Listen, sailor, you got a bum rap out of this. I'm going to say that straight up. I realize it, but this is how it is. Understand? We have to wait until the very end before we operate, in case there are delays with the game. Need to keep everything fresh. This was supposed to be Cesar, but since Cesar is now . . . unavailable . . . you're up. See how it works?" His voice dropped. "I'm gonna try to keep the girl safe, but I need some insurance policy. Can't just let her walk away and hope she doesn't talk."

He stood. "Come on, let's get this over with."

Christie was touching each one of his tools through his latex gloves, nodding to himself. It was a routine Brian had done himself prior to setting an outrigger in rough seas: First you lay out the plan, then you check to make sure your tools are in order. There was a small battery-operated circular saw, several scalpels and clamps, a bucket of rags. The tools were all stainless steel, and Christie had already wiped them down with alcohol. On the end of Christie's table was another syringe, much larger than the one he'd had before. It was half full, a drop of atropine hanging from the tip.

A small blue Igloo cooler sat by itself in the corner of the room.

"The girl is a stupid idea," Christie said, looking up from his inventory of his tools. "Let me do my job."

"We give her the option," Frankie said. "My call."

Thor escorted Destiny into the room. She glanced at Christie, her eyes dropping down to the tools lying on the table in front of them. When she did not look at Brian he understood what was going to happen. In some ways it was okay, better than the bloodless Christie, or getting it from snake oil Frankie. But it still wasn't good.

Christie pulled out his cell phone and held it up to her. "Say the words when I motion to you. Then insert the needle into the big thigh muscle and press the plunger. That's all there is to it."

Destiny picked up the syringe. Thor stood just behind her.

"Will it be quick?" she said.

"A couple seconds," Christie said. "And painless. Are you ready?"

"Yes," she said.

Christie motioned to her, and she looked directly at the camera, a hint of something coming over her face. Resolve, Brian thought. Good for you, Destiny. And if you get out of this, don't think about it anymore. He twisted on the couch, the plastic wrinkling underneath him. He closed his eyes as he heard her words, clear and strong.

"My name is Destiny Boudreaux, and I do this of my own free will."

Yeah, she would be okay. He kept his eyes closed as she moved toward him, kept them closed as he felt the needle jam into his thigh muscle. A small blossom of pain. The world would close in now and it wasn't so bad; it wasn't good, either, but it wasn't terrible. It was just the end.

"I think I hit a bone."

"What?" Christie said.

Brian opened his eyes. Destiny was staring at him. He looked down and saw the needle was in his leg, the plunger still not depressed. Christie stepped forward, still filming with his phone. He leaned over, craning for a better view, and as he did Destiny jerked the needle free from Brian's leg, swung it in a short backhand into the side of Christie's neck, and squeezed the plunger.

Christie yelled, bringing his fingers up to his neck and wiping frantically at the small hole on the side of his Adam's apple. Destiny held the needle up in front of his eyes, showing him the contents. Half of the atropine meant for Brian was in Christie's throat.

"You can't," Christie said, his words slurred. He took a step back, one arm waving in the air for balance.

Thor lunged forward and Destiny ducked under him, grabbing on to one massive leg. Thor started to reach down, meaning to pluck her off his leg, and froze. The needle was already buried in his calf, Destiny's thumb on top of the plunger.

"More than enough left, big boy," Destiny said.

Good girl, Brian thought. Good girl. He tried to push himself off the couch and managed to move his head a quarter-turn, just enough to bring Frankie into his field of vision. Frankie had backed away to the far corner of the room, his pistol in his hand but not pointed at her, just hanging along his side.

"Come on, Destiny," he said. "Put it down. This is silly."

"You put it down," Destiny said. "Or I inject him with the rest of it. I mean it, Frankie."

"So you kill Thor?" he said. "A guy I met three days ago? And then what, you tie me up and I go to prison? And Thor's family has to bury him?"

Destiny glanced at Brian, her eyes frantic, then back to Frankie. She twisted her wrist, positioning the needle. "I'll do it."

"Maybe," Frankie said, taking a step forward. "Push the plunger in or pull it out, either way I ain't gonna put my gun down."

"Chef?"

Frankie ignored Thor and took a step closer. "It's all right," Frankie said, his voice soft. "You aren't cold-blooded, I get it."

Brian hand pushed weakly against the sheet as he tried to sit up. He opened his mouth, garbled out something unintelligible even to himself. They both looked to him and he shook his head. "No," he said thickly, looking at Destiny. "It's no use."

Destiny looked from him to Frankie. Her hand holding the needle was trembling, and as he watched the tremble turned into a full-fledged palsy, Thor grunting as the needle worked a hole in his calf muscle.

"I'm sorry," she said. "I thought . . . shit." She pulled the needle free and threw it across the floor. "I'm sorry, Brian."

"It's okay," Frankie said gently. "Pick her up, Thor."

Thor leaned over and scooped Destiny up. For a moment Brian thought he was going to wring her neck. Then the big man shifted her in his arms, something about the new position almost protective.

"Does she go with us?"

"For now," Frankie said. "Take her up to the top. We'll figure out the rest of the arrangements when I'm done here."

Thor moved toward the door, stopping even with Frankie, and nodded back at Brian. "You need help with him, *chef*?"

"No, I can handle—damn it, Thor, don't put her down."

Thor pushed Frankie back a couple feet, positioning him at arm's length. Frankie understood and brought his pistol up, still quick, the gun almost to chest level when Thor's fist smacked into his forehead. Frankie staggered back, dropping the pistol from nerveless fingers. His legs wobbled and he went to his knees, staring up for a second like a penitent, then tipped to the floor, banging his head against the surgical tool table. One of the scalpels slid of the side and landed point first in the carpeted floor, quivering three inches from his cheek.

Thor stood looking down at him, his chest heaving. Not to see if he would get up, Brian thought. No, just savoring the sight of Frankie sprawled out on the cheap carpet. Then he shook his fingers, wincing. "Is bad place to hit a man," he said to Destiny. "Like hitting a concrete block. Someday I will learn."

"Is he . . . ?"

Thor shook his head. "The ones with small hearts, they are hard to kill. But he will have a very bad headache."

"What now?" Brian asked. His voice sounded drunk in his own ears.

"Drink water," Thor said. "It might help. When you

can, get to the top." He looked down at Frankie, who was breathing regularly. "Perhaps he made them send a rescue ship."

"I can't move Brian myself," Destiny said. "Could you help us?"

"No," Thor said, looking down at Frankie. "You did not kill me. I did not kill you. We are even, *ja?*"

"Even," Destiny said.

A massive tremor ran through the room, then stopped abruptly. From somewhere above them they could hear a man yelling, and the shrill sound of an alarm. Thor nudged Frankie one more time with his foot and walked out the door.

Destiny looked at Brian. "You need water."

"This first," he said, holding up his wrists. The simple gesture took an enormous amount of effort. He rolled his tongue in his mouth, trying to form the word he wanted to say. "Please." *Pluuu-uzz.*

Destiny pulled the scalpel out of the floor and severed the zip ties. She helped Brian to a sitting position, then went back over to Frankie. He had fallen on top of his pistol and she had to roll him on his side to reach it. She pulled it free and, holding it by two fingers, dropped it on the edge of the bed. Then she went through his pants pockets, removing his iPhone, a packet of gum, another of mints. The iPhone was half-charged but there was no signal.

Brian tried to swing his feet over the side of the couch and his vision darkened, little motes of green-black light zigzagging across the back of his eyelids. Destiny pressed her shoulder under his arm.

"When did you decide on that plan?" he asked.

"About three seconds before I did it," she said, turning to look at Christie. The doctor's eyes were open, his chest still. She dropped the Glock on the bed next to him. It was black, all rounded edges, sharklike in its efficient appearance. "You know how to work that?"

He breathed in deeply, concentrating, and then reached out and touched the safety. "Push down on this," he said. "Then pull the trigger." He paused, took another breath. "Don't forget to aim."

"Oh, no," she said. "One notch on the belt is enough for this chick. We're waiting right here until you can hold it. I'll find you some water."

She opened the sink in the little bathroom, was rewarded with a hiss of air, and searched the rest of the room. There was little to search. Christie's medical bag held nothing but his stethoscope, two more needles, rubbing alcohol, and a dozen bottles of atropine. She paused, then went over to the blue cooler. There was ice in a clear bag inside the cooler, partially melted. She opened a corner of the bag and poured it into a cup.

He drank greedily, washing the sour taste out of his mouth. When the water was gone, she pulled an ice cube out of the bag and plopped it into the cup. He pushed it from one side of his mouth to the other, crunched down. More coldness, sharper. Good.

"Brian? They never found the girl."

He pushed himself to the edge of the couch. "Give me a hand?"

"Already?"

"We don't have much time," he said.

Destiny got her shoulder under him again and he stood, weaving back and forth, his vision blacking out in waves. Destiny stayed with him, her shoulder propping him up and then, as his vision cleared and his legs stabilized, reached up to press her fingers against the side of his neck.

"Your heart is racing," she said. "I don't know if that's good or bad."

"It's pumping," he said. "I'll take it."

There was a noise at the door and he twisted around, feeling awkward and slow, caught in the nightmare slow-motion world of the atropine. There were two people blocking the doorway, a large person and a small person. Brian blinked. No, it was an adult and a child. Wells, and at his side was a young girl, rubbing her wrists and looking at Brian with a significant level of distrust.

"Hawkins?" Wells surveyed the room. "My God. What happened?"

Brian sat back down on the bed, suddenly overwhelmed with relief. It was not much help, but it wasn't the enemy, either.

"Did anyone ever call you a blister before, Dr. Wells?"

Wells cocked his head. "Come again?"

"A blister," he said. "Shows up after all the work is done." He reached down and tucked the Glock into his waistband. "Come on, help me get upstairs. We're abandoning ship."

* * *

"I tried to convince them it was a bad idea," Wells said. "Nobody would listen to me."

"Talk them out of what?" Destiny asked, readjusting her grip on Brian. "Your legs getting any better?"

"They're nice and sturdy," Brian said. "I just like leaning on you."

"I'm serious."

Brian straightened, taking some of his weight off Destiny. Yes, he was getting stronger, but it was coming back slowly. He put out a hand on her shoulder instead and motioned for them to continue down the hallway. "Where did you find Taylor?"

"They had her tied up." Wells said. "After I snuck out of the wheelhouse, I found her coming out of a room on C-deck."

"Why the hell did they tie you up?" Brian said. Taylor recoiled and slid around the far side of Destiny. "I don't know," Wells said. "She wouldn't tell me who did it, either." His voice dropped to a whisper. "She's awfully scared."

"You said something about trying to talk them out of it? Out of what?"

"Launching the lifeboats," Wells said. "There were about five or six people who insisted we needed to get off the ship, and they convinced others to help them. Graves is acting captain now, and he tried to stop them, too. They wouldn't listen to either one of us."

"We can launch the lifeboats ourselves?" Destiny asked.

Wells nodded. "It's a simple system. Passengers are supposed to be able to figure it out, even if the ship is going down fast. They had two lifeboats in the water within five minutes. I kept telling them not to, that it was going to attack—"

Brian swung his head to Wells. It was a ponderous motion, his temples throbbing. "Are there any lifeboats left?"

"Several," Wells said. "Not too many people willing to launch them anymore, though."

Wells opened the door at the end of the hallway and they entered the stairwell. "It waited," Wells said, facing away from them as he spoke. "Until they were away from the safety of the ship. It's beaten up from attacking the ship, and you wounded it with the flare gun. It doesn't want to hurt itself anymore, but it's not going away."

"The tug?" Brian said. "Will it attack that?"

Wells held a hand and tipped it back and forth. He looked down at Taylor to see if the girl was registering the conversation, but she appeared distant, in shock or just numb. "Either way, we can't stay here."

He motioned to Taylor, who placed her hands over her ears. Not very tightly, Brian saw with approval. She would be okay. Then he remembered she didn't know about her parents. That they had died, that they had left her.

Destiny said, "Kharkov shot both Prower and Hornaday. Shot them in cold blood, didn't even seem to think it was a big deal. Now Latham and Kharkov are waiting for Frankie to deliver the heart. Once they get that, they're going to get on a helicopter."

"What do we do?" Wells asked. "Can we commandeer it?"

"No," Brian said. "We steer clear, get Destiny and

Taylor on the tugboat, if we can." He gently pulled Taylor's hands away from her head. "You can listen now, okay?"

She looked at him. "I want my mom and dad."

"I know." The pressure changed abruptly in the stairwell, their ears popping. From below them water gurgled, followed by a hissing noise. "Come on," Brian said. "Let's get upstairs."

They labored up the stairs, pushing and pulling Brian, hearing the buzz of panicked voices above them. Their progress was painfully slow. Brian had to place one foot on the steps, both hands on the railing, and let them lever him up until he could swing his other foot up. It was much harder than walking. Finally, they reached the middle landing for B-level, the sound of voices louder now, individual voices punching through the din. Brian slumped against the wall. The next flight of stairs looked like the face of El Capitan.

As his breathing slowed he became aware of another sound, the steady rumble of a diesel engine.

"Someone's here," he said. "Another ship. Go up, make sure she gets on board. Hurry. I'm right behind you."

"Take her," Destiny said to Wells. "I'm going to help him."

"Go," Brian said, pushing her forward.

"No."

"Damn it. Take her up, Wells. We'll be there in a second." He glared at Destiny as Wells took Taylor's hand and they climbed the stairs, pushing the door open. Taylor spared one glance backward before they disappeared onto the deck, her eyes very round.

"Her parents are dead," Brian said. "They were on the lifeboat. Go with her." Above them the tugboat's horn bellowed, and its engines roared. They could smell the exhaust in the stairwell, and he could hear the passengers' voices, could feel the thudding of their footsteps as they pushed toward the tugboat.

"We'll both go," she said, grabbing his arm. "Come on."

Chapter 31

There was a new presence in the water.

The predator moved its fins slowly, its back brushing against the bottom of the ship's hull. Tiny vibrations tickled along its lateral line, the primitive network of nerves under its hide. There was the whir and slash of the approaching prey, new prey, and from its vantage point it could see the spinning fin was protected well. It could hear and feel the scramble of feet and understood, at some base layer, that the prey would move from one shell to another. It was then that the predator would finally gorge.

And far off, the other vibration continued to grow louder, different than the spinning whir, the old familiar sound. It was at once a disturbing and comforting sound; the predator did not want to share.

It dropped a bit in the water column, studying the new prey, letting the lingering pain from its ruined eye focus its thoughts. This was a distinct kind of pleasure, finding the cracks in the armor that evolution had layered on different types of prey. In the distance, the *swaying, lashing, vibration grew stronger, the smell more intense.*

It looked back to the prey. It had chosen its point of ambush well. Now all things were converging toward it, as they should.

It was time to feed.

Chapter 32

The *Santa Maria* was a squat, powerful open-sea tug, capable of pulling in thousand-foot tankers, now tucked alongside the *Nokomis*'s starboard flank. Brian didn't see any attempts to get the waterlogged *Nokomis* hooked up; at this point it would be like trying to haul an enormous anchor back to harbor. Graves and a man in a gray uniform, evidently the *Santa Maria's* captain, were shouting instructions to each other. Graves was gesturing in different directions; first the tug, then the deck of the *Nokomis*, and finally sweeping a hand out at the sea.

The tugboat captain was standing on aluminum planks that had been deployed between the *Nokomis* and the *Santa Maria*. Several of his crewmen blocked the passengers from boarding the tugboat.

Finally, the tugboat captain nodded, then held up both hands, fingers splayed, and opened and closed them three times. They could take thirty passengers.

Brian and Destiny stood at the back of the crowd of people, searching for Wells and Taylor. All around them people were jockeying for position, shouting at family members or friends who were in the jostling crowd. Someone was calling for their parents; a tall, blond woman was screaming for her daughter.

"You see them?" Destiny said.

"No."

Vanders came running up to Graves with a loud-speaker. Graves turned to the crowd, his amplified voice streaming over them. "We're going to put thirty of you on the *Santa Maria*," he said. "Children and their mothers first, then the rest. Only thirty people!"

It was like flipping a switch. The passengers streamed forward, pushing against the tugboat crew; others jumped over the *Nokomis*'s railings to land on the tugboat's curved deck. The tugboat captain retreated, first to his deck and then, as the passengers poured onto the *Santa Maria*, into his cabin. The tug's engines revved, diesel exhaust hanging over the deck.

Brian caught sight of Wells, just to the left of the gangway, shouting in the general direction of the *Santa Maria*'s wheelhouse.

"Stop!" Graves shouted into his bullhorn. "A cutter is coming! No more people on the tugboat!"

The passengers continued to surge forward, pushing aside the tugboat's crew, sweeping Wells along with them. Brian caught a glimpse of his balding head, bobbing in the crowd of people being pushed to the rear of the tug's deck. Waves splashed over her sides, drenching the passengers and sending several of them sliding along the deck.

They tried to shoulder their way forward, but the crowd was packed tight, and when Brian tried ramming forward he was rewarded with an elbow to the face. He went down, swearing, and Destiny helped him to his feet.

"Look." She pointed toward the railing of the *Nokomis*. Taylor was just outside the crowd of people, perched atop a low section of bulwark, calling out for her parents.

The tugboat diesel roared, sending a cloud of black smoke bellowing from its exhausts, and it separated from the *Nokomis,* the aluminum planks splashing into the ocean. The tugboat's cabin and decks were absolutely jammed; there were no more than twenty people left on the *Nokomis*. Wells was staring at them from inside the crowd of refugees. Brian gave him the okay signal and pointed to Taylor. Wells followed his finger and sagged in relief, then tapped his ears and pointed at the props. Then he motioned for Brian to get back.

In a flash of understanding, Brian pushed forward. "Taylor!" he yelled.

The sound of his voice surprised him. She jerked her head around, eyes momentarily lighting up and then dimming when she saw it was Brian who had called for her. He motioned her toward them with both arms, away from the railing. She took one more look at the crowd on the *Nokomis,* then slipped back through the remaining knot of people.

"They were looking for her," Destiny said before Taylor reached them, her voice low but fierce. "Her parents. You understand? They were looking for her."

"Come on." He pulled Destiny and Taylor with him, and then motioned them into the small alcove on the landing between B and A decks. He could still see

Wells's defeated face, his slumped shoulders supporting the sling for his broken arm, his eyes watching
them.

"Brian?" Destiny said. "What is it?"

"Cover her eyes."

"No," Taylor said, her first word since they'd met,
holding up her hand. "I don't want anything over my
face."

The tugboat's directional props continued to push it
away from the *Nokomis*. The passengers above decks
were hanging tightly onto the rail, the waves coming up
and over the tug's low sides. The *Santa Maria* paused
in the water as it rotated its props, and more exhaust
belched into the fog. Then it started forward, cutting
hard to starboard to begin its way back to shore.

"Hang on," Brian breathed.

The tug's blunt bow smashed into an oncoming
wave, and spray blew thirty feet into the air. One of the
remaining passengers on the *Nokomis* screamed out a
litany of curses at them, the words ripped from his
mouth by the relentless wind. "You bastards!" he bellowed. "There was more room! There was more—"

The sea split open. The kronosaur surged above the
waves, emerging from the water in long mass, the flippers pinned tight against its sides. It hung in the air
over the tug, head craned downward, eye trained on its
target.

The kronosaur crashed down on top of the *Santa
Maria*. The metal infrastructure of the wheelhouse crumpled instantly, and the tug tipped forward, props rising
out of the water and churning uselessly at the surface.
The massive head craned back away from the splinters
of metal as its flippers swept back and forth, sending

the *Nokomis*'s refugees cartwheeling off into the ocean. Others were pinned against the railing or what remained of the wheelhouse and crushed into red jelly.

A wave washed over them and the tug tilted hard to port. The kronosaur wedged its pectoral flipper against the rail and flexed. The tug, nearly ready to tip over, righted itself and began to sink, slowly, into the ocean.

Five tons, Brian thought. *Five tons, easy*.

"We don't stand a chance," he said.

"What?" Destiny asked. "My God. It's . . . Brian, it knows what it's doing. It *knows*."

The kronosaur was still partially submerged, its rear flippers just above the waterline. It surveyed the carnage below it, then twisted its body and forced another half dozen passengers into the sea, some of them screaming but the others silent, already mangled and battered. Those who had been caught against the railing were red messes, their bodies twisted, burst open. The kronosaur slid forward and the bow dipped again, lifting the props completely out of the water. The diesel engines whined for a brief second and then died.

The tug dove slowly, bow first, into the ocean. The kronosaur's head swung from side to side as it sank, twisting its massive neck at a hard angle to account for its missing eye, surveying the survivors. Marking them. Brian felt a fresh slug of horror at the measured reconnaissance.

"What's it doing?" Taylor asked. She had taken advantage of Destiny's shock to wiggle free.

"Making sure it has everyone," Brian said.

"What?"

"Nothing. You stay close to Destiny, okay? We'll be okay."

Just before the tug went completely under, the kronosaur swung its head over to survey the *Nokomis*. The remaining passengers retreated under its gaze, several turning away and running back toward the stairwell. The kronosaur lashed its tail, the lips peeling back. The waters had turned red around the tug, and bodies of the dead and dying were being carried away by the waves.

"Can it do that to this ship?" Taylor said. She was pressed against Destiny's side, one hand twisted in the untucked tail of Destiny's shirt.

"No," Destiny said. "We're too big. . . ." She surveyed the *Nokomis,* still tilted low on the water. The top of the swells now lapped at the bottom of the railing.

"Come on," Brian said. "Let's get up another level."

The kronosaur slid off the crumpled tugboat and entered the water. It moved steadily toward the *Nokomis*, bodies swirling in its wake. One of the survivors, a young woman, was flapping madly at the water, her blond hair streaked with gore. The kronosaur brushed against her and sent her reeling, the baleful green eye never leaving the *Nokomis*.

"It's staring at us," Taylor said, her voice no more than a whisper. "At me."

"No," Brian said, watching as the monster drew near, the four big flippers propelling it slowly toward the sinking ship. He pushed them toward the stairs. "Not at you. Take her up to A-deck, Destiny, right now. I'll follow you."

They went, and he stumbled after them.

* * *

He paused at the top of the stairs, panting. His stomach was clenching like a muscle about to cramp and there was a terrible taste in his mouth, adrenaline with a hint of atropine. Destiny steadied him as he staggered over to where she stood, looking across the helipad at Latham and Kharkov. Taylor was pressed against her back and looking down at her shoes, trembling. "Listen," she said. The thudding was getting louder by the second.

"Chopper," Brian said, then pushed Destiny across the way. "Convince them to take you."

She started to protest and he cut her off. "The only way out of here is by air."

"You, too."

"Think about the girl, Destiny. They won't take me, not a chance in hell." He peered into the fog; the sound was getting louder. He glanced over the side and saw that the water had washed over B-deck. The kronosaur was not in sight.

"Maybe Latham will let you come with us."

"No," he said. He looked at her face and managed a smile. "No more time to waste. If we can have one good thing out of this mess, if we can save her, this is it. This is our chance."

She nodded. "Be safe," she said. "Live."

"I'll try, Destiny." He motioned at Latham, who was talking into a phone, his face blotchy with anger. "Go."

Kharkov waited until she circled around the helipad, then swaggered forward. Destiny shouted at him, the words rising above the din of the approaching helicopter; Kharkov flapped a hand at her. She brought Taylor forward, letting him see the girl, and his face changed. At the same time, Taylor looked up from where she had burrowed into the back of Destiny's shirt, saw Kharkov clearly for the first time, and began to scream.

Latham glanced up, his eyes narrowed.

Above them the chopper appeared, its rotors sending the fog spiraling off. At the same time Taylor broke and ran back the other way, her hair streaming behind her, Destiny in pursuit. Taylor ran straight to Brian, still screaming, and he caught her, her arms circling around his neck. She was sobbing, her arms clenched so tight he could barely breathe. "Don't send me with him," she said. "Please, please, *please* don't send me with that man."

He shouted across the helipad. Latham peered at them. "What?"

"The girl!" he yelled, pointing at Taylor. "Take the girl! Keep her safe!"

"No-ooo!" Taylor screamed. "Please, no!"

Latham craned his neck upward to watch the chopper. He turned and said something to Kharkov and they laughed, and Kharkov turned to the stairwell and leveled his pistol. Two other passengers emerged from the stairwell, looking to the sky, their expressions falling when they saw Kharkov's pistol. He motioned with it, making shooing gestures, and the passengers reluctantly backed down the stairwell.

Brian gently pried Taylor loose and handed her to Destiny. He pulled Frankie's Glock from his waistband and started forward.

Destiny caught his arm. "No," she said. "He'll kill you."

The chopper landed, one runner on the canted deck

and the other hovering a foot above. The noise was deafening, the thudding of the rotors causing their eardrums to throb in and out, grit peppering their faces The pilot, his visor covering the upper part of his face, was speaking into his headset. Latham jumped onto the raised runner and disappeared into the cockpit in one swift movement. The roar of the chopper was tremendous.

Kharkov leveled the gun at Brian, his left hand cupped underneath the grip, the right finger on the trigger. A split second before Kharkov's hands bucked Brian crashed into Destiny and Taylor, sending them to the deck, one hand outspread to cover Taylor's face.

He lay on the deck. He was not hit. When he looked up Kharkov's hands were still bucking and his mouth was making *ka-pow* noises, his eyes merry. Then he turned and jumped into the chopper.

"I'm going to kill him," Brian said, bringing the Glock up. The helicopter had only risen twenty yards into the air and was hovering above the *Nokomis*, shaking and dipping in the wind.

"No," Destiny said, pulling on his forearm. "Maybe they'll come back. You said it, Brian—it's our only chance."

He glanced over the side and saw water spreading over the deck; the remaining passengers had retreated into the interior of the ship. The ship tilted another degree to starboard, the ship creaking and groaning. The chopper moved out horizontally and positioned itself just off the *Nokomis*'s side, carving out a large, shallow dish in the ocean's surface.

"What are they doing?" Destiny said.

"Waiting," Brian said. "Waiting for Frankie."

Chapter 33

He had managed to get up onto the bed. The water was lapping at the box spring, getting higher by the minute, and the room was nearly dark. To his side, Christie bobbed facedown, his long legs and arms spread wide. He knew he needed to move, and soon, but for the first time in a very long time, Frankie Rollins decided he deserved a break.

His head was . . . well, it was still attached. There were no other positives, other than the fact the scrambled, feverish sequences of thought, of deviousness and plan and strategies that had dominated his mind, seemed to have been broken the moment it met Thor's fist. What remained were small, isolated thoughts. *Head hurts. Water is cold.* He concentrated, was rewarded with something more complex. *Francis Rollins is a grade-A asshole.*

The idea he should take a break, though—that was good. He scooped up a double palmful of water and splashed it over his face. The cold water hit his eyelids, and his forehead seemed to contract, sending a fresh burst of pain deep into his skull. When it passed, he felt good enough to take stock of his situation.

No gun, no iPhone. The two tools that made Frankie a non-passenger, separated him from the unwashed masses. From the—what had Moore called them? Sheep. He was a sheep, then. He would learn humility in his old age.

He continued his reconnaissance, checking his shoes, the inside of his socks, under his belt. Nothing. He brushed over the inside pocket of his sport jacket and his hand lingered, feeling the hard edges. He caught movement out of the corner of his eye, heard the splashing at the same time. A light beam was bouncing down the hallway.

His eyes darted across the room and his gaze landed on a speck of brightness floating on the dark surface of the water. He took two steps and was just starting to reach for it when the voice came from the doorway.

"Stop."

Frankie froze, the hypodermic needle only inches from his hand.

"Or go ahead. But you get shot in the back."

He turned around, hands held high. "I wouldn't've believed you, you said that earlier."

"Yes," Thor said. "I know." He motioned with the pistol and Frankie sat back down, squinting. Thor had the flashlight beam trained directly on his face, and Frankie held up a hand to block it. The light stayed there, blinding him when he peeked around his hand.

"Come on," Frankie said.

The beam dropped to center on the middle of Frankie's chest, and Thor took a couple steps inside the door. He had a pistol in his other hand, and tucked inside his belt was Frankie's knife. He had wondered where that had ended up; he couldn't remember seeing it since he'd pulled it out of Thor's foot the day before.

"Time to settle the score?"

Thor reached behind him and closed the door, pushing a small wave of water into the hallway. It was only marginally darker with the door closed; the little bit of light was coming through the tiny porthole above his head, and it was already underwater. The emergency lights had gone out while he was unconscious.

"Listen," Frankie said. "I could do it again, it'd be different. But it happened, it's over. No need for bad feelings. Hell, I like you, Thor."

"It was only business," Thor said. "Correct?"

"Correct."

"I, too, am a businessman. Ever since I was young boy, working on my parents' farm outside Sundsvall, I knew good work meant good money. We cut up fat pig, we get more money. Skinny pig, we get less. So always I look for the fat pig."

"If that's a compliment," Frankie said. "Thank you. Right now I was thinking I was more of a sheep."

"The skinny pig," Thor said. "They are dangerous, less profitable, but sometimes are interesting." In the darkness, Frankie saw his big shoulders hunch once, then deflate. "It was not a good decision I made."

"There's more money—"

"No, skinny pig." He pulled the knife from his belt. "Now I do my own work."

Chapter 34

Destiny led them to the far side of the deck, across from the stairwell. They could see Latham and Kharkov in the seat behind the pilot, watching them. The chopper looked like a giant hummingbird in the wind, twitching and tilting in the strong breeze. There were still a few people between the swells, one of them swimming weakly. Another bobbed lifelessly, dark hair flaring around the head. Brian was reminded, suddenly and fiercely, of Gilly.

"What?" Destiny asked. "What's wrong?"

He started to turn away, to stew in his dark thoughts, then turned back and jabbed a finger at the ocean. "It's so goddamn *relentless*," he said. "Won't let us go, won't let us catch our breath."

She nodded. "Stubborn. Like you." She smiled, and it was the first time he'd seen her do it honestly. It opened up her entire face. "You have backbone, Brian, but you carry an awful lot with you. You can set some of it down."

"What do you mean?"

"We need you, Brian. Let the other stuff go and help us, right here and now."

There was a sudden constriction of his throat. Suddenly, he was not standing on the deck of a doomed ship but inside the hospital room, Sienna heaving and straining, her rounded belly pushing up the light blue hospital gown. They had gotten stuck behind a line of pulp trucks on the way in to the hospital and by the time they arrived at the hospital it was too late for pain medication, she was dilated to eight, and he was in a frenzy until Sienna reached up, between contractions, and took his hand. *It's okay*, she had said, with that calm in her voice. *It's like it's meant to be.*

"Brian? Look."

Thor stood at the top of the stairwell, holding a small blue cooler aloft. There was a smear of blood on the handle, and his hands and cuffs were stained pink. "Is here!" he bellowed into the air. "I have it!" He shook the cooler victoriously in the air.

The chopper tilted back toward the deck of the *Nokomis*, the downdraft flattening and contorting Thor's face. It stopped ten feet above him and Thor craned his ear toward them. Brian could see Latham's mouth working from inside the cockpit, shouting to Thor, who shook his head and put the cooler behind him. Latham shouted again. Thor took another step back, started to say something with his free hand out in front as though about to give a lecture, then staggered. He caught himself, then took two more halting steps backwards. Then he collapsed, three red blossoms spreading out on his shirt, and his outflung hand brushed against the cooler. It started to slide across the slanted deck.

Brian broke into a shambling sprint as the helicopter

tilted to the side, the pilot's head twisting around to yell something at Latham. The cooler was picking up speed as it neared the edge and Brian tried to force more speed out of his legs. It was like chasing a fly ball during high school, one that was just out of reach.

He broke into a slide at the last second, his left leg extended. The cooler hit his ankle, teetered as though it would tip over his ankle, and then came to a stop two feet from the edge of the railing. It would have slid underneath the bottom rail, he saw, lying there panting. It would have gone right over.

The chopper hovered over him, the downdraft pinning him for a moment, and then he was in the lee of its underbelly. He flipped the cooler open and saw a dull purple heart inside a gallon-sized plastic baggie, half submerged in blood, the remnant ice cubes floating in water around the bag. The large arteries had been cut off cleanly, the veins on the heart itself a purple so deep they were almost black.

He held the plastic-shrouded heart aloft, the cold water dripping down his forearm. The chopper backed off, circling to his right, then descended until it was nearly eye level. Latham crouched in the doorway, his blotchy face streaming with sweat. Behind him, Kharkov had leveled his pistol at Brian.

"Thank you!" Latham shouted.

"Get off!" Brian yelled. "We get on." He shook the bag, the organ thudding softly against the plastic. "Then I throw you the heart!"

"Or," Latham shouted, "you throw it onboard, and Kharkov won't gun you down. Only deal you get!"

Brian glanced back at Destiny. At Taylor peeking from behind Destiny's back. He knew better. There would be no mercy; they would not let them go. Latham had directed the murder of several people with no more thought behind it than a man swatting a mosquito. He wouldn't stop now.

"Give it to me!" Latham shouted.

Let it go.

Destiny's words, Sienna's words. The impulse started small, flared, and before he could stop himself Brian twisted around, his arm coming back, the weight and feel of the heart not so different than a baseball. He threw it as hard as he could, the plastic flapping around the heart as it arced out over the ocean. Latham turned to watch it. The heart curved slightly with the wind, just like a tailing line drive, and landed forty yards out in the ocean with a small splash.

"Run!" Brian motioned to Destiny and Taylor as the chopper roared behind him. He waited for the slugs to hit him, for the tilted deck to rise up to meet his face. "The stairwell!"

He ran toward the top of the stairs, reaching it at the same time as Destiny and Taylor. The chopper had spun in a tight circle and was hovering fifteen feet above the surface. The baggie was riding a swell, the plastic bag flapping, skittering away from the downdraft of the chopper. It rode the top of the wave, enough air sealed inside the bag for it to be buoyant, the purple swell of the heart pressed against the side of the baggie. Kharkov stepped out to place a boot on the landing skid, shrugging off his jacket. He paused, pointed.

The pilot looked down and then the chopper jerked, and Kharkov had to grab the side of the chopper door to keep from falling off. The pilot pulled back on the yoke just as the kronosaur leaped from the water, its jaws clamping down halfway between the cockpit and the tail rotor.

It wrenched the chopper hard to the side as it fell back to the ocean, a movement rehearsed on thousands of spines. The lightweight infrastructure of the helicopter bent back on itself, the main rotor spinning back in a scream of shredding gears. One of the blades snapped in half and spun wildly out to sea, skipping across the waves in massive furrows of water. Another blade, still attached, caught the kronosaur just behind the jawline.

The air exploded in shrapnel, and a huge gout of blood jetted out of the kronosaur's neck. Brian watched, not even ducking when a ragged chunk of blade hurtled past them in a buzzing whine, as the tangled mass of machine and beast fell into the ocean. Several more pieces of rotor blade shattered against the side of the *Nokomis*, and the surface of the ocean was suddenly pockmarked with fountains.

The kronosaur twisted, its giant tail writhing around the tail of the helicopter. The pool of blood around it colored the waves red and still it continued to bleed. Kharkov was pinned against the doorway, trapped in the mangled metal. A piece of steel protruded from just below his belly button, and he was looking down at it even as he went under.

Latham had climbed to the small pocket of air at the top of the chopper's cabin. He screamed. His voice was tiny inside the chopper, then it choked off to nothing as they sank lower into the water, the chopper's engine smoking and hissing into silence. The kronosaur twitched one more time, the chopper still clamped firmly between its jaws, and from somewhere under the surface a massive fin sent a whirlpool spinning to the surface. Then they disappeared, leaving a final gyre of swirling, red-tinged water.

They waited for several minutes, watching the water. Waiting for the monster to emerge, its wounds healed through some ancient alchemy. But the water was still except for the waves, the air empty except for fog and a few tendrils of smoke, quickly dissipated by the wind.

"It's dead," Destiny said after a while. "And you don't look happy."

Brian watched the water. "No," he said. Underneath them, the ship groaned, then yawed to the side.

"The lifeboat," he said. "We need to get on a lifeboat right now."

Chapter 35

All six lifeboats bobbed on the surface of the North Atlantic, the icy Kaala current streaming beneath them. They were eighteen feet long, with bright orange canvas enclosures and plastic windows. The hulls were aluminum, fitted with 50-horse Honda outboards. The small flotilla moved in circles a hundred yards from the *Nokomis,* which was slowly disappearing into the ocean. Destiny, Taylor, and Brian were alone in their own lifeboat; it could hold ten people, but the remaining passengers had decided it was better to deploy all the lifeboats.

"I thought it would go down faster," Taylor said, her voice muffled from the inside of the parka they had found in the captain's office. "Is it even going to sink?"

"Yes," Brian said, looking through the milky plastic. The lifeboats were better quality than he had expected, and the new Honda outboards had all started on the first or second pull. He watched the sea as they rode the swells, his hand making constant, minute adjustments to the tiller. "It'll sink."

"When?" Taylor said.

He looked at her, huddled deep in the parka in the bow of the lifeboat. "There are air pockets inside," he said. "The water has to push them out, all the way out, before it will sink. Some ships go down fast. Other never really sink, they just bob along on the surface, half-in and half-out."

"Neither dead nor alive?"

"Huh?"

"Nothing," she said. "Maybe the *Nokomis* won't sink, either."

"Maybe not."

He looked down at the fuel gauge on the six-gallon tank, trying to do the math. They were somewhere between forty and sixty miles from shore, not an impossible distance with the fuel-efficient Hondas. But the swells were twelve to fourteen feet, and many a small-craft sailor had swamped on the back side of swells half the size of these.

He scanned the horizon. If they spread out, the noise from the props might confuse the sound signature. At the same time, they would quickly become separated in the fog and heavy swells. *Pick your poison*, he thought.

"Mister?" She reached up and pulled on his sleeve. "Why do you look so worried?"

"Me, worry?" He patted the bench seat next to him. "Come here. We need to stay warm."

"You didn't answer me," Taylor said, moving closer to him. "Isn't the sea monster gone?"

He caught Destiny's eye. "Did you notice?"

"What?"

"The kronosaur that attacked the helicopter," Brian said. "It had both eyes."

She started to protest, then paused, looking at him. "Oh, shit. I think you're right."

"Maybe the original one left," he said. "Maybe this other one scared it off."

"Are you serious?"

"It's possible."

They motored in place, the prop spinning just hard enough to keep them pointed into the waves. After a while, Destiny and Taylor moved closer to him. Soon Taylor's breathing grew deeper, her mouth open slightly, the tip of her nose red from the chill. Destiny watched the sea, one hand wrapped in Taylor's, the other just above Brian's elbow. She laid her head on his shoulder, and after a while her eyes closed.

He adjusted the throttle, feeling their warmth as his eyes swept the cold and massive swells of the Kaala.

He woke with a start.

The *Nokomis* had disappeared in the few minutes he had been asleep. He ran his eyes along the horizon, trying to get his bearings, but everything was gray. He let the boat drift in the swells, took note of their bearing, then swung the boat around and traveled back in the opposite direction.

The sound of an outboard approached them, running at top speed, the pitch of the engine a throaty scream. It rocketed past, hidden by the fog, the bow smashing into the swells. The thudding went on and on, becoming distant, then there was a sudden crunching noise, followed by a strangled cry for help. It was followed by the monotonous sound of the waves.

He looked at Destiny. She was staring at Taylor, her lips moving but no sounds coming from her lips.

The *Nokomis* appeared in front of them, the ship's nose sticking almost straight out of the water like an iceberg. He nestled the lifeboat next to it, then maneuvered around the far side when he heard voices. The other four lifeboats were in a small circle just off the bow, the passengers shouting and gesturing. Brian heard the word *shore*, saw two men point at quartering angles. He motioned for Destiny to take the tiller and climbed out onto the enclosure, the canvas slick under his boots.

"Over here!" he shouted, motioning toward the *Nokomis*. "Get off the open water!"

They glanced at him and waved him over, mistaking his words for a cry for help. The two men were pointing toward an area that, to the best of Brian's reckoning, would take them out to the Flemish Cap.

"You'll die!" he shouted as the lifeboats headed out to sea in a single line, waves splashing over the enclosures. The boats motored on, the ones in the rear spreading out slightly to avoid the wakes of the boats ahead of them. The tiny armada disappeared into the fog, the whine of the outboards fading.

"You'll die," he said again, this time only loud enough that he could hear it.

He dropped back into the enclosure and motored closer to the *Nokomis,* maneuvering in the waves until he could touch the hull, the fiberglass sliding slowly downward under his palm. Around them massive bubbles broke the surface, and the ship gave off a litany of groans and creaks as the last of the air pockets were squeezed from the hold.

In the distance came the sound of splintering metal, the whine of a propeller spinning in air instead of water. More screams, and another kind of splashing, more irregular than the waves. The gnashing of teeth on metal.

He leaned down and began to unlace his boots.

The room had tilted almost ninety degrees. Frankie managed to climb up and over the bed, squatting awkwardly atop the headboard. His back was pressed where the ceiling met the wall, his right wrist was tethered to the headboard. It had been the last industrial-strength zip tie in the bag, Thor's final parting gift. The plastic band was indented into his swollen flesh, and blood was pouring down his forearm.

Below him, the water was coming through the closed door in surges. His ears popped just before each decrease in elevation, the pressure in the room building and popping.

He turned on Prower's satellite phone with his left hand, letting the light from the screen illuminate the room. Christie's body was floating faceup around the room, riding the invisible mini-currents as the water poured in. The dark cave in his chest revealed a hint of pink lung, the darker flesh interspersed by the red-gray ovals of sawn rib bones.

It was, Frankie thought, a colorful way to die.

He leaned down and began chewing on the zip tie. The plastic was slick and hard under his teeth, and the swollen flesh of his wrist made it impossible to reach it with his molars. The water was only a foot below him, the pressure building on his back as the bed tried to float upward. From outside the ship he heard a man yell *You'll die!*, his cry followed by the faint buzz of outboard motors.

He pulled his head back. The plastic had a couple tooth marks in it but was otherwise unaffected. His ears popped as the water surged in again, flowing up and over the top of the headboard. The water was red from Christie's blood, and Frankie was loath for it to touch him. He felt a stab of fierce unfairness that Christie hadn't had to scratch and claw his way to the bitter end.

Then, in the dark and stinking cabin, he laughed, and some of the bitterness went away. It was fair; it was the ultimate in fairness. In a moment, the bloody water would drown him. He had chosen to go on the ocean; he had elected to deal in flesh and blood.

"It's fair," he croaked, and his laughter echoed back to him in a gargle.

He closed his mouth. Maybe if it was just him who died, just the people involved in the game, it would have been fair. He thought of the scared eyes of the little girl, of Destiny's face losing its defiance as that single tear trickled down her cheek. She, at least, had been courageous enough to break free of the path Frankie was leading her down, the path he'd been on as long as he could remember.

He turned Prower's satellite phone around, the artificial light casting his face in stark detail. There was a single service bar, he saw, and the battery was still half-charged.

Perhaps the last few steps on his path could break him free, too.

* * *

The predator whipped its neck to the side, the violent action finally dislodging the last aluminum hull from its teeth. The remains of the lifeboat sank slowly, the long jagged gashes in the metal leaching blood from the predator's gums.

All around it, prey were dead and dying. The predator swam from one to the next, eying each one in turn. Its tail lashed back and forth, its nostrils flared.

The other predator, the one that it had felt approaching all day, the one that was to have been its mate, with which it would have coupled under the rough seas, was gone. Destroyed by the prey, the violent harmony of the world disrupted again. It could feel the discordant vibration, throbbing along the surface nerves. Alongside it was a deep and unfulfilled ache, not entirely physical.

A lone surviving prey flapped at the surface. The predator swam closer, moving faster when it saw the hairy face, the strong build. It circled around, heedless now in its fury, and saw it was not the prey it sought. The predator turned in a tight circle, its long tail slicing through the water. The sharp scutes along the edges sliced the man in half, sending a cloud of blood and offal blooming in the water.

The predator barely noticed. In the distance, something was pounding, the slap of flesh on shell. There was still prey left. Somehow, the predator was certain that this last survivor was the one it sought.

She had ceased arguing with him about the time he took his last boot off. He tossed it into the enclosure and motioned for Taylor to look away as he unbuckled his pants and dropped them, then stuck Frankie's

Glock in the waistband of his boxers. He dropped over the side of the lifeboat, sucking in a great breath as the icy water hit him. Destiny looked down at him as he released his hold on the side of the lifeboat and pushed away from them.

"Go," he said. "Please. This is the only way."

She turned the boat away, moving just fast enough to climb over the swells, and didn't look back.

He swam toward the great curved keel of the *Nokomis*. The entire back half of the ship was already underwater, and the portion of the keel that was normally underwater stuck up like a barnacled hand clutching for air. He swam next to it, feeling the strange downdrafts of current from the sinking ship. They would be much stronger once the rest of the ship sank, which would create a void, a new gravitational pull.

The ship was dying, her last words muted groans and creaks. He pressed a hand against the slimy hull and could feel her shuddering, the vibrations soft and loud, some long like a sigh, others short, hiccuping buzzings as infrastructure crumpled.

He began to slap the side of the hull.

The sound was weaker than he had hoped it would be, lost in the groaning of the ship. He pulled Frankie's Glock free and used the butt to tap against the hull, being careful to point the muzzle out to sea. His breath was short, his testicles drawn up tight and hard. He wasn't sure if it was the cold water or the fear.

My last great insight, he thought. Being very cold and very scared feels, physically, about the same.

Or not. Sometimes it was hot, a scalding rush of terror that seemed to rise up within him like a flood of hot vomit. And he had felt it as a pressure, the closing of the vise around him. He hammered the side of the keel. The important thing was to keep moving. There, that was a better philosophy. Forget the fear and keep moving.

The pounding did not seem to be working and he was wondering if he should try to shoot a round into the ocean when he saw a furrow of water erupt between the waves, a hundred yards in the distance. He smacked the hull again, and a few seconds later the kronosaur carved another furrow of water into the swells, now only seventy yards away.

He pulled himself around so that the keel of the ship was pressed directly against his back. The barnacles scraped against the knobs of his vertebrae as the ship continued to sink.

Easy, he thought. *Easy now.*

A large air bubble blossomed around him and he dropped suddenly, robbed of his buoyancy. The bubble dissipated and he pulled himself back to the surface, sucking in a shaky breath. It was impossible to swim in an air bubble. Perhaps that was the best philosophy of all. He had no idea what it meant, other than being true, but it sounded like it was a good saying.

Hold it together.

A spray of water shot out of a swell thirty yards away and he smacked the last bit of hull that was above the surface, then took a deep breath and let the last of the *Nokomis* take him under. His left hand ran lightly along the hull of the keel, his fingertips digging at the seams. In his right hand he held the Glock, his finger curled around the trigger guard. He was fairly certain it would fire underwater. He was also fairly certain that its effective range was no more than ten or fifteen feet.

Behind him, the *Nokomis* gave a long shudder and slipped deeper into the ocean, now completely submerged. In front of him, a portion of the gray depths solidified into a shape, propelling toward him with four large, rotating flippers.

He reached behind him and banged the hull one more time, then took his finger off the trigger guard and slipped the safety off.

It was there, waiting for him.

The prey was pressed against what was left of its shell. The predator could not tell if it was next to the shell, or some distance in front of it, but it hardly mattered. A few more surges from its flippers, and the prey would be inside the predator's killing circle. The predator could tell by its stance, by the way it looked forward, that this prey still thought of itself as a predator.

The predator reversed the motion of its flippers, coming to a stop. It was not scared, but neither did it want to be injured again. It was wounded, and its intended mate was dead already.

Now the prey was slapping at the shell again. It wanted the predator close, then.

It turned, its good eye watching the flailing prey, committing the distances and angles to memory. Then it turned in a long, slow circle so its good eye was on the offside. The prey could not hold its breath as long as the predator could, but to simply let it choke on water would not eliminate that discordant hum, would not restore the natural order. The only way to do that

*was to crush this hairy little prey between its jaws, to
feel the hot blood, salty as the ocean, trickle down its
gullet.*

*The predator turned again, angling its head so that
its ruined eye was on the prey's side, and went in for
the kill.*

It came for him with its good eye hidden, the jaws
opening wide to reveal the curved teeth, streaked with
blood and silvery smears of aluminum. Brian held the
pistol steady, waiting for it to turn its head for the final
strike. It could not hit him straight on without smashing into the keel; it would have to turn, and when it
turned he would have his chance. His finger tightened
on the trigger as he stared into the red rings of its gullet, the massive tongue. At those huge, ragged teeth,
designed to clamp down and not let go.

Wait until it turns.

He held the pistol up but made no attempt to aim.
There would be a second, maybe two, when the head
would straighten and he would have a chance at its
other eye. It would be like a grouse thundering through
an opening in the poplars, no time to aim, just point
and fire. His breath was coiled in him, a tight circle
below his Adam's apple. He was not good at flushing
shots, and unexpected turns and twists, but he would
have to be now.

Turn, he thought. *Turn, goddamn you!*

It straightened at the very last moment, and even as
his finger convulsed on the trigger he knew it was too
late, that the window in which he might shoot had

opened and closed faster than he could react. There was the briefest glimmer of that green eye, closed to a narrow slit, and then it was blotted out by the kronosaur's upper jaw. He fired anyway and his arm bucked under the recoil. The kronosaur twisted its neck around, its jaws unhinging, opening and opening and clamping down.

He fired again and again, directly into the gullet. The keel scraped hard against his back, and he felt a large tooth slide by his belly. He pushed against it, still holding the pistol, knowing that any second the tooth's sister would crush him from the opposite side. The keel scraped and shuddered behind him and Brian realized he was unhurt, that the kronosaur's jaws had not closed. He looked up and saw an imperfect triangle of light above him, teeth sticking into the triangle but not closing.

He looked down. The curved tooth pressed against his belly, smooth on the outside, the inside with those flesh-anchoring, infection-causing, nightmarish barbs, and he understood. Its jaws had closed on each side of the keel, puncturing the sinking ship. It was unable to close its jaws all the way, the equivalent of biting down on a stick. And now, judging from the way it was thrashing, it was stuck.

He began to climb his way up through the stairway of massive teeth.

He broke the surface and gulped in a great lungful of air. The kronosaur's tail was lashing the surface, the sharpened scutes slicing blindly at the waves. He could hear Destiny and Taylor screaming for him, Destiny's voice telling him they were coming for him, to stay where he was. He waved them back and took another breath, then dove back under.

The kronosaur's neck muscles were bunched as it tried to free its teeth, which were embedded deep into the fiberglass and steel infrastructure. There was a small gap between the keel and the back of its mouth where Brian had been, a small zone where the jaws had been unable to crush him.

The kronosaur's good eye faced the surface, the pupil contracting as Brian drifted down toward it.

He trailed a hand along the keel, lowering himself onto the side of the kronosaur's face. The pupil contracted more as Brian drew near, and it wrenched its head to the side. Fiberglass splintered, but its head did not move. The *Nokomis*, laden with many tons of seawater and still anchored, was all but immovable. The kronosaur's tail lashed around toward him, but fell far short.

You're mine, he thought, feeling a hunter's thrill. *You can't get away.*

He knelt on the rough hide, aimed carefully at the center of the furious green eye, and pulled the trigger. The firing pin clicked, then clicked again. He jacked the action back and the lone remaining shell, a dud, spun free and dropped away to disappear into the ocean.

The kronosaur twisted its head again with renewed energy. Behind Brian fiberglass ripped free, and the kronosaur's head moved slightly. No more than an inch or two, but more movement than it had a moment ago. It was breaking free.

Brian let the Glock drop away and studied the creature. It had come for him again and again. It would never stop coming for him.

He reached for the green eye. The eyelid, thick and heavy, closed before he could touch it. He punched it hard until it opened, the kronosaur bucking and writhing under him now, and when the eyelid opened he slid his left hand in and just kept going, wrenching the eyelid back and hammering away at the rubbery pupil with his right fist, all his muscles going into the ten square inches of the knuckles. He felt warmth on his hand and saw pink jelly seeping from the eye. He wriggled his fingers into the crack and pushed in, his wrist rotating, fingers digging. There was infrastructure here, too, there was substance in the goo. He ripped and shredded, pushing in and pulling out, until finally his hand wrapped around a thick bundle near the back of the eye socket.

He pulled, and the kronosaur roared through its open jaws, the air coming out in wash of bubbles around Brian. He barely noticed as he bent on the kronosaur's snout and pulled on the thick bundle of nerve. It would not pull free. He worked his other hand in and yanked on it with both hands as the kronosaur roared again and again, the tail lashing, the warm jelly of its eyeball cooling on Brian's wrists and forearms. The bundle was anchored somehow. It would stretch but not break free.

Finally, Brian paused, aware the pressure was growing around him, the water much darker. The kronosaur's teeth had punctured the last of the air pockets in the *Nokomis*, and they were sinking fast. The kronosaur's remaining eye was just a bloody hole, and its body was convulsing as it breathed in seawater. He stood, looking down at it, wanting to say something, to feel something, to be triumphant. All he felt was the need for air.

He kicked toward the surface. Below him, the convulsing kronosaur descended in trails of bubbles, following the *Nokomis* toward the ocean floor.

Chapter 36

He was shivering badly. They were moving across the swells, silently, the water in the bottom of the boat sloshing in concert with the motion of the waves.

"Brian?"

He did not open his eyes. It seemed like too much effort.

"Brian, I'm sorry."

He opened his eyes, saw Destiny looking past him. He followed her gaze, his eyes coming to rest on a darker-colored patch of hull on the starboard side, several inches below the waterline. He knelt and ran his hands along the jagged opening, feeling the gentle pulse of the water entering.

He looked back to Destiny. "From its tail?"

"Yes," she said. "It just grazed us. I know you said to stay back, but—"

"Not your fault."

He glanced around, saw a blanket draped over a seat, and pressed it over the hole. Water pulsed through the fabric, and after a moment he dropped it and began to search the rest of the lifeboat. There was nothing he could see that might work better than the blanket, and that was like trying to plug a sucking chest wound with a Band-Aid.

"Brian?" Taylor said.

He turned to her, checked her life jacket, double-checking the straps, and then let his hands fall away. They sat together and watched the water climb. Already they were riding lower in the swells. A wave came up to the edge of the hatchway and washed into the floor.

"Brian?"

He pushed a tendril of hair off Taylor's forehead. "Yeah?"

"Are we going to be okay?"

He looked out over the ocean. "We're better than we could have been," he said. "That's all I can say. Better than we could have been."

She put a small hand on his chest. "I can hear your heartbeat. It's beating really fast."

"You can, huh?" He patted her shoulder and smiled. Such a sweet, such an interesting little girl. "I bet—" He cocked his head and turned to Destiny, saw her eyes growing wide, her mouth opening in disbelief.

They moved out into the hatchway and the sound was much clearer, the thudding of rotors. They waited, wondering if it would pass overhead in the fog. It descended from the mists, hovering over the area where the *Nokomis* had sunk. Destiny screamed, her voice lost in the roar of the chopper. She stood and waved both hands over her head, Brian holding her waist to keep her from falling into the water. He was vaguely aware he was laughing, that Destiny was laughing, too, as she yelled.

His heart was beating very fast.

The helicopter rotated toward them, rotors sending out a circular field of ripples. They could see the pilot's face, could see him register their presence. And then he mouthed three simple words, their content clear even from the distance:

There they are.

Hundreds of feet below them, the upturned bottom of the lifeboat rode south on the Kaala, floating barely above the surface. The fog was starting to lift, and around them the great expanse of ocean revealed itself, the massive swells little more than ripples from their elevation.

"He's not Coast Guard," Destiny whispered.

"No," Brian said.

"Who, then? Prower?"

Brian leaned forward and shouted into the side of the pilot's headset; it was deafening inside. "When did you get the call?"

The pilot flipped on the loudspeaker. "Fifteen minutes ago." He glanced into the small convex mirror mounted near the overhead controls, right where a rearview mirror would be in an automobile. "You didn't make the call?"

Destiny and Brian looked at each other. Destiny pushed her hair away from her face and smiled.

She said, "Can we go back to land now?"

The chopper tilted forward and they raced over the water, the long lines of waves.

"Why are you smiling?" Destiny said.

"I've never seen it from up here," Brian said. "I've always been down in the slop."

She leaned over him, took in the view, and settled back into her own seat. "Looks almost peaceful."

By her side, Taylor was already asleep. *An orphan*, Brian thought. The chopper pilot would drop them off on land, maybe with no questions asked. To the outside world, Taylor Millicent did not exist, and would likely be presumed drowned, along with her parents. According to Taylor, her only living relative was a near-senile grandmother—her adopted grandmother—in assisted living. It was an interesting situation.

"Yes," he said. "I think I could watch it forever."

"That's right," Destiny said. "You have trouble letting stuff go."

He smiled. He was tired, more tired than he could remember being. A great warm weight on his chest, his neck, his eyes.

"What?" she said.

He closed his eyes. Below them, the helicopter's dim shadow raced it back toward shore, a dark line on the horizon.

It was good to let go, he thought as he drifted off to sleep. And it was wonderful to have something to hold on to.

Epilogue

Two months later a Jeep Grand Cherokee pulled into a short, weed-lined driveway forty-three miles southwest of Akron, Ohio. The trailer park was in a rural township, and each driveway had a mailbox on the end, dented or flaking or leaning or, in some cases, all three. The one on the end of this particular driveway said ROLLINS and was leaning back at a ten-degree angle, as if recoiling from the street.

The man who emerged from the driver's side was tall, his thick beard shaved close to his cheeks. He had the angular, rounded look of a man who tended toward burliness, now fresh off the heels of either a serious illness or serious diet. He glanced around, smelled the air, and his eyes drifted toward the treetops to check for the direction of the wind.

The woman who stepped from the passenger side was dressed in light jeans and a flannel shirt. Her hair fell to her shoulders, its color a honey blond at the roots, a darker orange near the tips. A shock of light green was enmeshed in the orange-colored hair.

She looked back toward the Cherokee, which was loaded with suitcases and boxes. There was movement in the backseat, and the woman asked the man a question. He glanced into the Cherokee, said a couple words, and smiled. Then he waved the woman forward.

In the distance, two or three trailer houses down, a dog barked. Someone shouted for it to be quiet and the dog gave one final bark, then fell silent.

The woman climbed the small wooden stairs set on cinder blocks, and rapped on the aluminum door. The door gave off a hollow, muted sound, and inside the trailer the babble of television voices went silent.

After a moment, the door opened. A heavyset woman in her sixties looked down at the younger woman, her face set in lines of suspicion. Behind her, a thinner woman, younger with hard lines around her eyes, watched with equal parts curiosity and mistrust. The older lady clutched a walker, the bottoms of the legs covered with tennis balls.

The woman with the multicolored hair began to speak. She talked of a ship, and how she and her friend— at this she motioned toward the man, who still stood by the door of the Cherokee—had lived when others had died. How they had lived because of her son.

The old lady stared at her for a moment, then spoke the name of her son, asking it as a question.

The woman on the stairs nodded.

The older lady said the name again, this time with a sigh. Then she turned and closed the door.

After a few moments, the young woman descended the stairs and they both got in the vehicle. The man backed out of the driveway, avoiding a fallen bicycle on one side, a deflated basketball on the other. As their tires crunched on the gravel between the rows of trailers the Cherokee's window rolled down, and laughter escaped into the summer air. Then the vehicle reached the main road and turned left and disappeared, heading east, leaving in its wake a faint trail of dust.